UNDEAD WORLDS

A REANIMATED WRITERS ANTHOLOGY

REANIMATED WRITERS   GRIVANTE

R.L. BLALOCK   JESSICA GOMEZ

DAVID A. SIMPSON   E.E. ISHERWOOD

BREA BEHN   CHARLES INGERSOLL

VALERIE LIOUDIS   SAMIE SANDS

JEREMY DYSON   MICHAEL PEIRCE

JULIEN SAINDON   DEREK AILES

MARK CUSCO AILES   JUSTIN ROBINSON

CHRISOPHER MAHOOD   ARTHUR MONGELLI

MICHAEL WHITEHEAD

CHRISTOPHER ARTINIAN   SYLVESTER BARZEY

T.D. RICKETTS

REANIMATED WRITERS PRESS

CONTENTS

Foreword   vii

Reanimated Writer's Newsletter   1
1. Alone Together   3
   About David A. Simpson   7
2. Defenseless: A Story of Death & Decay   9
   About R. L. Blalock   33
3. Before Safe Haven: Losing The Battle   35
   About Christopher Artinian   49
4. Fallen   51
   About Jessica Gomez   69
5. Damaged Goods   71
   About Samie Sands   95
6. Gone Fishin'   97
   About Justin Robinson   117
7. A Peaceful Town   119
   About Jeremy Dyson   145
8. Avery   147
   About Valerie Lioudis   159
9. Zombie Exterminators   161
   About Grivante   187
10. When I Grow Up, I Won't Be   189
    About Brea Behn   207
11. JIMMY   209
    About Arthur Mongelli   227
    Undead Worlds 2 Available Now!   229
12. In the Beginning, God   231
    About Charles Ingersoll   265
13. To The Hills   267
    About T.D. Ricketts   283
14. The Fort   285
    About Michael Whitehead   301

15. Adam   303
    About Sylvester Barzey   337
16. On the Rocks   339
    About EE Isherwood   345
17. Morning Of The Living Dead   347
    About Mark Cusco Ailes   367
18. Brain Waves   369
    About Julien Saindon   383
19. The Horror at Roswell Mills   385
    About Michael Peirce   417
20. The Festival   419
    About Christopher Mahood   451
21. The Undead Pool: The Zombie Night   453
    About Derek Ailes   471
    Afterword   473
22. More From The Reanimated Writers   475
    Undead Worlds 2   477
    The Reanimated Rumble   479
    Reanimated Writers Podcast   481
    The Reanimated Reader   483
    Facebook Fan Group   485
    Reanimated Merch   487

Cover art by Christian at Covers by Christian

FOREWORD

Welcome to The Reanimated Writers "Undead Worlds"
Anthology!

The Reanimated Writers was born from the idea that
authors working together could accomplish more than
authors in competition with one another. Not only could we
help each other out, we could also help expose our mutual
fan bases to more great stories!

I started reaching out to other authors in late 2016,
asking if they were interested in being a part of a collective
to share knowledge and support each other. The response
was and continues to be overwhelmingly positive. We have
over 200 authors in the group and we also have a group just
for interacting with you, our fans. You can find it and join us
on Facebook by searching for, **The Reanimated Writers Fan
Group.** We look forward to seeing you there.

We decided a great way to expose more readers to our
zombie filled worlds would be to craft a collection of new
stories from each of our universes and this is that project,
The Undead Worlds Anthology. We hope that you find

some new authors you love to read and go on to explore their worlds further.

We thank you for joining us and the growing horde of fans that hunger for our stories!

Kevin M. Penelerick
　　Reanimated Writers Founder

REANIMATED WRITER'S NEWSLETTER

Want to hear about upcoming projects from The Reanimated Writers first?

Want to score free books and get to know some of our authors?

Then come join our newsletter where you'll get all of the latest news as well as 5 free books from different authors in our network!

http://subscribe.reanimatedwriters.com/

1

ALONE TOGETHER

Her breathing was ragged as she sat down beside me on the steps outside the back door of the makeshift club in the warehouse. I could smell her sweat, she was fresh from the mosh pit.

I didn't look over, I wasn't interested, I had problems of my own.

I'd been outside the barricades, I'd seen my whole unit wiped out, my friends torn to shreds. I'd seen the innumerable hordes of the undead screaming after us as we fled to the end of the island. They were unstoppable, unrelenting, uncountable. They flowed like a river over every obstacle they came across, leaving everyone and everything dead in their wake.

I stared into my mug of beer.

I don't know how long we sat apart, yet together. It was late September on Long Island and the night air was chilly.

Time passed.

Her sweat cooled and a hazy steam rose off of her. She said nothing and slowly her panting breaths returned to normal, winding down from the violent thrash dancing she had been doing. Trying to not remember, pretending to not know, dancing in violence and anger and rage and pain.

Even out here the band drowned out the sound of the generators and they were so loud that normal conversation was impossible. They played hard and raw. Angry and desperate.

A half mile away at Saint Mary's, the orchestra played sad and slow and older couples waltzed with their finest clothes and jewelry.

I had hoped coming here would pull me up out of my despair for a few hours but it hadn't worked. I couldn't forget and I couldn't get drunk enough to not remember, it wasn't possible. I had been with my National Guard unit on our weekend of live fire training, living off of MRE's, beef jerky and candy bars. We got to pretend we were real soldiers every fall, when we would camp out at the local gun range and do our annual weapons qualifications.

The silence between us was nice. It wasn't strained or uncomfortable like some silences are. She knew the truth. I knew the truth. Hell, the whole town knew the truth. There was no place left to go. We were on the edge of the ocean and the last of the boats, overloaded and sitting low in the water, were gone. The walls we threw up with semi-trucks and sandbags were fourteen feet tall. The horde stumbling towards us was a million strong, drawn East like lemmings marching towards the sea, always searching for fresh meat. The barricade was strong, it would hold but the horde would simply swarm over the top. There were too many coming out of New York.

The beer cupped in my hands was warming, the bubbles I had been watching rise to the top were slowing, now only coming up occasionally.

I pulled out a cigarette.

She pulled out a straight razor.

I still hadn't looked over at her and I had a feeling she hadn't looked at me since she'd sat down. She saw from my haircut and dirty uniform as she came out that I was a soldier. One of the very few that were left. One of the very few who had retreated back to this quiet little town at the very tip of Long Island, surrounded by the ocean. I was one of the very few that managed to out-run the horde as they lost interest in the Hum-V. They would rather chase a person fleeing on foot than the metal box.

When I arrived, I had no more ammo and no extra guns. I only had tales of an incalculable number of the undead slowly making their way East. They would be here by morning. Once the first wandering zombie found its way to the barricade and sensed we were here, it would start up with that ungodly keening scream they do. It would call the others and they would come on the run.

Earlier that evening, the whole town had sat around and listened to the radio as an Army Sergeant told them the new government was rebuilding in Oklahoma. He asked everyone to get there if they could. It was too late for the people at the very tip of the island. The only road out was impassable, clogged by hundreds of thousands of the undead and anything that would float had long since been put to sea.

Her tangled mass of black hair obscured her face completely as she mimicked my casual slope-shouldered stoop, elbows on knees, hands forward.

Only mine held a beer.

Hers held a razor.

I put the lighter to my cigarette and she still didn't move, just stared at the surgical steel in her hands. She turned her wrist towards me and I saw the scars of prior attempts. Horizontal and vertical, but not deep enough. Scars of one who had lost her nerve. Scars of one not quite fully committed.

The blade glinted in the harsh sodium lights and the pounding bass was relentless as the band played like it was the last time they ever would. The people in this nothing club, in this nowhere town, were counting down the minutes and living each one to its fullest.

She moved the blade slightly towards me, holding it in her open palm, her head still hung.

An offering.

I took a drag off of my cigarette, the surreal orange glow brightening the scene that burned itself into my mind. This last concert, in this last town. Dancing while the Titanic sank. I sat down my beer and reached for the razor, staring deep into her eyes as she finally faced me. I saw a bleakness, an understanding and a raw terror barely held in check.

I saw my own eyes mirrored.

I took the blade and before I could lose my nerve, I slashed deep and long into my own wrist, all the way to my elbow.

My eyes never left hers.

I smiled, silently thanked her for showing me a way.

Her silent eyes were begging me to take her with me.

The blade flashed again under the lights and we sat side by side, leaning into each other, our lives flowing warm down the stairs.

Alone.

Together.

ABOUT DAVID A. SIMPSON

.

David Simpson is a starving writer living in Atlanta who got tired of starving, so he drives a truck. He's married and has a passel of great kids, most of which are in or have served in the Army.

Over the years he's done a lot of things to put food on the table, always writing and thinking he had a book in him, or hustling some crazy notion or get rich scheme! Here's a list of paid jobs he recalls while not yet divulging the many unpaid jobs or entrepreneurial start-ups that he lost his ass on.

Golf course grass cutting boy. Carpenter. Burger King employee. Steel mill worker. In the Army. Licensed broker (stocks, bonds, insurance, etc). Repo Man. Bounty Hunter. Leather shop co-owner. Farmer. Factory worker. Cross country truck driver. Lime hauler for the mines. Fuel hauler. Construction company owner. House flipper. Restaurant delivery driver. Cookie and snack cracker hauler. Regional truck driver.

Thank you, Tamra Crow for editing my work.

The Zombie Road books are on **Amazon.**

To find more information about David A. Simpson, go to **Davidasimpsonauthor.com** or follow him on **Facebook.**

DEFENSELESS: A STORY OF DEATH & DECAY

Day 1

3:29 pm

"Daddy!" Dylan launched himself out of the car door like a rocket. His red-and-blue shoes lit up as they hit the ground. In the last few steps, he leaped up and threw his arms around his father.

"Hey, buddy!" His father wrapped his arms around Dylan, returning the enthusiastic hug.

"I missed you," Dylan said, pouting as his father picked him up.

Brushing a stray lock of dirty-blond hair out of the six-year-old's eyes, his father said, "Well, I missed you too. Have you been good for your mom?"

"Uh-huh." Dylan nodded.

"That's my big boy." His father beamed down at Dylan. Creases formed in the corners of his father's eyes and mouth, his smile rippling across his face. The two looked a lot alike. They both had the same gray-green eyes and the same dirty-blond hair. His father gave him a final strong, loving squeeze before setting him down. "Now go inside and put your stuff away. Maybe we can see if Ben can come out and play."

Dylan ran back to where his mother stood by the driver's side of her little black car. Her short black hair clung to the edges of her face. Her lips turned up slightly into a thin smile. Her hazel eyes shimmered in the sunlight, and she swiped at them quickly. She crouched down in front of Dylan and held out his Spiderman backpack. Most of the things he needed were already here. He had two of every-thing: two beds, two rooms, two sets of clothes, but there were a few things that he didn't have two of. Like his blan-ket. The same one he had slept with since he was a baby.

"Now you be good for your dad, alright?" His mother pulled him into a tight hug, her embrace firm and reas-suring but not crushing like his father's.

"I'll miss you." Dylan kissed her cheek.

"I'll miss you too, honey." She pressed her lips to his forehead. "I'll talk to you tonight before you go to bed."

"I love you." He nuzzled against her shoulder.

"I love you too, sweetheart." His mother held him until he released her.

"Go put your stuff down inside," his dad said. Dylan ran to the door, dropping his bag in the entryway.

"Be careful going out with him," he heard his mom say quietly to his dad. "Things haven't calmed down yet."

"I know," his dad said, nodding. "I don't have any plans to go anywhere this week. We'll be fine, Rebecca." His mom nodded. "I'll have him call you tonight before bed."

"Thank you." His mom opened the car door before turning to Dylan. "Bye, baby. I love you." She waved and blew him a kiss.

"Why can't Mom stay here?" Dylan waved to his mom as she pulled out of the driveway and drove off. He wished his parents lived together. He wished he could live with them both at the same time. He still didn't understand why they didn't live in the same house.

His father's mouth opened and closed a few times before he was finally able to say something. "Adults don't always get along, buddy. Just like you don't always get along with all of your classmates."

Dylan nodded. He had asked the question before and usually got the same kind of response.

"Come on." His dad tugged on his hand. "I bet Ben will want to come play. He was asking about you yesterday."

Dylan's face lit up. He liked Ben. Ben was only three-years-old, but he liked to follow Dylan around and Dylan liked teaching him new things.

Dylan bounced up the steps to the house and knocked on the door. A woman with a broad, friendly smile opened the door, her sable eyes lighting up. Her thick, chocolate-brown hair was pulled back into a loose ponytail that bobbed back and forth as she moved. She was a petite woman with a wispy frame.

"Hi, Dylan!"

"Hi, Mrs. Ward! Can Ben come play?"

"Sure! Just let me get some shoes on him and we'll be right out." Mrs. Ward looked past Dylan and waved to his father. "Hi, Robert!"

Dylan's dad waved back. "How's it going, Sarah?"

Mrs. Ward shrugged. "Wyatt is at work. Just Ben and I today."

"He's working around here, though, right? They haven't called him in to go deal with the riots yet, have they?"

"No." Sarah knelt down next to Ben and slipped on his

shoes. "His time will come, though, if things keep going this way." She smiled down at Ben and kissed him on the forehead. "Go play!" She gently swatted him as he darted past her.

Ben was a bundle of energy. In the last few months, his baby fat had begun to melt away. He looked more like a kid than a baby now. His feathery blond hair was always a mess, sticking out from his head at odd angles. He had the deep brown eyes of his mother. They were always bright and intent, watching and absorbing everything around him.

"Let's go explore!" Dylan said to Ben.

"Don't go too far!" his dad shouted after him. "Stay in the yards."

Dylan rolled his eyes but ran between the houses towards the open backyards. None of the houses had fences around their yards. This left them all connected in one continuous stretch of green. Behind the yards was a copse of trees. Dylan liked to pretend it was a vast, untamed forest. That he was an explorer setting foot in an untouched jungle full of wild animals.

He and Ben ducked through the branches of the shrubs, weaving around tree trunks. A flash of movement caught his eye and Dylan jump back, bumping into Ben. The small boy cried out as he stumbled. The movement came again and Dylan's eyes narrowed as he focused on it.

"Ben!" He grabbed the other boy's hand in excitement, dragging him towards it. "Look at this!" He knelt down in the dirt, small twigs and rocks biting into his knees.

"What is it?" Ben asked, standing back a few feet to inspect the creature.

"A toad!"

The tiny animal hopped again and Dylan crawled after it. It wasn't big, only about the size of his palm. The toad was covered in brown bumpy skin that helped it blend in with the dead leaves on the ground.

Dylan reached out tentatively and lightly stroked the creature's skin. It was soft and dry, not slimy, as he had expected. The toad jumped again at his touch. Dylan leaped, a nervous laugh escaping his lips as excitement coursed through his veins.

He scurried after the toad, clamping his hands down over the creature. He could feel it frantically squirming underneath his fingers. He didn't want to hurt it. He just wanted Ben to be able to feel it too.

Carefully, Dylan scooped the toad up in his hands, cupping them together. Slowly, he closed his hands until he had a firm grip on the toad. One by one, he peeled back his fingers until he could see the little creature staring up at him.

"Ben, come see!" Dylan held his hands up to Ben. The younger boy inched forward. "Want to touch it?"

Ben reached forward cautiously. As his fingers brushed against the toad, it began to struggle again and he sprung backward.

"Feels cool, doesn't it?"

Ben's eyes darted between Dylan and the toad as he nibbled on his lip. Finally, the little boy nodded.

"Come on! Let's go show my dad!" Dylan stood up shakily, his attention focused on the toad staring back warily at him.

Dylan shouldered through the leaves, clutching the toad close to his chest as the branches scratched his arms and legs. As they broke out of the trees, Dylan blinked in the bright sunlight and looked around. They had wandered a few houses down but not far from his house.

"Do you like frogs?" Dylan asked as they started back towards the house.

"Yeah." Ben nodded, though he still eyed Dylan's hands warily.

"I've never been able to catch one. Toads are slower, though." Dylan continued chattering to his younger friend. "You know there is a difference between frogs and—"

Thuds sounded behind them, and Dylan froze. Ben turned around first. Not wanting to look like a coward compared to a three-year-old, Dylan slowly turned around. A woman lay face down at the bottom of her back steps. The storm door swung shut again, smacking hard against the frame.

The woman stirred, slowly trying to pull herself to her feet. Dylan thought she must have been hurt, but she didn't cry. Dylan wanted to call out for his dad to come help her, but he couldn't find his voice.

As the woman rose, he could see that her face and shirt were stained red. Her head hung awkwardly to one side. Her face was covered in scratch marks, and her shirt was torn at the shoulder. She looked like a monster.

Ben let out a whimper and Dylan's breath caught in his chest at the sound.

The woman's head whipped around, her eyes locking on the two children. A shriek ripped from her throat, and suddenly she was sprinting towards them.

Dylan dropped the toad and ran. His arms and legs felt jerky and uncoordinated as he forced them to move.

He could hear Ben's terrified cries behind him. Dylan chanced a look over his shoulder. Ben was a dozen feet behind him, tears streaming down his face as his short legs struggled to catch up to Dylan.

"Dad!" Dylan shrieked, his voice high and frightened. "Dad!"

Dylan looked back again. The monster reached out, her hands inches from Ben's shirt.

Someone grabbed ahold of Dylan's arm and Dylan screamed again, trying to claw at whoever had grabbed him.

"Dylan, what's wrong?" His father's eyes were wide and wild.

"Ben!" Mrs. Ward's shriek cut through the air.

"Stay right here! Don't move!" Dylan's father raced after Sarah, towards Ben and the woman.

Ben was on the ground. The monstrous woman was on top of him, but Ben wasn't crying anymore.

Why isn't Ben crying? Dylan was shaking. He could feel the tears running down his cheeks as he wrapped his arms around himself.

His dad grabbed the monster by her ankle, dragging her away from Ben. Mrs. Ward collapsed next to Ben, scooping his limp body up in her arms. Dylan finally got a look at his friend. There was blood everywhere. It covered his face, soaked through his shirt, and matted his hair.

The woman twisted and lunged for Dylan's father, her teeth snapping in his face as he struggled to push her away.

"Dad!" Dylan took a few steps forward.

"Stop! Stay back!" His father's grip slipped. The monster lunged forward, her teeth sinking into his bicep. He roared as blood bubbled up around her lips. Dad pushed the monster back, her teeth peeling back the meat from his arm like string cheese as she held on tight.

When she finally ripped free, a chunk of flesh held tight in her mouth, the monster tripped over her own feet. She didn't even try to catch herself as she toppled, her head cracking hard against the corner of the concrete patio. In an instant, his dad was on her. He seized her head in his hands, lifting it up and slamming it back down on the concrete. The monster snarled and hissed, her fingers scraping down his arms and face as she tried to pull him closer to her mouth.

Finally, as he slammed her head down on the concrete again, a sickening crunch reverberated through her skull and the woman went limp.

Dylan saw his dad stand up. He looked around wildly before his eyes locked in on Dylan. He sprinted towards the boy and for a horrifying moment, Dylan wanted to run. His father looked so much like the woman. Scratched up. Covered in blood. His eyes vacant, like the eyes of his teddy bear.

But it was his father? Wasn't it?

"Dylan." His father breathed as he scooped his son up. "Are you hurt?" His eyes frantically searched over the boy for wounds.

Dylan shook his head.

"He won't stop bleeding." Mrs. Ward's frantic words broke through the silence. Her hand was clamped over Ben's neck, blood oozing around her fingers. She looked up at them, tears filling her eyes and spilling down her cheeks.

Dad released Dylan, though Dylan wrapped his arms around the man's waist, holding on tightly. His dad pulled his cell phone from his pocket and punched three numbers in before putting the phone to his ear.

He frowned as he promptly pulled the phone away from his head. "It's busy." His voice was distant and detached.

"What do you mean it's busy?" Sarah snapped.

"Nine-one-one is ringing busy." His father punched the numbers on his cell phone again and raised it to his ear. He quickly lowered it, shaking his head.

"I-I-I have to get Ben inside. I have to stop the bleeding." Mrs. Ward suddenly scooped up Ben and sprinted towards her house.

"Come on." Dylan's father scooped him up with a wince, jogging towards their house.

"What about Ben?" Dylan asked.

"You need to get inside." His father shouldered the front door open, leaving a long streak of blood. A large German shepherd scrambled around their feet, whimpering and licking Ben's legs with concern.

"But what about Ben?" Dylan insisted.

"Dylan." His father knelt down in front of him, cupping Dylan's face in his hands. "I need you to listen to me. You need to stay here. You don't open the door for anyone. Do you understand?"

"Are you going to help Ben?" Irritation flitted across his father's face. Finally, he sighed and nodded solemnly. "I'll be back as soon as the police get here, but I need you to stay here. I need to know that you are safe."

"Okay, Dad."

His father darted around the corner and reemerged a few moments later with a small first-aid kit and some towels. He kissed Dylan's head and ran out the door.

Dylan wrapped his arms around Apollo. The large dog nuzzled his head against Dylan's side, licking his hands and whimpering. Dylan threaded his fingers through the dog's long caramel and black-colored fur. The dog smelled musty. It was light and pleasant, like the smell of the outdoors. Dylan buried his face in the dog's fur, letting the familiar smell fill his nostrils.

The dog's closeness was comforting. Apollo had always been around. For as long as Dylan could remember, Apollo had been his shadow. The beast slept at the end of Dylan's bed at night, banishing the monsters that crept through the dark. He stuck to Dylan's side during the day, gratefully gulping down table scraps and playing whenever Dylan needed a friend. As Dylan watched television, he'd curl up on the floor, using Apollo's fluffy body as a pillow rather than lying on the couch.

As Dylan sat back up, he noticed streaks of red in Apollo's coat. His hands were covered in the red. It was on his shirt too. Dylan walked to the bathroom, turning on the light and standing on a stool to reach the tap. The water turned pink as he stuck his hands underneath it.

Dylan pulled off his shirt and shorts, tossing them to the floor and heading to his room. He pulled open a dresser drawer and fished out a new shirt. This one had a bunch of superheroes on its front.

Dylan wished they were real. He needed Spiderman to come swinging in to save Ben. Or Superman could fly him to the doctor for help. Or the Hulk could have beaten the woman before she ever touched Ben. Dylan could feel tears welling up in his eyes again as he looked at the shirt.

A cold nose touched his back and made Dylan jump. Apollo nudged his hand expectantly. Dylan smiled and obliged the dog, rubbing his ears. The dog leaned into Dylan's hand, bowing his head as he enjoyed the affection.

The front door opened and quickly closed. Dylan froze as Apollo perked up at the noise, a low growl rumbling in his chest. Dylan pulled on his shirt, along with a new pair of shorts, and cautiously stepped out into the hallway, with Apollo glued to his side.

His dad stood in the entryway, his forehead resting against the door.

"Dad?" The man jumped and spun around. His eyes were wild and afraid. Dylan thought there was more blood on him than before. He shrank back, Apollo's fur clutched tightly in his fists. For a moment, Dylan didn't see his father. He saw a monster.

Finally, Dylan took a breath, forcing himself to speak. "Is Ben alright? Did the police come and save him?"

His father ran his hands through his hair, his mouth opening and closing a few times.

Dylan could feel the tears welling up in his eyes once again. Remembering how Ben had been lying on the ground, the crazy lady on top of him. How Ben had cried.

His father sighed and knelt down, pulling Dylan into a tight hug. "Ben is going to be just fine, bud. The doctors are going to make him all better. Don't worry."

"Why would she do that to Ben?" Dylan wailed, trying to wrap his mind around what had happened.

"I don't know." His father hugged him tighter. "I think that lady was sick. Very sick. She needed help."

"Is someone going to help her too?"

His father's lips pressed into a tight line, and for a moment his eyes grew distant. "I don't know."

Dylan leaned into his father. His eyes fell upon the gash that the woman had ripped into his arm. It was scabby. Delicate black lines ran across the skin around it.

"Does it hurt?" Dylan asked, his eyes never leaving the wound.

His father suddenly stiffened as he looked at the bite. His fingers carefully probed along its edges. "No." His brow furrowed. "It looks worse than it is." He forced a smile at Dylan. "I should probably clean it up though. Then we'll make some dinner."

Day 1

6:02 pm

Dylan looked up from his tablet. It was taking his dad a long time to get cleaned up. His stomach rumbled impatiently. Dylan set the tablet down. With a stretch, he stood up and look around. Apollo sat up from his spot on the couch, watching Dylan intently.

"Dad?" Dylan called out. The house remained quiet. Dylan started to tremble. He didn't like the silence. Where was his dad? His father wouldn't have left him here. Not by himself. He didn't see his father leave.

Dylan moved down the hallway that led from the living room to the bedrooms.

"Dad?" Dylan's voice was quiet as he called out again. He didn't want to go down the long hallway, which seemed to be too dark. He didn't want to look for his dad. He wanted his dad to walk out, laugh at him for being silly, and give him a hug.

His heart began to race as he approached his dad's room. Quietly, he pushed the door open. His dad was sitting on the edge of the bed, unmoving. The hair on Dylan's arms rose and he could feel every muscle in his body tense.

Monster. Monster. Monster.

The word repeated over and over in his head. It couldn't be a monster, though. It was his Dad.

Dylan stood perfectly still in the doorway, afraid that if he moved he would draw the monster's attention. He wanted to call out, but his voice was caught in his throat as he watched the motionless figure.

He trembled as he gathered his courage. "Dad?" His voice was barely more than a whisper.

His dad sprung up and spun around, making Dylan jump back. "Jesus, kid, what are you doing in here?"

"I-I-I'm hungry. When are you going to make dinner?"

"Make dinner? How did you get in my house? Where are your parents?" He frowned.

Dylan stepped back, grabbing ahold of the doorframe and hiding behind it. "But..." He could feel the tears coming again. "I-I-I don't like this game, Dad. It's not funny." He sniffed, struggling to hold back the tears.

His father's mouth opened and closed. Suddenly, his eyes locked on the dresser, on a framed picture that stood on top of it. It was a picture of Dylan and his father from a few years ago. Dylan was sitting on his father's shoulders, smiling with his arms out wide. His father was smiling at the camera, his eyes hidden by sunglasses as he held onto Dylan's legs.

His father walked over to the dresser and picked up the picture. His eyes darted from the picture to Dylan and back again. He swallowed a few times as he stared down at the picture for another few moments, running his fingers along the glass. Finally, he placed the picture back on the dresser.

"Hey, buddy, I'm sorry." His brows were knit together as he knelt down in front of Dylan. "Where's your mom? When is she coming home?"

"Mom doesn't live here." Dylan took another step away from his father. He was acting so strange. Perhaps his father was mad at him. Mad that he hadn't kept a closer eye on Ben. Dylan's heart twisted as he thought about his friend.

His father scratched at his head as he thought about what to say next. "Why don't we try calling her?"

Dylan nodded. His father stood up and patted down his pants pockets, pulling the phone from his back pocket.

"Do you know her number?" He held the phone out to Dylan.

"It's in your phone." Dylan didn't move to take the phone. His father knew his mother's phone number. This felt like a trap. If he played along, something bad might happen.

"Right. Right." His father nodded. He chewed on his lips as he opened up the contacts list. "What's her name?"

"Mom."

His father sighed. "Can you pick her out on here?" He offered the phone again.

Cautiously, Dylan took the phone. Even if it was a trap, he wanted his mom. He scrolled through the pictures of people and names. He tapped the picture of his mother and handed the phone back to his father.

His father tapped a button on the phone and brought it up to his ear. Within a few seconds, his frown deepened and he ended the call.

"Alright, buddy. It seems like there's some trouble with my phone. How about I make us some dinner and you keep trying to call your mom? Does that sound like a plan?" His father offered him the phone again.

After a moment of consideration, Dylan nodded and took the phone from his father.

"Good! What do you like?" his father said enthusiastically.

"Mac 'n' cheese," Dylan said quietly as he trailed his father to the kitchen.

"That sounds like a plan!" He opened a cabinet, frowned, closed the door, and opened another.

Dylan watched his father rummage through the cabinets, producing a pan and filling it with water. He was wearing a clean shirt now. The bandage poked out from underneath the sleeve. It was clean and white. The black lines emerged from underneath it, snaking down his arm past his elbow.

Dylan looked back down at the phone. With a sigh, he went back into the living room and plopped down on the couch. He touched the phone icon next to his mother's picture and lifted the phone to his ear.

"We're sorry. All circuits are busy now. Please try your call again later."

Dylan stared at the phone as it repeated the same message. Is that what his dad had meant by trouble with his phone? He hit the red "end" button and waited a few seconds before calling again. The same message played again.

He could feel his panic rising. What if he couldn't get ahold of his mom? He had always been able to get ahold of her before.

Just as Dylan was about to hit the "end" button again, the phone rang. His heart raced as he held it to his ear.

"Hello," his mother answered.

"Mommy!"

"Hi, baby!" His mother's voice was soothing. Just hearing it made him feel better. "Have you been having fun with Daddy?"

"No." Dylan lowered his voice, whispering into the phone, "Daddy is acting strange."

"Strange? What's wrong, baby?" He could hear the concern in his mother's voice.

A lump formed in Dylan's throat as he thought about Ben and the sick lady. "Something bad happened."

"Baby, what's wrong? Are you alright?" The worry was plain in his mother's voice now.

"Someone hurt Ben." He sniffed into the phone.

"Oh, baby," his mother crooned. "I'm so sorry. Are you alright?"

Dylan nodded then remembered his mother wouldn't be able to see the gesture. "Yes, but she bit Daddy."

"Baby, everything is going to be alright." Even as she tried to comfort him, Dylan could hear the strain in his mother's voice.

"Mommy, I think Daddy is pretending like he doesn't know me. I think he's mad at me."

"Like he doesn't know you? Baby, I'm sure he's not mad at you. He's probably just worried." He could hear shuffling in the background.

"Mommy, I'm scared. Can you come over?" Dylan swallowed around the lump in his throat, his chin quivering as he fought against the tears.

"Of course, baby. I'm on my way." He could hear the car door slam in the background. "Can you put your dad on the phone?"

"Sure. I love you, Mommy."

"I love you too, sweetheart."

"Dad." Dylan entered the kitchen and held out the phone as his father stirred pasta on the stove. "Mom wants to talk to you."

"Hello?" His father took the phone.

Dylan wandered back into the living room. He could hear his father's hushed whisper. It quickly turned frantic. The fear in his father's voice scared Dylan. Maybe his father was just playing pretend because he was afraid. Maybe he wasn't mad at all. That made sense. Whenever Dylan heard a strange noise at night, he'd pretend he hadn't heard it.

Dylan plopped back down on the couch. Apollo stood there, shaking himself off, and moved to Dylan's side, resting his head on the sofa next to Dylan. Dylan wrapped his arms around Apollo's large head and nuzzled his musty fur. The dog gently licked his arm, as if trying to tell him not to worry.

Day 1
10:32 pm

Dylan's eyes fluttered open. It was dark in his room. The only light came from a small nightlight plugged into the wall. The light it cast created long, distorted shadows out of his toys.

He reached down towards the end of the bed. It was empty. Dylan began to frantically feel across the sheets for the warm soft body that usually lay there.

A growl rumbled through the quiet room. In the dark, Dylan could see the dog's silhouette near the door.

"Apollo," he called quietly.

The dog didn't come. He stood rigid, facing the door, the fur on his back standing on end.

"Apollo," Dylan called a little louder. The dog finally looked back at Dylan. His ears lay flat against his head, his hackles stood on end, his tail was raised and rigid. As Apollo turned back towards the door his lips peeled back revealing his long, sharp teeth.

Dylan slid out of bed, tiptoeing to the door. Apollo was rooted firmly in place, not moving as Dylan reached for the doorknob. After a moment of struggling, Dylan pulled the door open. Apollo bolted into the darkness.

"Wait!" Dylan cried out, suddenly alone. The entire house was dark. Slits of pale light filtered in through gaps in the blinds, leaving most of the house in deep shadow. Dylan's heart raced as he stared out into the dark house beyond his room.

A thump echoed down the hall and Dylan whirled around. Apollo stood in front of the door to his father's bedroom. He snarled at the door.

Dylan approached the door. He could hear footsteps shuffling through the room on the other side. They were uneven and heavy. He reached for the knob, his heart thundering in his chest. His palms were slick as he twisted the doorknob and pushed the door open a crack.

His father stood in the corner of the dark room. He wasn't doing anything. Just standing there.

Monster. Monster. Monster.

The voice screamed in his head. A whimper escaped Dylan's lips.

His father whipped around, his lip curling back in a snarl that mirrored Apollo's expression. As Dylan shrank away from the man's gaze, his father let out an ear-piercing shriek.

With a roar, Apollo lunged. As his father darted forward, Apollo sank his teeth into his left leg. His father pitched forward, falling hard.

Dylan turned and ran, his heart thundering in his ears. He sprinted down the hall and towards the front door. His fingers felt thick and clumsy as he fumbled with the deadbolt. As it clanked open, Dylan threw the door open and stopped.

It was dark outside. The other houses were shrouded in shadows. The air was hot and heavy. Outside looked just as threatening as inside. Dylan could imagine all the monsters that were lurking in the shadows, just waiting for him in the darkness.

A yip sounded behind him, and Dylan spun back towards the house's interior. He didn't want to leave Apollo. He didn't want to leave his dad. He didn't know what to do. He wasn't supposed to leave the house without his dad, but his dad was scary. His dad was a monster.

Claws skittered across the floor and a second later Apollo slid around the corner. The dog darted out the door. He paused on the porch, looking back to Dylan and whining, his muzzle wet and glistening in the moonlight. Dylan bolted after the dog, not wanting to be left with his dad in the dark house.

Dylan's head whipped back and forth as he tried to decide where to go. The neighborhood was shrouded in darkness with only sparse patches of light cast down by the street lamps. His heart hammered in his chest. A tremble started in his fingers and began to work its way up his arm and throughout his body.

Heavy, clumsy footsteps echoed through the house behind him. Dylan jerked into motion, his breath coming out in quick, wheezing puffs as he dashed across the lawn towards Ben's house. Apollo was glued to his side, his ears up and alert. The dog's presence was comforting but did little to alleviate Dylan's fears. He was out in the dark of the night on his own. Something terrible had happened to his father, and he didn't know where his mother was. Dylan leaped up the short three steps, nearly tripping on the landing.

"Help! Mrs. Ward! Please, help me!" A heavy thump resounded on the other side of the door. Dylan took a few steps back as the thumps turned into a steady beat that shook the door.

Suddenly, the ground fell out from underneath him. His arms pinwheeled as he tried to catch himself. All too quickly the ground came up, sending a bolt of pain through his back and elbow. Tears started streaming down his cheeks anew as he clutched his scraped elbow.

Dylan looked around at the dark street through the haze of tears. He didn't know where to go. He didn't know what to do. He wanted his dad to be his dad again. He wanted his mom. He wanted them to hug him and tell him this was all just a bad dream. But he couldn't wake up.

Apollo's deep rumbling growl broke him from his self-pity with a start.

A man was running down the street towards him. The man was wearing nothing but a pair of boxers. As he darted underneath a street lamp, Dylan could see the horrible snarl that contorted his face. Gore dripped from his lips and coated his chest.

Apollo's furious barking cut through the night, and Dylan bolted down the street. The dark houses were a blur as he ran. He didn't know where he was going. He didn't know what he was going to do. He just knew he couldn't let that man catch him.

A terrifying shriek echoed from behind Dylan, sending a chill up his spine. Throughout the neighborhood, more screams responded. Dylan pumped his legs harder, but he could hear the slap of the man's bare feet behind him, drawing nearer.

A house reared up out of the darkness. Dylan looked around for another road. None of the houses looked familiar anymore. He couldn't remember what streets he had run down. He couldn't remember what turns he had taken. He didn't know where he was or how to get back home.

He had run right into a cul-de-sac.

There was nowhere left to go.

Dylan's bare feet skidded painfully across the pavement as he came to a stop. His chest heaved as he desperately tried to take in the oxygen his body needed. His heart roared in his ears.

Soft fur tickled his leg. Apollo inched closer. The fur along his back stood on end. His lips curled back from his teeth. His ears flattened to his skull as he ducked his head low.

Three.

Three people were running up the street towards them. Dylan inched back with a whimper. They were going to rip him apart. Just like Ben.

It was going to hurt.

Dylan wrapped his arms around his body, hugging himself tightly.

A loud scream erupted to his left, and suddenly he was knocked to the ground. Dylan couldn't even scream as the air was forced out of his lungs. Fingers dug painfully into his shoulders as crushing weight bore down on him.

Dylan looked up into the face of the monster. Snapping teeth filled his vision, and Dylan finally found his voice. He screamed, tears streaming down his face as he tried to push the woman back, but she was so heavy and so strong.

Suddenly, the teeth were gone. Apollo lunged forward, seizing the monster's throat in his massive jaws. Her snarls turned into wet gurgles. He shook his head furiously, ripping her throat to shreds. Warm, sticky blood poured down onto Dylan's chest, soaking into his shirt. The monster's fingers loosened and Dylan quickly scrambled out from underneath her.

She was still fighting. Still moving. She didn't even notice her injuries. The woman reached for Apollo, her fingers curling into claws as she reached for him, but Apollo gracefully dodged out of her reach. Darting in again, he took hold of her arm and shook it violently, tearing skin and muscle. His muzzle and chest glistened with blood as he jumped back.

But the fight wasn't fair.

As the other people reached the fight, one reached out and grabbed Apollo's back leg, pulling it out from underneath him. As the dog fell, he whipped around, his teeth clamping down on the man who had ahold of him.

In that moment, the woman lunged forward, sinking her own teeth into his back. Apollo let out a high-pitched yip, snapping at the woman, but unable to fend her off. The man bit down into the dog's leg. As the next monster dove in, Dylan momentarily lost sight of the dog. The first friend he had ever had. The best friend he had ever had.

Apollo wasn't fighting anymore. Instead, he thrashed wildly, whining and whimpering as he tried to free himself, but he couldn't get free. The more he struggled, the more they tore into him. Blood pooled underneath him on the pavement, glinting in the moonlight as Apollo finally fell still.

Dylan slowly scooted backward. Inch by inch. Putting distance between himself and the monsters, between himself and his best friend, as silently as he could.

His foot slid across a pebble, scraping across the pavement. The monsters' heads snapped up. Their faces were coated with fresh, shiny blood. Apollo's blood.

The man let out an ear-piercing scream. Dylan cried out

as he scrambled up. But the monster was faster. A hand clamped onto Dylan's ankle, pulling him across the pavement. Dylan frantically kicked out. His foot connected with flesh, but the monster only snarled and continued to pull.

A roar and a screech.

Dylan recoiled from the sound and from the bright lights suddenly blinding him.

Fast footsteps.

The man wrapped his other hand around Dylan's foot and pulled hard. The concrete scraped along his stomach.

A wet smack.

The monster's grip loosened and Dylan clawed at the pavement, desperate to drag himself away. He pushed himself up. He didn't care where he was going. He just had to get away.

A heavy thump.

A strong hand locked around Dylan's wrist and he cried out, pulling frantically.

"Baby." With the single whispered word, Dylan froze. The hand pulled at him again and Dylan collapsed against his mother. He wrapped his arms around her, burying his face into her chest and sobbing.

"I'm here, baby." She wrapped her arms tight around him, her embrace protective and comforting. He could feel her chest heaving as she cried with him.

Shrieks rose in the night. They were close by. Dylan tightened his grip on his mother, his fingers digging into her back.

"We have to go." Her voice was tight, fearful, as she scooped him up, sliding into the driver's side of the car and depositing him on the passenger seat.

She looked into the rearview mirror and grimaced. "Get down on the floor, baby." She motioned for him to get down on the floorboards. Dylan shook as he did as he was told, curling up into a tight ball.

"I love you, baby," his mother whispered, smiling at him from the driver's seat. "We're going to be OK."

Warmth flooded through Dylan as he settled into the floorboards. "I love you too, Mommy."

ABOUT R. L. BLALOCK

R. L. Blalock's love of reading started young, but her love of zombies started later in life. In 2008, when R. L. Blalock first watched the remake of Dawn of the Dead she instantly fell in love with the genre. Born and raised in Sacramento, California, R. L. Blalock now lives in St. Louis, Missouri with her loving husband, precocious three-year-old daughter, two dogs, and a bird. Stay connected with R. L. Blalock at **rlblalock.com**!

I would like to give a special thank you to my wonderful and supportive mother who endures the nightmares of reading my work.

The rest of the Death & Decay series can be found at **Amazon**.

facebook.com/RocBlalockauthor

twitter.com/rocblalock

instagram.com/rlblalock

BEFORE SAFE HAVEN: LOSING THE
BATTLE

There was a knock on the door. "Doctor Blair, we've got a call out," said the gruff voice.

Lucy's head dropped. She looked at the tatty copy of *Charlotte's Web* she was holding and traced the title with her fingers.

"Doctor Blair?"

"Yeah! On my way," she said, bringing the book up to her mouth and kissing it before putting it back into her bedside drawer. She looked at a photo of a little girl on a swing. "See you soon, sweetie," she said before grabbing her shoulder bag and heading out of the small room.

On the other side of the door, there was a soldier waiting for her. He was holding a clipboard and scanning through a document. "Usual call. Scratch victim - cessation. Reanimation prevention equipment used successfully, just a case of collection and checking on the family."

"Another day at the office huh?" asked Lucy as the two of them walked along the corridor. The soldier didn't answer but continued to the reception area where a small team was waiting for them.

Two men were in full hazmat gear; both were carrying side arms. There was another soldier, fully armed and in combat fatigues. A few seconds passed, and a nurse joined them.

"Dr Blair?" the nurse said.

"Hey," replied Lucy.

The group continued out of the building to a waiting military ambulance. There was no polite conversation. There was no camaraderie. There was only the task at hand. It was a dismal, grey, cold task, that mirrored the dismal, grey, cold morning. The nurse and Lucy climbed into the back of the ambulance with the two men in hazmat suits. The soldiers climbed into the front. The driver turned the key, and the engine coughed into life, filling the tired ambulance with a breath of exhaust fumes.

Other than the sounds of the engine and the muffled chink of apparatus as the ambulance weaved and turned, the journey was silent. Lucy looked around at the faces. None returned her gaze. Their expressions were all too familiar now. No pleasant smiles, no pleasant anything. Their thoughts were way down deep and all they had left of their former selves. They weren't about to give them up to a relative stranger.

The ambulance pulled up at a block of flats, and Lucy immediately checked her watch. Ten past eight. *Thank God*, she thought to herself. The rationed electricity would have kicked back in ten minutes ago. She really didn't fancy a long climb as well as what else awaited her.

"Seventh floor," said one of the soldiers, looking into the back of the ambulance, almost as if he'd heard her thoughts.

They all climbed out of the vehicle. The hazmat team pulled one of the gurneys out of the back and released the brakes. The six of them headed into the building, the soldiers well and truly on the job. They had their SA80s at the ready and at the first sign of trouble they wouldn't hesitate to use them. The hazmat team had side arms, but they were more concerned with steering the gurney over the uneven ground than anything else. These calls had become routine now. Everything always went to plan, there were never any surprises.

They entered the block of flats, and Lucy suddenly shivered. There was something about the place. It wasn't the bland brown carpet or the cold white of the breezeblock walls. It was a feeling, a sense that something wasn't right. They proceeded down the hallway to the lift. The nurse pressed the button, and the juddering clunk of an old mechanism rang down the shaft as the familiar whirring sound began.

"Nice place," Lucy said with a half smile on her face.

"My sister lived in a block of flats like this before she died," said the nurse. "Five years battling cancer. Five years battling staircases when the lift was broken."

Guess that conversation's over, Lucy thought. Note to self: Don't speak to anybody... ever.

The lift finally arrived, and the clumsy movement of the doors did nothing to instil confidence in the team as they stepped over the threshold. There wasn't much room with the gurney sitting uncomfortably in the middle of them, and with another juddering lurch, their ascent began. The lights flickered, and Lucy was about to come out with another little quip but then looked at the dour faces of her companions and remembered the advice she had given to herself.

The doors opened, and the hazmat men with the gurney stepped out first and stopped dead. They had a routine to follow. The soldiers raised their weapons and proceeded to sweep the nooks and crannies looking for anything deemed a threat. When they were confident all was well, they signalled for Lucy and the nurse to leave the lift. The group moved down the long hallway, stuttering when they found two apartment doors ajar. For the first time since leaving the field hospital, the nurse shot Lucy a glance.

Why were the doors open? Nobody left doors open these days.

The soldiers paused outside of flat 7E. One of them pressed the bell. A chime sounded and the door opened simultaneously, revealing a girl of about fifteen. Tears had left shiny trails down her cheeks, and as the team entered, they heard muffled sobs from another room.

"Hi sweetie," said Lucy, trying to displace some of the fear in the girl's eyes. "My name's Lucy, and this is..." she gestured towards her female companion.

"Nurse Harper. Now, where's your mother, we have to give you all an examination." The nurse guided the girl by the shoulder towards the sound of the sobs.

Nice, Lucy thought to herself. Nice bedside manner, Nurse Harper. I bet you are a pure joy to be around when you're not comforting recently bereaved teenagers. What a bitch!

Lucy and the nurse passed several doorways as they walked down the hall. She looked back to see the soldiers and the hazmat team were standing in the hallway. They had left the cumbersome gurney outside. There was no need to bring it in. The majority of the scratch victims had withered away to not much more than bones by the time they got called out, so carrying them a few metres wasn't an issue. As Lucy and the nurse entered the living room, they saw the familiar sight of a huddled family. The mother was in the centre crying heavy tears, while her older son and youngest daughter clenched her tightly. The sadness Lucy had felt dozens of times and more came flooding back. Another family gone. Another painful exit. Lucy knew it wasn't just the suffering of watching a family member succumb, but it was the guilt of finally having to put a family member down.

She would not allow herself to close off from the emotion. She would not allow herself to be like Nurse Harper. She was Lucy, the girl from Maine who used to spend hours after school running errands for senior citizens or helping out with food drives for the homeless. She was proud of who she was. She was proud of what she did. It cost her nothing to try and make someone feel a little better. She wouldn't let anything beat her. She walked up to the grieving family, crouched down in front of them and gently put her hand on the crying woman's knee.

"I'm Lucy. I'm sorry for your loss. This is Nurse..." She stopped suddenly. Between heartbeats her world changed. A sound... a feeling. A violent thud as a body flung itself against a bedroom door and the frigid touch of death.

Everything moved in slow motion now as her mind raced to catch up with the events that were unfolding. The thud sounded again from down the hall, and the soldiers started talking in raised voices of panic. Lucy looked down at her hand. It was placed firmly on the woman's knee. The knee was stone cold. She looked at the children. They were sobbing, clutching their mother tight. The boy was squeezing a cushion against her in his vice-like embrace. Lucy saw now. The cushion was pressed against a wound. She looked up at the woman's face. Her pallid skin, seconds before contorted with grief, was now unmoving. The woman's eyes were closed.

"Oh, sweet Jesus," Lucy whispered.

Lucy's hand immediately sprang from the knee, and she let out a gasp.

The woman's eyes shot open, revealing the all too

familiar gaze of a world gone to hell. The colour and life had been replaced with an opaque greyness interrupted only by a shattered pupil of nothing human or natural. Seconds before, this thing had been a woman and a mother, now it was just a creature of malevolence. A beast whose sole purpose was to feed and spread the infection it held within itself. It let out the angry gurgling growl that Lucy had heard before but never in such close proximity.

She backed away, losing her footing and landing on her bottom. She continued to shuffle back, almost crab walking until she hit the wall, too scared to do anything but stare. Nurse Harper began to scream, but before her voice sliced into the air, the newborn creature tore a piece of flesh from the face of the boy who was too bewildered to register anything.

The echoing crack of a door being booted in was followed by gunfire and another scream, this time that of a man, one of the soldiers. The apartment filled with terrifying sounds. Lucy looked up at the girl who had answered the door, standing motionless and soundless as she watched a chunk of her brother's cheek drop from her mother's bloody mouth. The creature turned to bite into the scalp of her other daughter, who pierced the air with a shriek of agony. Dripping crimson skin and hair hung from the creature's mouth as a symphony of pain played around the room. The boy, the young girl, the nurse - all screaming different cries of terror and pain while the malevolent growl of the RAM, the reanimated corpse of the woman, gurgled a hellish undertone, making Lucy's blood curdle in her veins.

She sat there... frozen, her back to the wall, watching everything unfold like some gory flip book. Another pained roar bellowed from down the hall, and the chime sounded as the outer door reopened. She heard a shout, "They're everywhere! Let's get the hell out of here!"

The two children clutched their wounds, screeching in pain. How could their mother have done this? The beast, satisfied her work was done with them, leapt from the black leather seat towards Nurse Harper. The nurse's scream of terror turned to one of agony as the creature's teeth tore through her flesh like it was wafer-thin ham.

The girl who answered the door just stood, watching it all happen...bewildered. The voices from the hazmat team disappeared down the outer corridor. They were abandoning them. Lucy heard a shot ring out. The familiar sound of a Glock 17, the standard issue weapon for the hazmat soldiers. Only seconds had passed, but it felt like more.

Lucy, what are you doing? The adrenalin finally kicked in.

She leapt to her feet and ran at the creature, throwing both her hands out in front of her. She barged into it, causing it to lose its balance and crash into the sideboard where shelves and decorative plates collapsed on top of it. Nurse Harper put her hand up to her neck as arterial spray squirted like a fire hose onto the furniture and carpet. She stumbled a few paces, then her legs folded underneath her, and she fell on top of the writhing creature.

"Run!" Lucy shouted, grabbing the girl's hand and dragging her out of the room while the RAM struggled to get to its feet.

The pair sprinted down the hall and past the shattered door that the soldiers had kicked in. A RAM laid dead, its mouth bloody, a single bullet hole in its forehead. The two soldiers were on the floor. Dark red patches had formed underneath them, and their bodies were beginning to move once again, not as the people they had once been, but as this new thing, this new subspecies.

Lucy noticed a keychain attached to a belt loop of one of the soldiers - it was the ambulance keys. Like an athlete, she ducked and grabbed, releasing the clasp in one swooping movement before grasping the girl's hand once more.

"Don't look, sweetie, don't look at anything, just run" cried Lucy as she glanced back to see the mother RAM getting to her feet and letting out a long, angry growl.

They stopped at the outer door, and Lucy angled her head around the corner. The two men in hazmat suits were down. There was no sign of anyone else, but she could hear guttural, gurgling echoes somewhere.

"C'mon," she said as the pair began to run.

Lucy let go of the girl's hand to take the Glock and an extra clip from the prone hazmat operative. Blood dripped off his yellow suit as he clutched his shoulder wound. "I'm sorry... I'm so sorry," he started to cry.

"Piece of shit," she replied as she signalled for the young-ster to follow her once more. Lucy put the extra clip in her shoulder bag and continued down the hall. She checked to make sure the safety was off. She knew these creatures were lightning fast, and she couldn't afford mistakes.

Lucy suddenly heard pounding feet and growls from behind as the girl's former mother charged towards them. Lucy looked at the girl. For the first time, she saw something other than indifference. She saw sadness and fear. The reality was finally sinking in.

"I'm sorry sweetie," said Lucy as she took aim and squeezed the trigger. The RAM crumpled to the floor in midstride. A hand seized Lucy's leg, she looked down. It was the other operative. His yellow gloves grabbed her as he tried to drag himself up. Not missing a beat, she aimed the gun towards his head and pulled the trigger. The figure fell back to the ground.

"May as well finish the job," she said and took aim towards the other yellow suited coward. There was a small explosion of red, and one more threat was gone.

"Okay sweetie, let's go."

The pair began moving down the corridor toward the lift. Lucy looked back as a growl bounced off the walls behind her. The soldiers and children had emerged from the apartment and were now storming down the corridor towards them. At the same moment, the girl began to scream. Lucy turned to see a group of ten RAMs heading around the corner.

"Shit!" she yelled.

There were just seconds before one of the two groups caught them. She grabbed the girl, and they ran through the first open door, slamming it behind them. Lucy put the bolt and safety chain across before the first clawing hands began to scrape and bang against the wood. She took a breath and realised this was no time to pause. Raising the Glock, she began sweeping the apartment as she had seen the soldiers do many times before. The door continued to judder under the hammering weight of the raging creatures. Once satisfied there was nothing lurking within the apartment, she took a breath.

The living room was modern, minimalist, almost antiseptic. It showed no signs of apocalyptic interference but for a single streak of blood down one white wall. It was almost a piece of modern art. Lucy placed the Glock in the back of her jeans and looked down the hallway. "Come away from the door sweetie," she said to the girl who just stood, almost hypnotised by the rhythmic beats of the creatures.

Lucy walked up to the large window. The drizzle had

turned into a constant rain. It was a depressing picture but for dazzling beds of hydrangeas that had been planted by the council to liven up what was ultimately a fairly depressing landscape for anyone who casually passed by. There was no movement, no pedestrians. The city was in lockdown, quarantined... this should have been so straight-forward. They had been told the reanimation prevention equipment had been used successfully. It should have been a simple health check on the rest of the family. And why the hell didn't the soldiers sweep the house? They saw the girl and got lazy.

Damn it. This should have been easy.

Lucy realised there was no point getting angry now, she had to figure a way out. She looked around for a phone, but couldn't see one. Probably in one of the other rooms. She began to head back out through the hall but stopped dead. The pounding and growling continued, but Lucy was suddenly deaf to everything but the sound of her own voice.

"What are you doing?" she asked in horror, as she watched the girl slide the chain free and then put her fingers around the bolt.

The girl turned to look at Lucy. "Don't you see? This is how it's meant to end," she said, sliding the bolt across and pulling the door open.

"Nooooo!!!!" screamed Lucy.

The girl flew back against the wall, her head smashing the plaster. She turned to Lucy and smiled as hands and teeth tore at her face, shoulders, breasts, and stomach. Blood dripped from her lips and down her chin before she finally slumped to the floor.

More RAMs barged into the flat, and Lucy ducked into the nearest bedroom, slamming the door shut behind her. The sound of thudding bodies and guttural growls filled the air. She pushed a chest of drawers up against the entrance, followed by the double bed. The inner doors were far less secure.

She wouldn't have much time.

Lucy looked around the room, desperate to find a spark of inspiration, desperate to find a way out. She went across to the window as the volume from outside increased further. Nothing, it was the same scene from a different angle.

Think Lucy, think!

She looked towards the bed. As she had pushed it across the floor, a blanket had rolled and twisted, it almost looked like a ship's rope. That was it. Her only option. The pounding continued, each time the jewellery box on top of the chest tinkled.

Lucy ripped the bedding off and began tying the pieces together in knots she hoped would not fail her. She pulled down the curtains and separated them from the blackout lining. Her nerves were starting to get the better of her. She kept throwing looks towards the door, searching for movement.

Then it came, a loud crack.

She paused in mid knot. Her breathing fluttered as fear engulfed her. She dropped her makeshift rope and pulled the Glock from the back of her jeans. She pointed it hopelessly towards the entrance. The wood around the top hinge had splintered, it wouldn't last long, but it was still holding for the moment. She fired a few head height shots... had to be head height through the door. She heard at least one RAM collapse to the floor.

This was no time to give up. She put the Glock back in her jeans and continued with the rope. It needed to be longer. She opened the built-in wardrobe. Towels, dressing gowns, anything and everything, she tied them together, frantically, hopelessly, as the door finally began to give.

"Fuck, fuck, fuck!"

She took one of the bedside cabinets and threw it at the window with all of her strength. The glass exploded outwards and somersaulted into the perpetual rain. The sound made the RAMs go wild, and suddenly there was another loud crack as the door began to shift in its frame.

Lucy's brow creased as she took off her trainer, put her hand inside and swept hard up and down the window frame, removing any errant pieces of glass. She twisted the handle and opened the window, then tied her homemade rope around the frame and pulled it tight and hard.

She looked back at the door as the chest of drawers moved, and the first grey arms reached around the wood. She let out a half sob and lowered the rope. She was short, by about fifteen feet, but she didn't have any more time. She pulled her shoulder bag off and dropped it. The laptop probably wouldn't survive, but what the hell. A growl broke through, and she looked round to see the first grey faces emerge.

Lucy took a deep breath, grabbed hold of the rope, sat on the sill and swivelled her legs over the ledge as the first RAMs forced the door, pushing the chest of drawers and bed out of the way.

"Here goes nothing."

Lucy allowed herself to drop. She felt the rope and moving window frame take the strain as she swung from side to side, desperate to hang on. She shimmied down a little, and as the first reaching arms and malevolent faces emerged above her, she exhaled. She continued her descent, holding on for dear life, closing her mind to the danger, only hearing her own heartbeat. Lower, lower as the growls became more distant and finally she was there. More like twelve feet, she now realized.

One, two, three, drop!

She landed amid the hydrangeas, as soft a landing as she could have hoped for in the circumstances, but a jolt of pain shot up from her ankle and through her leg at the second of impact, and she collapsed heavily. There was a winded moment's pause before she stood, brushing pink and purple petals from her hair and shoulders. She looked up at the window to see one of the creatures leaning out further than the others, too stupid to register the danger. She picked up her shoulder bag and began to climb out as a single growl suddenly got louder. She looked up again to see the RAM falling towards her.

Lucy leapt from the bushes as a bone crunching smash filled the air. The flowers and branches bristled as a deformed, broken creature dragged itself through the greenery. It was one of the soldiers. Lucy reached into the back of her jeans for the gun. She flicked the safety off and fired point blank. She turned and stumbled towards the ambulance, climbed in, started the engine and pulled away.

"It should all have been so easy."

There was a knock on the door. "Doctor Blair, we've got a call out," it was a female voice with a friendly Yorkshire accent.

"Just give me a minute," replied Lucy, as she swung her legs out of bed. There was a bandage strapped around her ankle. She winced as she gave it a rub and scratch. Lucy reached into her bedside cabinet and removed a small pill bottle labelled oxycodone. She tapped a tablet into her hand, placed it in her mouth and expertly cocked her head back to swallow it before she started to get dressed.

Five minutes later, she opened the door to reveal a pretty young nurse with pale skin and red hair. The nurse extended her hand. "One of the soldiers was going to come and get you, but I really wanted to meet you. My name's Samantha, Samantha White."

Lucy chuckled to herself at such formality. "Okay Samantha White, pleased to meet you," Lucy replied shaking her hand. "What have we got?"

"Scratch victim - passed away. The reanimation prevention equipment was used successfully, so it's just a case of collection and exams on the family".

Lucy burst out laughing until a tear appeared in the corner of her eye.

Samantha looked confused. "What is it? What's wrong?"

"You'll see sweetie, you'll see."

ABOUT CHRISTOPHER ARTINIAN

Christopher Artinian was born and raised in Leeds, West Yorkshire. Wanting to escape life in a big city and concentrate more on working to live than living to work, he moved to the Outer Hebrides in the north-west of Scotland in 2004, and has lived there ever since with his wife and dogs.

He released his debut novel, Safe Haven: Rise of the Rams in February 2017. This was the first installment of a post-apocalyptic zombie trilogy. Book two, Safe Haven: Realm of the Raiders continues the fast moving and often terrifying story and book three is expected to be released later in the year.

The Safe haven Series is available on **Amazon.**

For more information on his past, present and future work follow Christopher at the social media sites below or visit **www.christopherartinian.com**

facebook.com/safehaventrilogy

twitter.com/Christo71635959

FALLEN

A FLASH PREQUEL

Told by Harold Fossek, Anchorman

Repetitive.

This is how I describe my days, now that my darling wife, Evelyn, has passed. Even though it seems like yesterday that she was here with me, it has been one year, three months, twelve days, and I miss her terribly. Material possessions fill our home to the brink, helping me remember her each and every day. My memory is not as sharp as it once was, so having her clothes and perfume around settles my nerves. The higher power thought not to bless us with children, so our ten-year-old dog, Betsy, is the closest we'd come. Even at ten, she's still as rambunctious as a pup.

"Now, you be a good girl, Betsy. I'll return home after work and take you for your walk."

Betsy wags her furry little tail. Even for a Pomeranian, she has a lot of hair. I tried to convince Evelyn to name her Gizmo, but she fell in love with the name Betsy from the get-go. I smile to myself, thinking of my darling wife and the wonderful years we lived together. Some days, all I think about is the moment we will finally reunite. We met in our twenties, and Evelyn was the president of her sorority. She was young, blonde, had a nice body, and she was full of spunk. She drew me to her immediately. But it was more than just her beauty and her crystal blue eyes that captivated me, her soul called to me. As soon as the first "Hi" left her mouth, I was a goner. Of course, it didn't hurt when I flaunted my hazel eyes back at her. I'm not in as good a shape as I once was, but I was heavily muscled and toned then. We couldn't keep our young selves away from one another.

Chuckling to myself, remembering the carefree youths we once were, I lean down and pet Betsy. Now, almost 50 years later, my hair's streaked with gray. My once hard body is now soft and pliant. The only remaining fixture of my youth is my light hazel eyes. They're just as boyish.

Leaving Betsy panting after me, I head into the news station. Vanessa, the station's assistant, called about 20 minutes ago in a panic, stating we received a tip that could devastate people if released. This is the big break Vanessa's waited for. At the end of this month, I'll end my 33 year career at the news station, and Vanessa will take over my time slot as host at 8:00 PM on channel three news. If this story's as large as she's portraying it to be, she'll have a set place at the station.

"Good morning, Harold," Vanessa announces when I enter. She makes her way to my side as she does each evening. She has dark, waist-length hair, a slim frame, and dark hazel eyes. My entire being softens towards her. If Evelyn and I would have had a daughter, I imagine she would have looked like Vanessa. I began mentoring her several years ago. She's hoping to gain insight in to how I've maintained a high-ranking position for so long when most new stations hire young and fresh every few years. Honestly, there's no trick to it. The station is loyal. I signed on when they first aired, so the people who watch have only ever seen me.

"Good evening, Vanessa," I greet her tenderly. "What's the rush to get me down here, dear?" I smile and wave at the rest of the camera crew.

Vanessa guides me to a private corner and finishes telling me about her tip. "This is dangerous," she begins, piquing my interest immediately. She looks around to make sure we're still alone. Her behavior is odd. Her skin is flush, and slightly sweaty.

"Are you alright?" I ask, placing my hand on her shoulder, attempting to draw out an answer.

She shakes her head, leaning against the wall for support. She meets my eyes and says, "I don't think any of us are alright."

Concern crosses my features as my eyebrows dip down. "What do you mean?"

"The contact I told you I was meeting..." I nod, encouraging her to continue. "He told me things. Things he shouldn't have, and there's nothing I can do to help. We're all doomed, every one of us." She chokes on a small sob.

"Vanessa, you're not making any sense. How are we all doomed?" My concern is deepening as I wrap an arm around her waist and turn her further away from the crew.

"I've known my contact since we were children. He works for the government... several of them actually." She hesitates, clearly reluctant to reveal too much about her friend. "He knows things. Secrets that are always meant to remain secret. Only this time, he says there's nothing anyone can do." She pauses again, readying herself to give me the horrible news. "The launch codes to a number of chemical weapons placed around the world have been stolen and are about to be unleashed."

Disbelief covers my face. "What?" I ask, dumbfounded.

"I'm telling you the truth. The only question now is, do we tell the rest of the world what we know?"

Silently, I shake my head as she speaks. "I'm still not sure what's going on. I'm not telling millions of people until I fully understand what exactly we are facing. Tell me everything you know."

She nods. "Yes, okay." She combs her fingers through her long hair, and begins reporting as if she's giving a speech. "He came to me this afternoon, frantic, trying to steal me away. He's never given me a straight answer as to what he does, only that he works for the government. He's let things slip here and there, that tell me I don't want to know what he does. This time was different. He was pacing, muttering that there's no way to avoid *it*. Once I got him to calm down and explain himself, he told me more than I ever wanted to know. Our government worked with several other countries to create a self-defense weapon. They contracted a chemical weapons manufacturer to create and test it. The weapon worked so well, they secretly placed them all over the world, keeping control over territories with the threat of their country's destruction, kept governments pliant. The objective of this weapon is to infect everyone with a disease. He did say that some people will remain immune to the weapon." Her voice lowers. "Most will not survive. And the ones that do... will wish they were dead."

I couldn't wait any longer, I had to ask. "Where are these bombs located? And what kind of disease are we talking about here?" My heart is pounding. Vanessa doesn't lie and she certainly doesn't make up stories.

"They're not bombs... they're rockets. In roughly..." She looks at her delicate wrist, reading her watch. "One hour, they'll launch into the air and release this disease all over the world. No place will be left untouched."

"That's before tonight's show." By 6:00 tonight, everything as we know it will be changed.

"Yes." She ran her fingers through her hair again nervously, barely containing her hysteria. "He said, *a giant flash will light the sky, most will drop where they stand.* The impact is immediate. The chemicals will trip a trigger in your brain that shuts off, stopping your life in its tracks. Those who survive the initial flash will become ill. They'll turn into bloodthirsty monsters that lack any humanity."

"Does he have proof, or is this just his word?" I ask. I like to have more to go on than someone's word. Especially, someone I don't know personally.

"His word. But it's enough for me. I'm leaving with him. He would have taken me with him earlier, but I begged him to let me talk to you first." Tears swim in her eyes, as if she's saying goodbye already. "Come with us," she pleads. "Please! I can't take the thought of leaving you behind." She begins to cry silently and clutches at my arm, already knowing the answer before I speak.

"I can't and you know that." I take her hand and fold it between both of mine. "You go. Get as far away from this place as you can." I pause thinking. "Is there even a safe place to go?"

She swallows hard. "I don't think so. No matter who you are, or where you live, this is going to end all. Except those who are immune. I'm not sure if I'll want to live through this. I'm hoping it's over quickly."

My chin trembles. It's the only time I've felt relieved that Evelyn is no longer with me. I'm ready to be with her, but before I go, I can help others through this devastating time. "Does he know who is releasing this, or why?"

"Another country. A civil war erupted and the wrong side won. The radicals are part of a religious group, that believe that if they end the world, we begin life in another. The US attempted contact, but the radicals wanted no part of it. They started the countdown on the weapons, before disabling the detonator. There is no way to stop them." Her hand is trembling.

"Is there anything else? Hopefully, there's a chance I survive long enough to relay as much information as possible to the people." Living long enough to inform the American people is my top priority. Then making it home to Betsy for her walk. A small smile finds my lips. I might see my lovely wife today.

"That's everything. I know it's not a lot to go on... And who knows, maybe it's not true... but deep down, I think it is." She wipes at the tear that runs down her cheek.

A large male wearing all black, barges through the side entrance. He glances around until his wild and frantic eyes land on Vanessa. *This is her friend.* The expression on his face tells me he's serious, this is not a scam, this is real. His longs strides head in our direction. I cup Vanessa's cheek, she's the closest I've had to a daughter. I've worked beside her for years, and this is probably the last time I'll see her. "Go. Get yourself somewhere safe. It sounds like you're the safest with your friend. May we meet again." I kiss her forehead and nudge her towards the man.

She stumbles as she hugs him. "He won't come," she whispers, heartbroken.

He pulls her tightly against him, eyes locked with mine over her shoulder, before shoving a needle into her arm.

She falls limp against his chest. He holds her up easily, keeping his eyes on mine.

My heart lurches. "What the hell are you doing, boy?" I move to reclaim Vanessa.

"Stop," the stranger growls, pulling her tighter against him. "This is her only chance at survival. What I gave her in that shot, just might help her live through this shit."

"She said you couldn't stop it. Don't you have this antidote for everyone's use?" Why wouldn't he want to save everyone?

"There are only a handful of these. They gave me the shot a long time ago, in case I encountered the disease. The one I gave Ness is the only other one I could find." His expression pleads with me to understand. Vanessa's important to him.

After watching them for a moment, I nod. "Go, then. Save her."

The man nods, silently picking up Vanessa and cradling her in his arms, before he exits through the same door he'd entered. My heart is leaping frantically in my chest. The set is eerily calm as panic courses through me.

Looking around the office, I watch my coworkers, and no one notices Vanessa's departure. I've known most of these faces for years. *Do I warn people? Are they going to even believe me?* More importantly, *would it even matter?* No. Warning people that they may only have until 6 PM to live, would only create chaos. Or get me thrown in the loony bin. I round the anchor desk to complete my setup before the news. Shuffling my papers for the umpteenth time, my mind begins to drift back to Evelyn. My heart thumps heavily against my chest. I, in no way, want to die, but the thought of seeing her lovely face again is exciting.

"Where's Vanessa? She should be here by now," Walter, the cameraman, asks.

"I gave her the night off. She wasn't feeling well," I explain away her disappearance. He opens his mouth to question me, not surprising since Vanessa hasn't missed a day of work since she started four years ago. "Food poisoning. She's throwing up everywhere and we can't have her doing that in the studio."

Walter nods, looking ill with the thought. He turns back to his camera and takes a drink of water.

I check my watch. *Twenty minutes.*

At this point, I'm clueless as to what to do next. You'd think tons of things would run through your head, but mine is blank. I'm banking on making it through the initial wave. Long enough to make it home to Betsy. Hopefully, she'll stay alive until I get there to walk her.

When ten minutes past six strikes and all is well, it would seem Vanessa's friend's story is no longer as credible.

As the thought crosses my mind, a pure blinding white light flashes over the windows. Closing my lids and covering my eyes does nothing to stop my retinas from burning. Lasting only seconds, but feeling like years, the high wattage blocks out all other senses. Minutes later, my eyesight returns, and what greets me is horrific.

Walter's body is slumped over the camera, beginning a slow descent until he lands with a loud thud on the floor. The rest of the crew litters the ground like fallen mannequins. No movement. No breathing. Just as Vanessa's friend said, immediate. They dropped where they stood. No one remains standing on my floor, but me.

I spend minutes that seem like a lifetime looking around at the fallen. Young or old, it doesn't matter what age. They all lie lifeless in awkward angles, as if taking part in some gruesome game. Realizing I still need to deliver as much news as I can—prepare anyone who may have survived for what is to come—I move toward Walter's camera. I face the lens toward the anchor desk, trying not to step on Walter in the process. Heading back to the desk, I catch my reflection in the makeup mirror. The glance halts my steps. The person staring back at me has a misshapen head, yellowed out eyes, and skin that resembles sweaty melting plastic.

I'm *Infected*.

My energy is zapped, but I finish moving behind the desk, and wipe the sweat from my brow, before situating myself in my seat. The little red light on the camera is blinking, signaling that I'm live.

"Good evening, I'm Harold Fossek. If you're still watching this broadcast, then you've seen the light. The blinding light in the sky has taken almost everyone with it. The person next to you, your family, friends... It appears I'm the only one left in the newsroom." I sigh, collecting myself before I continue. "We received a tip a few moments before the Flash appeared." I provide all the information Vanessa relayed to me before she left. *I really hope she's alright.*

When I finish recording, a weight lifts off my shoulders. I've provided what's left of the American people with as much information as possible, in three separate recordings, hopefully giving those remaining a fighting chance to live. Most are no longer able to hear a word I said, but if I reach even one person, it's been worth taping these final airings. Moving to the control room, I set up our system to repeat the same three recordings at various times of the day, for as long as the station has power. I watch each one, making sure there are no glitches. In each recording, the signs of my infection are more obvious. In the first taping, my head is only slightly warped, but by the last one, it's almost double its size.

Once everything's in place, I grab my coat and hat from the hook for the last time. Turning, I look at all the dead surrounding me, friends and colleagues, and wish their lives could have ended differently. Saying a silent prayer, I turn and head home to walk Betsy.

Stepping outside, seeing the carnage left behind stuns me. I'm locked in place, a sound like buzzing mosquitos in my ear. Wasted lives lie before me, a blanket of human bodies covers the ground. Men, women, children, regardless of age or color, they all fell to this chemical weapon. That abrupt. Our way of life, destroyed.

I'm living to see a massacre.

The horror jolts me from my thoughts. Sound slams into my eardrums. Screams fill the air. Even though most lay motionless, lifeless on the ground, there are still people, some running. Running for their lives, as others give chase. I tilt my head, as if the motion will somehow reveal the answer. There's something terribly wrong. The humans doing the chasing are horribly deformed. They're *Infected*, like me.

Processing information is becoming harder by the minute. As I touch my brow, I notice the large lump growing out from my forehead is substantially bigger. The infected are grotesque and I look exactly like them. There's nothing further I can do here.

"Help!" A woman runs by me. Pretty, with her dark hair and middle-aged features. She pauses next to me, as if to ask for assistance. Then she notices... notices the *Infected* features marring my skin.

What am I supposed to do?

I stare at her, waiting for her to say something. She

opens her mouth, poised as if to speak, when someone slams into her from the side. Growls and screams emanate from the two on the ground. My feet shuffle back a step, my mind wondering why I'm not processing this, while I quietly freak out. The screams are silenced, when the *Infected* snaps his head in my direction, challenging.

Challenging?

He thinks I want a part of his kill. The thought shocks me out of my haze, and I stumble back further, hands up, warding off any advances. Instead of attacking me, he slowly turns back to the woman whose stomach looks to be ripped from her body, and continues to enjoy his kill.

A flash of Evelyn's face replaces the carnage, reminding me of my goal. *Betsy.* We always walked her when I returned home from the station. One last evening walk for my old girl. I turn away from the carnage and head home.

There's a logical part of my brain that is rioting, fighting against this haze, knowing the gruesome acts going on around me are surely a version of hell. Still, that voice cannot scream loud enough to fully penetrate. I'm on autopilot as I head home, the sound is still there, but it fades to the background. My own rambling thoughts take over. I'm forced to step over dead people, but it no longer bothers me. I know it should, but it doesn't, and I'm not sure how I feel about that. Everything is slowing down and becoming less important, the closer I get to the house.

A man runs by me, screaming, not slowing down to ask for my assistance. For some reason, his presence annoys me and forces a territorial streak to the surface.

I growl at him, long and deep.

The shock of my actions snaps me straight.

I was about to attack that man. For a second, the predator was the only thing that existed.

Seconds later, a body slams into my side, almost knocking me over. Not slowing in her pursuit, an *Infected* female chases after the man, who passed me moments ago. I stare after them, in a trance, as I finish walking up the steps to my door. Standing at the door, I try to remember how to enter.

Again, I tilt my head, trying to decipher a puzzle that I know I have the answer to. My gaze locks on a round silver disk on the door.

Keys.

Reaching into my pocket, I pull out my keys. Looking back and forth between the lock and the keys, I finally remember to fit it in the hole. I try the first one. It doesn't work. The second one doesn't work. The last key finally slides in all the way, and I turn it. Opening the door, I walk in. Betsy's normal greeting is not waiting for me at the door.

"Bmmthy." My tongue won't form the words I'm attempting to speak. I try to call her to me, but I get no response.

I shuffle my way down the hall, my feet dragging. *I better get her evening walk out of the way.* Rounding the corner to the living room, I see her curled up on her bed. Words still elude me, so I hum instead. *Humming always makes me happy.*

I clip Betsy's leash to her collar and we turn to leave out the door. Taking her out is probably not the best idea, but I know she loves her walks. We leave the porch, forgetting to shut the door, not that it matters much anymore.

Next door, Nancy leaves her townhouse. I wave, just as I do every evening, except this time Nancy looks scared. I smile, trying to soothe her nerves, but still, her eyes grow large, as they move frantically between Betsy and me. I look down and Betsy is lying down, resting again. Glancing back up, Nancy is running down the road, in the opposite direction.

"Hmm... I woner wa wong wiff er?" I ask, Betsy. Not that she'll answer, she is a dog.

I continue down the sidewalk, stepping over people where they lie in our way. Betsy took her time and climbed over them slowly. Betsy's age is concerning me for the first time, as I watch her move at the slower pace.

I'll have to make her an appointment at the vet. Dr. Glenn will make room for her.

As we walk, I observe the neighborhood Evelyn and I lived in for over 30 years. Nancy is the neighbor to our left. We have the corner townhouse, which gave my Evelyn a wide view of the area. She knew that Nancy is a cheater. She was sleeping with a man half her age for the past three years. Every Wednesday. Evelyn always joked about it being hump day. Nancy doesn't know it, but my Evelyn used to watch the people in this neighborhood like a hawk. I teased her all the time, calling her the town stalker. She'd laugh and tell me to shush.

As Betsy and I move on, I see most of our neighbors haven't made it out their doors. The next stoop over belongs to Kathy, the cat lady. Evelyn said she never leaves the house and she was pretty sure she's a hoarder. Piles of random things stuff her house to the brim. There's no way she'd leave her stuff behind. She's more than likely slumped over her hoard, surrounded by all her cats. It may be harsh, but Kathy was never a nice lady, yelling at the kids on Halloween to get off her porch. Anyone who can yell at a child is no friend of mine. Especially since Evelyn and I never had the chance to become parents. My wife would have made a wonderful mother.

The sidewalk is surprisingly clear of the fallen, other

than Stanley, our mailman. His mail truck sits idling next to him. It looks like he took all of three steps before he dropped. His arm outstretched, with fingers clasping the mail, only seconds away from stuffing the letters in the box. He was a nice enough man, giving suckers to the little ones in the neighborhood. Except last Christmas, when Evelyn baked him some cookies and he said he couldn't eat them, giving some excuse about his sugar intake. Now, I know my Evelyn doesn't bake or cook well, but it's the gesture that counts. His refusal upset her terribly for the next couple days, until I told her they were amazing, and ate the entire contents of the tin myself. My stomach hurt for three days, trying to digest those things. Fitting that he only made it three steps. Maybe he should have been kinder, and eaten her cookies.

I smirk as I step over his fallen corpse. Betsy has small legs, so she gets stuck behind Stanley, having trouble hopping over him. She doesn't whimper, but I know she doesn't like it when I'm too far ahead of her. I give her a tug and she jumps right over top of him, stumbling for a couple of steps before she catches up.

Glancing over at Mrs. Smith's townhouse, I see she's in her normal spot, watching everyone in the neighborhood. Shelly Smith has always been nosy. She and Evelyn got along famously. They'd watch the happenings and then report back to each other in a gabfest. This person was doing that, and that person was doing this. They were the first to know about Nancy's indiscretions, Kathy's hoarding, and Jerry's constant need to wash his hands. I think they called him OCD.

I could never keep up with those two. Ever since Evelyn's passing, I swing by a couple times a week to see if she wants to sit and visit with me at the dog park. Rocco, Shelly's dog, is Betsy's brother from the same litter of Pomeranians. Shelly is the one who talked my Evelyn into getting Betsy. For this reason, she'll always have a special place in my heart.

Heading in her direction, I smile and wave to let her know I saw her. A look of panic crosses her face, before she pulls the curtain closed. My eyebrows scrunch as I tilt my head. *That's funny. Normally she's very excited to see Betsy and me.* I head down her path regardless of the unwelcoming response.

Reaching her porch is quite a challenge, I may just say hi and go home for a nap. I'm feeling rather exhausted.

Her door cracks before I begin my trek up the stoop.

"What the hell are you doing, Harold?" Her question throws me for a loop. Confused, I look around, trying to assess where this is coming from. "Wha you mean, elly? I come to see if you and Wocco wan come to the ark." The words come out grumbled, barely understandable.

My alien speech snaps her eyes unbelievably wide, as her mouth hangs open. Her lips begin to tremble, attempting to form words, but no sound emanates. "H... Ha... Harold? Wha... What happened to you?" She stumbles on her words.

What does she mean, what happened to me? Her question confuses me and makes me rather irritated. An overwhelming feeling of anger surges through my veins, from the tips of my toes to my fingertips. Shaking my head clears some of the misguided anger. "Nothing is wrong. I want to see if you and Rocco want to accompany us to the park."

She's shaking her head, the movement becoming more violent with each passing second. "*No!*" She screeches. "I can barely understand a thing you're saying! Look at your reflection, Harold!" My subconscious prompts me there's something I should remember—something very important—but for the life of me, my mind is drawing a blank.

Confusion and agitation are crawling over my skin. I've never lost my temper with Shelly before, but she's pushing every one of my buttons. Her demand resonates as I happen to look at the window level with the street. The reflection slams into me.

I'm Infected.

The disease has spread; my forehead is the size of a basketball, and white pustules and lesions cover my face. Yellow skin, red veins, sunken and hollowed out eyes looking at me. Jekyll and Hyde are playing a game of tug-of-war within my brain. One wanting me to remember the good, to hug Betsy tight, and remember I'm going home to Evelyn soon. The other whispering cruelly to drag Shelly out to the street, and devour her. Looking around, I'm reminded of the death surrounding me. *How on earth have I forgotten these crucial details?*

Still fighting against the darkness, Shelly picks that moment to open her stupid mouth again. "Harold! Get off my porch! Go home! Everyone outside is dead! For heaven sake, look at Betsy! She's dead! You're dragging around a dead dog!"

Each shout has me retreating farther. I'm now standing in the middle of the road, anger flicking its fiery tentacles up my neck, consuming me. Looking down at Betsy, I see what I should have before I hooked her to the leash, and dragged her from the house. Her limp form is lying on the ground next to me. Dirt is covering her beautiful cream-colored, fluffy fur, as blood seeping from her eyes dyes it red. She's been dead this entire time. The realization angers me more. Steam must be shooting from my ears, as a red haze clouds my eyes. Mr. Hyde is beginning to take over.

Bloodlust devours me.

At this point, the peaceful Harold is screaming from the dark recesses of my mind, trying to overpower this evil version of me. Inside, I still know right from wrong, even though the awareness is growing smaller by the second. An all-consuming urge to hunt and maim is taking over. I look down, attempting to shake these horrendous thoughts from my head, when I realize I'm losing the battle. There are only a few threads of restraint holding me back, as I lock my body in place.

When the last two strands of sanity snap, I feel it.

All my troubles, *gone.*

My head lifts slowly, as a snarky smile pulls at my lips. I open my eyes and focus on Shelly. *She's mine.* A feral growl rips from my throat, at the thought of decimating her. I drop Betsy's leash, she's no longer important. She's dead, after all.

Shelly must sense my change as well, because her eyes fly impossibly wider, as she backs into her door. *Silly woman, should have left it open. Now she'll have no escape.* She's frantically trying to open the door to get to safety, when I step in her direction, thoughts of carnage clouding my vision.

The sound of an engine revving has me turn to the right, just as a silver Chevy Silverado bears down on me. I'm thrown several feet, bones cracking, and skin slicing. A snarl leaves my lips, as I immediately start choking on blood. Surprisingly, the pain is absent. As I begin slipping into the dark abyss, clarity once again surfaces. Damn that Tracey, she should have never passed that drivers test. My wife, Evelyn, said the girl's a few crayons short of a box. Her words, not mine. Evelyn said it took her seven times to pass her written exam, and her driving test, six tries. She apparently hit a parked car on her second attempt. Now, as I lie in the middle of the road, I'm glad Tracey sucks at driving. This plague is robbing people of their humanity, but I'm still getting annoyed by bad drivers

Shelly, now inside her house and looking out the window, is screaming for me. Screaming in fear, and screaming because she's left alone in this unforgiving world.

My body spasms, as the final shallow breath leaves my lips.

ABOUT JESSICA GOMEZ

Jessica Gomez is a bestselling author of Suspense, Romance & Paranormal, Apocalyptic books. She's best known for her Paranormal novel, Infected. She independently published her first book, After the Before, in 2014, and reached #1 in Bilingual, Suspense, & Romance genres. She's currently working on book 3 in the Flash series, Evolved, which is to release Fall/Winter of 2017. As well as a new Alpha, Suspense, Romance series, schedule for early 2018. For more about this author, visit one of the sites listed. She enjoys hearing from and chatting with her readers, who have the same passion for reading.

Deds and Creds

The person that planted this story in my head is Colin Ginn. A BIG thank you for reminding me that even the smallest character has a story to tell.

Thank you, Tracey Parker for allowing me to use your name as the Truck driver who couldn't drive.

You can find the Flash series on **Amazon**.

To find more information about Jessica Gomez please follow her on the social media sites below.

facebook.com/BooksbyJessicaGomez

twitter.com/Author_JGomez

DAMAGED GOODS

An AM13 Outbreak Series short story

Chapter One

ow the hell did this happen?

H I still, even now, can't work out how I allowed myself to be so stupid. I'm a smart girl, aren't I? At least that's what I've always been told. The teachers at my school have always said to me: *'Ava Jones, you are a smart girl. One of the cleverest in the class. You'll go far in life'.* Maybe if they could see me now, none of them would be half as quick to say that.

I mean, what sort of girl allows themselves to get bit in the middle of the damn zombie apocalypse? I'm sure as hell not going far in life now!

I tentatively glance my eyes downwards to look at the injury on my trembling arm, but it's hard to stand the sight of it. As soon as I spot the slightly brown, coagulating blood that's forming on my wrist, my eyes squeeze shut and my lips clamp together so tightly it's as if they fear vomit might fall out if I dare to part them.

The pain is much worse than the sight though, so it's not like I can ignore it. It's hot and radiating all over me as if it wants to swallow me whole. In all honesty, I've never experienced anything quite like it before.

I'm not an idiot, I know what the bite means. I've been out there enough to know what it'll turn me into, I just don't know what to do about it. I know my skin will grey, my irises will pale, my body will slow as my brain shuts off. I'll become one of the monsters that are outside my door right now, waiting for some human flesh to consume. Hoping someone will be dumb enough to stumble into their path. I'll become the one thing that everyone wants to avoid these days, the nightmare that no one can stand to even discuss.

The worst part is I could've avoided that fate, too, if only I'd listened.

I thought it was the end of the world when the Lockdown was announced, I felt like the Government was just trying to punish me. Very early on, it was suggested that everyone needed to be quarantined inside their own homes while this disease was dealt with, meaning no one could go to work or to school or anything. To me, that was hell, a complete and utter nightmare. I couldn't see the bigger picture then because no one had seen any infected in real life, only online and occasionally on the news. I didn't really understand the impact of the virus or what was going to happen afterwards. All I could really think about was Noah.

Ah, Noah Marks, the love of my life. With his cropped brown hair, his piercing green eyes, and dimples that show up only when he smiles. He's the definition of utterly adorable, and he'd only just become all mine. It was quite an achievement to make that happen, I can assure you. Every girl in my class wants to be his girlfriend, and some of them have been, so I had to really make myself stand out in the crowd to get his attention.

I did it, then two weeks later we were told that we would have to spend a fortnight indoors, locked away from the outside world. That's a lifetime, anything could happen in two damn weeks. I couldn't stand the idea of such a long time away from Noah, so I made a plan. I decided that we wouldn't stay indoors during the Lockdown, and that actually we'd find a way to still spend time together. I had to do something, didn't I? I couldn't risk losing him...

Or so I thought.

Luckily for me, Noah is always up for breaking the rules, so he instantly agreed to the plan. Instead of dreading the looming quarantine, I actually started to look forward to it so I could see the boy that I was definitely falling in love with more intimately, on a one-to-one basis, while sharing a taboo secret that was only for us.

Only now, as I sit here with this gaping wound on my arm, do I think that it might've been a mistake. Even my intense love for Noah isn't worth losing my life over. Tears fill my eyes as it hits me again that I'm going to die. It's hard to accept the concept that it won't be long until I no longer exist. My life will be no more. My parents and my sister will have to find a way to carry on without me, my friends' lives will move on, and Noah will end up marrying someone other than me...all because I couldn't keep away from him for two weeks.

It wasn't worth it. I've been an idiot.

"Ava?" Mum yells up the stairs, completely oblivious to

my inner turmoil. "Dinner will be ready in a moment. You might actually have to leave your pit to join us all."

I thought it was a good thing that I never left my room so my family wouldn't notice me missing as I went out to see Noah, but now I just feel sad. Maybe if I'd been more sociable, or if Mum knew that I could easily use the garage roof to escape my room, I wouldn't have run into that zombified man on the way back from seeing Noah. I wouldn't have gotten close enough for him to bite me because I was so lost in the memory of the lovely kiss I just shared with my boyfriend, and I wouldn't be about to die now. I'd still be able to have the positive future that awaited me.

This is a punishment, it has to be. There's no one to blame for this but me and now I have to suffer the consequences of that. Of course, I'll have to tell my family eventually, there's no escaping the inevitable, but I don't want to do it just yet. I want to process and accept it myself first. I pull my sleeve tentatively down over my arm to cover up the wound. Then I grab another tee shirt and I throw it over the top as extra coverage to hide all the blood. I should be able to keep it a secret just for now.

I'll tell them, they deserve to know, but not today. I just want to have one more nice day with my family.

"Coming, Mum."

Chapter Two

I can't look at anyone as I take my seat at the table for dinner. I don't want to see myself reflected in any eyes because the truth's sitting firmly on the edge of my tongue as it is. I fear it might come out if I open my mouth at all. Just one more night, that's all I need. One more day of normal and I can be honest. I haven't seen many of the news reports but I'm pretty sure it doesn't happen that quickly. And even if it does, I'll feel it, I'll sense it happening and I can take action then. It'll be fine.

Just one more night.

"It's pie and mash tonight, is that alright?" Mum asks briskly as she plates up the food. "That's all I have left, so it'll have to do."

"How are we supposed to get food again?" my sister, Sadie, asks. Being six years younger than me, it takes her a while to understand things. In a way, I'm jealous. This is one situation where ignorance would be bliss. "Will we just starve?"

"There are supposed to be food deliveries while we're all in quarantine, but I haven't seen one yet." Mum gazes out of the window as if the answer lies out there somewhere. "I don't know, we'll see. They'll have to sort something out soon because they can't leave us all with nothing."

"Couldn't we go to the shop?" Sadie continues as if she can't sense the impending doom that lies just outside the door. "I want some chocolate."

"No, it's too dangerous. Plus, everywhere is closed anyway, it isn't just us locked inside."

I gulp down the thick ball of guilt that lodges itself firmly in my throat. It could become dangerous in here, too, if I'm not careful. If I remain in this house until I become a monster, then I'll end up endangering everyone. Much as I'm scared to tell them what's happened to me, I don't want to end up killing everyone else because of that. I know I need to go, I just hope I don't miss out on the opportunity through fear.

"Hey, kiddo." My dad claps me on the back as he takes

his chair next to mine. "What's going on with you? I haven't seen you all day long."

I turn my head to face his, unable to resist that look of love my father always gives me no matter what I do. I've always been a daddy's girl, he's always been my best friend, and up until recently, I thought we'd always be close. I guess that's just something else that I've sacrificed for Noah. Since liking him, I've distanced myself from everyone in my family. I've wasted precious time that I should've spent with them. Now, at sixteen-years-old, I need fully comprehend that soon enough, I'll never see any of them again.

This is all a load of regrets that I'll have to carry with me forever, whatever version of myself I am. I'm sure that even as a mindless zombie, I'll hold onto that sadness deep inside.

"Are you alright, Ava?" he asks me with concern plastering his expression. "You don't look like yourself. You look...ill."

My heart hammers painfully in my chest as he searches through my eyes. I don't want him to see the truth because I know for sure that he'll freak. At the same time, I kinda do want him to work it out...to save me from having to confess. I imagine that he'll wrap me up in a bear hug and he'll somehow find a way to make it right.

"Maybe it's Rickets," he finally decides in a self-satisfied tone. "That's what you get from getting no sunlight, isn't it?"

"Maybe in Victorian times." My mum laughs loudly at the accusation. "No one gets that anymore. I don't think there's been a recorded case in years."

"You don't know that. We're all stuck in our houses

unable to do anything...why wouldn't old illnesses come back? It makes sense, don't you think? Maybe that's what this virus is, something old returning..."

Sadie rolls her eyes and sticks her tongue playfully out at me as our parents continue to bicker about the aftereffects of the AM13 virus and the Lockdown. I smile weakly back but inside my heart shatters. Sadie might be a lot younger than me, and particularly annoying at times, but I think I'll miss her most of all. I'm sure it'll be her face I think of last before I go.

I hate the fact that I won't get to see her grow up, I won't be able to help her through her difficult teenage years, that I'll never be her role model...but I'm only getting what I deserve, I suppose. In all the self-pity, I cannot forget that I brought this on myself.

I push the food around my plate feeling far too sick to actually eat it, and as I do, I try to remember all the important parts of my life. I know they say that when you die your life flashes before you, but that seems like the sort of thing that comes with a quick death, so I'd rather do it now just in case. I want to recall it all so I can have something pleasant to carry in my heart.

I've always been a good kid, I haven't ever done anything wrong. I had a happy, average childhood with odd trips to the seaside to break it up. I was well-behaved in school, kind to my friends, mostly pleasant to Sadie. Nothing particularly exciting happened to me until Noah moved to our town. I always wanted things to get more thrilling, and it's safe to say that they have now. It's just a shame that it's in a terrible way and that I've ruined everything for myself.

I wrap my hand discretely around my wrist and wish that none of that had ever happened. My boring, average life was much better. Now I'm starting to see that excitement and drama isn't great. It's downright dangerous.

Things were way better before.

Chapter Three

Ugh, what the hell?

It's a real struggle to open my eyes as the bright light of morning streams through my bedroom window. My head pounds, my heart thumps violently, my nose feels like it's stuffed to the brim to the point where I can't breathe. My lungs feel flat and deflated as if they were totally useless limp balloons in my chest.

I blink rapidly as I force my aching body into a sitting position. Why now do I have to feel like crap when I've already got enough going on? Trust the common cold to come for me just as I've been bitten...

Wait!

My pulse stops dead as I realise something horrible. Words that I've heard rolling in the background as this whole mess with the virus has been unveiled. They've been spoken that many times that they've become a small buzz somewhere in my brain. They've blurred into the wallpaper...until now.

Flu-like symptoms. That's how the virus starts gripping onto you. Victims feel sick and achy, they have what feels like a cold. I glance down in shock as it becomes increasingly clear that my body is already failing me. I haven't had time to adjust to what's about to happen next, and it's already starting. I can't physically see any changes, but I can feel them which is just as terrifying. AM13 must be creeping through my veins, slowly swallowing me up and changing me.

I'm filled with an image of the infected and I desperately want to throw up. They're something to be disgusted by, something to fear or pity, not something to become. When it started to become obvious that this virus was something real, I completely dissociated myself with it. I never thought it would be me. I suppose everyone out there, all the corpses walking around once thought the same, but just like me, they've had to learn the hard way.

What happens next? I rack my brain, trying to recall everything I've heard but the only words that come to mind are far too unpleasant to accept. *Pain, organ failure, brain closure.* I don't know if I can deal with that prospect however long I have, I'm not sure I'm strong enough. Then again, would anyone be okay with that?

I feel like I want to cry. I wish to weep for what lies in my future, but it's as if all the liquid has been drained from my body and there isn't anything in there to create tears.

I glance at my arm, noticing the blackness that's overcome the wound. Without even really thinking about what I'm doing, I lean in and take a deep sniff. The stench is unbearable, it causes me to wretch. I already want it gone. If I had access to some form of knife then I'd probably attempt to remove the injured part of my body just to get it away from me. I don't think I'd be able to stop the journey of the virus that's already cascading through me at a million miles an hour, but I want that part of me gone. It feels alien, disgusting. It belongs to someone else, it belongs to that infected man, it can't be mine.

Bleep, bleep.

The sound of a message bursting through my phone doesn't fill me with the usual glee. I know it'll be Noah and that he'll want to spend time with me today. I wish I could see him too because the normality of that would help me to forget, but I can't. I don't want him to look at me when I'm like this.

With a tentative, trembling hand I pick up the phone and I glance my eyes through the message: 'Hey Ava, what time are we meeting today? Miss you xxx'

My heart yearns, but my brain shuts down any possibility. Not now, not yet. Maybe not even ever. Unfortunately, it's going to take a lie to make this work.

'Sorry, Noah, Mum caught me coming in yesterday. I don't think I'll be able to get away. Miss you too xxx'

With a heavy heart, I set my phone down and I completely ignore it when it goes off again. Then I pad my way into the bathroom to get some cold and flu tablets. There might not be any real way to combat this sickness, but I have to at least try.

"Alright, Ava?" my dad's voice calls out from behind me, making me jump. "You sound like you've got a cold. I thought you didn't look well yesterday." I stiffen, my blood runs ice cold as I expect him to put two-and-two together. "Typical, huh? Just as we can't get out to the pharmacy. Still, I'm sure we've got something in the cabinet."

Of course, he isn't going to suspect. Why would he? To suspect, he'd have to assume that I've gone outside and my dad trusts me too much to believe that I'd do such a thing. Maybe I've distanced myself from him recently, but he still only knows me as the good girl that I've always been.

"Erm, yeah thanks, Dad." I don't how to reply to that, so I barely say anything. "I'll probably be in bed most of the day."

"No different to usual then," he half smiles. I think I can see a glimmer of something behind his gaze, like maybe he misses what we once had. I want to acknowledge that, to tell him that I miss it too, but those words are too overwhelming to say aloud. "You get better, kiddo." He ruffles my hair playfully. "Take care of yourself."

"Right, yeah." Say something! Tell him how you feel. "Thanks."

Cowardly until the very last minute. I can't express my emotions because I'm afraid of falling apart. As I watch the most important man in my life walk away, I don't know if the aching inside my body is because of the virus, or because of my dad. Either way, it hurts like hell.

Chapter Four

It's so hard not to scream aloud, I've never experienced agony like it. It feels red hot and fiery, yet somehow icy all at the same time. I thought the virus was supposed to take forever to ravage my body, but I only got bit yesterday and I can almost feel everything giving up on me. My heart aches like hell, my stomach is all twisted up as if someone has hold if it and they're squeezing it tight, and it's an absolute challenge to get any air into my lungs. I've never had to concentrate on breathing before, but now I'm having to suck back air as if there's no tomorrow.

The tears are streaming hard and fast down my face and I think my lip is probably bleeding from how hard I've spent the day biting down on it trying to keep the pain inside. At one point, Dad came in to check on me but I told him to let me rest until I felt better. I had to practically bark those words at him, but at least I got the message across.

I suppose it's lucky, really, that he's so relaxed in his

approach to parenting. Again, he and mum are letting me be, leaving me alone to be myself.

Wonderful.

Since this is pretty much the final stage before the virus consumes me completely as far as I can remember, I need to take action now. There's no more waiting around for me to come to terms with this change inside of me, it's moving too quickly. Everything is spiraling out of control ,which leaves me with no choice. My brain already feels very fuzzy, and I want to make my choice before it shuts off completely. I fear it could happen any moment, and while I might've been scared and selfish up until this point, I won't be that way anymore. I'll protect those that I care about because it's the right thing to do.

It's hard to think through the pain, every thought is tainted, but I'm pretty sure that I only have two serious options; I tell my family and let them take control, or I leave. Much as I'm tempted to take the childish way out and to let my parents make the hard choices for me, I also know that isn't fair. Making my parents kill me would be the most selfish choice that I could ever make in my life. They won't want to do it, and I won't want to say goodbye, which will make it all a slow and involved process. It seems I don't have time for that anymore. I'll turn before I die, and that'll kill them too.

I got myself into this, I need to get myself out of it.

Plus, most importantly, there's Sadie to think of. I can't even begin to consider how my death would affect her. It'll be hard enough for her to learn that I'm missing, but I think it'll be kinder in the long run.

At least I hope so.

I clutch onto my stomach as I push myself towards my phone. I don't have enough strength left in my arm to write a goodbye note, nor would I know what to say, but there is one person I could talk to who'd pass the message on for me. Noah. I think he might take the news better too, especially if we're outside where he can just send me on my way. Much as I'm in love with him, we've only been really involved in one another's lives for a short while. Our bond isn't as strong as I'd like to think, certainly not as powerful as the one I share with my family, which makes him the perfect candidate.

Admittedly, there's also a part of me that wants to see him again. I want to put my eyes on his face before I die. Just to give me one more lovely image to keep me going. I would love to hold onto a little bit of who I am up until the end.

*The end...*even now, with all this pain, it's hard to think of it as 'the end'. It's hard to envision a world without me in it. Or this version of me anyway. I guess until they really do get this virus under control there will be a part of me that still exists. But then...nothing.

Hopefully, none of that will matter if I find a way to say goodbye.

'Noah, change of plan. Meet me in the usual spot in an hour. I can't stay for long though.'

I grip onto my bedside cabinet until my knuckles turn white while I wait for an answer. It would be just my luck that now he won't want to see me, just when I need him more than ever. I try to work out what I'll do if he doesn't get back to me, but my mind reels with totally useless ideas, proving to me that my brain definitely doesn't work in the way it did before the virus. That bit of me is being stolen away, piece by piece.

Luckily, just as I'm about to drive myself insane, the familiar bleeping sound rings out once more, flooding me with relief.

'*Sure, look forward to it. See you then xxx*'

Okay, great. I breathe deeply as I plan. I just need to hold it together for another hour, that isn't too hard. I'm already dressed, I don't need to do anything until then, I don't even need to take anything with me. I just need to hold it together. I need to keep hold of my faculties, to remember who I am and who's in the house with me. If I can keep control of that then everything will be fine. Then I can see Noah, and plan my next step from there.

Simple. Nothing to worry about at all. It's all going to be just fine.

Chapter Five

My soft bed beneath my head...the view from out of my window...the grass beneath my feet...

I don't know what's happening really, it's as if someone keeps hitting fast forward on my brain, leaving me with only small snippets of information. I'm getting important parts, I know just about what's going on around me, but I'm missing all the filler details in the middle which is very disconcerting. I know I'm outside and that I'm moving in the right direction, but I don't recall making the choice to leave, or the jumping out of my window part.

I probably should be panicked about that, shouldn't I? It feels like something that should be troubling me, but I don't feel that way at all, I've simply accepted it for what it is. I have a sense of peace about it, just because I still have *something* left of myself for now. It feels nice to hold onto the little bit that's still *me*.

I'm slipping away, I can feel Ava Jones slopping off me like a wet towel. I have no idea where she's going or what's going to happen to her, but soon I'll only be a vessel. I'm more aware of that than I've ever been anything else. It's strange to know that so casually, when before, everything sent me into a tailspin. I suppose it's because I've held it together for an hour while I waited at home, and that was my only aim. There aren't many good things left happening to me, this is officially the worst day of my whole entire existence, so I need to cling onto any victory, however small it is.

Huh?

All of a sudden I feel dizzy and disoriented as if I don't know where I am at all. The last thing I was aware of was the outside of my home. I feel like I was looking up wistfully at my bedroom window wishing I was still inside. Now though, I'm near the DIY warehouse in my town...which isn't anywhere near where I'm supposed to be going. I narrow my eyes in confusion and try to work out what I was thinking. Why did I end up here? Every decision I've made up until this point made sense, but this...I can't see the logic in it at all. I don't know what would've brought me to a part of the town that I almost never go.

What the...?

There's a smell in the air, a scent that I've never inhaled before, and there's something sweet and tantalising about it. It's new but exciting. Maybe a little bit exotic. I can almost feel it coating my tongue, luring me in...

No! I need to remember what I'm doing. I shake my head and try and pull myself back into reality. I need to meet Noah, I need to tell him what's going on so he can understand and also so he can pass the message on to my family. I don't want them to think that I just left, and that thought alone should be enough to drive me in the right direction. I need everyone to know that I'm sorry for all my mistakes and that I've done what I can to rectify it without causing any issues. I also need to ensure that from here on out, Noah stops rebelling and he obeys the Lockdown. If he doesn't, he might end up losing his life just as I have.

I twist my body and start stepping in the direction that I actually need to go in. I focus on my feet as I go, counting my steps to ensure I don't lose my mind again. There's something terribly frightening about losing a chunk of time. My brain desperately wants to know what I missed during that little period.

I don't know how people drink so much they forget about things, it's horrible. Not that I'll ever get to be a grown up now, but if I could find a way to make that happen I don't think I'd be able to ever touch a drop. If this messy, horrible experience has taught me one thing it's that I like to be in control.

As I walk towards the lush green park where I've been meeting Noah every day because we can hide among the trees to kiss and talk, I can't help but wonder what's going on with the quarantine. We were all supposed to be put under house arrest so the Government could get this virus under control. There were supposed to be food supplies delivered, Mum was right about that, and people rounding up everyone sick to get them treated (or maybe killed, I always thought killed) but there doesn't seem to be anyone doing anything at all, about the food or the virus. Noah and I have met up pretty much every single day without any interruption, we haven't had any food delivered, and the number of infected seems to be rising every single day.

I pray all hope isn't lost. I hope they haven't given up on humanity.

Losing myself is one thing, I don't like to really think about it at all, but losing all of humanity is something else entirely. It makes my stomach drop out and my insides curdle bitterly like out-of-date milk. The image of everyone that I've ever known becoming a zombie leaves me feeling hopeless and sick.

This can't happen. The human race cannot become extinct, that's just too much. There needs to be someone out there doing something, I refuse to accept otherwise.

No, I can't keep focusing on any of that though. For now, I just need to get to Noah. He's my new end goal and another one that I'm determined to meet. If I take things one step at a time, then I'm sure it'll be fine. All I need to do is see his face again. Just one last time before the virus envelopes me completely.

And hopefully, he won't hate me forever for being damaged goods.

Chapter Six

N...Noah?

I look at my shaking hands, unable to avoid the bright red, fresh blood all over them. I can't quite work out what happened, only that somehow everything is red. I don't remember much, I was on my way from the warehouse, I was walking towards the park thinking over everything that needed to be done...then nothing. Now I'm here and that damn vital middle bit is nowhere to be found. It doesn't matter how hard I scour my brain, nothing's there and I just know the part that's gone is the one bit I really should have. Somehow, I *need* to fill in the missing pieces.

My knees knock together as I force myself to glance downwards. Red liquid flows from my mouth down to the ground, giving me answers that I don't want to accept. I want to stare at the sky forever because that's blue and freeing, whereas the redness beneath me locks me in a cage forever, but if I don't do it then I risk never filling in that blank. Maybe not knowing would be better, but I just can't resist.

Oh God, Noah.

I don't know if I was expecting it or now, I have no idea where my brain is, but there he is, lying on the ground, with chunks of his body missing. His cheek, his thigh, his stomach...the jigsaw pieces are all there, I'm just in too much shock to fit them all together quite yet.

How?

Why?

What now?

It's like I'm in the middle of the most horrific nightmare ever, and there isn't any escape from it. I should feel disgusted as I look down at the mangled body of the love of my life with the, surely accurate, assumption that I'm responsible, but mostly I'm just numb. I'm annoyed that he won't be able to pass any messages on to my family, but that's about it. I guess the part of me that loved Noah has died alongside him. Or maybe I never loved him and it was all just childish infatuation. Either way, that bit of Ava Jones is no more.

Noah is dead and so am I.

I knew I would end up capable of murder like that. I guess I didn't think it'd happen so quickly but it has. I've transformed into a monster, all through my own fault, and now I need to decide what I want to happen next.

I suppose I should move really, start making my way out of here because there's nothing left for me to hang around for. The virus has got enough control of my brain to have me killing someone I love, which means every scrap of humanity I once had is on its way out. I'm slowly becoming a shambling, cannibalistic monster and there's no turning back now.

I need to leave. Yep, I definitely need to move.

I don't though. The thought circles my brain over and over again but I ignore it. Instead of going anywhere, I slump onto the ground to sit next to the remains of Noah. Once my butt hits the ground with a thump, I slowly run my fingers over the parts of his skin that are left. I caress him in the way that I used to in between kisses, as if we're the lovers that we were only yesterday, touching each other because we can't bear for any bit of us to be apart.

I can't speak to him, I don't think I have that part of myself left, so I try to communicate my apology through my mind instead. It's not much, but it's something...right?

Noah, I didn't mean to do this to you. I'm sorry. I didn't even know that I was doing it, to be honest. I wasn't myself when I killed you, but I assume you already know that. I never would've wanted to hurt you. I stare at his eyeball, wishing this conversation wasn't happening. I wonder what went through your mind when you first saw me. Did I look like a monster, or couldn't you tell until it was too late? How strongly did you fight me when I started to attack you? Or were you too shocked to do anything?

I brush my fingers over my lips as I try to imagine the scene of horror. I'm glad I don't remember what happened because that's something that'd stick with me forever. This is bad enough, that definitely wouldn't have been the sweet picture that I wanted to be left with forever.

I guess I just want you to know that I did love you. I think. If it wasn't love, then it was certainly a whole lot of like. I know we're young and we hadn't been together for a long time, but I admired you for such a long time, before we were even together, that it had to be love and I really didn't want things to end this way.

Then again, back when we started, 'this way' wasn't even a possibility...

It isn't until I look at my hands again to see the intestine trailing towards the ground that I realise I've been snacking on Noah's organs as I silently communicated with him. As I thought, I was stuffing parts of my boyfriend into my mouth like he was a bowl of peanuts. How messed up is that? I'm sick. I need to get the hell away from here!

I jump up and push myself away from Noah so I don't look at him anymore. That's really freaked me out, I feel even worse than before for doing that. Just because he smells sweet, just because I'm starving, doesn't mean I need to eat him.

Although...

Would it be so bad to just have one last bite? The damage is already done, isn't it? He's already dead and I *am* desperate for something to sustain me. Maybe just a tiny bit more, then I'll leave this place forever.

I drop to my knees with what feels like a twisted grin on my face. Yes, one more bite. That'll be just fine.

Chapter Seven

My eyes are blurry. I can't even see anymore. I don't have the slightest clue where I am, but I'm walking regardless. I honestly don't really know anything apart from the fact that I need to get the hell away from Noah. I've eaten too much of him already, I'm an absolutely terrible person. I need to make my escape before I hurt anyone else I care about which is why I'm heading towards the outskirts of the town as quickly as I can make my ailing body go, before I do something else I regret.

"Ava?"

Huh? Who the hell is that? I spin around wildly, but of course, my eyes aren't working. My ears seem to be on fire though, I feel like I could hear for miles. Either that or my brain is creating sounds for me, allowing me to hear things that comfort me. Maybe that's what happens right at the end, just to make that last bit of losing myself a little more pleasant.

"Ava?"

I open my mouth, trying to reply, but nothing but a low groan falls out of my mouth. It seems my voice box has switched off and I'm merely primal in that respect.

"Ava, what are you doing out there? It's dangerous, come inside."

Oh, okay. That's my mother's voice. I've definitely gone a little insane and I'm starting to make things up inside my mind. That's alright, it's quite nice actually. I might've been a daddy's girl but I still love my mum a lot. It's nice to have her with me, although it does encourage me to keep on moving. Knowing what I did to Noah keeps me going because I have to get far away from everyone I love.

Of course, I'm tempted to go back home. I would love to see my family again, but I've already proven that I cannot be trusted. I don't want to be responsible for any more deaths.

"Ava, stop walking away." The tone is sharper now, which somehow makes it feel less like an illusion. "Come here. Why are you all covered in blood, have you been fighting?"

All of a sudden, a scrap of my vision comes back. Just enough for me to see a familiar shock of brown hair. My heart stops dead in my chest as I realize what this could possibly mean. Maybe, without even meaning to I've followed through on my impulse to get back home to my family. I've walked to places before with absolutely no intention to. I could've easily done it again...

It's either my mother or an image that shares her features very clearly. And her smell. Her very tempting smell.

I move closer to her, slowly and purposefully dragging my feet as I try to work out how accurate my vision is, and as I do the smell becomes overwhelming. It wafts up through my nostrils and races over all of me, consuming me.

I'm Ava Jones, I think dreamily to myself, almost as if I'm wasted drunk and I'm trying to recall the vital details of my life. *This is my mother, not someone that I want to harm. As long as I remember that everything will be alright.*

"Ava, what are you doing out here?" Mum asks cautiously. "What's going on here? Why are you outside? The Lockdown started days ago, you're supposed to be indoors."

I open my mouth but all that happens is my teeth bare at her. I can't see Mum's fear but I can almost taste it on the tip of my tongue.

"Ava, I don't like this." I hear her footsteps shuffle. "Why are you acting so strange?"

I'm sorry, Mum, I didn't mean to do this to myself. I desperately wish that I could vocalise my emotions, that I could express my feelings properly but of course that opportunity is long gone now. This will have to do. I was foolish, naïve, stupid. I'm sorry for upsetting you, I apologise for ruining our family, now all I can do is make things right by getting as far away from here as possible.

I turn to walk away, to leave her alone, but there's an anchor within me, weighing me in place, keeping me by the only home that I've ever known.

I'm going now, I promise you. Any minute now...

Then I feel myself dive for her, and everything goes black for the very last time. The world is gone to me forever. I didn't pay attention to the Lockdown which has turned me into a monster.

Ava Jones is no more.

6

GONE FISHIN'

Eli Burns

Ten years after the end of the world, there were a couple things you don't think you'll ever hear again. Stuff like a child's laugh. The ding of a microwave. A quiet dead guy.

Michael Jackson's "Thriller" was pretty high up on that list.

Eli Burns had to wrack his brains to try to come up with what he was hearing. Like trying to match an actor's name to his face, or what those sons of bitches at the back table *should* have tipped on their bill. This sounded like something sliced off at the edge of a dream. Something you don't remember soon as the muzzy morning light hits you, takes you from that world to this. In a way, it was. Michael Jackson was a relic of the old world. Gone, same as Harley Davidsons, same as Coors, same as a woman didn't taste as skunky as she smelled.

Eli and his boys might live on the bones of the old world, but they sure as shit didn't hear its words anymore.

He and his boys were out past the walls clearing out an infestation of geeks. The last thing anyone wanted was those things piling up. Like junk mail that stank and bit. The thing was, geeks attracted geeks. One day you might have one of them at your fence, pawing and jawing to be let in for a quick bite, but leave the son of a bitch alone, and the next day there were ten, then a hundred, and pretty soon a whole sea of rotting flesh that smelled like bad cheese. So it was good civic responsibility for Eli and his boys to go out once every couple days, and Little Bunny Foo Foo any geeks that might have piled up. There was a price to ruling Geektown, USA.

The name wasn't Eli's fault. He always told new arrivals not to blame him, before he figured on what to do with them. The name had been decided back when Luther Childs was in charge, but old Luther got his ass shot during a raid down south, so Geektown was Eli's now. He never liked it, but he figured that Luther had made enough people afraid of it, that the name had some value. Geektown wasn't the biggest settlement around either, so a little fear could go a long way. Keep what was theirs, and when the time came to raid, might encourage folks to surrender without a fight.

Eli and his guys, that was Filthy Pete, Rock, and Lewis prowled through the ruins of the town that had once been Olympic Beach, Washington. A tiny tourist burg for people who wanted some time at the shore, but didn't want to do anything silly, like wear bikinis or go swimming.

Eli had walked these streets enough to have sketched the lot of them from memory. Most important were the traps Geektown's people had set for the geeks and maybe a breather who wandered through without knowing whose house they were in. Open manholes made effective pits for the bastards to fall into, clotheslines hung at neck height kept them corralled, and the occasional hammer-from-a-doorway gag could pick the odd one off. Though much of the buildings were overgrown, either by ivy consuming the walls and rusted-out cars, or weeds and grass sprouting through split sidewalks, a trained eye could see the streets were kept clear. Now, the four men, armed with makeshift crossbows and hatchets, wrapped in old riding leathers and fading ink, hunted through the asphalt thoroughfares, bopping the occasional geek on the head and dumping the corpse into the sluggish river flowing out to sea. Like responsible municipal employees.

Until, of course, "Thriller."

"You hear that?" Lewis asked. Lewis was a skinny kid they found out in the wilds maybe four years ago. He'd grown into a hell of an asset, though it had taken some time, and they'd had to break his eye socket when he wouldn't stop whining. Now his right eye kind of listed to the side, like a boat in a bad storm. He had skin the color of bad milk and a personality to match.

"Hear what?" Rock wanted to know. Eli called him Rock because he looked like one and was almost as smart.

"Imagining things," Filthy Pete said. He and Eli had known each other since before the world fell. Pete and the rest of his buddies from the Devil's Due M.C. used to drink in Eli's old bar. A couple of them worked on and off as bouncers. Kept the place the way everyone liked it, with the right people on one side of the door and the wrong ones on the other side. Sometimes Eli still thought about that place. It had been a good fortress for a couple months when the shit originally hit the fan. Then the geeks had torn down those walls, and Eli, Pete, and a couple others – all dead now – had busted out to live on the corpse of the world.

"No, no, I ain't. It's a song," Lewis said.

Eli *could* hear it. He didn't know how. A lifetime in a shitty roadhouse should have turned his hearing into a tinny whine, but there was Michael Jackson's girly voice, singing about the monsters closing in.

"Kid's right," Eli said. "It's a song."

"It's…" Lewis fumbled. A grin broke out over his face like finding the last beer in a shattered fridge. "It's 'Thriller.'"

Now, Eli had heard the song before. He didn't really go in for that kind of music. Eli liked badass music. Real man's kind of stuff. Like Kansas, or Queen. Jackson had been popular, though. Damn near inescapable for the year or so before the end of the world. Even some of the slabs of beef who'd frequented the roadhouse had liked it enough that Eli put it on the juke. Winced when someone picked it, but that quarter went straight into his pocket anyway.

Lewis started softly singing along. Filthy Pete hit him on the back of the head.

"You lost your damn mind, son? You hear music and you think that's a good thing? Means somebody's found us."

Eli felt the ice water clench around his heart, and the way Lewis's eyes got big, he was feeling it too. It had been some time since Geektown had to fight any battles. They only had about eight fighters, then the women, but they weren't going to help. Ungrateful. If one of the other settlements was coming for Geektown, Eli and the boys were at the front lines.

"Nobody shit his pants just yet," growled Eli, mostly to calm himself. "Let's see what we're looking at."

They holstered the hatchets and clutched their crossbows a bit tighter. They followed the music, creeping down a few more streets, before reaching the main drag of the town. This was lined with shops, long since looted. Now every window was broken, the displays bare, greenery steadily reclaiming the whole thing.

Down main street, they found the source of the music. Eli didn't see something he thought he'd lost to the apocalypse. No, he saw something he never thought he'd see in his life.

At first, he thought it was a woman. A big one. Six feet of lean muscle with big shoulders and narrow hips. The little pink skirt and a flash of panties when the figure moved had been enough to get Eli stirring. She was wearing shitkickers halfway up her calves. Her top was a sweater straining over a flat chest. She wore an old surgical mask splattered with geek gunk over her face. Her hair was blonde and cut in a Ziggy Stardust mullet. Her eye makeup, even from fifty feet away, was stunning. Looked like her eyes had purple and gold wings on them.

She was waving around a pair of goddamn samurai swords, and she was doing a butcher's work with them too. The mob of geeks on her, all green and pretty ripe, looking like they'd hauled their asses from the river, were getting filleted by this chick. She removed limbs as afterthoughts, before dispatching one with a slice through the cheeks, separating the top part of the head from the bottom by way of the mouth. Didn't kill the top part, but a geek couldn't bite without both halves of the jaw. Good enough for baseball.

The music was blaring out of an old silver ghetto blaster, sitting not far from the chick samurai, and it was belting out Thriller.

The samurai sword knifed through the last geek. The top of his head when tumbling away with a sound like a wooden block, only wetter. The rest of the green and slimy dead guy fell into a heap at the girl's feet.

Only now Eli could see this wasn't a girl at all. Just a guy in a skirt. Eli's half hardon didn't go away though. He wanted to punch the freak for that. How dare he look that way and make Eli think... Eli didn't want to acknowledge what he had been thinking.

"Hey," the freak said, waving to Eli and his boys. "What's up?"

The boys exchanged a worried look. It was like the freak didn't realize he had four crossbows trained on him. Maybe they didn't look like much, but they could punch an arrow right through bone.

"Who the fuck do you think you are?" Eli asked him, mentally chastising himself for being so polite. Freak threw him off his game.

"Oh, shit. Sorry. Name's Dave Pulaski."

"Lewis Thatch," Lewis said, then looked guiltily at the others. No one else spoke.

"You want to shut that fucking thing off?" Eli said. "Gonna attract more geeks."

"Oh yeah," Pulaski said, hitting *STOP* on the tape deck. Then he stood up. The surgical mask crinkled and Eli realized the freak was smiling.

"What the fuck are you doing here, *Dave*?" Eli spat enough contempt on the name to choke a starving geek. Dave Pulaski barely noticed.

"Looking for you! Heard a rumor there was a community of survivors around here."

"And you were lookin' to join?" Pete asked, laughing.

"Oh, hell no," Pulaski said genially. "I got my own community and everything. I was looking to see if any of you want to trade."

"What do you have to trade?" Eli wanted to know, mostly out of morbid curiosity.

"We got fish coming out the ears. Whale meat, whale oil. whale bone, if you got anyone who wants that. Makes a nice corset."

"The fuck are you getting whales?" Pete asked.

"From whaling."

"Oh," said Pete, an *ask a stupid question* look on his face.

"Why are you dressed like that?" asked Rock.

"I like to look as pretty as I feel," said Pulaski. "And I feel pretty as *hell.*"

"You a fag?" Eli asked. "We don't deal with fags."

"Cap'n Stew is as gay as the day is long. His husband, too." Pulaski frowned, as though he was having trouble dredging a thought up from the muck of his brain. "That's probably a good thing."

Eli slapped a grin on his mug. It was pretty easy. His natural tendency was to grin because he had himself a plan. Wasn't often the good Lord dumped a thing like this into his lap, and he was going to take advantage. This community of Dave Pulaski's, with their wealth of whale, had sent this fruitcake as an emissary. Sure, his bladework on the geeks was something, but anyone who lasted the apocalypse knew a thing or two about chopping up the dead. If they had to resort to Pulaski as an emissary, they couldn't have many people to choose from.

"You got women in this community?"

"What kind of community doesn't got women?"

Eli's grin got a little wider. The last time they'd gotten a new woman was Keisha, and she was kind of mouthy for Eli's taste. He was already thinking of ways to solve that. New women would make that loss hurt a little less.

Eli looked around. The street was quiet. No more geeks, but chances were a few were still shambling their way in, chasing the strains of "Thriller." The last thing Eli wanted was to let his guard down out here.

"Where is this community of yours?"

Pulaski pointed. A few blocks away was the marina, and past that, the Pacific Ocean. "Out at sea. They sent me here to see if anybody might want to trade. In a day or two, they'll be sailing on into the harbor for your answer."

"That's wonderful news. Just top notch."

Rock furrowed his simian brow, but Lewis and Pete got it. They got it with aces.

"Now how 'bout you drop them pig-stickers, *Dave*?" Eli said, raising his crossbow. The rest of the boys followed suit.

"Aw, shit," Pulaski said. "This is one of those places. Look, between you and me and this dead motherfucker, it's better if you trade with us. We have been trading all up and down the coast. Queen Mary, Republic of Chumash, Hearst Castle, Alive Here... they're cool. You want to follow their example."

"What are you going to do if we don't?"

Pulaski's shoulders slumped. "C'mon, dude. I've killed a lot of people. Like, a lot a lot. Like, we're talking a full Laker game's worth."

Eli laughed. He didn't believe it for an instant. A fairy like Pulaski couldn't even kill shame. If he had some kind of body count, it was all ambushes. Sneak attacks. Pussy shit. Pussy shit that didn't fly in Geektown, USA.

"Drop the pig-stickers, fairy. I ain't telling you again."

"Okay, dude. Your funeral."

The samurai swords clattered to the ground. Eli clocked the fairy's face with the butt of the crossbow. The beating only got worse from there.

Annie Doe-Eyes

Rock and Filthy Pete each had a hand up under the figure's armpits as they dragged him along. Though the figure was male, and Annie figured that out from the second she saw the slim hips, he was dressed as a woman. Pretty cute outfit, too, all told. And *clean*. That might have been the weirdest part. This wasn't a before-times-clean, sure, but by the standards of after the apocalypse, it was spic and span. The bulk of the soiling looked recent, too. Some black and green spray from geek chopping, and a waterfall of still-wet blood from face onto the sweater.

Eli marched along behind, crossbow over his shoulder like he'd just slain an elephant on safari. Annie hated Eli like she hated no one else in existence. She wanted to spit in his face, claw out an eye, bite out his tongue, but she knew what happened if she tried anything like that. Eli kept around the evidence of the last time one of his girls "got smart" as he put it. She was mewling in the next cage, shitting all over herself.

Lewis was last, carrying a pair of samurai swords in one hand and a beat-up old ghetto blaster in the other. He disappeared into the armory.

So instead of open defiance, Annie and the other girls pointed their faces at the floor and stole glimpses up through the hanging vines of their hair. No one was getting smart.

"Annie! Got yourself a roomie!" Eli said with a guffaw. "His name's *Dave*."

She slunk backward, out of the way of the cell door. With a clank, it opened, and the two thugs dropped the body of the man into the center.

"Once he's fixed up, maybe he can be in the same line of

work as you ladies," Filthy Pete said. "He's damn near pretty enough."

Eli gave him a raised eyebrow.

"You ain't never done time, Eli. It's an okay change of pace. You know, every now and again."

"This is why they called you Filthy, huh?"

"No, I once went a year without showering on a bet."

Eli and his boys disappeared up the stairs. Annie stayed still until she could only hear them as faint echoes above her. Then she turned her attention to the man on the floor. *Dave,* she reminded herself. *Eli said his name was Dave.* Normally, she never would have gotten so close to a man. They'd been the source of all her hurts for the last ten years. But for some reason, the fact that Dave was in a skirt made him feel a lot safer.

He was stirring a bit, which was a good sign. They'd opened a couple gashes on his head, and he was bleeding from his nose and mouth, but Annie'd seen a lot worse. Hell, if she looked up at Broken Suzy, she could see it again.

"Annie!" whispered Keisha from the next cell. "Who the fuck is he?"

She shrugged. "I dunno. I'm gonna ask him."

Dave's eyes opened and they were a fetching shade of blue, even if they were swimming in trauma. He had them made up elaborately too, but blood from his temples obliterated a lot of the makeup. He unhooked the surgical mask over his face and put it aside, revealing a pretty face like a rock star. He blinked the wooziness away and looked Annie in the eyes. She found herself withering.

"Hey," he said. "Name's Dave Pulaski."

"Annie."

Dave's face lit up. "Annie? No shit? Annie, are you okay?

Man, I keep hoping I'll meet a Billie Jean, but this world ain't so big anymore, you know?"

"They call me Annie Doe-Eyes."

"They? Oh, shit. *They*."

Annie didn't speak, locked in the old superstition that speaking something summoned it.

"Where the fuck am I?" he asked. Then he waved to the other girls, all five of them. Even Broken Suzy.

"This was the cop station," Keisha said. "Got us in the old jail underneath."

"Don't gotta ask why," Pulaski said. "Jesus, what the fuck is it with assholes and dungeons?"

"I'm sorry to say it," Annie whispered, "but you're stuck here with us."

"This ain't my first dungeon. Ain't my first group of assholes either." Dave pushed himself up to a sitting position. Annie flinched, her body locking up in fear. None of Dave's energy was directed her way. No, his hatred was the same as hers, pointed upward and ready to let fly.

"You saying you can get us out of here?" Keisha asked. "Pretty little fag like you ain't doin' much against them."

"Why does everybody think I'm gay?" Dave asked.

"You dressed like a whore on Sunset."

"I'm dressed like I look *good*."

Annie had to agree. Dave had nice legs and a pretty face. More than anything, he didn't exude an ounce of threat to her. He was dangerous only to the men who'd brought him in.

Keisha laughed. "You either crazy or stupid, but you funny as shit."

"You ain't the first to say that," Dave said, completely seriously. "So, ladies, when they brought me in here did you see any swords or are those upstairs?"

Annie pointed. "They're in the armory. Special kind of sadism. They keep their weapons close to us. We can see what we need, but they're too far to get to."

"What kind of weapons do they got?" he asked. "I saw crossbows and hatchets."

"That's about it," Keisha said. "Got some bows and hammers too. A couple guns, but no ammo."

"Yeah, ammo ran dry about two years back," Dave said. "Trust me, we've been trying to get our hands on some but no dice."

"Who's we?" asked Annie.

The other girls had started leaning forward, listening. They weren't as bold as Annie and Keisha. They'd been there longer. Endured worse.

Dave sighed. "Look, I didn't name it. The thing is, when we found the first boat, it was this sweet sailing yacht called the *Wet Dream*, and I tell Cap'n Stew we gotta name our place that. I mean, who doesn't love a good wet dream? I had this one where I was on Jabba the Hutt's sail barge with the entire cast of *Charlie's Angels* and all my sister's friends—"

"Dave," Keisha said. "Who the fuck are your people?"

"Oh. We're called Pacifica. Whole fleet or flotilla of us or whatever. Bunch of boats on the high seas."

"Geeks can't swim," Annie said. A smile crept into her voice. An alien sound in her voice.

"Damn straight. And assholes have a hell of a time doin' to us what they do to everyone else."

"So what are you doing here?"

"This."

"Getting your ass thrown in a cage?" Keisha asked.

"No. I mean, kinda. We hear about a community, Cap'n Stew sends me in. Calls me an ambassador. See how they treat me, and if they're cool, we add them to our ports and we trade. If they're assholes, then they get the high hard one."

"From inside a cage?"

"No, I usually get out first."

Annie felt the bright heat of hope inside this crazy man, but she didn't want to turn into it. Didn't want to find out it was fake. Not a flame, just a Christmas light and some fluttering plastic.

"Crazy *and* stupid," Keisha said.

"How many times have you done this?" Annie asked.

"Beats me. Doc Bloch calls me the leading cause of death for assholes. I mean, when the kid's not around. Gotta watch your language around kids."

"You have a doctor?"

"Yeah, a good one too. She figured out the whole geek thing. Somethin' to do with mushrooms. No vaccine or cure for a bite. I mean, not yet. We got us a network in the other places. They got a scientist and a doctor out in Fuck You—"

"Fuck You?" Annie asked.

"Fuck you too," Dave said genially.

"No, you said it."

"Oh, that's what they call themselves. They're right on the border of Oregon and California. This fortified plateau. Used to be a military camp and mobile lab back when the outbreak first happened. They're still around, and they're pretty cool, you ask me. We trade research. Only a matter of time, Doc Bloch says."

Annie shook her head. This really was insane. There was no cure. No hope. When a person was bitten, there was no mercy. You killed them or they got up and tried to kill you. But Dave Pulaski was walking hope. He was a bright light thrown into the darkness and he was blazing with no sign of fuel.

"So how many fighters they got topside?" Dave asked.

"Maybe eight?" Annie said. Keisha nodded.

"And civilians?"

Keisha laughed. "Ain't no civilians. Just those mother-fuckers and their pets down here."

"So, if I kill all of them, you're cool with that?"

"If you kill them, I will do things to you make your eyes roll back and your toes curl."

Dave started, then grinned. "You want me to take a bit longer with any of 'em, I take requests."

Now all the girls save Broken Suzy were leaning in, their faces alight. This was a campfire tale, told by a madman, but it was hard not to be swept up in his infectious enthusiasm.

"Cut Filthy Pete's fingers off," hissed Raven Mama.

"Show Rock his own guts," suggested Wendy Gams.

"Make Eli Burns *hurt*," whispered Annie. Murmurs of agreement chased her request.

"Rad," said Dave. "Now, this is a little like a Gallagher show. First couple rows might get wet, so everybody sit back."

The girls moved back against the blockhouse walls. Annie couldn't allow herself to imagine Dave Pulaski would do what he promised to, but the story was too good. Her heart was crawling its way from her chest, and tears wobbled in the corners of her eyes. Let him be the focus of their will. Let him take their rage and humiliation and turn it into death.

Pulaski cast about, then settled onto the shit bucket. There was nothing else in the cell. Ever since Broken Suzy tried to escape, there would be nothing dangerous allowed. Dave rapped it against the bars, back and forth, back and forth, releasing waves of stink, but he didn't seem to notice.

"Hey! Hey, assholes! It's Dave! I got some information or something!"

Annie wanted to hiss at him to shut the fuck up. To huddle in a little ball in the corner. Wasn't too late. She was wrong. She should have stopped this before it got out of hand. Before they were going to turn him into another Broken Suzy. But she couldn't move. Couldn't speak. And Dave didn't even seem to know what fear was. Dave didn't give a fuck about any of that. He hollered and banged and caterwauled until he got results.

Results in the form of Lewis. As the bastards went, Lewis was the least bad. He never hurt more than he had to, and there was something behind his green eyes. Something brittle and wobbly, that would only break in the dark.

Lewis came down the stairs holding his crossbow.

"Eli wanted me to tell you to shut the fuck up," Lewis said.

"Yeah, I figured," Dave said. "Could you come here for a second?"

Annie thought there was no way Lewis would keep coming, but he did. Something about Dave hypnotized him. This bloodied, beaten man in a skirt couldn't be any kind of threat. Annie saw it right then: Pulaski was wearing camouflage. The skirt, the makeup, that made the bastards think of him as a woman, and in their minds, women were walking weakness.

"What do you want, *Dave*?" The way Lewis said it, it was obvious he was aping something Eli had said. But it was tough guy pretension. Lewis tried to be them, but he never truly could.

"I wanted to ask you a question."

Lewis was all the way down the stairs now, padding forward, step after step. Annie wasn't even certain he knew he was doing it. The crossbow dipped and weaved, trained between the bars at Dave's face.

"What question? You eat when we feed you, you shit in that bucket, and when we throw the bitches in from your faggot country, you make 'em understand what happens when they fight."

Dave set down the bucket. "Right, right. Not that, though."

"What?"

"Annie said you cry after every time you fuck her and you won't stop calling her 'mother.'"

Annie's heart just about shattered. Now when Lewis beat Dave, he would beat her too. Probably do worse, just to prove he was all man. She wanted to shriek, but she was paralyzed. The fight had been ruthlessly beaten from her.

Lewis's eyes grew large. A snarl played at his lips. "You motherfucker—"

He took two more steps, and that was what doomed him. Pulaski was faster than a rattlesnake. His arms snapped between the bars and he yanked Lewis into them. The crossbow hit at the same time as Lewis's face did. His nose split open, hot blood streaking down it. The crossbow went off, the arrow shattering against the blockhouse floor, then the whole weapon clattered from his hands.

"No, no, no," Pulaski whispered. "Way she tells it, *you're* the motherfucker."

Dave let go of Lewis's lapels with his right hand, then gripped the back of his head. Annie looked away. A wet crunch split the air, and Lewis's body fell to the floor. Pulaski knelt, finding the keys in Lewis's pockets, and opened the cell door. For years, the heavy creak of that cell door meant only one thing: pain. Now it was an end to torment. Now it was freedom.

Pulaski tossed the keys to Annie. "Have fun."

He went into the armory and emerged carrying his two swords and the ghetto blaster. By that time, all the cells were open, and Annie held up poor, drooling Broken Suzy with an arm around her neck and under an armpit. Dave hit rewind. "Okay, ladies, don't come up till Thriller's over, got it? Unless you want to grab a crossbow and help out."

"Fuck yeah I do," Keisha said. Raven Mama made a guttural sound in her throat. Pretty soon, both had retrieved crossbows and full quivers of arrows from the armory.

"Annie? Hit play, please."

Thriller boomed out in the cellblock. Pulaski executed a quick spin, then a graceful moonwalk. "Sometimes I think the worst thing about the apocalypse is that it killed Michael Jackson before the follow-up to this one." He sighed. "Now let's go have a conversation."

Pulaski, Keisha, and Raven Mama disappeared up the stairs. The screams started shortly thereafter. By the time Thriller ended, a river of blood flowed its way downstairs.

Broken Suzy made a contented sound deep in her throat.

Cap'n Stew

Stew sailed the *Wet Dream* into the small marina to join the few rusted hulks still there. Stew burned with some small embarrassment at the thought of potential allies seeing the name, in looping calligraphy, on the hull of the yacht. Pulaski wouldn't let him change the name to something dignified. They were trying to build a goddamn civilization here and Pulaski couldn't let go of a juvenile sex joke. Problem was, Pulaski was the finest killer Stew had ever known, and he'd known quite a few. These little fishing expeditions didn't work as well without Dave Pulaski. So he got to win the less important arguments.

This was getting to be a habit. While he hoped Pulaski would be by the marina with some mayor, or president, or even petty warlord, ready to open up a trade negotiation, Stew knew it was a long shot. The world ending took the brakes off morality. Gave the world permission to embrace the desires that only whispered in the dead of night. Sometimes it felt like those who wanted to do right were a guttering candle in a blizzard.

Pulaski was out on the pier where his little boat, the *Even Wetter Dream*, was tied up. He'd collected a handful of strays: skinny women with haunted eyes that Stew wished weren't so damn familiar. They wore clothes sized and styled for men, packed over them in layers, most of which was shiny with wet blood like the hides of fresh kills. The littlest of them, holding up a drooling and broken woman, had a crimson-stained trucker hat shoved down over her eyes. Two of them, one sturdy with a large afro and the other a feral who looked like a Halloween witch, carried makeshift crossbows.

On the horizon behind them, a pillar of greasy smoke reached into the sullen skies. Stew guided the ship next to the pier.

"Ahoy there, Cap'n," Pulaski called out, waving. A few of the hands threw lines out to Dave, and he secured them to the pier. Dr. Judy Bloch stepped out from the ship to greet the new arrivals. Some tension bled from them when they saw a woman, whole and confident.

Stew looked Pulaski up and down. Most of the blood on him wasn't his. "I suppose this says everything I need to know."

"Geektown, USA was full of assholes," Pulaski said. "Now it ain't full of shit."

"These women want to join us?"

"Yep. I thought maybe they want to keep Geektown for them, but they wanted to burn it. So we burned it." Pulaski turned to the women. "This is Cap'n Stew. He's our leader, and he's super gay to boot, so you ain't got nothing to worry about."

"Thank you, David," Stew said. He turned to the women, careful to keep his energy directed inward. He had put on a little bit of weight now that they were at sea, and had decided to shave off his graying hair. The beard, though, he kept, and it had turned to the color of wet iron. His deep brown skin was wind-scarred from four years at sea, and he thought he looked maybe a decade older than he actually was. He addressed them with his hands behind his back, an avuncular smile on his face.

"Welcome to Pacifica. I'm Christopher Stewart, but most just call me Cap'n Stew. You can stay with us as long as you've a mind to. You can direct any questions to myself, to Dave here, or to Dr. Bloch."

Doc Bloch tended to the women as they boarded. They stayed out on the deck with her, under the open sky and in the kiss of the wind. Pulaski joined Stew as the crew fixed the tow cable to the bow of Pulaski's little boat. Stew glanced over at the bloodied swordsman. They'd been together a long time. Longer than anyone else. Stew had only just gotten used to the idea that they might even be friends. Each one of these trips, as successful as they were, took a little bit out of Pulaski. Maybe it was the beatings. Maybe it was the killing. But one day, Stew would send Pulaski out, and the swordsman wouldn't come back.

"You should let Judy look at your head."

"Bullshit, it's fine. They hit like grandmas."

"That's an order I'll give you, David."

Pulaski rolled his eyes. "*Fine.* I'll go see the Doc. So what's next?"

"Heard rumors of a place up the coast, calling itself Indian Fort."

"Gimme a couple days, skipper. I ain't as young as I used to be."

"Thought you said they hit like grandmas."

Pulaski offered a lopsided grin. "Like grandmas who pump iron a little bit."

"Take all the time you need," Stew said to his friend. Maybe one of these times Pulaski would say it was the last one. But he never did. And Stew knew the swordsman never would. This was what he was good at. What he was made for. He'd do it until he was used up. Until that razor-bright luck ran out. Maybe Pulaski had just figured out the riddle no one knew the world was asking: the dead were living and the living were dead. He'd put both of them into the ground until the day he joined them.

The yacht sailed out into open sea and met the rest of Pacifica. Other sailing ships of various makes, patched and repaired, tooling the Pacific Coast. Making a home. Founding a nation in the ashes of the old world. Stew figured he could do a hell of a lot worse. He just hoped he wasn't going to have to carve through half the human race before they saw some sense.

ABOUT JUSTIN ROBINSON

Much like film noir, Justin Robinson was born and raised in Los Angeles. He splits his time between editing comic books, writing prose, and wondering what that disgusting smell is. Degrees in Anthropology and History prepared him for unemployment, but an obsession with horror fiction and a laundry list of phobias provided a more attractive option. He is the author of more than 10 novels in a variety of genres including detective, humor, urban fantasy, and horror. Most of them are pretty good.

Thank you to my editor, Norma Krautmeyer, and of course my wife and daughter.

Undead On Arrival can be found at http://captainsupermarket.com/undead-on-arrival.html or his **Amazon** page.

To find more information about Justin Robinson please follow him on the social media sites below.

facebook.com/weirdnoirmaster

twitter.com/JustinSRobinson

A PEACEFUL TOWN

Mondays are always the worst, but today, everything is going wrong. I'm sitting in gridlock when I realize that the clocks are still set for the wrong time. I always leave it to Blake to change them and he forgot, just like every other thing I ask him to do. I tried calling to make sure he knew he made me late to work, but his phone must be off or something since the calls went straight to voicemail every time. Figures. I toss the phone on the passenger seat and then it begins to ring.

"Blake?" I answer the phone. "I was just trying to call you."

"I'm stuck in Arlington Heights," he tells me. "There's a car accident at the railroad crossing or something."

"I just heard about that on the radio during the traffic report."

"Yeah," he sighs. "I don't think I am going anywhere very soon. I can't get ahold of anyone at the office. The phone lines are messed up."

"I know. I tried to call you, like ten times, but it wouldn't go through."

"I think I am just going to head back to the house as soon as I can figure out a way back there," he tells me. "You should too. Call out today. Pick up Abby and meet me back at the house."

"I'm sitting in a ton of traffic right now. I can see the light is out up at the intersection. Maybe it'll clear up after that."

"No," he says. "Go home."

I roll my eyes. It's just like Blake to think I can skip work because it is too inconvenient today. He doesn't understand these things because he has never had any real responsibility.

"I have to get to the school," I explain to him. "Especially if something goes wrong today while all the kids are there."

"Listen," Blake says. "I'll go get A-"

His voice cuts out and the phone goes silent.

"What?" I say. "Blake, I'm losing you, the phone is cutting out. Blake!"

The line goes dead and I look at my cell phone to see the call failed. I call him back but only get a message telling me the circuits are all busy due to high call volume. With a sigh, I toss the phone onto the passenger seat again and stare at the line of cars in front of me and turn up the radio. Instead of cracking jokes or making prank calls like usual, the morning disc jockeys voices sound urgent and terrified. They're talking about riots and the national guard. My heart begins to race.

"What is happening?" I mumble to myself.

A driver blares his horn behind me and I hear people arguing on the street. I twist around in my seat to look out the back window at the car at the line of cars behind me and I notice Abby's jacket on the floor of the car. The sight of it makes me realize that Blake was right. I need to get Abby back home. That's all that matters right now.

A loud bang startles me. I look up and notice a hole punched through the back window. Like someone threw a rock at my car or something. I have to get out of here. After I shift the car into reverse, I start to wheel around, but I stop when I feel a sharp pain in my abdomen. My hands reach down as I hit the brakes and I feel the blood rushing out of me.

Someone shot me. It takes a moment for my brain to even make sense of it. I have no idea why someone would want to shoot at me. My bloody hand finds my phone in the passenger seat and I clutch it. I try to call Blake again to tell him what is happening but I only manage to smear blood all over the display.

This can't be happening.

I throw the car in park and open the door. Maybe getting out of the car is a bad idea, but I don't know what else to do. I don't want to stay there and get shot again. The pain really hits me as I climb out the car. I double over in agony and collapse on the street.

Other people are getting out of their cars and scattering in all directions for cover. I hear sirens approaching. More gunshots. A woman screams at the top of her lungs.

"Help," I gasp. My voice is barely audible and drown out by the sounds of chaos.

I crane my neck around toward the police sirens up the street where people are getting out of their cars. The driver of a black Camaro with red racing stripes spins his vehicle around in the road, clipping a cop that fires a few rounds through the windshield of the vehicle. Instead of stopping, the guy in the Chevy floors it and the cop stumbles to the ground. He howls in pain as the tires roll over his body. The car jerks toward the side of the road and crashes into a towering oak along the road. The door opens and the driver spills out onto the grass, blood gushing from the bullet wounds in his chest. I watch in shock as his body goes still on the ground.

"Can you get up?"

My head twists around to find a man in a stylish leather jacket and sunglasses reaching for me.

"I've been shot," I tell him. My voice cracks from my panic. "I don't know."

Instead of waiting for me to move, the guy just crouches down and grabs me roughly by the arm and pulls me over his shoulder. Before I know it, he is carrying me down the road. The pain surges in my lower back with every step and my vision begins to blur.

"Stop," I gasp, but the words are hardly more than a whisper as I struggle to breathe. Then everything goes black for a moment and I start to feel nauseous from the motion. I lift my head up and spot a car speeding right at us. I try to yell and warn the man that is carrying me, but by the time he whirls around the vehicle is too close. The man darts for the shoulder of the road and the vehicle swerves slightly but clips the man and sends us both sprawling on the ground. My head bounces off the gravel along the road and everything spins and blurs.

I know if I lose consciousness I'm going to die here. I twist around and get to my hands and knees and crawl alongside the road. The man that had been carrying me groans as he sits up. After he gets to his feet, he hobbles over and grabs me and pulls me to my feet.

"We need to get off the streets," he says as he drapes my arm over his shoulder and wraps his arm around my waist. We shuffle down the grass embankment and into the thick woods alongside the road. I trip over sticks and rocks every few feet and a couple times I drag him to the ground alongside me. Eventually, we emerge into a backyard in a subdivision of mansions. The man helps me up to the back patio and sets me down on a patio chair beside the pool. A pair of scruffy terriers growl and bark at us through the glass of the french doors to the kitchen.

"You still with me?" the man asked me. He waves his fingers in front of my face to get me to focus on him.

Once my eyes focus on his face, the man tries to calm me with a pained smile.

"Can you tell me your name?" the man asks me.

"Amanda," I gasp.

"Don't try to move, Amanda." The man presses a hand to my chest to keep me still.

I can't manage to say anything else, but I nod my head to let him know I understand.

"I have to go inside for a few minutes," the man tells me. "See if I can find a first aid kit or something. You should be safe here while I'm gone, but if you see anybody, and I mean anybody, you call me. My name is Eric. Just yell as loud as you can."

I nod again and watch as he scans the backyard before leaving my side. A moment later, I hear the sound of glass breaking and the terriers begin barking wildly inside. The man speaks softly to quiet the dogs. I stare up at the sky and try to ignore the throbbing pain in my abdomen. It seems like the man is gone for too long. The pain subsides enough for me to think clearly for a moment and I begin to panic at my situation. When my thoughts return to Abby at her school, I try to sit up but a crippling pain causes me to collapse back down on the lawn chair and start crying. It isn't just the pain, but the feeling that my child needs me and I'm physically unable to do anything to help her, which drives me to tears.

I let out a wail of agony, and then the man emerges from the house and hurries over.

"Shhh," he hisses as he scans the surroundings. "Easy, Amanda."

His right hand rests on my chest and he brushes the hair out of my face with the other.

"I need to see the wound so I have to take off your top," the man tells me as he begins to undo the buttons of my blouse.

I panic at the thought of this stranger undressing me in the open like this, but the excruciating pain is severe enough that I simply nod and let him undo my shirt buttons. He lowers the chair and rolls me over to check the entry wound on my lower back.

"Who are you?" I ask him.

"I told you. My name is Eric," he tells me.

"No," I roll my eyes. "I mean are you a doctor?"

"No ma'am," he shakes. "Just a corpsman."

I don't know what in the world a corpsman might be, but it's not like there is anyone else trying to help me and he seems to know what he is doing.

"There isn't too much blood," he says as he rolls me back again. He presses his fingers to my wrist as his eyes dart to the watch on his wrist. "But we have to get you to a hospital now."

"I can't," I groan. "I need to get my daughter from her school."

When I try to sit up he presses his hand firmly on my chest.

"What school is she at?" he asks me.

"Lyons," I tell him. "I need to get there."

"No," he shakes his head. "I'm going to find us a ride and get you to a hospital. I promise I'll look for your daughter when I can. Just lay still and I'll be right back to get you. Can you do that?"

He waits until I nod before he stands up and limps back to the house. Even though he got hit by a car and has to be in plenty of pain himself, Eric put himself aside to help me. I don't know too many people like that. Several minutes later he returns and helps me inside the house. The terriers bark and growl at us as we pass through the dining room. We move through the kitchen and a laundry room before we reach the garage door. Eric gets it open and helps me into an idling pickup truck in the garage.

"Buckle up," he tells me before he races around to get behind the wheel.

He shifts the car in reverse and backs down the drive. I jerk forward when he slams on the brakes, and the seat belt digs into my wound and causes me to groan in pain. I close my eyes and dig my nails into the armrest.

"Damn it," I curse.

"Sorry," Eric says as he shifts the truck in drive. He slams on the gas and wheels the truck around causing another surge of pain in my gut.

When I open my eyes again, I see he isn't just driving like a maniac through the subdivision to try and kill me. There are people in the road. Dozens of people. But something is all wrong about them. They stagger towards the car in bloodstained clothing with blank expressions on their faces.

"What's wrong with them?" I ask Eric.

"I don't know. They're not right," he mutters as he swerves to avoid a woman that is hunched over a body on the ground.

Once we pass her, I glance at the side mirror and see her face covered in blood. Her hands rip out another chunk of flesh and shove it into her mouth. For a second I wonder if I am losing my mind or if what I just saw had actually happened.

"Where are we going?" I ask him.

"Try not to talk," he tells me. He reaches across the seat and puts his hand on top of mine and presses it harder against the wound. "Just keep pressure on it."

We come to the end of the subdivision to a road that is clogged with traffic in both directions. Eric curses and slams on the brakes then reverses the truck and spins back around to drive in the opposite direction.

I begin to feel woozy, and the world begins to spin around me. My head rolls from side to side, and my eyes begin to close.

"Stay with me, Amanda," I hear Eric say, but his voice sounds far off like he is not in the truck beside me.

The world around me begins to dim and then everything goes black.

❧

When I open my eyes again, I am staring at the sunlight coming through the blinds in a quiet room. When I move, I notice an IV stuck in my arm. The wound to my stomach is bandaged, and I am cuffed to the bed. Fear strikes me suddenly. This isn't a hospital. I'm in a house. I debate calling out for someone, but I decide against it. Someone cuffed me to a bed, so it wasn't likely that it was someone I could trust. They certainly didn't seem to trust me.

My entire body feels weak, and I can barely move anyway. I try to piece together the last memories before I lost consciousness. There was a handsome man helping me on the street. Eric. That was his name. Maybe this is his house.

I look down and realize my clothes are clean. Even my underwear. And they are my clothes, but not the ones I remember wearing last. If I went back home, I have no memory of it.

For a few minutes, I stare at the clock on the wall until I hear footsteps outside of the door. I hold my breath as I watch the handle turn to the side and the door creaks open. The smile of the young woman that enters the room calms my unease.

"You're finally awake," she sighs. "Eric will be excited to hear that. He has been coming by every few hours to check on you."

I try to speak but my throat is so dry and hoarse that only a croak comes out. The woman grabs a bottle of water from beside the bed, opens the top, and pours it into a glass.

"Just small sips," she orders me before she hands me the cup and watches as I take a small sip of the lukewarm water.

"How long was I unconscious?" I manage to ask her.

"Four days," she tells me.

"Four days?" I gasp.

"You're lucky to be alive at all," she says. "You developed a pretty bad infection. I thought you were dead for sure."

"What is this?" I say and jerk my arm to indicate the cuffs that confine me to the bed.

"It's just a precaution," the young woman explains. "In case you didn't make it."

"I have to get up," I grunt as I try to sit up in the bed. I only manage to get halfway up before the pain in my abdomen becomes excruciating and I collapse back onto the pillow.

"Please," I beg the young woman. "I have to look for my daughter and my husband."

"Eric said to keep you cuffed to the bed no matter what," she says. She brings her hands together and squeezes her fingers as if to keep them from doing something they shouldn't. "I can't take them off."

"What?" I say. "What the hell is going on?"

She pinches her lips together and forces a smile like she wants to tell me something but she won't.

"What is it?" I ask her.

"I shouldn't even be talking to you," she says. "Eric said not to."

"No," I beg her as she turns towards the door. "Miss, please tell me."

She pauses in the doorway and looks back at me.

"My name is Lacey," she says. "If you need anything just call for me. Eric should be home soon. I wish I could do more for you, but I'm actually just a dental hygienist."

The door closes and I pull my arm against the restraints even though I know I am probably too weak to even walk across the room right now if I managed to free myself. I begin to cry because deep down inside I feel a sense of loss and I know it is because something terrible has happened and I dread finding out what it is.

A truck pulls up outside and I hear the loud engine shut off and a door slam shut. The sound of boots on the porch and then the front door opens and closes. I can almost make out the conversation on the floor below between Eric and Lacey. His deep raspy voice and her sweet delicate tone with a hint of southern roots go back and forth for several minutes before I hear footsteps coming up the stairs. The door opens and Eric smiles when he sees me awake and sitting up in the bed, even though I only scowl back at him. I can't help but feel a little unnerved by waking up to find myself in these circumstances.

"Finally," Eric says. "I was worried you'd never wake up." He walks over to the side of the bed as he removes a key from his shirt pocket. I watch as he unlocks the handcuffs and releases me.

"How are you feeling?" he says. His eyes wander over my body as if to check if everything was where he expected it to be.

"I'm scared," I roll my eyes. "I want to know what is going on."

"Easy, Amanda," he says. He reaches for my hand but I pull it away before he can touch me. Eric shakes his head and turns to pull a chair in the corner of the room closer to the bed. He yawns as he sits down and rubs his tired eyes. It looks like he has hardly slept for days. "Do you remember me?"

"Yes," I tell him. "You saved me."

"Right," Eric says as he takes a seat. "So I'm not about to harm you now." I wait for him to continue but he just stares at me for a long moment.

"Please just tell me what is going on, Eric," I beg him.

"You remember anything from the morning when I found you?" he asks.

I scan my memories for a few seconds. Some of it is clear but I struggle to fill in the gaps.

"I remember people started acting crazy," I say. "They were killing each other. Eating each other. It was like they were out of their minds. I've never seen anything like that."

"Those people," Eric says. "They weren't crazy. They were dead."

"Dead?" I scoff. "They were walking around."

"That's exactly right. I still don't know why this is happening," Eric admits. "But it is."

I feel lightheaded and numb, like I might pass out at any moment.

"Don't worry, though," Eric says. "You're safe here now. It might be the only safe place left. It is worse out there than anyone could ever imagine. But this is still a peaceful town. I'm going to do everything I can to make sure it stays that way."

"Eric," I interrupt him. "What about my family?"

His eyes lock with mine for a moment before he lowers them.

"Listen, Amanda," he sighs. "After I brought you here, I went to the school. It was the most awful goddamn nightmare I've ever seen in my life. All those kids..." his voice trails off.

"What about Abby?" I plead.

"We managed to pull a handful of kids out of the classroom, but none of them were your daughter," he explains.

"No," I shake my head. "I have to go look for myself. Take me there."

"They're all gone, Amanda," he says. "You don't ever want to see something like that."

I know then that my gut was right. My daughter is gone. I cry into the palm of my hand.

He reaches for my hand again and I let him take it this time. He gives me it a slight squeeze and offers a consoling smile.

"I also checked out your house," he tells me. "Saw the address on your license and went to look for any sign of Blake... That's his name, right? I saw it on some of the mail on the desk in the office."

I nod.

"Well, I checked the house but it doesn't look like he ever made it home," he says. "I'm sorry Amanda, I wish had better news for you."

I shake my head. I was expecting the worst, but I still can't accept what I am hearing. He must be telling the truth, but I still can't believe that Blake is gone. If it wasn't such a shock, I probably would have completely lost it right then and there.

"How could this happen?" I finally manage to say.

"No one knows," Eric says. "But anyone that dies turns into one of those... things. It's happening everywhere and no one knows how to stop it. So help won't be coming either. We have to protect this town. It's the only hope we got left."

"How?" I say.

"I'm doing everything I can," he says. "There are some good people here. They listen to me, I got them organized. And we have everything we need. We're building walls and defenses. There's only one road in or out of town. It took a few days but we managed to clear the dead. We're okay here."

A gunshot echoes on the streets outside. Eric swivels in his seat and looks outside.

As much as I want to believe it is safe here, I heard the apprehension in his voice. He knows we are never truly safe. Not anymore.

"Thank you," I tell him. "I can never repay you for helping me."

"Don't worry about it," he smiles. He releases my hand and stands up. "Just rest up. I'm going to need all the help I can get out there."

"I'm just a teacher," I tell him. "I'm not going to be much help."

"There are still kids," he says as he heads for the door. "Somebody needs to educate them."

The door closes again and I shut my eyes and begin to sob for a long time. I still can't accept that my daughter is gone. My baby. The thought ties my stomach into a knot. I want to believe that there is a possibility Blake managed to get to her in time, but I know it's wrong. I know him and he would have brought her home. So, he must be gone too. The last time I talked to him, I didn't even get to tell him I loved him. Even if I didn't feel that way most of the time anymore. He was still my husband. I know I will regret not letting him know what he meant to me when I had the chance.

For the next few hours, I work on getting out of bed. The pain from the wound is pretty bad if I stand too long or sit or lift anything. The only thing Lacey gives me to eat is some chicken broth for lunch to help my stomach get used to food again. Eric comes back again in the afternoon to check on the wound and hands me antibiotics and two different kinds of pain medication. By the time Lacey returns with dinner, the pills are starting to kick in and make me drowsy. I can only manage a few bites before I fall asleep.

I wake up half a dozen times during the night with my heart racing. I'm not used to the sound of gunfire. Whenever I hear it, I feel my body tense. As soon as I relax, someone will fire off a few more rounds to take out one of the dead outside. Even though Eric assures me this town is still safe, I can tell he just doesn't want me to worry. The reality is no place is ever safe anymore.

By the time morning comes around, I'm mostly back on my feet and feeling restless. Lacey brings me a breakfast of eggs, crispy bacon and salty hash browns that I devour while she watches me with a smile.

"How can you smile with all this going on?" I ask her at one point.

"I don't know," she says. "I reckon I'm used to having bad stuff happening all around me. Frowning all the time won't fix nothing. Plus, I was in the military. That helps, too."

"You?" I say.

"I might be small, but I can take care of myself," she snaps. "Not everyone is perfect like you."

"I didn't mean that," I say. "You just seem very sweet."

"I can see why he likes you," Lacey says.

"Who?" I ask her.

"Eric," she says. "I seen how he looks at you. I know that look."

"I'm married," I tell her, but then I remember my husband is probably gone. There was a time I secretly wished something might happen to Blake, and even welcome the attention of another man, but now I just wish he would hold me and kiss me one more time. I might not have been the best wife, but there is nothing I can do to make up for that now.

Lacey takes the cuffs off while I eat and tells me all about growing up in Arkansas. How she ended up in a foster home and being kicked out of school for fighting. Then she moved to Colorado and had her first kid at nineteen and the awful marriage she got stuck in. No wonder Lacey seems able to handle the end of the world better than me. She makes me realize just how good I had it all my life and never realized it. I married a millionaire. So even if I was a teacher, most people always thought of me as some trophy wife.

"How did you end up in Chicago?" I ask her.

"I fell in love," Lacey confesses. "I moved out here to be with him. Had no idea what I was getting myself into. I done lots of stupid things for love. I just can't help it. If I hadn't done that—" she pauses.

"What?" I ask her.

"I'd be with my kids right now in Pueblo," she says. "I sent them back home last month to stay with their dad and grandparents. I thought they'd be safer out there. I'll never forgive myself if something happened to them."

"Lacey—" I start to say but the sound of gunfire outside interrupts me. I'm about to start speaking again when more gunshots ring out. Moments later, people run passed the house shouting and screaming.

"I better check it out," Lacey says as she grabs her handgun off the dresser and tucks it into her waistband. "Stay here."

"No," I insist. "I'm coming with you."

"Eric will kill me if he catches you out there," she groans. She takes a long look at me and realizes I'm going outside whether she likes it or not. "You stay right by me, you hear?"

I nod and follow her down the stairs and out to the street as a couple of men run by with hunting rifles and windbreakers.

"What's going on?" Lacey asks them as we hurry down the sidewalk behind them.

"Some bikers just hit the south blockade," the guy pants.

We reach the intersection of Hough and Main in the center of town and turn south but the sounds of gunfire are tapering off by now. There are bodies all along the road. I nearly trip over one in the darkness of the unlit street.

I feel a cramping pain in my abdomen and slow down. Lacey stops when she notices me struggling and turns to help me. She scowls when she sees the fresh blood on my shirt.

"You done ripped open your stitches," Lacey says.

"I'm all right," I tell her.

"Eric is gonna kill me for sure," she says. "Shit!"

Lacey yanks my arm to move me to the side and steps over to the man I nearly tripped over on the ground. He groans as he pushes himself to his knees and turns his head in time to see Lacey fire off the round that punches through his forehead. The body collapses to the ground and Lacey reaches down and picks up his handgun. Lacey turns back toward me and brings up the gun again like she is going to shoot me. I drop to the ground as she fires the gun again. I collapse onto the sidewalk in agony and then a body crashes down on top of me.

"Get up," Lacey barks as she hauls the body off me. "You're fixing to get us killed out here."

She helps me to my feet and we hurry down the road. Lacey spots another shape coming towards us from across the street and raises the gun and fires off a couple of quick rounds. Even with me hanging on her shoulder in near total darkness, this young girl manages to hit the thing on her first or second shot. With her focus on the other side of the road, she doesn't see the corpse that plows into us as we pass by a doorway.

The thing latches on to her and we both lose our footing and tumble to the sidewalk again. Lacey wrestles with the dead man on top of her and grabs his neck as he snaps his jaw inches from her face. She tries to feel around on the ground for the gun but she quickly moves both hands back to hold him off.

I slide a few feet away and watch in horror as she struggles. I twist around to run away and leave her to deal with him, but then my hand lands on the gun. I pick it up and point it at the thing and fire several times, missing wildly and hitting the shoulder before finally hitting it in the head.

Lacey flinches when the blood splatters down on her face and shoves the limp body to the side.

"I'm sorry," I say. I don't know if she realized I was ready to run away.

"You're fine," she says as she gets to her feet. "Come on."

She helps me up and we slowly climb the hill. The gunshots continue to dwindle and after another couple of minutes the town is quiet again. At the top of the hill, a large group of people gather in the middle of the road in the darkness. A couple hundred men carry flashlights or torches and it seems like everyone has a gun. Eric is standing in the middle of them on the bed of a pickup truck waiting for them to quiet down enough to speak. He spots me in the crowd and then glares at Lacey.

"Shit," she mutters. "I'm dead."

He returns his attention to the crowd and waves his arms to encourage everyone to settle down.

"Calm down, everyone, please," he begins. "The situation is under control now. Go back to your homes."

The crowd rumbles anxiously. Everyone is afraid now and no one is leaving.

"How do we know they won't come back?" yells a voice from the middle of the crowd.

"Listen," Eric continues. "It was just a matter of time before something like this happened. As much as I like to believe otherwise, I guarantee you this won't be the last time."

He pauses to scan the faces in the group surrounding him.

"We can't afford to let our guard down. If we do, we die. It's that simple. I have been saying the time will come when we need to fight to protect what we have here. We have to treat anyone outside this town as a hostile whether they are dead or alive. No exceptions."

He stops again for a minute to let his words resonate.

"I need volunteers to clean up the bodies," he says. "I want to double patrols on watch for the next 24 hours and we need to set up overwatch positions on the rooftops in town. Let's get this mess cleaned up."

He steps down off the bed of the truck as the crowd disperses. His eyes find me and Lacey and he heads for us.

"What are you doing out of bed?" he says to me. He shoots a sidelong glance at Lacey. "Maybe I wasn't clear enough about that."

"I wanted to know what was going on," I tell him. "I want to help."

His gaze lowers as he considers my words, but he catches sight of the blood on my shirt and shakes his head. He grabs me by the elbow and turns me around back toward town.

"Lacey, get her back and I'll be by in a bit to look at those stitches," he says to the young woman.

"Yes sir," she answers like she is addressing some drill sergeant.

"I'm fine," I insist, but I let Lacey take hold of my arm and lead me back down the road.

"Told you he'd be mad," Lacey reminds me. "Now you done it and got me in trouble, too."

I glance back over my shoulder to see Eric directing some men to pile bodies in the bed of a pickup nearby the road.

"I will talk with him," I assure her. "I promise it'll be fine."

"I know him," she tells me. "And I can promise you it won't."

We return to the house and I climb back into the bed

and take off my shirt so Lacey can clean up the wound. Her hands tremble as she dabs the damp cloth against my skin.

"You're really afraid, aren't you?" I ask her.

She pauses to look up and meet my eyes.

"If you seen what I seen, you'd be afraid too," she says. She returns her focus to the cloth and the task of cleaning blood off my skin.

"Just yesterday I thought he seemed so nice," I say.

"That's what I thought at first, too," Lacey says. "That's why I fell in love with the bastard."

"Eric?"

"It wasn't until later I found out just how cold he can be," she says. She drops the cloth in the bowl of pink water and stands up to leave. "Trust me, you ain't seen nothing yet."

After she closes the door, I sit in the silence of the bedroom for as the sun rises until I hear the sound of a truck pulling up to the house. Boots on the porch. The door downstairs opening and slamming shut.

"Lacey?" Eric barks into the quiet house.

There is no answer. Then I hear boots on the stairs. The door handle turns and Eric peers into the room from the darkened hallway.

"Where is Lacey?" he asks me.

"I don't know," I say, and can't help but notice my voice is shaky. "She was just up here a few minutes ago."

He grumbles quietly to himself as he approaches the bed. I clutch the sheet to my chest. He gives me an irritated look when he tries to pull them down and I don't let go.

"What's wrong with you?" he asks me. "I just need to take a look at the damn stitches again."

"They're fine," I insist. "Lacey checked them already."

"That so?" he says. His hand releases the sheet and he

walks over to look out the window at the street. "Did I do something wrong?" he asks me.

I don't know what to say so I just wait for him to continue.

"I'm just trying to understand why you look so afraid right now," he says. "Did Lacey say something to you?"

I shake my head. I get the sense that telling him what I heard might be a very bad idea.

"I'm fine really," I lie. "Just a little anxious after everything that happened."

"Good," he says as he swipes his palm over the stubble on his jaw.

"Why would Lacey say anything bad about you?" I ask. I regret it the minute I said it as his stare turns cold.

"Lacey," he clears his throat. "Sorry, there is no nice way to say it. Lacey likes to make up stories. Especially when it comes to me."

"She told me she came out here to be with you," I say. "That she loved you."

"Ha," he laughs. "She did? Damn, that's a new one."

"What's so funny?" I ask him.

"Lacey is my little sister, Amanda," Eric tells me. "She might be the loon of the family, but she is still my family. She probably just feels a little threatened by you being here. Probably doesn't help that she has been off her meds all day."

I let out a sigh and rub my forehead with my fingers. I don't know what to believe and now I feel afraid of everyone around me. I just want to leave, but I have no idea where I could possibly go.

"Just get some rest," Eric says. "I'll straighten Lacey out tomorrow. I'm really very sorry to put you through that."

He bends down and gives me a kiss on the forehead. It

would have been really sweet if I wasn't still concerned that he was a total psychopath.

"Goodnight, Amanda," he says as shut the door. I wait to hear the front door and the truck engine starting so I know that he is gone, but he doesn't leave the house. I am not sure what I will do when he leaves, but my instincts keep telling me to get out of here as soon as I can. I'm too scared to move for hours until I am too tired to do anything but sleep.

By the time I wake up, the late afternoon sun is spilling warm light into the bedroom. I catch a faint scent of meat grilling through the open window and my stomach growls. When I look around the room I find Eric sitting in the chair flipping through pages of a photo album. After my eyes can focus again, I recognize it as my album with all the photos from modeling shoots I did when I was younger. It creeps me out to know he has been digging through my life.

"Good afternoon," he smiles. "Thought you'd never get up."

"I had trouble falling asleep," I explain.

"No need to explain," he said. He stands up and fills a glass of water from a pitcher on the dresser and brings it me in the bed. "I understand."

"Where is Lacey?" I ask him.

"I'm not sure," he says. "I was hoping you might be able to tell me. She never came back home last night. So I've been waiting here for you to get up because I hope maybe you might have some idea where she went."

"No," I shake my head.

"You sure she didn't say anything?"

"Sorry," I tell him. "If she had mentioned anything I can't remember it."

"I guess I will just wait around with you until she gets back then."

Damn it. As if it wasn't hard enough to figure out what was going on around here, now he seems suspicious of me, too. I reach up to grab the glass of water and find my hand is cuffed to the bed again.

"Sorry," he smiles. He brings the cups to my lips and pours a bit in my mouth. "Since you decided to take off last night, I thought I'd better make sure you don't hurt yourself again."

"I'm not going anywhere, so I'd appreciate it if you'd take them off," I say.

"Sure," Eric says as he retrieves the key from his shirt pocket and releases me. "I'm just here to look out for you."

He returns to the chair across the room and sits down and folds his hands in his lap and stares at me for a few minutes.

"I appreciate everything you've done for me," I tell him. "But I think I'd like to leave."

"Leave?" he laughs. "And go where exactly?"

"Anywhere," I tell him. "I don't feel safe here."

"Well, that's unfortunate," he sighs. He scratches his forehead for several seconds while he considers how to respond. "I tell you what, as soon as you're healed up we'll set you up with some supplies and you're free to go on your way."

"Really?" I ask.

"I don't want anyone here that doesn't want to be here. That will only lead to trouble. I told you before. This is a peaceful town and I want it to stay like that."

A truck pulls up outside and the doors slam shut. I hear

the voices of several men approaching the house. Eric sits up in his chair to look through the window.

"This can't be good," he grunts as he gets to his feet. He walks over to the door and looks back at me on the bed. "Stay put," he tells me then he closes the door.

Downstairs the men begin to argue. Eric tells them all to calm the fuck down and then starts explaining something at length. I don't know what is going on, but this might be my chance to get the hell out of here while I still can. My feet touch the creaky wooden floors as lightly as I can manage as I cross the room to get my shoes and clothes. By the time I get dressed, the men are moving back out the front door. They hurry back to the truck and pile in. When they drive away, I hear boots on the stairs I hurry back the bed and cover myself with the sheet.

The door swings open and Eric barely notices me as he walks over to the closet.

"What's going on?" I ask him.

He doesn't seem to hear me as he tosses aside some clothes and retrieves a case.

"Eric?" I ask him louder.

"They spotted another group heading toward town," he tells me as he begins attaching a large scope to a rifle. "Sounds like they have some serious firepower, too."

"Maybe they aren't looking for trouble," I say. "Eric..."

"Listen," he whispers. "I know you're scared, but I need you to pay attention. This could get bad so I need you to promise me you will stay inside no matter what. Can you do that?"

"Okay, I promise," I say. I try to sound sincere even though I'm leaving the first chance I get.

"You have to trust me, Amanda," he says. "I'd never let anyone hurt you."

He turns to leave and shuts the door behind him. I listen as he heads outside and climbs inside his truck and fires up the engine. After I climb out of bed, I watch as Eric pulls onto the street but only drives a block away and parks outside of an old movie theater near the center of town. A few minutes later he appears on the rooftop and takes up a position behind the neon sign. The orange light of the setting sun fills the empty streets.

If I leave now, he would spot me on the street for sure. I have to wait until the shooting starts. That's my best chance of getting out of here alive. I hear a faint gunshot in the distance and wait for a long time for more to follow as the sky continues to darken.

It's almost dark when I see Eric shifting his body on the rooftop. He points the rifle down the adjacent road at someone out of sight. There is a sharp crack as he fires off a round. Eric reloads another round and fires off a second shot which is followed by the sound of shattering glass. A few quiet seconds go by and then the sound of an automatic rifle fills the streets. Bullets spark off the sign as Eric ducks and takes another shot. I turn and hurry down the stairs and out the front door. I pause in front of the house to glance at the movie theater just as there is an explosion on the top of the building.

"You messed with the wrong fucking hombre!" yells a man down the street.

This is my chance to escape. I turn away from the theater and start to run. Halfway down the block I turn and notice a pickup coming up fast behind me. I keep moving as fast as I can in spite of the terrible pain in my gut. I spot a handful of the dead up ahead moving in my direction. They moan as they spot me and start to converge around me. The truck speeds up and then veers off the road onto the lawn in front of me to cut me off and comes to a stop. I am shocked when I see Lacey behind the wheel.

"Don't just stand there," she says. "Get in."

I look back toward town as other pickup trucks race down the street in search of the outsiders. Corpses begin to wander around the street, drawn here by the sounds of battle.

A peaceful town, my ass.

I limp around the truck and climb into the passenger seat and Lacey hits the gas, tearing up the grass as she skids onto the road. She races around the block and back up to Hough Street and heads south toward the edge of town.

"What about your brother?" I ask Lacey. "You'd really leave him like this?"

"Brother?" Lacey laughs. "I bet he done told you I was crazy or something, too."

ABOUT JEREMY DYSON

Jeremy Dyson is the author of the ROTD zombie series. His first novel, Rise of the Dead, was named as one of the best new zombie novels of 2016 by Ranking Squad. He is a member of the Chicago Writers Association. Look for book three in the ROTD series coming soon.

A special thank you to my wife and editor, Sarah Dyson, and my trusted beta reader Erin Braden.

The ROTD series can be found at **Amazon**.

To find more information about Jeremy Dyson please follow them on the following social media.

facebook.com/jeremyrdysonauthor

twitter.com/jeremyrdyson

instagram.com/jeremydyson

8

AVERY

The hoarding started sometime after the outbreak. It became one small way I could recapture the life that no longer existed. It was one simple object that pulled me in with the siren's call, a glass cookie jar in the window of the local thrift shop. I was hiding in my boarded-up home trying to drown out the moaning when I felt that pang of regret that has now become so familiar. The jar became my obsession. It was an itch that refused to leave.

Days later, I finally gave in knowing I would not be able to sleep until the object was safe in my home. So, I loaded up with gear, trying to convince myself that this was not just a trip to grab a cookie jar but a full-scale supply run. Only a lunatic would venture out into the nightmare to get a glass jar that had no value or use. But the pull was so strong, and I was so weak. My heart raced as I crept down the side streets. All those years of being picked on for my tiny stature, but who was laughing now? Small is silent. Small is nimble.

The zombies aren't hunters. They are monsters of opportunity, so the best plan is stealth. At least that has been true for me. I have killed a few but it was a close call every time. I know if I was ever really backed in a corner, it would all be over for me. I just don't have the strength needed to behead them, or poke through the skull. I also have not had the great fortune of finding a gun, not that I would know how to use one anyway.

Thinking back on zombie shows and movies from before the outbreak, it amazes me that the writers believed that once someone had a gun, they would not only know how to load and shoot the thing, but maintain and service it as well. Plus, every person is suddenly able to make a head shot while running. They wrote it, and we watched while guzzling soda and flinging popcorn down our throats. Reality is so much more boring. You hide because when hidden, you may survive.

I could see the thrift store's plaza off in the distance. Just a few more blocks and I might be able to sleep tonight. I had a spot in the kitchen waiting for my prize. Two zombies shambled across my path. I had become so preoccupied with my mission that I almost missed them coming. I stood perfectly still next to a pickup truck that someone had wrecked against a tree. What I hadn't accounted for was the dude who wrecked the truck still being inside, and starting to smash his face against the window trying to get to me.

That alerted the other two to my presence. "Frig!" I muttered. There was no way I would be able to have it out with the two of them and make it out of there with my life. Running was my only option. I tried to travel light when I headed out, but any gear weighs you down when you need to flee. It didn't take long before my small backpack felt like it was filled with bricks. Lucky for me, the street was littered with broken down cars. The zombies didn't have my agility, and as long as nothing popped out from underneath one of the cars, I would be able to get a pretty good distance between us.

I know it seems ridiculous now, but I headed towards the two zombies because that was where the store was. I knew I might die for it, but I would be damned if I wasn't getting that jar before I went home. Each step brought me closer to the store. I could hear them in their awkward chase behind me, but as my mother always screamed during my races, "Never look back!" So, I didn't.

I made it to the glass windows, and could see the jar staring back at me. Relief washed over me. I hadn't thought until that moment that it may not have even been there. Someone could have bought it months before this all began. The raspy groans were nipping at my heels. Somehow, I had to find a way in to the store. I gave the windows a quick bang to make sure I wasn't going from one danger zone to another. Nothing but silence.

There was a tree at the corner of the building that looked sturdy enough to climb. I was going to have to be fast about it. The two creepers were gaining ground. I scanned the parking lot for other options, but didn't see any. If I broke a window or door at ground level to get in, I was just asking for them to follow me. So, up I went.

One of the branches snapped as I put the full weight of my foot on it. A sharp pain went in my leg. No time to check the damage. The two zombies were right below me now. Their moaning and groaning caused my heart to race even faster. They were so close now. One more wrong branch, and I would be on my back getting my guts torn into. Since I was just out of reach, I forced myself to slow down and take my time. Zombies don't climb. Thank god for that!

I pulled myself up on the overhang. There was a set of windows on the second floor, but I wasn't about to rush through them. I needed to catch my breath. Scooting myself as far away from the ledge as possible, I popped off my backpack and removed a bottle of water. I always waited until my breathing was calm and steady, and my heart rate had returned to normal before I entered a new place. I have never been one to make good decisions in a panic.

Scooping up a few pinecones from the gutter, I eased my way back to the wall of the building. I tossed one across the parking lot, hitting the side of a busted up pick-up truck. The noise caught the attention of one of my friends below. I tried again, but my arms were exhausted and my aim suffered. It didn't matter, though. The last one I lobbed had landed loudly enough that he decided it was worth investigating. I said a silent prayer of thanks, then tapped on the window again.

This time it was a light tap, I didn't want to attract the zombies below. The longer they were away from me, the more likely they would move on from the parking lot. That would be a good thing in case I needed to make a hasty retreat after entering the thrift shop. Satisfied that no one was behind the glass, I said another silent prayer before trying to slide open the window. This was why I loved small towns, the window opened instantly. Most people in this area never thought to lock their front doors, let alone a window on the second story.

I plopped my bag down on the floor, and waited another minute before lowering my leg in after it. I haven't stayed alive this long by being reckless. It is a lot like the saying "measure twice, cut once", but instead, it's "test 40 or 50 times and don't die." The air in the room was stale. Most thrift stores have that musty, my-stuff-has-been-in-the-attic-or-basement smell because, well, the things have been in the attic or basement. What I didn't smell was rotten flesh.

That didn't mean that there weren't any undead wandering around in here, but it was a good sign. A door leading onto a landing sat open in front of me. As quietly as possible, I tiptoed over and gently shut it. Each room would need to be checked. There were so many things that I had on my wish list. The longer this nightmare lasted, the more supplies I either used or lost. It would be great if there was a place I could go and just fill up a cart, but they haven't existed in forever. Most of the big box stores and supermarkets had been ransacked and looted before filling up with zombies. Your best bet at this stage in the game is to get creative.

A giant comfy office chair was calling my name. It was old ripped leather, but it was worn in like an old shoe. Molded in all the right places, and ugly as hell. As soon as my rear hit the chair, the adrenaline I had been running on ran out. I thought about barricading the door, or even locking it, but it was too late and it was lights out. Running for your life can turn you into a narcoleptic.

I awoke with a jerk. It was suddenly too quiet and my fear sensor went off. The room around me was blurry and for a moment I had no idea where I was or how I got there. The room was still lit, but it was with a soft orange tone now. Sundown was coming. Mentally, I counted to 100, listening intently as I did. There was not a sound. My heart began to beat at its regular pace again. My bag sat on the floor near the open window. I pulled it shut as I picked up my supplies.

All I had was a small can of fruit, another bottle of water, and a half empty pack of Tic Tacs. They were orange. Not my favorite, but not gross either. After my measly dinner, I rummaged through the drawers and closets. I netted a small flashlight. It was one of those strange ones you shook to get to work. It wasn't as bright as my other lights, but the no batteries thing was a great advantage. I also found a small multi-tool.

Once this room was searched I headed to the next. I worked my way around the top floor. There were so many things I wanted to bring with me, but I had to think of my ability to carry them. I only grabbed the most useful of the items, then filed the rest in the "maybe later" column. Food, water, tools, lights, and weapons. I just kept repeating that list over and over. By the time I made it downstairs it was dark. I was hungry and tired again. I resigned myself to spending the night in the store.

I wasn't going to draw attention to myself by using a flashlight to search the main store. I gathered as many cushions and blankets as I could carry and brought them back to the room I first entered through. One more trip downstairs and I had a small kitchen setup from some of the donated camping gear. This time, I barricaded the door and made myself really comfortable. There was a cache of non-perishables downstairs that people had donated to the thrift store, having mistaken it for a food bank.

They were going to warrant a second trip to the store. I would need something to transport them in, though, there would be no way I could carry it all myself. Once I was full and tucked in, I turned on a portable radio that I had snagged from downstairs. It was a long shot but I had hope. Slowly, I dialed through the FM stations. Nothing. Then the AM. Also, nothing. I was disappointed but not surprised. There was a tape in the deck, so I flipped it on and hummed along with the mixed tape from the early 90's.

I was warm and safe. It was more than I could say for most people at the same moment. I knew for the first time in weeks that I would get a good night's sleep. It was sad, and maybe a bit pathetic, but as I gazed over at the glass cookie jar, I felt calm and happy. It was as if, in that moment, all was right in the world, and I had finally calmed the voice screaming in my head. Little did I know that laying there would be that last time that I would feel at peace.

Morning came far too fast, my body screamed for more sleep. There were days pre-downfall that I would complain about being achy and stiff. Nothing I had experienced then had held a candle to the pain that I felt now. Malnourishment and lack of actual sleep turns your body into an enemy. There would be no more sleep, though, despite my definite need. The noise of motors shook the windows and rattled my insides. With the glass jar tucked safely in my bag, I climbed out on the overhang to investigate what all the hub-bub was about.

I pressed my body close to the outer wall of the building and said a silent prayer that I wouldn't alert anyone to my position. Curiosity killed the cat, hopefully, it wouldn't kill this human. Three oversized mudding trucks tore ass up and down the street beside the thrift store. With each rev of their engines, more zombies gathered in the road with the hope of getting a taste of one of the street outlaws. At first, I thought there was no rhyme to the madness the drivers were exhibiting, but the longer I watched, the more apparent their plan became.

All three were pulling in the dead from the area. The original laps had cleared the middle of debris, and had pushed it in an incomplete ring around the track they were forming. They were herding the dead, but what I couldn't figure out was why. The engine revving stopped when the flow of dead had ceased. Each truck sat idle in one of the openings into the circle so they blocked the dead from leaving. A whistle signal came from one of the cabs.

Each truck pulled a piece of debris to fill the hole that they had occupied. That left the dead trapped for just enough time that the trucks began to smash the barricades into the center. With each shove, the circle became smaller, and the dead were either smeared underneath a few tons of broken down vehicles, or trapped like sardines in a can. The trucks slammed against the outer rim until there was no more room left for the debris to move. There was a honk, then the engines died.

All three doors opened, and three equally psychotic looking men leapt into action. The sound of three chainsaws ripping through the skulls and necks of zombies would have brought more dead to the area if the truckers hadn't already drawn them all in. Any stragglers, few as they were, were dispatched before they could harm any of the executioners. Once they had reduced the hoard to ground meat, they crawled up on the hood of one of the trucks and lit up some celebratory cigars.

"That never gets old." The largest and, by far, youngest of the three men celebrated the carnage around them.

"Hell, no, it doesn't, and we just get better and better at it," a man who looked to be his father assured him as he took another drag from his cigar. "We should probably get our asses in gear. This area won't stay clear for long, and as fun as that shit is, we need supplies."

That was my cue to slink back into the window. If I was lucky, the group would ignore the thrift store and focus more on the traditional places to find food, weapons, and gas. I positioned myself at the top of the stairs and waited, shaking, for the group to come through the door downstairs. They didn't seem like the kind of people I wanted to get involved with.

I had done my best to stay on my own since the beginning. Really, I had done my best to stay on my own my whole life. I didn't have the kind of personality that trusted easily, and it only took one incident of letting my guard down to learn that I had been correct in my distrust. One night, a few drinks, and a man I considered a friend, left me scarred and scared.

I sat there for hours on alert, not entirely sure what I would do if they walked through the door. Eventually, after it got dark enough, I braved a peek through the window to where their trucks were parked. The three of them had made a half ass camp next to the pile of dead undead bodies. Their sense of smell had to be numb, because I couldn't even imagine the putrid aroma that pile must have been giving off.

From what I could see, it looked as though we would all be spending the night in our current positions, so I spent the rest of the evening packing myself for a hasty retreat, then hunkering down for another restless night. If I had only known that they would soon be drunk and passed out inside their trucks, I may have actually slept for two nights in a row.

It was a shame, but that knowledge only became clear at dawn when I put all my gear and treasures on and slipped out the window and down the tree. Empty bottles were shattered around the campfire the trio had erected the evening before. I could see feet propped up against each of the three truck windows. Even with them passed out, I felt that heading home in the opposite, and much longer, direction was a wise choice.

The thrift store had too many treasures for me to take in one trip, but I wouldn't chance it until those three had moved on. As I beat feet back to my house, the glass jar clanked noisily against the cans I had packed in with it. I would have to slow down to make sure it didn't shatter. The area was eerily devoid of creepers. Maybe, the ole truck and chainsaw show wasn't as crazy as it looked. Or, maybe it was, but was also effective.

I engaged the locks on my doors and headed straight into my kitchen to place the jar in its rightful home on the counter. It was the first of thousands of times that this ritual would be repeated. Each time I would tell myself that it would be my last, or I would lie to myself and say that it was a run for more than just a bike wheel, painting, or book. Every item fell into a category and was sorted as such. I would brave the streets with dead men and women dragging themselves along as they tried desperately to eat or turn me, just to add another piece to the growing pile. It was like this, rinse and repeat for over a year.

Then, one night, I awoke to the smell of smoke. Fearful that someone would try to come into my sanctuary and steal the treasures I had worked so hard to acquire, it never occurred to me that what I had really been doing was creating my own death trap. Something, God knows what, had sparked a fire in one of the overflowing rooms. Once the reality of what was happening hit me, I knew I needed to find the jar. I wouldn't be able to live if I couldn't at least bring my beloved first piece with me. I was about to lose everything and the weight of that felt like it would crush me.

Items cracked and popped from the rooms as the fire spread, and smoke filled the few spare inches that I had allowed to stay empty as a pass-through from one space to another. I choked on thick black smoke and my vision blurred as my eyes watered in pain. The one blessing was that I didn't need my sight to navigate the enormous piles. Each item had a place, and even though an outsider would never understand my system, I knew what each pile contained.

The fire was closing in on me. There was just too much fuel for it, and regardless of how fast I was, it was faster. The jar felt cold and smooth in my hands, and tears of pain mixed with tears of relief rolled down my cheeks as I pulled it close to my chest. I prayed that I could escape through one of the windows before I triggered a landslide. The kitchen was the worst of all the rooms. The compulsion had started there, and no matter how hard I fought it, there had always been just one more thing to add. I snatched up the backpack I had waiting on the back porch. The jar got zipped inside as I pulled it onto my back. As I walked away from the place I had called home since childhood, I couldn't find the strength to turn and see the scene behind me. Everything was dying again, just like it had when everyone got sick. My world was crumbling, and I cried as I tried to remember each piece that would be lost. Then, it started again, that same familiar pull. Order in chaos. There was a ceramic bird with tiny blue flowers painted on it. I headed off down the street with a drive in my step. I hoped that chair in the thrift store is as comfortable as I remembered.

ABOUT VALERIE LIOUDIS

Valerie had a busy year writing in 2017. She is releasing the second book of the Aftershock Series in October. She also released her first solo novel in late August. The Many Afterlives of John Robert Thompson is available on Amazon, along with the numerous anthologies she has contributed to this year. Her work is scattered across genres, but always has the same sarcastic yet human touch.

Valerie would like to thank Jack Kelly from **Redline Editing** for cleaning up the mess of words that get sent over, and as always her family for letting her get words on paper every once in a while.

The Aftershock Zombie Series can be found on **Amazon**.

To find more information about Valerie Lioudis please follow her on the following social media.

facebook.com/AuthorValerieLioudis

twitter.com/AuthorVLioudis

instagram.com/valerielioudis

9

ZOMBIE EXTERMINATORS

I. Lab Rats

The technician adjusted his white lab coat, making sure the buttons were clasped tight. He counted six, sticking through their proper holes. Rosario, the ex-lead of this department had been fired two days ago for having one undone. Adrian Fisk glanced across the busy lab, past the dead bodies lying on stretchers and past the live ones studying beakers and mixing solutions. His gaze continued all the way to the office at the back, with its tinted windows and the lone female form visible through them.

He could make out the bottom edge of her black pencil skirt, following the curve of her hips until he saw the sharp points of her blouse's collar jutting out. It was only a silhouette, but he averted his eyes in case she was looking at him. He didn't want to get caught staring by her or the ever-present bodyguards who stood sentry at the CEO's office door.

A light blinked on a console before him. He pushed a button and spoke. "Yes. What is it?"

"Yeah, this is the front gate, there's a Mr. Edison here. He says he has a delivery for the lab. His car has government plates, but he's not on our expected visitors sheet."

Finally!

Adrian turned and looked to the desk nearest him where two other technicians waited. He spun his arm above him in a wind-up motion, letting the others know it was 'go' time. They turned and alerted others throughout the lab. "Send him right over. Direct him to park in the empty spot near the bottom of the stairs by the door marked 'Research'. I'll meet him there."

"Yes, sir." The security guard set the phone down and stepped out of the booth.

The car's window sat half-open and the man in the driver's seat, bald, wearing reflective sunglasses and a business suit, waited.

"You can go on in, sir. Park over there," he said, pointing a short distance across the parking lot to one of the large warehouse-sized buildings on the property, "next to the staircase, someone will meet you at the door marked 'Research'."

The man didn't reply. He rolled up the window and drove into the Nitsau Pharmaceuticals manufacturing and research complex.

A smaller man, also dressed in a security guard uniform walked over from the other side of the entrance. Together, they watched as the car parked and the man got out, removed a silver briefcase from the trunk, and was greeted at the door by one of the many lab coat wearing men that worked in that building.

"What was that all about?"

"No idea, Judas. We're not paid to know anything more than who comes and goes."

Adrian led Mr. Edison to the door of an office at the rear of the lab. He stopped before the large man standing to the right of it and looked up. "She's expecting us."

The towering bodyguard studied the sunglass and suit wearing man for a moment, then nodded as he punched a code into the keypad. The door slid open with a 'whoosh'.

Inside the office, the air felt even cooler than the always chilly main lab. Dimmer too, from the tinted windows. Dr. Nitsau sat behind her desk, nylon clad legs crossed, fingers intertwined across her knees, her back straight as she looked with expectation at her guests.

They entered without words. Adrian stood beside the desk while Mr. Edison sat in front of it. He placed the briefcase on the desk, held his thumb over a sensor, and waited. After a few seconds, there was a click and a hiss as the pressurized case opened.

They all smiled.

"Mr. Cross," the man spoke, "was able to secure what you requested from the Russian Biodefense Ministry." He lifted the lid on the case as a haze of mist drifted up from the special cooling system it contained.

Dr. Nitsau peered across the desk and into the case. Her smile twitched at the corners of her mouth as she fought to contain her excitement.

Inside the case, two vials, each about an inch long and half that in circumference, sat equidistant from one another, surrounded on all sides by foam padding. In the top half of the lid, fan blades slowed to a stop. The vial to the left was yellow and marked with a 'Z', while the one on the right was blue and marked with an 'X'.

"These are the only samples left?" the doctor asked,

removing her hands from her knees as she slid forward and centered herself at the desk. She drew her hands up into a steeple before her.

"Yes. The storage facility suffered a systematic environmental failure brought on by an electrical malfunction. It burned to the ground. They won't even know to miss them."

Dr. Nitsau grinned. "Such a waste of potentially catastrophic bacteria. Alas, we can't leave the competition with a leg up."

"No, we can't," the sunglass-wearing man replied. "Mr. Cross thought you'd appreciate that extra touch."

"Oh, I do," she said, "very much. Speaking of, how are his own plans coming to claim the prize?"

The man didn't acknowledge her question and a moment of awkward silence ticked away in the room.

"Very well," Dr. Nitsau's smile vanished. She reached out and pushed a button on her desk. There was a slight buzzing sound as the office door slid open and one of the large men posted outside stepped into view. "Show this gentleman out, give him the case with his payment."

Mr. Edison stood, nodded, and left.

The door closed behind him with a soft whoosh. Adrian found himself alone with Dr. Nitsau and the open case. He glanced down, once again checking to see if all the buttons were clasped on his coat. They were. He breathed a sigh of relief and looked up to find the CEO of Nitsau Pharmaceuticals staring over the tops of her still-steepled fingers at him.

"Is your team ready?" she asked, her voice sharp and clear.

Adrian's tongue felt thick in his mouth as he began to explain that there had been some delays. The firing of Rosario just a few days ago, for instance, had thrown the lab into chaos. Or how about the departure of the lead researcher, Professor West a few months back? Instead, he answered, "Yes, ma'am. We have plenty of hosts ready to try the reanimation formula on."

She nodded. "Good. What about a live one?"

Adrian's stomach tightened. "Professor West's notes didn't say anything about live human trials."

"And they shouldn't have." Dr. Nitsau stared him down. "Nor will yours. Begin preparations." She reached for the phone on her desk. "I'll order the test subject."

A passenger van pulled up to the front gate of the sprawling industrial complex. Dusk had fallen and its headlights were on, making it hard to read the words on the dust-covered van, but the Sheriff's symbol on the hood stood out clearly enough.

Jonah Zee stepped from the gatehouse and read the words stenciled on the side, 'Arizona State Corrections', and walked to the window. The man in the driver's seat wore a guard's uniform with a tag on the sleeve that read, 'Cross Enterprises Security'. In the back of the van sat another man, this one in an orange jumpsuit, with a black hood over his head and a thick steel chain bolted from the floor to the cuffs around his wrists.

"I think you might be at the wrong location." Jonah glanced from the prisoner to the guard as he rolled down his window.

The driver pulled a piece of paper from his pocket. "Yeah, I'd think so too, but this is the address the warden gave me. I'm supposed to ask you to call extension 231," he explained as he handed the piece of paper to Jonah.

Jonah read it. It had the facility's address on it, 467 Industrial Parkway, and the extension. He nodded at the guard and walked back into the gatehouse. Judas looked up from a checklist he had been making marks on as he scanned the various monitors in front of him.

"Is that a Sheriff's van?"

"Yeah."

"He lost?"

"No. He doesn't think so."

Judas turned his attention from the monitors to Jonah. "What's he here for?"

"I don't know. I'm supposed to call extension 231."

"Who's that?"

"I don't know yet." Jonah scanned various pieces of paper pinned behind the computer monitor. He found the one with the list of numbers on it and ran his finger along it until he came to the correct one. "Hmm." His brow furrowed.

"What is it?" Judas asked.

"It's the extension for the CEO's private office inside the research building."

"The CEO? You mean that hot chick that came in the limo this morning? Escorted by those guys straight out of 'Mercenaries Weekly'?"

"Yep. That's the one."

Judas stared at the van and caught sight of its passenger. "What the hell? This job's getting weirder than working at Pests B' Gone."

"Hello. Yes, this is the front gate. There's a..." he paused. "Yes, ma'am, right away." He set the phone down.

Behind him, Judas asked, "What is it?"

Jonah ignored him, stepped back outside and raised the arm on the barricade before pointing toward the research building. He then gave the man directions on where to park.

As the van drove off, Jonah turned to find his brother staring at him from the doorway.

They both watched as the van parked in the same spot that the sunglass-wearing man had used earlier in the day. The door to the research building swung open and the CEO's two bodyguards emerged, walked over to the side door of the van, and opened it.

"What's going on here, Jonah?"

His brother's question snapped him out of his own curious fixation and he turned, motioning his brother back into the booth. "It's none of our business."

And it still wasn't their business a few minutes later when the van left, empty of its passenger. An hour after that, however, when the sounds of muffled gunshots rang out and the door to the research facility burst open, that changed. When a young female wearing the tell-tale white lab coat of a research technician ran out screaming that "he'd gotten loose", they found that it all of a sudden was their business.

II. Formula ZX

As the hood came off, the man in the orange jumpsuit closed his eyes. The bright lights blinded him. He tried to raise his hands to shield them but found they were bound to the chair he sat in. He could hear voices talking in hushed tones, but none of it made sense to him.

"Almost ready."

"This is what she's been waiting for."

"Are we really testing this on a living person?"

Vague snippets from a world he knew nothing about. Then, he heard the clicking of heels on tile, a sound he recognized. A favorite of his from back in the day when he and his crew would hit the strip joint after turning some lifted merchandise into easy cash.

He looked up to find a tall, slender woman with long, straight black hair and a thin, angular face approaching. She wore a white leather lab coat over a white blouse, black pencil skirt, nylons and black stilettos. Two large men dressed in black with sidearms strapped to their hips flanked her. In a different environment, this would have excited him. He squinted and looked away, his eyes quite adjusted yet.

When he opened them again and looked to his right, his heart stopped. Four bodies in various states of decay lie strapped to stretchers.

"What the fuck?"

He looked around as the clicking heels came down a set of stairs and stopped before him. Monogrammed above the left breast on the lab coat, it read, 'Dr. Nitsau'. On the right-hand side, two intertwined letter N's sat in the middle of a circle.

"What do you want from me?" he asked, then pushing his luck, "Did you come to give me a dance, mamacita?"

The woman before him didn't respond. Instead, she looked behind her and nodded at one of the men in black. "Teach him not to speak unless spoken to." She turned in the direction of a man in a tight-fitting, buttoned-up lab coat who had his gloved hands inside a sealed biohazard container. The man drew a greenish liquid into a series of syringes from a petri dish.

That was the last thing the prisoner, one David Marquez, saw for a bit, as a fist slammed into his jaw, plunging him back into darkness.

When he awoke, blood dripping from his swollen lips, he heard the woman speaking.

"Give the second one a larger dose. The first hasn't responded more than a twitch. Just make sure we'll have a full dose to give our live subject."

A pair of scientists wearing thick gloves injected one of the strapped corpses with a syringe full of green liquid. David watched in silence as did everyone in the large space.

The quiet ticked away for a full minute, broken only by the occasional tapping of the doctor's foot on the ground as she waited. The room drew in a collective gasp when the corpse spasmed. It passed through it like a wave, beginning in the foot, then its leg bent at the knee, its hips thrust upward, and its chest strained at the straps. Someone in the crowd of onlookers let out a cry.

Dr. Nitsau grinned as she stared. "Yesss," she spoke in a low hiss.

The body on the stretcher groaned, its hand flexing and grasping. Suddenly, the dead man's eyes shot open and he gazed around the room, growling and gnashing his teeth at the onlookers.

The doctor turned to look at David, her grin unchanging. "Adrian, bring the final syringe. We need to try it on our other test subject."

David glanced between her and the moving, growling corpse. "No!" He spat warm blood from his bloated mouth as he strained against the restraints that held him. He felt some slack on the one holding his left arm, but he couldn't get free.

"Don't make me have Thomas silence you ag—" But her threat was cut short by a voice from the back of the crowd.

"We can't do that to someone who's alive!"

The room, aside from the moaning and groaning of the strapped down corpse, went silent.

Dr. Nitsau's head snapped toward the voice and the sea of scientists and technicians parted, revealing a young blond woman with her hair in a ponytail. She was staring at David.

David wiggled his arm back and forth, trying to loosen the strap further.

The woman's cheeks flushed as she looked up to meet the doctor's gaze.

"Lila, is it?" Dr. Nitsau asked.

"Y-Yes."

"Second-year intern?"

"Yes."

"So, Nitsau Corp. is helping to cover your tuition costs, correct?"

"Yes." The woman glanced away, then opened her mouth to object but was cut short by the doctor.

"Stop and listen, girl," Dr. Nitsau interrupted as she pivoted on her foot to face her. "Are you familiar with the U.C.A. Penal Code? Specifically, Part 47, Clause XXII?" She paused only a moment, then continued. "Which states, prisoners who are unable to be rehabilitated, whose crimes include bodily injury to minors, are stripped of their rights and are subject to disposal by the state in which the crimes were committed?"

A thickness hung in the air as the young woman shrank back, tears rolling down her cheeks. "N-No."

"That's too bad. Now you do. Pack your things and leave. Your internship is over." Dr. Nitsau stared at the young woman who trembled. "And don't forget the NDA you signed. Breathe a word of what you've seen here, and our lawyers will make sure your next job will be cleaning public urinals."

A river of tears flowed as she turned and quickly made her way back to her workspace to collect her things.

III. The ZX Experiment

Adrian stood before David Marquez, the loaded syringe at the ready. Behind him, Dr. Nitsau smiled in anticipation.

"No way am I letting you stick that in me!" David spat through his bloodied lips. He thrashed against his restraints and lunged forward, head-butting Adrian in the chest. His teeth seized one of the coat's buttons and he yanked on it. The button tore loose, hanging by a thread, blood smeared across the white fabric.

Behind them, Dr. Nitsau signaled her bodyguards. The larger of the two stepped forward and landed another blow across the prisoner's face.

"Beat me all you wan—"

Another fist sent his face sideways, silencing him. Blood poured from his mouth and ran the length of his arm, coating it.

Adrian moved back into position, stuck the needle in David's arm and swiftly pushed the plunger down. Before it was empty, David's body started convulsing. Adrian pulled the empty syringe free and set it on a small metal stand. He turned from Dr. Nitsau's view and rushed to get the undone button back in place before she noticed, the blood made it slimy and it kept slipping from his fingers.

The prisoner's body continued to shake and twitch. The blood that had run down his arm lubricated his wrist under the loose strap and it easily pulled free. Voices cried out from the crowd of onlookers. Adrian, whose attention remained focused on his loose button didn't notice until Dr. Nitsau's sharp command sent him scurrying.

"Mr. Fisk, fix that strap now," she hissed.

He turned and found the prisoner's arm free of the restraints, swinging wildly. Adrian's fingers still grasped at the button on his coat and he looked at the CEO in a panic.

"Now!" She snapped at him before turning to her body-guard. "Help our newest lead researcher to keep his test subject in place."

The large man stepped forward, grabbed the flailing limb and wrestled it back onto the armrest. There was a snapping sound as he did so and the prisoner fell silent, his head lolling forward.

Adrian rushed over, unfastened the strap and wrapped it back around the man's wrist. His hands shook as he worked the brown leather restraint back through the loop. Next to him, still holding the arm down, the foreboding presence of Thomas loomed. Adrian cinched the strap tight as it would go and then struggled to get the small metal prong in the hole.

"Hurry up!" Dr. Nitsau's impatience manifested in a growl.

Adrian's hands shook. He couldn't quite get it buckled. He heard an intake of breath and a low growl. The prisoner lunged forward and bit into the bodyguard's bulging tricep.

Thomas cried out, slammed his elbow into the prisoner's face and stumbled backward. Blood ran through his fingers as he grasped at the throbbing wound on his arm. Within seconds, he began feeling woozy and sat in an empty office chair behind the prisoner to catch his breath.

Ramone, the smaller of the two guards, rushed over to check on him.

Without it being held down, the arm slipped free of the

strap again, causing Adrian to cry out and jump back into the panicked crowd. There were gasps and cries as the other scientists and technicians finally got their first unobstructed view of the changed prisoner.

The life energy of David Marquez was no more. Instead, a growling, hissing madman with a green tint to his skin and a mouth full of bloody gristle stared back at them.

Dr. Nitsau's grin widened. "Yes!"

Adrian stood straighter and felt a sense of wonder fill him. They had done it. They had reanimated both a corpse and transformed a living human into... what exactly? He knew the corporate research program was about anti-aging and extending life, but he also knew Dr. Nitsau had other plans as well. Secret plans. For years, they had studied various viruses, compounds and even crazy legends meant to bring the dead back to life. The goal had always been to find a magic anti-aging drug that was marketable, but its effect on the prisoner was not what he had been expecting. He turned to face the CEO.

"Dr. Nitsau," he cleared his throat. "I don't understand the results. This man seems to have lost his mind. There's been no change in—"

"This man is dead. He is something more now." She stepped closer to examine their test subject.

Thomas, still clutching the oozing wound on his arm, was doubled over in the chair.

"Get this arm strapped down," the doctor said through gritted teeth as the flailing fingers grasped at her. She turned to Adrian, who was fiddling with his loose button again. Her expression changed from irritated to pissed. "You're as bad as your predecessor. Thomas—" She spun and found her bodyguards off to the side behind the prisoner.

Ramone turned away from Thomas, who remained

slumped forward in the chair groaning. The expression on Ramone's face showed concern, rather than the look of obedience that he typically wore.

Dr. Nitsau paused, taking things in for a moment, then gasped.

Thomas lunged from the chair and grabbed Ramone by the shoulder. He sunk his teeth into his partner's neck and tore a chunk of flesh free.

Ramone swung backward, knocking Thomas away. He then fell to the ground, clutching at the bleeding hole, and scrambled across the floor in an effort to get away from him. He rolled onto to his back and fumbled for his sidearm. Thomas rose, turned to a nearby lab technician, and moved toward him.

Cries rang out from those gathered, but few moved. They watched in fascination, not realizing the potential threat, as Thomas tackled the technician. The man he attacked howled and thrashed, then Thomas stood once more and turned his bloodied face toward the watching crowd. They screamed and ran.

In the chaos, a heavy-set man pushed a smaller man out of his way and into the stretcher containing the reanimated corpse. He fell atop the cadaver and knocked the stretcher over. Both the dead and the living toppled, with the corpse biting at and tearing free pieces of the man's flesh.

Shots rang out as Ramone pulled out his gun and emptied the entire clip into Thomas's back. The shots tore through him, striking the ceiling tiles above. He didn't fall, nor did he stop. He turned and glared at the CEO, one of the last people standing nearby, and lunged for her.

Adrian, who was still to her left, beside the restrained and flailing prisoner, stared as Thomas approached. When Dr. Nitsau suddenly grabbed him by the arm and threw him forward into Thomas's path, he screamed. Thomas sprang at him, knocking him to the ground with ferocious hunger.

The doctor spun around to discover the thin lab technician lying on the floor near the stretchers, grasping at his bleeding wounds. Beside him, the corpse from the toppled stretcher was attempting to take a chunk out of his leg. Dr. Nitsau pivoted in her heels and ran straight to her office.

Once inside, she opened a panel on the wall next to the door and smashed her hand into the big red button it had concealed. The door slammed shut behind her and locked with an audible click. The windows dimmed and a hiss sounded as the room sealed, regulating the atmosphere through pressurized tanks.

After catching her breath, she stepped in front of the large windows and stared out at the chaos erupting in her lab. She watched Ramone rise from the spot where he had fallen and lumber toward several screaming lab personnel.

"It spreads so fast," she whispered, then smiled. "Perfect."

Lila, the intern whom Dr. Nitsau had fired moments earlier, had been furthest away from the madness when it started, but turned back from the exit at the sound of the first shocked cries. She stood there, with her cardboard box of possessions from her desk, mesmerized as she watched the crowd scatter. She had seen the prisoner flailing, but it wasn't until she watched Dr. Nitsau shove Adrian into the path of the crazed Thomas that she turned and ran from the building.

IV. The Zee Brothers

The slamming of a door followed by the sound of heels running on concrete distracted Judas from the tedium of staring at perimeter security monitors.

"What's that, Jonah?"

Jonah turned from the front window through which he had been staring blankly to glance back into the compound. He saw a young woman, wearing a white lab coat and carrying a cardboard box, running in their direction. Judas walked up beside him and they both stepped out of the gatehouse.

The woman arrived panting and crying, with flushed cheeks and a half-empty box. Behind her, a trail of debris led from the door to the front gate.

"What is it? What's the matter?" Jonah asked, putting his hands on the sides of her arms to steady and reassure her.

"They've gone— mad! She... they." She shook her head. "He's attacking them."

"Who? That prisoner they brought in earlier?"

She pulled away from Jonah as the research door slammed open and two more forms rushed out. "Let me go. I have to get out of here!"

Jonah did and watched as she ran toward the employee parking lot. He looked at Judas.

"What do we do?" Judas asked.

Jonah's brow wrinkled. "We're security. We better go investigate."

"Are you sure, Jonah? Doesn't the CEO have her own security team?"

"Yeah, but something's going on and it looks like it's getting out of hand."

The other two forms rushed passed them. It was a pair

of male lab technicians, glancing over their shoulders and not saying a word.

Jonah and Judas ran toward the research door. As they approached, it swung open again and a large heavy-set man burst through.

"What's going on in there?" Jonah asked.

The man continued passed them, shouting over his shoulder. "They're eating each other."

Jonah looked at Judas, both shared wide-eyed quizzical expressions.

"Be ready for anything," Jonah said, then opened the door.

Shouts and screams filled their ears as soon as they stepped into the narrow hallway that led into the facility. Ahead of them, they could see desks and little else. On the wall to their right there was an emergency fire station, containing a fire extinguisher, a rolled-up fire hose and an axe.

They made their way to the end of the hall where it opened directly into the lab. From there, they could see the entire expanse filled with desks and workstations, analyzers, contraptions with beakers and tubes. Everywhere they looked, people were running, screaming, and attacking one another.

The Zee Brothers stood in the opening for a moment, shocked into silence.

Judas broke their paralysis. "Oh my God, Jonah. What's gotten into them? What do we do?"

Jonah shook his head. "I don't know. Let's help get some of these people out of here." He stepped into the room and around a desk, then halted, staring at the ground.

Judas came up behind him. "What the fuck?"

Before them, one of the CEO's bodyguards crouched on

the ground holding a young female lab technician to the floor. He had his face buried in her neck as blood gushed out, pooling on the floor. The bodyguard turned his head at the sound of Judas's voice.

Jonah watched as the woman's body convulsed, blood spurting from the gaping hole in her neck as the color drained from her face.

"Oh shit," Judas cried out as Jonah backed into him.

Blood dripped from the bodyguard's chin. He growled as he chewed a chunk of flesh between his teeth and stood, glaring at the brothers.

"What's going on here, Jonah?" Judas cried out as they inched their way back down the entry. The guard followed, his shirt thick with congealing blood. They could see the bite marks on him.

"They're eating each other!" Jonah said, dumbfounded.

"Buy why? What the hell is going on?"

The large man stepped toward them, a red hand jutting out at Jonah.

"What's wrong with you?" Jonah asked as he continued to back into the entry.

The man didn't answer. He just kept coming.

"Are you sick? We can get you help." Jonah looked into the man's eyes, searching for some sign he'd heard them. "Oh my God, Judas, I think they might be zombies!"

"What are you talking about? Mom always said it was make-believe. That they were some filmmaker's commentary on the state of humanity."

Jonah raised his hands up defensively as the man approached. "I don't think anyone is home. Look at his eyes."

Judas continued to inch back but answered. "Yeah. So?"

"When have you seen someone look like that before?"

"Never. Well, maybe in the movies."

"And the last time you saw someone eating another person?"

"The movies."

"Is this a movie set?"

"No." Judas shook his head. "What the hell are we gonna do? I'm not ready for the zombie apocalypse!"

They found themselves back at the entrance, next to the emergency fire station. The bloody bodyguard was only a few feet away.

"Let's get out of here," Judas cried.

Jonah nodded and turned when— "Help!" A loud cry came from back in the lab.

"Crap!" Jonah bit his lip. "There are still people alive in there. We can't leave." He turned his head and caught sight of the fire station. "Judas, hand me the axe and grab the fire extinguisher."

"But there isn't a fire anyw—"

"Just do it!" Jonah barked as he lunged forward and slammed his fists into the approaching man's chest, knocking him back but not stopping him. "Stand down, sir! Don't make me hurt you!"

"Graaahh," the bodyguard growled as he charged at him again.

Jonah reached out his hand to Judas and felt the solid handle of the axe placed in it. He spun it around and used the head like a pole and smacked the man in the chest. "I repeat. Please step back. I don't want to hurt you." The man growled in response and lurched at him again.

"Judas, blast him in the face with that extinguisher, maybe that'll shock him out of it."

"You got it, bro!" Judas stepped next to his brother, aimed the nozzle and pulled the trigger. White fire retardant blasted out, spraying the man's face until it looked like he was wearing pink shaving cream.

The man shrieked, growled, and thrashed around.

Jonah stepped in, slipped his right leg under the man's left ankle, and slammed the head of the axe hard against his chest.

The bodyguard stumbled, tripping over Jonah's foot and falling to the ground. It only took a moment before he was trying to get up again.

"Stay down," Jonah shouted.

Judas stepped in and kicked one of the man's arms out from under him. He fell but grabbed at Judas's ankle, seizing it and diving in for a bite.

Jonah brought the axe down right atop the man's head. It cleaved through his skull with a crunch and splattered his gray matter. The man went still, his fingers loosening their grip on Judas's ankle.

"Did... did you just kill him?" Judas stared at his brother.

Jonah, panting, nodded. "Yeah, I did."

"Oh my God, Jonah. What are..."

Another form entered the hallway, casting shadows in their direction. They both looked and saw that the woman the bodyguard had been eating was now stumbling toward them, a river of blood rushing from her neck. Screams and cries of pain continued to come from inside the lab.

"Wh-what is going on here?"

Jonah pulled the axe from the man's skull. "I have no idea but we've got to try to help those that aren't—" He shook his head, "Whatever these things are."

"But Jonah, that woman shouldn't be..."

"I know." Jonah cut him off. "Get ready with that fire extinguisher. Miss, I need you to stop!"

The woman kept coming. Jonah's commands to halt only seeming to egg her on.

"Blast her," Jonah said.

Judas did, then Jonah slammed her backward using the axe as a pole again. She shrieked and fell to the ground with a smack.

"Fuck," Jonah muttered and swung the weapon as the woman looked at them, her mouth open and savage. He slammed it into her chest. They heard the crunch of bone and then saw the rush of red staining through her lab coat, yet she only growled louder, her arms outstretched, hands grasping at them.

Judas backed away, panting with his mouth hanging open. "I think I'm gonna be sick."

Jonah pulled the axe out of her crushed chest, raised it up, then brought it down on her skull. The woman stopped moving. He yanked the weapon free and turned back to his brother.

Judas looked at him with wet, wide eyes. "What have we done?"

V. Zombie Exterminators?

Screams, cries, and the groans of the dead and dying echoed through the hallway.

"I don't know what's going on, but people need our help," Jonah said. "Hitting them in the head seems to work."

Judas, who had been hyperventilating to keep steady, nodded. "Jonah, I don't..."

"Judas, whatever is going on, these things are already dead. You saw what they were doing to one another, you saw what happened when I hit that one in the chest. She didn't even say 'ow'! She just kept coming for us. We need to stop this."

Judas took two slow, deep breaths, nodded, and reached for the fire extinguisher. "You got it, bro. Let's do this."

𝕶𝖍𝖍𝖍𝖍𝖍

Inside the main lab area, a dozen or more blood covered figures lumbered around, heading to where another female, this time an older one with reddish-brown hair, stood atop a counter in the back corner, she kicked and screamed at those nearest her.

"Stay away!" Blood oozed from a wound on her exposed ankle.

The brothers made their way in her direction, alternating between blasting their attackers in the face with the fire extinguisher to distract them and then finishing them with a blow to the head.

Jonah continued trying to talk to the first few, telling them to stop, but soon he became a quiet, axe swinging, killing machine. A trail of pink-faced corpses lay behind them.

They had no choice but to move, to swing the axe, to stop those that came for them. Blood and fleshy bits of gore covered their faces, their clothes, and their minds.

When they finally made it to where the woman stood just out of reach of her attackers, there were only six crazed people still standing.

"How are we gonna do this, Jonah?"

"Blast the ground in front of us. Make it slick."

Judas let out a long stream of the fire-retardant foam, coating the tile floor before them.

"C'mon you crazy bastards," Jonah shouted, waving the axe in the air. "Come and get us!"

The flesh-hungry group came towards them, slipping and falling, making easy targets for Jonah's blows. He crushed skulls, severed limb and brought death to the living monsters.

A moment later, silence descended as the brothers and the wounded woman stood in the aftermath trying to catch their breath.

"Are you all right, miss?" Judas asked, putting the extinguisher down and walking over to help her off the tall counter.

The woman shook her head and clutched at her bleeding ankle.

Judas offered a hand and slid her onto the floor. The woman slumped, leaning against a shelf.

Jonah rushed over and knelt beside her. "What happened in here?"

The woman's eyes blinked sluggishly. "The experiment..." she took in a long breath, "it worked." Her eyes closed and her head lulled forward.

A groan sounded behind them and the brothers turned to find a man in a tight white lab coat with one bloody button undone coming at them.

Jonah handed the axe to Judas. "I've got nothing left man. That one's yours."

Judas took the weapon and walked to meet the man.

Jonah turned back to the woman, lifted her head and let it go. It fell back, lifeless.

"Crap," Jonah shook his head and stood, turning to watch as Judas approached the man.

"Hey, you've got a button loose!" Judas shouted and knocked the man back with the head of the axe.

Dead Adrian growled and lunged forward.

Judas brought the weapon up and aimed for the man's head. He missed, the blade taking the man's ear off before sinking deep into his shoulder.

The dead man screeched and swung around, yanking the axe from Judas's hands. He was on top of Judas in a heartbeat. They fell to the ground, the axe bouncing free as the handle struck the floor.

"Ahh," Judas cried out as the man grasped at him, growling.

Jonah rushed to his side, grabbed the man and yanked him off, then slammed him onto the ground on his back. Jonah put a foot on the man's chest, then swept his hand down, grabbing the fallen weapon.

K-thunk.

He severed the man's head at the neck. It rolled to the side, the mouth just inches from Judas's ear and still biting. "Rargh, rargh."

"What the fuck!" Judas cried out and scurried away, getting to his feet. They watched the man's eyes move to follow Judas, its mouth still gnashing away.

Jonah raised the axe again and swung it down, spattering the severed head into silence.

They breathed in a moment of silence until yet another groan came from behind them. They turned to see the woman they'd saved getting up off the floor.

"How is that even possible?" Judas cried, glancing from the woman to his brother.

Jonah shook his head. "I've got nothing."

The other bodyguards black-clad body lay nearby. Jonah walked over and removed the gun from the man's holster.

He raised it and pointed it at the woman's face as she approached.

"Grag—" Blam!

The woman's body fell to the ground, leaving the brothers in the deafening echo of the gun blast, surveying the carnage all around them.

Then a whooshing sound broke the silence.

The brothers spun to see a dark-tinted glass door about a dozen feet away sliding open.

A tall woman with waist-length raven colored hair and wearing a white lab coat stepped out. They'd only ever caught glimpses of her before as she exited or entered her limo, but they both knew who she was.

She smiled at them, taking a moment to look at each in turn. "Hello, boys. My name is Dr. Nitsau" She looked around the room at the wreckage and her smile widened. "How would you like a promotion?"

ABOUT GRIVANTE

Grivante, pronounced "Gri-von-tay" for anyone wondering, is the author of The Zee Brother's series. What you have just read is a special origin story that tells us exactly how the brothers got into zombie exterminating in the first place. It also officially introduces Dr. Natasha Nitsau into the mythos. She plays a large role in the final two books in the series.

Special thanks to Jack Appell for his editing skills in fine-tuning this story into all it could be!

The Zee Brothers series can be found on **Amazon.**

To find more information about Grivante please follow him on the social media sites listed below or visit his websites, www.grivantepress.com and www.thezeebroth-ers.com

BB   bookbub.com/authors/grivante

f   facebook.com/grivante

twitter.com/grivante

instagram.com/grivante

10

WHEN I GROW UP, I WON'T BE

"Get out of there! That's our spot and you know it."

Niki startled awake and froze.

"If you don't come out now, we'll use you as bait to get away from the Flesh Fallers."

She could hear them laughing. She wouldn't come out, no matter what. Not this close to darkness. Not when they would be coming out soon.

A hand reached inside the only opening of the empty dumpster tipped on its side. Niki pressed herself tighter into the corner. It was so dark, she couldn't even see the hand that grabbed her ankle, making her squeak.

"Come on out, you filthy, nasty Vaxxer. We don't want you to stink up our space."

Niki kicked out, but missed. "You're all Vaxxers, too, dumb ass."

A hand clamped around her ankle again and started dragging her across the dirt and metallic edges of the dumpster. She felt pain in her hands and elbows as she clawed to stay in place and her skin tore, making her cry out.

Half of her body was out from the dumpster. Another

hand grabbed her other leg, then another pulled at her shirt. She managed a few kicks, hits, and even a bite, but in the end, she was helpless as the group of teenage girls dragged her out.

They pulled her several feet away from the dumpster before dropping their hold.

"Bitches!" She spat at them.

They laughed and crawled into the dumpster one at a time.

Niki didn't bother to try again or to tend to her bloodied hands and elbows, there was no time. The sun was already down and only a bit of orange was left in the sky. They would be here any minute.

She ran back up the alley the dumpster was in. When she reached the end of it, she looked both ways. No humans dared to be out at this hour. No zombies were in sight either. Not yet. They didn't like the light.

Niki ran to the closest safe place, an abandoned vehicle, hoping against hope it was unoccupied by humans or the undead.

By the time she got there, only the faintest bit of light was left. She peeked in the windows one by one. No one was in the rotting rust-colored car, human or otherwise. The hairs stood up on the back of her neck as the groaning started all around her. They were coming out. Throwing herself in, she irrationally locked the door and huddled on the floor.

The moans and random bits of noise of the creatures that were once kids close to her age filled up every space of the car. Even with the glass still intact. Niki didn't dare move any more than shallow breaths. She was probably screwed anyway, considering the blood still oozing out of her hands and elbows. The Flesh Fallers had incredible senses, especially for the liquid they craved most. The same liquid that was dripping steadily on the car floor as she tried to wrap a raggedy piece of cloth around her wounds without gasping in pain.

A bang came right behind Niki's head. Against her will, a squeak came out of her mouth. Another bang came and she knew they would certainly be able to hear the pounding of her heart and her rapid breathing. She pulled out her only weapon from the cloth bag at her waist. A serrated hunting knife. A lot of good it would do her.

Glass shattered and rained down on her. She dropped even lower.

The smell of hundreds of naked, rotting teens fell over her and she gagged involuntarily, temporarily paralyzed by it. She pulled a wad of cotton out of her raggedy jeans pocket and shoved it up each nostril. The smell still lingered in her open mouth, but at least she could function.

"What a stupid way to die," she muttered.

A rotten hand grabbed on to her short brown hair.

"Ah!"

A Flesh Faller dragged her upwards. She only had seconds before rotting teeth would break open her veins and they would drain her dry.

Without a target, she flung the knife backward. It sunk into a very rotten head and the hand in her hair let go.

She fell the few feet back to the car floor. Body fluids from the dead Flesh Faller rained down onto her hair, back, and face before she was able to scramble out of the way, gagging again.

She brushed her bare arm across her face and gore stuck to it. The dead Flesh Faller hung in the window. Three more had gotten stuck trying to wedge in past the dead one. Their teeth gnashed and their white eyes rolled in their sockets.

Niki didn't dare reach for her knife, still stuck in the head of the dead one. She scrambled to the floor of the front passenger side. She had stripped this car of anything useful months ago, so she didn't bother looking. Trembling, bleeding, starving, and exhausted, Niki allowed herself to let go. To disconnect herself like she had many times in her fifteen years.

The noise outside the car lessened, breaking her out of her daze.

After a few minutes, the only sound was the four still wedged in the broken window.

A series of screams sounded in the darkness a little distance away. Niki was just thankful it wasn't hers.

She carefully leaned up enough to look out the far window. It was pitch black. Not even the one or two stars usually visible above the crumbling buildings were out tonight. Not good. She couldn't stay here.

Taking a risk, she unlocked and opened the door behind her in one quick motion. Opening it a crack, only the sounds of the ones in the window came to her. In one movement, she pushed open the door, stumbled out and ran.

Her eyes were not completely used to the dark, but shapes were moving in the darkness all around her.

Not even sure where she was running, she bolted in the opposite direction the horde had gone. This was her city and lucky for her she knew it well.

An idea came to her. A place she could hide. There was no guarantee it wasn't occupied, but there was no way the Flesh Fallers could get to it.

The sound of them was all around her in the darkness. Her eyes had adjusted better and she saw one of them nearby. A boy. One of his eyes hung on his cheek and bounced when he moved erratically in stops and jerks. It turned toward Niki, smelling the air. Time to go. Fortunately, the hideout was close.

She stepped onto the ladder to get to it. A cold hand grabbed onto her leg, followed quickly by teeth as they clamped onto her pants. The layering she had taped there saved her life. She kicked out with her other foot, which sunk into the creature's head, making her gag. She kept going up the ladder, the body and gore falling off to land below her with a wet thud.

Launching herself into the opening she crawled as far from it as she could.

A male voice yelled out, "Ow!"

A blade of some kind was at her throat. It was cold and deadly.

"I'm human!" she gasped.

"So what? So am I."

"Get that blade away from my throat, dick. You could hurt someone."

She pushed his arm away and she didn't feel him try to put it back.

"I could kick you out, you know. I was here first."

"I would fight you."

He sighed. "I don't have the energy to fight you."

His shadowy figure slunk further into the darkness.

She went the opposite way until her back hit a rough wooden wall.

Her torn elbows and hands burned, reminding her of her injuries. She would have to deal with them soon or they could get infected. Although fatigue hit her hard, she was afraid to fall asleep with the strange boy there. She fought off sleep, drifting in and out of it for a long time.

"What's your name?" his voice said, startling her out of her stupor.

"Why?"

"That's a unique name. I met a kid named Can before. I think it's because he lived in a trash can though."

Niki was momentarily stunned to silence. His voice sounded deep and somehow alluring. Yet his joke made him sound like a child. She guessed he was close to her age.

"My name's Raker."

"Good for you," Niki muttered.

"It's getting cold. Can I come sit by you? To keep warm?"

"No!"

He shuffled closer anyway.

Niki instinctively moved further away from him, but he had her cornered. She could smell him coming. Not that she smelled fantastic either, especially with the fresh gore still drying on her hair and shirt.

"Don't touch me or I'll kill you," she threatened.

He chuckled. "You don't have any weapons or you would have killed me already when I put the knife on you."

"I don't need a weapon."

"Right. Gonna kill me with your bare hands I suppose?"

"Yes."

She could just make out his figure in the moonlight now shining in. He sat down next to her, not touching her.

"You killed people?"

"Only if they touched me."

His deep laughter shook his body. "Where are you from?"

"Why?"

"I don't know. You're not very good at conversation, are you?"

Niki didn't answer.

"If I sleep, will you kill me?" he asked. "I don't have anything to steal, so it would be a waste of your energy."

"No, as long as you don't touch me."

"No touching, that's pretty clear."

"Then no."

"Good. I'm tired."

They said no more. Niki thought about trying to stay awake, but decided he didn't seem dangerous. She couldn't fight it anyway.

𐤊𐤊𐤊𐤊𐤊

She woke the next morning with warm light shining in the doorway of the room. The bare wooden walls, floor, and ceiling in the small space made her claustrophobic, even with two open windows and a door.

For once she wasn't cold at least. It didn't take her long to figure out why. Raker was wrapped around her. At first, it freaked her out, then she relaxed into his warmth. Still, she wanted to be out of there before he woke up. She learned a long time ago not to try to make lasting connections with anyone. It never ended well.

She wiggled out from under his weight and crawled toward the open door, stepping out of it.

"Want to meet here again tonight?" the boy said above her, making her look up.

He had black hair that was crudely cut short. To her surprise, he had a piece of metal in each ear similar to the one in her eyebrow. He looked older than her and had fierce green eyes that were a shade brighter than her own. He was smiling in a cute, crooked way with amazingly nice teeth.

"Maybe," she called up, surprising both of them.

As soon as her feet hit the overgrown lawn, she pushed her way through the tall grasses away from the house that looked ready to fall down.

She found a place to do her morning business before setting off to one of her hidden food stores. She never slept where she ate or brought anything with her. Another lesson she had learned the hard way. People attacked people who had stuff to steal.

Her favorite place to hide food was in the metal boxes attached to houses. Most of them were hidden behind overgrown bushes. Plus, most of them were dry and kept bugs out. Today, it was at a house that had once been green. Looking around her to make sure no one was watching or following her, she jumped in the bushes. Her breakfast consisted of an ancient jar of peaches and a bar whose wrapper was faded, hiding its flavor.

Once she was finished, she put the jar back, which would also be her dinner later, and closed the lid. Her reflection made her pause.

"Ugh," she said out loud. She looked worse than usual, which was saying something. Her brown hair was a ratty mess and her pale skin and sharp cheekbones made her look gaunt. Probably lacking something in her diet, ha ha. She sighed.

A couple of blocks down was a house that was still a plastic gray color where Niki stored emergency medical supplies. She cleaned and bandaged her elbows and put salve on her hands. They were already crusted over, so she wasn't worried. She changed her shirt and cleaned up her face as best she could. Her hair wasn't worth wasting the water on.

Her next goal was to get her knife back. The two Flesh Fallers that were stuck in the window were gone and no one had taken her knife, much to her relief. She pulled it out, managing to avoid the gore that came out with it. She cleaned it with more of the seat fabric. Using the mirror in the car, she cut all of her hair off as short as she could without cutting herself. When she was done, she smiled at her reflection. She couldn't remember the last thing that had made her smile.

She spent the rest of the day scavenging and resting, hunting and fishing.

As the day neared the end, she decided to go to the treehouse early, after first retrieving a glass jar of soup she had been saving, planning to share it with Raker. Call it as close to an act of affection as she was capable of in this messed up world.

It took forever to get dark, with no sign of Raker. Just as well. She would be able to sleep without fear of being molested.

She must have fallen asleep, because she was jarred out of it when a light came into her vision.

"Raker?" she whispered.

The light came straight to her and it took only a second to realize it wasn't him.

"Give me your food," a gruff voice demanded. An adult male voice. He looked sick or starving.

"I don't have anything."

The man came closer and Niki jumped to her feet.

"Everyone has something."

She braced herself, pulling her knife subtly out of the cloth in her pocket she kept it in. "Don't come any closer."

The man smiled wickedly, showing brown, broken teeth and a ratty beard. The light went out.

Hands grabbed her out of the sudden darkness and she was pushed roughly into the wall of the treehouse.

"Get off me!" Niki screamed.

"Be quiet, little girl. You'll bring them here," the man whispered in her ear.

He pawed at her, his intent clear. She fought him and he backhanded her. She had no choice and plunged the knife into his side with a fierceness to survive that took her over.

He gasped and his weight pushed off of her. She pulled her knife out ready to do it again. Niki could hear him scuffle into the dark nearby, but the moon wasn't bright enough to see where.

A scream ripped through the dark near her, making her jump.

A light burned to life in front of her. She prepared to defend herself, but Raker's face glowed behind, it a look of panic in his eyes. "Are you okay?" he asked.

Niki swallowed and relaxed. "Yeah, I'm fine."

He took a step closer to her. "You're bleeding."

He reached out and gently touched the blood on her cheekbone with his knuckle.

She winced. "Is he dead?"

Raker turned to hold the lighter close to the face of the man that had attacked her. He was on the floor. His eyes were open, no life in them.

"Help me push him out," Niki said.

"It will bring them."

"He deserves to be drained."

"It will smell."

"He's going to smell in here too. We can bury him in the morning."

The sound of Flesh Fallers coming closer proved her point. "See? They smell the blood. How else are we going to get him out of here?"

Raker set the light on the floor and together they dragged the man to the opening and pushed. The sound he made hitting the ground was horrifying, but not as much as the sounds that followed as Flesh Fallers drained him of his bodily fluids.

Soon the sounds of Flesh Fallers all around them was deafening. Luckily they couldn't climb. Niki was still keyed up and sleep wouldn't come. "You still awake?" Raker asked.

"Yeah."

"Me too. Now that I saved your life, will you tell me your name?"

"Niki. You hungry? I brought soup."

"Sure."

The treehouse shuddered a few times as the Flesh Fallers smelled the blood and pounded themselves against the tree.

Ignoring them, Niki found and opened the jar with her knife she had wiped clean, scooped some out with her fingers, and passed it to Raker. Beef stew. Amazing, even cold.

Raker flicked the light off when the moonlight was enough that they could see a little through one of the windows.

"You didn't save me, by the way," Niki said as they passed the jar back and forth. "I stabbed him first."

Raker snorted. "I stabbed him last. Doesn't that mean I technically killed him?"

Niki heard something in his voice. "Was this the first time you killed someone?"

"No!"

Niki guessed it was. "He was going to hurt me."

"I know."

Once the soup was gone, Niki scuttled over to the opening and chucked the jar at the relentless creatures below. It bounced off one's head and hit another, making her chuckle.

Raker laughed too. "I've never met someone quite like you," he said after she had settled back against the wall farthest from the dead man's blood.

"Me neither."

He chuckled again.

Silence fell between them for so long, Niki thought he had fallen asleep.

When he spoke again it startled her. "Want to have sex?"

"No!" She yelled and instinctively scooted away from him.

He laughed and moved closer to her again. "Worth a try. Do you want to stick together?"

"What do you mean?" Niki asked.

"We could hunt together or fish or look for stuff."

"Why?"

"I don't know. We can watch each other's backs." He paused and said, so quietly that Niki could barely hear him, "Besides, I'm tired of being alone."

"I don't mind being alone. It's safer," Niki answered bluntly. "But alright, we can try it. You don't own me though. I go where I want, when I want."

"Of course. Has someone tried to own you?"

"No."

"They have with me."

"Really?"

"Yeah, this crazy group of girls who wanted me for—"

"I don't want to know."

"It wasn't so bad. They gave me food."

"Some things aren't worth food."

"Yeah, that's what I decided too."

They went quiet then. Neither of them slept until the light of morning scared off the horde below.

Once again, Niki woke first. She thought about running off anyway, despite what they had decided, but she liked this boy. More than she had liked anyone in a long time. She felt drawn to him. She watched him sleep. He looked peaceful. He stirred and his eyes opened.

"Morning," Raker said, sitting up.

"Morning."

"You look different in light."

Niki raised an eyebrow.

"No, it's good. You're pretty. You cut your hair."

"A Flesher got ahold of it the other night. Decided I'd like less to grab. By Fleshers or jerks like that guy last night."

They both peeked out the door to see his remains below. It was not a pretty sight.

"We better get to it," Raker said.

They climbed down and went their separate ways to do their morning business.

They came back and were both staring at the mess that was the dead man, now drained dry, making him look shriveled.

"Know where a shovel might be?" Niki asked.

"Nope, you?"

Niki sighed. "Let's get some food, then we'll deal with him."

"Sounds good to me."

Niki was surprised when Raker led her to one of the ponds in the area. It could be dangerous there since the water was contaminated with dead Flesh Fallers who gorged themselves on water until they died permanently.

He led her to a large rock that was jutting into the water and surrounded by weeds. There were no bodies in this part of the pond since the weeds were too hard to get through, although the smell was still horrific.

"You keep a lookout," he said to her.

Raker leaned over the rock on his stomach and with some effort pulled a metal box out of the water with a string attached to it.

"This is my stash," he said after he had set the box down with a clang.

He opened it and handed her a jar of water. She looked at it suspiciously.

"It's from the spring and boiled. It's safe."

She drank from it thankfully and handed it back.

After getting a drink himself, Raker pulled out some jerked meat in a cloth. It was salty and delicious.

"Where'd you get this?" Niki asked.

"I know a lady that makes it. She trades me for fish."

"Nice!"

"Just don't ask what kind of meat it is."

Niki wasn't picky.

Once they were finished and he had re-sunk his stash, they started back to the thick of the city, walking down a weed-choked path that had once been a road. The rotting city in front of them twinkled in the sunlight.

"Why would you show me that?" Niki asked.

"What? My stash?"

"Sure. I mean, I've seen people killed for less."

He shrugged. "If you wanted to kill me, you would have already."

A roaring sound broke them back to their reality.

"Run!" Niki yelled.

They ran, but it was too late. Several cars and trucks roared around the corner behind them and sped up at the sight of them.

They screeched to a halt and people poured out of the vehicles. Niki and Raker ran in between buildings into the weeds, but could hear footsteps catching up to them and vehicles coming closer.

Niki spun around just as hands were reaching for her. Her knife was out and in a man with a black mask before her brain caught up with her actions.

"Niki!" Raker yelled.

She watched helplessly as three men dragged him into a rusty truck. Hands grabbed her from every angle. She fought using her hands, feet, and even her teeth.

She was punched several times. The last one to the head made her vision fade for a moment. By the time she came back, they were loading her into a different truck than Raker.

"Damn," one of the men said as they bound her arms and she continued to fight. "This Vaxxer has some spunk."

Niki was unable to move her arms or legs at all. They were pinned in such a way that they quickly went numb. A black bag was pulled over her head. She was able to breathe fine, but was claustrophobic.

What felt like hours later, she was dragged back out, still fighting. Her body was dropped painfully onto a cold cement floor, knocking the wind out of her. Her captors walked away laughing and making comments on her strength.

The bag was pulled off her head, but she still couldn't move.

The face of a boy crouched in front of her came into focus.

"My name is James. You're okay now. We're going to cut you lose."

Niki was in a cage. Metal bars made up one complete

wall. The other three were cement walls with small windows high in them which also had bars on them.

Her arms and legs were freed, but it took a full five minutes for the numbness, tingling, and pain to diminish and the feeling to return. Her entire body hurt. She sat up and then stood, looking around.

About 20 or 30 kids were sitting around, working out, eating, or sleeping. One couple was in the corner blatantly enjoying each other.

"Raker!" Niki yelled out loud.

"They took him that way, to another cage," a younger boy said, pointing.

"Niki?"

She pushed herself hard against the bars. His voice was faint, but it was him.

"You okay?" he asked from a distance.

"Yeah, you?"

"Been better."

"Keep it down, Vaxxer!" a man yelled and a metal against metal bang made her go quiet. A man with a gun came into her view. Raker was okay, though. She spun around, her attention back to her own situation.

"Where am I?" Niki asked James, who was watching her closely.

"Don't know. None of us do. We all came the same way you did."

"Who are they?"

"They're VETs."

"Damn it. I thought so."

"Vaxxer Elimination Teams," a girl behind her said. "I'm Abby."

"I know who they are. What does this group do with us?" Niki asked, remembering what she'd heard. There were many groups with many different purposes, none of them good for teens close to changing.

"We don't know," James answered. "They wait until we turn and then take us."

"Like a weapon," Abby said.

"I hear they take big groups out sometimes too," another girl, younger than Niki, said.

"How long have you been here?" Niki asked James.

He shrugged. "Too long."

She looked around at the other teens' clothes, which were tattered and falling apart. That was normal in this world, but still, Niki didn't like the sound of this.

"What do we do?" Niki asked Abby.

Abby laughed. "Now, Vaxxer, we wait."

ABOUT BREA BEHN

Brea Behn started writing at the age of fifteen, when she wrote a memoir for her twin brother. Currently, she writes dystopian, children's fiction, nonfiction, and is building her career as an author and public speaker. Brea speaks on topics ranging from social medial, being a hybrid author, and on the more personal topic of grieving as a teen. Brea is represented by the Purcell Agency. When Brea is not writing, she is reading, crocheting, canning or watching movies. Brea lives in Wisconsin with her husband and their two children.

Brea Behn's books can be found on **Amazon.**

To find more information about Brea Behn please follow them on the social media sites listed below.

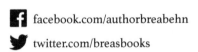

facebook.com/authorbreabehn

twitter.com/breasbooks

11

JIMMY

"Don't you think it's time for him to get out of bed, Martin? It's nearly twelve o'clock."

"He's a teenager, Mary, that's what they do. They sleep."

"Still. . .noon?"

Martin shrugged, not bothering to look up as he flipped to the sports section of the Sunday paper. He shifted in his seat a bit when the sun coming in through the kitchen window obscured the words on the page. They had arrived home from morning Mass barely ten minutes before and he wanted nothing more than a quiet cup of coffee with his paper.

"I think I'll just pop my head in there to make sure he is okay."

"Leave him alone, Mary. He'll be down soon enough," Martin replied, looking at his wife for the first time since they left church. "Teenagers need their sleep. Teenage boys need their privacy. Besides, it's Sunday morning, he prob- ably didn't come in until late last night."

"Well, I'm getting tired of his door always being locked. I

haven't even seen him since he left for school on Friday morning."

Martin shrugged the comment off, knowing he was right. He wasn't interested in discussing it further and waited patiently for Mary to move on to something else. As soon as he saw her disengage from the conversation, he flipped the paperback open and returned to his Sunday morning ritual. Mary paced about the room for a moment before moving purposefully to the refrigerator.

"Well, if you want the roast for supper, I'd better get it started," She said, bringing a plate out of the fridge with a bloody hunk of meat on it. "Have you heard from William?"

Martin sighed audibly, annoyed at the continued banter.

"Not since he needed to borrow money for groceries last month."

"Did you give it to him?" Mary asked, accusingly.

"Of course, Mary. Can't let him starve. I just can't get over how expensive everything in New York is."

"Do you think Jimmy is going to go away to college too?" Mary hissed, afraid that the boy who was halfway across the house, behind his closed bedroom door, might hear her talking about him.

"I hope so. Working at that fast-food restaurant isn't going to pay the bills once he graduates high school."

"Martin! Cut him some slack, at least he's working."

"I just don't understand why he didn't want to come work with me. It certainly pays better."

"He wanted to do something on his own. Maybe he didn't want his father breathing down his neck at work as well as at home."

Martin just shrugged and turned back to the newspaper. An article about the Packer's offensive line had caught his eye. In truth, he was actually relieved when Jimmy had chosen not to come to work with him. He had only secured the seasonal office assistant position because Mary had insisted on it. He loved his sons to death, but if Jimmy were to have come to work with him it could make things uncomfortable for him around the office and at home.

Jimmy had recently been showing some tell-tale signs that he was gay, and while he personally couldn't care less about his son's sexuality, he also knew that this part of the country was still a bit behind the times. The words 'gay' and 'fag' were thrown about on a regular basis by his co-workers, who seemingly had no concept that it was both offensive and inappropriate. Given the choice, he would rather his son not see him associated with such things. He also didn't want to be put in a position where he would be forced to alienate his office in defense of his son.

The sound of a piece of furniture sliding across the hardwood floor sounded from upstairs, indicating that Jimmy was finally up and about.

"See, Mary, the boy is awake. Teenagers." Martin sighed, fully absorbed in the article.

"I better go see what he wants for breakfast." she said, sliding out of the kitchen and moving through the sitting room towards the stairs.

Martin finished reading the article, which reassured him that McCarthy had solved last years woes. He stood up and moved around the table to the sliding glass doors to look out, across the back deck, into the fields beyond. *Stay healthy boys.* he thought, referring to his team, as he sipped his coffee. The weather had just taken a turn for the cold, and he wanted to try and relax and enjoy what might be the last quiet weekend for a month. With hunting season in full swing, he knew that his weekends were going to be busy in the coming weeks.

There were three separate hunting outings that he was forced on as an annual tradition, one trip with the guys at work, one with his brothers, and one with Mary's father and brother. Since Sundays were already filled, being the holy day as well as game day, Saturday was the only time any of them were able to get away from their families and out into the woods. Martin's thoughts were ripped from the bucolic scenery by the sounds of Mary yelling for him from upstairs.

"Yeah, Mary. What is it?" he shouted back, his moment of peace shattered.

"Get up here, Martin. I think something is wrong!" she yelled back, her voice laden with panic.

Martin sighed heavily and started off towards the stairs, feeling deflated. He paused to set his cup of coffee down on the table as he walked by.

"There's music playing and I can hear him moving around in there, but he won't answer me and the door is locked," Mary called down, wringing her hands at the top of the stairs.

Martin didn't respond as he mounted the long flight that led to the upper floor of the house. He was getting quite aggravated with the drama of the morning and wanted to get to the bottom of it before it led to an argument. *Kid is probably hung-over or cleaning up a mess of Kleenex and dirty magazines.* he thought as he moved in front of his youngest son's bedroom door. He rapped heavily on the door with the back of his hand, loud enough to shake the solid wooden door in its frame.

"James, it's Dad. Open up," he demanded, anticipating a response from within. "It's one thing to come and go at all hours, but if you are going to disrespect your mother and me, then we are going to have to talk about the hours you've been keeping and set some boundaries."

There was no answer but a low moan from inside. Martin was now sure that the boy had been drunk the night before.

"Can you please get my keys, Mary," Martin said absently.

They did their best to allow the kids their privacy, but always kept a copy of their keys, just in case a situation arose where they needed them. Mary moved off, down the hall to fetch the keys from atop his dresser, returning a moment later. It took Martin a few tries before he found the correct key. He slid it home and twisted the knob. The knob turned freely, but the door still wouldn't budge.

"Sonofabitch," Martin swore under his breath, drawing a scowl from his prim wife. "He must have blocked the door with a chair or something."

Martin, now thoroughly aggravated, started hammering the heel of his fist against the door.

"James Martin Norman, open this door right now!" He snarled, unable to control the volume of his voice as it lifted to a low roar.

Again, there was no response but for the sounds of Diana Ross singing and a low moaning from within.

"James, open the door!" Mary urged from behind him. "Martin, please open it."

Martin took a breath to steady himself and flush his frustrations before responding.

"Mary, something inside is blocking the door from opening. . .that door is original," he said, referring to the mid-nineteenth century roots of the house. "If I break it down, it'll cost an arm-and-a-leg to replace."

"Well, what do we do then, Martin?"

"I don't know, Mary. Why don't we just go downstairs and take a breath? He'll come out eventually."

"I'm worried, Martin," Mary said, again wringing her hands in worry. "Do you think he is on drugs?"

"I don't know, Mary," he answered absently, as he started down the stairs.

Martin poured himself a fresh cup of coffee as they moved through the kitchen. He did so out of habit more than a desire for another cup. It was a reflex to keep his hands busy, a habit that he carried home from the office, while he mulled whatever his son might be up to. Mary stood where the sitting room opened to the foyer, nervously staring up at the closed door of Jimmy's bedroom. She finally moved from her position, broken from her reverie, by the tell-tale whooshing sound of the sliding glass door opening.

With a warm mug of black coffee in Martin's hands, the two moved out onto the back deck. They almost invariably came out here to discuss their problems. Ever since the kids were old enough to listen in on them, the deck was the most convenient place they could come and speak in private. The quiet pastoral beauty of the acreage behind the house had a calming influence on both of them. That calm lent to a discussion of problems rather than arguing about them.

"Did we fail Jimmy, Martin?" Mary asked, moving to the far railing and looking out over the disused horse pasture.

"I don't think so, I don't know." he started before petering off.

"We put so much pressure and attention on William. I feel like we ignored everything with Jimmy."

"Don't say that, Mary." he replied.

Though he refuted her statement, he also recognized the truth in it. They had been a lot more attentive with William, their eldest. While it was obvious, in hindsight, that they needn't have worried, it wasn't at the time. Martin pondered the question for a moment longer before forcing a follow-up statement.

"Teenagers are secretive, we can only do so much. A lot of it is up to them, you know."

William had been studious by nature which had landed him acceptance into NYU, where he had been for the last five years, much to the chagrin of their bank account. They still worried about William, though, their worries now were mostly focused around terrorism and crime with him living in the Big Apple, rather than the poor life-choices they had been so concerned with in his adolescence. The same studiousness did not appear in their second child. Jimmy was a social butterfly and had no interest in school other than to find something to rant about on social media or to hang out with his friends.

"Do you think it's crack-cocaine?"

"Mary. . ."

"Heroin?" Mary gasped before she finally broke down and started to sob.

Martin moved in behind his wife and held her.

"We don't know anything, Mary. He could be hung over. Even William drank as a teenager. He could be ill, with the turn for the cold, he might have caught the flu. We should calm ourselves until we can talk to him and find out exactly what is going on."

Mary was almost beyond her ability to accept his response at this point, nearing hysterics.

"Is that why he is taking all those weekend trips to Duluth with that Meyers boy? Are they going there to buy drugs?" she managed to ask through her tears.

Martin was caught flat-footed by the comment. He and Jimmy had agreed to keep the trips a secret from Mary. He didn't want to worry her, assuming that the boys were just going to Duluth to be around other like-minded people. Sam Meyers was Jimmy's best friend and his own eccentricities caused Martin to make the same assumptions about his sexuality that he had with Jimmy. Martin had never even entertained the idea that the trips might be for more nefarious purposes.

He was suddenly struck by how Mary could be right about them failing the boy, and for the first time, Martin saw the chasm between him and his son. He began to worry that he was a failure as a father. The truth was, he had given Jimmy a lot of leeway, suspecting he was gay. He wanted to let Jimmy figure things out for himself, without he or Mary sticking their noses in. But now, he honestly couldn't discount the idea that the boy had gotten mixed up with drugs. He sat down heavily on the railing bench and finished his coffee in silence.

With his cup drained and the mystery still pressing, Martin took a deep breath and stood up. He stared at Mary's back for a moment, before she noticed him waiting and turned to join him. He took her hand in his, trying to reassure her with touch, and slid the door open. As they stepped through the sliding glass doors into the kitchen, Martin was the first to notice the sounds of hammering of fists on wood coming from upstairs. Without a word to Mary, he let go of her hand and set off, moving quickly past the wood stove in the sitting room and around the corner to the stairs.

"James, are you okay?" he called as he strode up the stairs, taking the steps two at a time.

"Jimmy!" Mary shouted from just behind him, her voice filled with maternal concern.

The two moved up to the door and the low moans they had previously heard, were much louder now, seemingly more insistent. The boy's hands pounded rhythmically, one after another, against the door with the sounds of Katy Perry playing in the background.

"Martin, get the door open, please!" Mary pleaded.

"Okay. Stand back, Mary," he replied.

Martin waited until she stepped back, well clear of the space he thought he would need to break the door down. He cursed silently to himself as he took a position in front of the door.

"Jimmy, this is your last chance to open this door. If I have to break it down, you're going to pay for it to be replaced."

Martin waited patiently, hoping for a response. None came, only the continued sounds of fists slamming on the inside of the door and the low breathless moaning that accompanied it.

"I'm giving you to the count of three, Jimmy. One. . .two. . .three!"

Martin rocked slowly from front foot to rear, and back again a few times before hurling himself forward. He led in with his shoulder, slamming heavily into the hardwood door, hoping that his body weight would be enough to sunder it. The door shuddered in the frame and the sound of creaking and splintering wood issued from it, but it held. Martin rebounded painfully back from the collision. He pushed aside the pain in his shoulder and threw himself forward again, committed to finishing the job and getting the answers that Mary and he needed. Again, he bounced off the solid door, though the sounds of splintering and cracking were much louder with the second blow.

Martin took a deep breath and threw his shoulder, once again, into the door. The top hinge gave with the shriek of nails pulling free of century-old wood. The door tilted inward on a pivot, still held by the latch and bottom hinge.

Martin tried to keep his balance, but when the base of the door kicked out, it scooped his front foot out from under him. His forward momentum sent him tumbling over the ruined door, spilling him into the dark room.

Martin rolled clumsily over the end table that had been blocking the door, twisting about and landing painfully on his back. The room was cast in a hazy darkness, the only light came in from the ruined doorway and what little bit diffused through the heavy draperies that James had hung over his windows to blot out the sun when he was trying to sleep.

His breath was blasted out of him on impact with the floor, and as he drew in a fresh breath, the first thing that he noticed was the horrific stench in the room. James' room usually smelled of incense or his body spray. The aroma in the room lay somewhere between that of a backed up septic tank and that of a weeks-old deer carcass left to bake in the sun. His first thought was that the boy was sick, and the whole morning of mystery and worry was due to the boy's embarrassment over a toileting accident. He was almost relieved, but a flash of movement from the other side of the darkened room put him on high alert.

"James. . .Jimmy, you there, Son?" he asked nervously, his mouth suddenly dry.

The only answer was in the form of a shuffle of movement and the sound of a low moan, growing slightly louder. Still, the sounds of Katy Perry drifted loudly, coming from the laptop in the corner of the room, next to the closet. He heard Mary scream from the hall outside the door as he righted himself to a seated position.

"Turn on the light, Mary. I can't see a damn thing in here." he barked, just as the form of his son bore down on him, startling the last word into a shriek of surprise.

As Jimmy's full weight pressed down on him, Martin's stomach could no longer handle the abhorrent stench emanating from the boy. Unable to restrain it any longer, he vomited, coating himself and his son in bile and coffee. As he fought to regain control of his stomach, a flash of intense pain erupted from his shoulder. He screamed in agony as Jimmy's teeth sunk deep into his trapezius, where the shoulder meets the neck. The light on the ceiling fan overhead flicked on and Martin caught sight of Mary's arm, extended in from the doorway. He managed to get his hands on the sides of Jimmy's head and heave him clear. As Jimmy's head tore from his shoulder, he tore a large ribbon of flesh from his neck. Martin continued to scream in pain and fear as his son tumbled over to the far side of the bed.

Martin scrambled to his feet, clutching the wound and shifting further from the boy. He cast a glance at the doorway thinking of escape. Mary stood there with her mouth agape in horror, drawing his eye back to his son. Jimmy's once handsome face was slack and pale. Sores riddled the flesh of his cheeks and arms, his eyes were filmed over and void of all emotion. Jimmy sat where he landed, atop a heap of laundry on the floor, busily chewing on his father's flesh that hung in a strip down his chin. Blood ran freely from his mouth, coating his chin and his chest. Mary, standing outside the door, started screaming in terror as she processed the scene inside her son's room. As Jimmy stuffed the last of the flesh into his mouth, he turned toward her. The low moan filled the room, accompanying the sounds of Lady Gaga coming from behind Martin. The boy started to his feet, moving towards his mother in the doorway. Martin knew he had to do something.

"Jimmy!" he shouted, hoping to draw the boy's attention away. "Jimmy, over here!"

Jimmy didn't respond to his calls as he lurched, reaching over the top of the door, laying off-kilter and still partially blocking the doorway. The boy's mouth opened, spilling blood and bits of chewed flesh as he moaned, reaching towards his mother. The sound of an inhuman roar sounded from behind Martin, sending a ripple of fear up his spine, paralyzing him. The roar was followed by heavy, furious pounding coming from the inside of Jimmy's closet.

"Run, Mary. Get the fuck out of here!" Martin yelled as his paralysis finally broke and he propelled himself towards his son.

"He's on drugs!" Mary shrieked, still standing on the other side of the door.

Martin grabbed Jimmy by the back of his bloodstained shirt and hauled him back into the room, just as the boy's reaching fingers brushed the front of his mother's church blouse.

"Run! Get help, Mary. Call the police!" he screamed at her, from barely five feet away.

Mary just stood there shaking, staring in disbelief at her son. Jimmy was growling like an animal and clawing at the air between them as her bloody husband wrestled the boy away. Her heart broke and something else inside her did as well. She stopped screaming and watched in horror as Martin was struggling to keep Jimmy's head at bay when the boy turned and started attacking him. The sound of Jimmy's closet door slamming open, crashing into Jimmy's computer desk was followed by a flash of movement coming from the darkness within the closet. Sam Meyers came rushing out in a blur and slammed into Martin. The three were on the ground in a heap of flailing limbs and screaming.

Martin, busily keeping his rabid son's mouth at bay, had no warning as the boy rammed heavily into his side. He found himself laying prone, atop his son, with something feral atop his back. Teeth sunk excruciatingly into his thigh, as Jimmy was finally freed of the hands restraining him. A second set of teeth scraped painfully down his back, struggling to find purchase. Another blinding flash of pain tore through Martin as Jimmy wrenched his head back, tearing off a chunk of his thigh. Martin lashed out, shoving Jimmy back down to the floor and struggling to extricate himself from the tumult, even as the new assailant thrashed about on his back, furiously clawing and trying to sink its teeth into him.

In the process of twisting and heaving himself off of his son, he managed to throw the other attacker clear. He twisted about on the floor and Sam Meyers came into view, thrashing and snarling as he righted himself before he came barreling in again. Sam threw his arms wide around his waist before Martin could react, putting him in a bear-hug. Sam immediately sunk his teeth into Martin's stomach.

"Mary!" He shouted, his voice warbling through the excruciating pain. "Run!"

He tried to move clear of Sam, but the boy was incredibly strong. Every effort was met with furious resistance and pain as the teeth shredded through his flesh and into the muscle. Jimmy crawled atop him, moving next to Sam. The next flash of agony was followed by a rush of endorphins that both numbed him and made him nauseous at the same time. He watched, almost remotely, as coils of his own intestines were pulled free of his stomach. The two boys were feasting on his entrails and he had no strength left with which to try and stop them. The sight horrified him, and though he was numbed due to the endorphin release, he could still feel changes in pressure as his organs were pulled out of him. His screams were those of agony, regardless of the lack of pain and he knew that he was watching his own death. His consciousness lasted much longer than he wished as they fed on his body.

Martin looked up at her with a mixture of fear, pain, and desperation as the boys ripped furiously at his midsection. Mary's legs collapsed beneath her. She drifted into unconsciousness at the sight of her husband being torn open and devoured by her son and his friend.

Mary awoke an indeterminable time later, feeling both scared and confused. The tension from panic still gripped her muscles, so she assumed that she hadn't been out too long. She took a mental inventory, working hard to remember the events that led up to her fainting, hoping that it had been a nightmare. The sinking pit in her stomach told her it was not. She immediately recognized that Martin was no longer screaming and her heart sank. Adrenaline wrought from fear surged through her and she had to force herself to remain still and listen carefully before daring to move.

The sounds of wet slurping and chomping drifted to her ears once she focused her attention. She opened her eyes and peered through the wreckage of the doorway. Between the legs of the end table, she saw the forms of her son, Jimmy and his friend, Sam, devouring the body of her husband, barely five feet from her. A pool of blood widened across the hardwood floor beneath the three. The overhead light cast a glare off the crimson fluid as it crept slowly towards the threshold of the room where she lay.

Oh, dear. Oh, dear. Oh, dear. she thought, racking her brain for a course of action. *Martin told me to get help, to call the police,* she thought. *But the Meyers boy was so fast!* her mind fearfully argued. She lay there immobile for the span of nearly a minute with her mind racing in fear-ridden circles. She shrieked uncontrollably at the sensation of her husband's blood soaking through her stockings when the still-warm puddle of blood finally reached her. The silence inside the room that followed her scream spurred her to action, she could no longer hear the sloppy sounds of the boys devouring Martin. Even the music had stopped playing when the closet door had collided with the desk. She crawled backwards to the banister and rose warily to her feet. The sight of Sam Meyers's eyes, staring blankly at her over the ruined door sent her in full flight.

Mary propelled herself down the flight of stairs, around through the sitting room and into the kitchen as fast as her feet would carry her. The sounds of heavy crashing sounded from upstairs as she spotted Martin's keys on the kitchen counter. As she scooped them up, an inhuman roar issued from upstairs, followed a moment later by the sounds of running feet, moving downstairs. Panic welled and Mary screamed again, uncontrollably. She turned and ran through the laundry area and mudroom and stepped out the side door into the brisk autumn wind. She looked around the side yard for a moment, hoping someone had heard the commotion and called the police. Nothing moved but the fallen leaves carried by the winds. The sounds of running feet behind her got her moving again.

Mary swung the door shut behind her and started down the short flight of stairs that ended at the driveway. The door slammed into something noisily before rebounding into her arm. Her whole body clenched up in terror at the glimpse of the blood-soaked boy right behind her. His mouth snapped as he reached out for her, barely missing her shoulder. She bolted down the stairs and ran around the rear of the Camry parked there. Sam's cold and fiercely-strong hand clutched her elbow for a brief and terrifying moment. His hand slipped free when his momentum carried him past the car as he hurtled after. She cast a quick glance to the side to see him cutting back towards her, his eyes wide and milky, locked on her. A loud roar boomed from his gore coated mouth as he surged in.

She jumped into the unlocked vehicle, slamming the door closed and locking it before she hurriedly twisted the key in the ignition. The motor roared to life as Sam Meyers bore down on the side of the vehicle at full speed. Mary gritted her teeth and threw the sedan in reverse, starting its course back down the driveway.

As soon as the vehicle started rolling back, the side window blasted inwards, showering her with glass and blood. Sam's upper body came in through the shattered window, grabbing, ripping and tearing at her. She screamed and slammed her foot hard on the accelerator. The vehicle hurtled down the drive with Sam's legs hanging out of the driver's window. Mary punched and slapped at the boy in a feeble effort to keep him at bay. When the car bumped down onto the roadway, the boy was thrown clear of the window and sent rolling on the road. She cut the steering wheel and the tires bounced heavily over some part of him as the sedan skidded to a halt in the middle of the unlined road.

Mary cast one final forlorn look at the home she had lived in for the last twenty-five years. She stared long at the house she shared with her beloved husband and raised two wonderful sons in. Tears streamed down her face and she almost lost her fight with the overwhelming grief she felt when the shambling form of Jimmy staggered out from the side door. She watched, both horrified and pained as her baby, soaked in the blood of his father, staggered down the driveway towards her. The sounds of Sam's hands slapping about in the undercarriage of the car wrenched her attention from the miserable sight of her son. She dropping the shifter in drive and starting the Toyota down the roadway.

"I'm coming for you, Willy. Hang tight, Will, Mama's coming," she said through her snot and tears.

ABOUT ARTHUR MONGELLI

Apocalyptic fiction has been a passion of the author's since he was probably 5 years old, watching movies he had no business watching, such as The Road Warrior and Dawn of the Dead. He dabbled in writing for many years, though, it was only recently that he figured out his process for writing long fiction.

Arthur Mongelli is the author of Harvest of Ruin (Severed Press, 2017), his first published work. He has written the forthcoming sequels to the story, which concludes in the third installment. Arthur Mongelli resides with his wife, child and two dogs in a zombie-proof home in the Hudson Valley of New York State.

The Harvest of Ruin is on **Amazon**.

To find more information about Arthur Mongelli follow him on **Facebook**.

 facebook.com/Arthurmongelliauthor

UNDEAD WORLDS 2 AVAILABLE NOW!

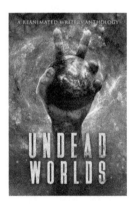

15 Brand New Stories!
Get it now at the link below!
www.reanimatedwriters.com/uw2

IN THE BEGINNING, GOD

I

Keep on Truckin'
Day Zero minus 4 – 2033 hours CST

A lone semi-tractor trailer sped through the fading light on I-80 West toward Rock Springs. After cresting a low hill, the rig accelerated too quickly down the backside. Practiced, but tired, hands and feet worked the clutch as he downshifted through the set of double gears.

He took in a long draw of air and adjusted his oil-stained Mack Truck cap.

Its perfect adjustment was short-lived as a hand slapped him on the back of the head.

"What the hell you trying to do, Cecilia?" he asked, readjusting the cap and tucking his hair under the edges.

"What am I doing, Ed?" Cecilia asked, emphasizing the "I". "I ain't the one pushing so hard!"

"We got a schedule to keep," Ed reminded her.

"Shouldn't have taken the job to haul this thing halfway across the country in the first place."

"You know we need the money."

"There ain't gonna to be any time to enjoy the money if you jack-knife on these twists," Cecilia said. "Just take it easy, will ya? You're scaring the crap out of Ozzie."

As if on cue, a miniature black poodle popped up onto the center console. Ozzie wagged his nub, his back haunches shaking more than the remains of his tail.

"You want me to take it easy? Is that it?"

Ozzie growled his agreement from the back of his tiny throat and tapped his front legs on the leather.

"You dancin', kiddo?" Cecilia asked, slipping into the passenger seat. Ozzie launched into her lap as she clicked home her safety belt. "Ouch. You sure know how to kick a woman in the va-jay-jay."

She cradled him up in her arms, making loud and exaggerated kissing noises on Ozzie's head. He responded by craning his neck and nipping Cecilia on the nose. He soon felt bad for his actions and apologized by licking her directly on the mouth.

"Gross," Ed exclaimed. "You know Ozzie licks his own balls and asshole, right?"

"You know they say that dog's mouths are cleaner than ours."

"Yeah?" Ed asked. "Who are *they*?"

"You know I'm right."

"Do I?"

Cecilia swatted Ed on the right arm, the second assault in as many minutes. Ozzie let loose a soft growl from the back of his throat in support of the woman who was keeping him warm.

Ed shot a sideways glance at his wife for a moment before smiling. Cecilia smiled back. She always said his grins were contagious. Even Ozzie smiled, his tongue hanging out to one side where several teeth had been extracted.

"ETA?" Cecilia asked.

"In about an hour," Ed replied, "if traffic holds up. We just passed Point of Rocks."

Cecilia looked past the chrome bulldog on the hood to the empty road. The rig's headlights reflected off the yellow dotted dividing lines. "Traffic? I think we'll be good."

"Yep."

"Gotta W-A-L-K the fur baby, too."

"Yep."

"You're a real asshole."

"Yep," Ed said again, shifting the rig's massive gears again as they approached another incline. "But you love me in spite of it, don't ya?"

"Against our better judgment," Cecilia said, holding up Ozzie as a co-conspirator. "Yep."

2

Half Baked
Day Zero minus 4 – 2054 hours CST

"Billy!" A muffled shout came from the other room, thankfully separated by a least two layers of thin walls.

Billy turned onto his back with his elbow crooked over his eyes.

"You better get up!" the same insistent voice called. "You need this job and I ain't letting you skip another month's rent!"

"Alright, ma," Billy croaked through a dry mouth full of phantom cotton. "I'm up."

The effort to speak sent up a wave of nausea.

Billy swallowed the bile down toward his sour belly.

He reached over a dirty T-shirt on the nightstand for a stained coffee mug.

A stack of envelopes fell to the floor, one with a red Final Notice emblazoned on it landing on top of the mess already on the threadbare mustard shag carpet.

Billy slowly propped himself up and swung his legs to the floor, a groan escaping before he slurped the remains of day-old coffee. He swished the muddy brew around his mouth before swallowing it down.

"Definitely needs more sugar," he mumbled as he put the mug back.

Tiny clumps of cream and grounds remained.

Billy stepped into a pair of wadded up khaki pants and zipped up.

"Where's that shirt?"

He sifted through the floor's dirty laundry with his left foot.

"You're gonna be late again, Billy," the voice whined. "You can't be late."

"Coming, Ma! Christ!"

Billy widened his search for the only dress shirt that he owned. You would think that would make it easier to find. He did find two dress socks on his way across the room. He opened the bedroom door, knowing that his mom's voice would be shriller without the hollow door to muffle it.

Black military-style lace-up boots sat in the hallway, standing at attention across from the door.

His navy blue cotton dress shirt hung from a wire hanger on a sconce.

Billy's mom, at least, respected the sanctity of his room and did not enter it... ever.

He leaned against the wall to wiggle on the black sock.

Shrugging, he pulled up the dark red sock on the other foot. He wrapped his pants cuffs around his ankles and pulled on the boots. Lacing them up was a pain in the ass, but he fumbled through it well enough. Finally, he swiped the pressed blue shirt from the hanger and shrugged into it. Buttoning the shirt was also a pain in the ass. He tucked in the shirttails as he wandered down the hallway toward the smell of pancakes and bacon from the kitchen.

He was sure mom had a nice "to-go" breakfast waiting for him, as well as a well-stocked lunch for mid-shift. He liked breakfast any time of day, especially before night shift at the facility that employed most of the township.

3

Close Calls

Day Zero minus 4 – 2310 hours EST

A tall slender man in a pressed dark suit stood with his hands behind his back, one flat palm resting over the other. The middle finger of his left hand tapped absently into the palm of his right as he gazed down at the vast Manhattan skyline, the sun having long fallen prey to the west.

His plans were heading west now, too.

The deserts of the Middle East had been a wash for him and the company.

He'd had high hopes for the Marine, but the weeks spent observing that experiment had resulted in nothing profitable. The other one, the female, could still prove to be an asset. She would just need the proper motivation to join the program.

As the red and white dots crawled along the avenues

below, the man in the black suit wondered if they had an inkling of what truly powered the world.

A soft knock from the massive double oak doors took him out of his revelry.

"Yes," he called out.

The left door swung open, slightly dragging across the deep carpet.

The visitor remained in the vestibule.

"Yes?" Black Suit asked, his patience already waning.

He had heard whispers that he was considered a cold and calculating executive, unapproachable and aloof. He didn't mind. His focus was always on the future.

"Sir," the meek visiting voice finally answered. "The Farson facility reports the shipment is twenty minutes out."

"And is Regis onsite?"

"Uh... Emerson expects him in five minutes, sir."

Plenty of time.

Even though R&R underfunded and understaffed the Farson facility, Regis still ran a tight ship.

He waved the messenger away.

The door clicked closed, leaving him to ponder just how bright the future was going to be.

4
Hairpins
Day Zero minus 4 – 2121 hours CST

The Jeep Wrangler roared northbound on I-191 at seventy miles an hour.

The phone in the driver's pocket buzzed. He tapped his bluetooth earpiece.

"Go for Regis."

"Hey, boss," crackled in his ear. "New York asked when you're getting here."

The voice was laced with pops and static. In spite of all of the most modern technology in communications, Wyoming still managed to shrug off those advancements in favor of a technological black hole where all cell reception went to die.

"Hey, Harvey," Regis replied. "Yeah, I'm a few minutes out."

"Shipment is almost here."

"That's why I'm coming in."

"I ain't a fan of these last minute deliveries," Harvey complained. "Plus, Shaw's bachelor party has got me four out sick."

"I told those idiots the Satin Maiden food was suspect."

"They're idiots, alright," Harvey agreed. "Now I have an empty warehouse and no lift operator."

"I'll take delivery myself," Regis promised. "It'll be quick and easy."

"Okay," Harvey replied. "You're the boss."

"Yes," Regis said with a smile. "Don't you forget it."

"You remind me too much for me to ever forget," Harvey said. "Do you have a time table on fixing the exhaust fans in the SCV?"

"Dampeners still sticking open?"

"Yep. I know our maintenance budget is slashed to almost nothing, but this is bullshit."

"I'll get Harold to come over and take a look over the weekend."

"I appreciate it," Harvey said. "Boss."

"Now you're catching on to why I'm the top dog, Harvey."

"And the second stall in the first floor men's room keeps

backing up," Harvey reminded Regis, hoping that this was a good time to add to the complaint list.

"And the tear in the chain-link in the eastern corner by the tree line," Regis recited from his own mental list.

"Exactly."

"I got it all covered," Regis assured him. "Everything's going to be okay. It ain't the end of the world, hombre."

"Maybe." Harvey chuckled. "I'll be happier when you get your ass onsite."

"Roger that," Regis confirmed.

The connection dropped with a click.

Regis put just the slightest of pressure on the accelerator, watching the speedometer needle climb to eighty. The wind whipped against the canvas soft top, flapping the material like the inside of a bass speaker. Only a few more weeks before the soft top comes off for the spring.

Soon enough.

A road ahead curved to the left, three yellow signs warning motorists to reduce speed to 40 MPH.

Regis always challenged himself to see how fast the Jeep could take the corner. Everyone lectured him on how off-balanced the Wrangler was, but Regis knew his baby better than them... and knew how to handle her.

Regis slowed into the beginning of the curve, leaning into it like he was riding a motorcycle. He accelerated and felt the outside edges of the oversized tires bite into the asphalt as the centrifugal forces dragged the Jeep outward. Regis gripped the steering wheel tighter and finessed out of the curve on the road he traveled every day.

What he hadn't anticipated after three years of repetition was the coyote on the outside single line that was tearing into a dead jackrabbit on the still warm asphalt. Its amber eyes glanced up as Regis turned the steering wheel hard to the left.

"Shit!"

The tires, having already flirted with loss of traction throughout the curve, lost their purchase with mother earth altogether.

The Jeep caught air and rolled from the asphalt to the soft shoulder.

From the gravel and grass, the Jeep dropped from view of the road altogether, crashing against an outcropping of boulders nestled on the edge of a deep gulley.

The canvas had been ripped through, its corners pulled away from the snaps of the crushed frame. The Jeep's tires still spun and the beams of the headlights were swallowed in the cold, fast-moving stream. As Regis bled out from a crushing blow delivered by a sliver of boulder, it was evident that spring had come earlier than expected.

5
Special Delivery
Day Zero minus 4 – 2130 hours CST

Ed downshifted the rig as Cecilia and Ozzie tidied up in the sleeper cab. Ozzie dug under the covers as quickly as Cecilia had smoothed them out.

"Worse than a child," Ed commented as he gazed on the empty I-191 highway.

"Well," Cecilia answered, blowing a stray auburn lock off her forehead, "we could always try for a real child."

She stood up and jutted out her belly, rubbing it with both hands.

"You're all dried up, kiddo." Ed laughed. "Even if I was interested in rearing a clingy offspring."

"Oh, you would be alright. You ain't your father."

"Small favors," Ed admitted. "Although here we are in the same trade driving the same truck."

"Maybe." Cecilia shrugged. "But I don't think your daddy ever had a payload like you."

"That's what she said." Ed laughed.

"Gross," Cecilia replied. "Right, Ozzie? Daddy's gross?"

Ozzie stopped digging under the bedspread long enough to poke his head up and let out a gruff. When he realized no one was going to give him any extra attention, he returned to his work.

"Watch this corner," Cecilia advised, pointing to the road ahead. "Looks a little treacherous."

In fact, Cecilia was right. Only fifty yards past the last Reduce to 40 MPH sign was a fresh set of tire skids. There was no vehicle, but those tracks still looked menacing. Ed ground down through the gears, using low-end torque to power around the bend.

"Good job, baby," Cecilia said. "It's almost like you've been doing this for a couple dozen years."

"Definitely feels like it," Ed replied, shifting his weary bones and sore muscles in the captain's chair.

"ETA?"

"Five minutes."

"You did make good time."

"I do it all for you, baby. All the time."

6

Time Tables

Day Zero minus 4 – 2134 hours CST

Harvey stood on the loading dock with a clipboard pinched in his armpit. He blew out nervous smoke from his lungs in spite of the rules. This was a No Smoking Zone. This was a No Cell Phone Zone. This was a "do not discuss this zone with anyone outside the zone" Zone.

Regis was a no-show.

Regis was never a no-show. That was why he was in charge of this facility.

Harvey's nephew was also a no-show, although that was typical. If it weren't for the fact that Billy was his sister's kid, Harvey would have canned him nine months ago. This time may be the time–

A late model Dodge Dart skidded to a gravelly stop at the main gatehouse occupied by the square-jawed, heavily armed, and always-imposing Sgt. Fernandez.

Dust wisped over the car as Billy put the car into Park. Billy scoured the front dash and passenger seat for his ID badge. Fernandez waited for Billy's identification, showing the practiced patience of a man who has seen much in his covert ops military career. Billy threw his arms up in frustration and defeat. Fernandez pointed at Billy's chest where the badge had been clipped to his breast pocket all along.

Fernandez flipped a switch and the security bollards receded flush into the pavement. Billy and his rusty Dart drove to the employee parking lot located west of the loading docks and the 30,000 square foot warehouse. Billy found a spot in the near-empty parking lot and got out, not bothering to roll up the windows. He jogged over toward Harvey, taking the concrete steps two at a time up to the loading dock.

"You ain't supposed to be smoking," Billy warned.

"You're supposed to be on time," Harvey shot back.

"I'm only a couple minutes late," Billy said defensively. "Fernandez took his time letting me in."

"Go clock in." Harvey sighed.

"Why you out here anyways?"

"We have a delivery."

"Where's Regis?"

"Do I look like I fuckin' know?"

"Whoa. Sorry, man," Billy said, his hands raised in surrender. "Geez."

"This ain't my responsibility," Harvey mumbled, cursing Regis in his head.

"Don't you need a lift operator for deliveries?"

"Yeah," Harvey said, the calm of his prohibited cigarette fading much too quickly with Billy's arrival.

"And ain't he supposed to be on the dock already?"

"Yes," Harvey said through gritted teeth. "Shaw never showed up."

"What an asshole," Billy said in commiseration. "Glad I only drank at his bachelor party. You want me to run lift?"

"When the hell did you get trained?"

"Last week," Billy said with his chest out and a proud smile on his face.

"You got your certification letter?"

"It's supposed to be in my mail slot this week. Don't think Shaw's gonna get around to it tonight."

A semi-truck chugged up to the guardhouse and squeaked to a stop behind the bollards, the air brakes hissing in compliance.

The driver handed Hernandez a manila envelope. The guard reviewed the documentation and studied the smiling driver, going as far as climbing up to better appraise the interior of the cab.

When a little black dog popped his head out the

window, Fernandez smiled and patted it on the head. He hopped down to the concrete pad, reached inside the gatehouse and activated the bollards again. He waved the driver through and the rig soon crept forward with a lurch.

"Get the bay door open and get in the lift," Harvey ordered. "Don't screw this up."

7
Precious Cargo
Day Zero minus 4 – 2145 hours CST

Ed maneuvered the trailer back, gently pressing into the loading dock rubber bumpers. The air brakes hissed again and the rumbling of the diesel engine cut off. Anticipation hung in the air with the new silence. Even the cicadas hadn't decided whether to start up their conversations.

"Let's do this," Ed said, opening the heavy driver's door.

Cecilia scooped up Ozzie in her arms and followed her husband down from the cab to the ground. Once on the concrete, she snapped the latch of a retractable leash onto Ozzie's collar and put him down. Considering himself the Alpha of the pack, Ozzie bounded away as far as the leash would extend in search of a private place to do his business.

Ed walked up the loading dock steps with his documentation.

A man in a dress shirt, windbreaker and a clipboard waited for him.

"Are you Regis?" Ed asked after referring to his paperwork.

"No," Harvey replied. "He's offsite at the moment. I'm Emerson. I will supervise the offload today."

A second young man sat in a pristine idling forklift, leaning on the steering wheel.

"Alright," Ed said. "Let's see what we see."

Ed unlocked and unlatched the rear door, pulling up the strap. Overhead LED lights clicked on, casting a brilliant wash of white to the interior. Five feet from the rear edge was a steel pallet. Strapped to it was a stainless steel tank, four foot tall and three foot in diameter. Other than four struts that were welded to the cylinder's sides, the item was free of any distinguishing characteristics.

Ed walked inside the trailer, his footfalls echoing off the steel deck.

Stranger than a single pallet in a too big truck trailer was the fact that the steel cylinder started to hum as he approached it. The vibrations made the hairs on his arms and on the back of his neck stand on end. The hum made his stomach churn. The spaces behind his eyes pulsed with the deepening daggers of the start of a migraine.

Ed removed the dog clamps keeping the palette stationary on the deck. His dad never had sweet technology like this. These little devices saved him from having to strap everything to the side strap rails. Ed secured the clamps, happy to make his way back outside to the cool fresh night air.

He nodded to Harvey just as Cecilia walked up with Ozzie trotting along behind her. His wife dropped a full doggy pick-up bag into a nearby trash receptacle, both of them pleased with Ozzie's performance.

"Billy, go ahead," Emerson said to the lift operator. "Miss, you should keep your dog off to the side, please."

"Absolutely," Ed agreed.

"No worries," Cecilia answered, scooping Ozzie up into her arms. "There you go… all out of the way."

Billy started the lift. The flashers started spinning and the backup alarms started beeping. He lined up the machinery with the cargo, used the levers to extend and drop the tynes of the forks closer to the trailer's steel deck. He nudged the lift slowly forward, craning his head to each side of the lift's mast to keep an eye on the pallet. Taking a moment to wipe away beads of perspiration from his forehead and neck, Billy then drove the lift forward until the forks slipped under the cargo. The pallet tapped against the load carriage frame.

With a deep breath, Billy used the levers to raise and tilt the forks back. The flashers continued to spin and the backup beeps became more insistent as Billy reversed the lift back onto the locking dock with the thrumming cargo.

Ed felt a wave of nausea erupt in his throat.

Ozzie growled.

Cecilia hushed and bounced the dog.

Harvey looked at the clipboard, swallowing hard.

Billy whistled as he drove away through the loading dock bay roll-up doors.

After the hum of the lift's electric motor receded, Ed's dinner came up between the side of the trailer and the concrete wall.

"Ed," Cecilia said in surprise. "You alright?"

After another wave of partially digested food splattered across the concrete of the delivery bay lane, Ed looked up to Cecilia and Emerson with tears in his eyes. "Sorry about that. You got a bathroom I can use?"

8

Off-Load
Day Zero minus 4 – 2209 hours CST

Billy stood up a little straighter as he navigated the shiny metal cylinder down aisle B4. He couldn't help but smile as he and the forklift rumbled down the aisle toward the Special Containment Vault. It was weird to drive around an empty warehouse.

"Graveyards have more life in 'em," Billy said to the cylinder.

He slowed to a quiet electric stop as he approached an unmanned security station next to the SCV massive doors. Bobby was supposed to be manning the desk. His Mustang was in the parking lot, but he was nowhere to be found. Dude was going to be in trouble for abandoning his post.

Probably was another victim of the Satin Maiden strip club buffet.

No matter.

Billy hopped off the lift and went to the desk.

He had been friends with Bobby since first grade and had been on first-string varsity together. It took three attempts on the security desk's partially hidden keypad before Billy was rewarded with more lights and the hydraulic hiss of the heavy Special Containment Vault doors swinging open. Billy would have to remember Bobby's football jersey number and the date of his birthday for future reference. It probably was his pin number, too.

Billy looked at a still-steaming mug full of coffee on the desktop. Bobby might not be at his post, but he was around here somewhere, at least.

From far off a dog barked.

9

Clean-up on Aisle 3

Day Zero minus 4 – 2210 hours CST

"Quiet, Oz!" Cecilia warned the dog as they watched both of the closed bathroom stalls. "Hush!"

Ed was definitely not quiet as he retched again into the toilet. After he spit the last of his food from his mouth into the bowl, he struggled to his feet and flushed twice for good measure. He emerged from the stall and headed to the sink. With a splash of cold water on his face and more into his hands to swirl around his mouth, Ed spit again before turning off the faucets.

"You gonna live?" Cecilia asked.

"I think so," Ed replied, his mouth feeling cleaner.

The sound of grunting echoed out of the other stall.

"Poor guy," Cecilia commiserated.

"I don't remember that pallet humming when I strapped it down to the deck."

"At least it's delivered. And on time."

"Correct."

"Let's get squared away and depart, dear."

"Yeah," Ed said, staring at the dark circles emerging under his eyes. "I just want out of here."

The door opened and Emerson poked his head in.

"You alright?" he asked.

"Getting there," Ed replied.

Emerson opened the door wide and came inside to use the other sink. He looked at the redness in his own eyes. He washed his hands, shook them off in the sink, and went over to the hand dryer. "All the paperwork is in order so you're all set to go."

"Thanks," Cecilia said as the dryer motor revved up loudly, echoing off the hard surfaces of the restroom.

"Sorry?" Emerson asked once the dryer stopped.

"Thank you," Cecilia repeated.

"No problem," Emerson replied. "You can find your way back to the loading bay okay?"

"Shouldn't be a problem," Ed commented.

"Great," Emerson said. "Thanks for the delivery."

"It's what we do," Ed answered, proud of his customer satisfaction.

"And we appreciate it," Emerson said. "Now I got to make sure we get things put away."

"Have a good night," Cecilia added with a smile. "Although you may want to check in on one of your guys."

"Who?"

Another bout of intestinal evacuation churned into the toilet bowl from the far stall.

"Another one?" Emerson said with a sigh, knowing that following up with Billy would have to wait. "Damn strip club."

10

Put-Away
Day Zero minus 4 – 2216 hours CST

The barking quieted down after a minute.

Billy guessed the delivery couple got their dog under control.

It was crazy that the driver threw up all over the loading bay. Billy hoped Harvey didn't expect him to clean it up. Although, playing with the high-pressure power washer would be more fun than counting munitions inventory, going through invoices for order accuracy against what the computer said. That stuff hurt his brain.

With the SCV doors open, Billy returned to the forklift and turned the key. The motor's electric hum matched whatever was vibrating in the metal cylinder. He didn't know why everyone reacted so strange to it. The driver got sick. His old lady looked upset. Even Harvey had gotten a little bristled. Billy guessed that he had a better constitution – a stronger stomach – than these other folks.

He smiled at that idea.

Billy had proven that he could operate the lift, even without any certification. He had watched Shaw plenty of times. It wasn't that hard to figure out. He swung the steering crank handle and stepped on the accelerator pedal.

Crunch.

"Shit!" Billy cursed under his breath as red plastic fragments scattered around the warehouse floor.

The lift's right mast had clipped one of the emergency alarm flashers mounted to the frame of the closest metal warehouse rack.

"Don't know why they don't put a cage around those things," Billy muttered as he stepped down to look at the pieces. Glancing around, he swept the pieces under a low shelf full of polymer rifle cases with his foot. Once all of the most noticeable shards were hidden, Billy looked up at the busted light. Even the bulb was cracked.

"Shit!"

Oh well. Maintenance would have plenty of replacements.

He'd better get this pallet offloaded before something else could go wrong. His smile turned grim as he hopped back up on the lift platform. He turned the steering crank and drove the cargo forward through the open doors into the SCV.

It was decidedly cooler in this section of the warehouse.

The walls were a brilliant white and the metal shelving was a gleaming stainless steel, the LED ballasts lighting every inch of the space. It was painful to open his eyes more than slits, like sitting in a boat in the middle of a lake and trying to look past the sunlight reflecting off the water.

He navigated down an aisle with seven-foot capsules stacked upright on each side. They looked like giant-sized Tic-Tacs. The only difference was that these had tubes and wires running all over them. Odorless compressed gas vented out from pressure valves every few seconds to regulate whatever was inside the chambers. He was tempted to lean over and wipe off the frost on one of the curved windows to see what was inside, but the brilliant white surroundings and the chill in the air kept him from lingering.

He drove the lift forward to the first cross-aisle.

Billy fumbled for the receiving invoice to verify the bin location where the cylinder was to be stored. With the paperwork still in hand, he crumpled it against the steering lever and swung the cargo left to the first bin location. Toying with the levers, he raised the pallet to an elevated rack space that was twelve feet in the air. The forklift groaned as its center of gravity got higher.

Billy hadn't seen Shaw do this.

Even in the cold, Billy started to sweat.

"Come on," he whispered. "Come on."

Once Billy had the pallet lined up to the shelving, he drove forward and tilted the fork tynes down until the pallet squeaked against metal. He lowered the forks another couple of inches and slowly reversed back into the aisle. He re-oriented the lift with the forks facing the way he had come in.

With a sigh of relief, Billy stepped on the accelerator and hummed up the aisle. As he nearly cleared the aisle, he wiped the sweat off his forehead with his free sleeve.

The steering lever slipped in his grip, the receiving invoice still smashed between his fingers and the metal handle. The forks drifted left, still several feet off the ground. They caught on the tubing above the oversized Tic-Tac capsules.

"Fuck!"

Billy swung the forks back to center, taking the hoses and wiring with it.

In a panic, he took his foot off the accelerator.

The lift stopped.

The forks stopped.

The hoses and wiring stopped.

Billy slowly reversed the lift.

The hoses and wiring slipped off the edges of the tyne. They swayed a bit before returning to their natural hanging state above the capsules.

All was as it should be.

Billy took a minute to lower the fork blades to the deck, tilted them back just a little bit, and drove back to the SCV doors.

II

Runaway
Day Zero minus 4 – 2231 hours CST

"Feeling better?" Cecilia asked, handing Ed a cup of coffee from the vending machine.

"I've been better," Ed answered. "Whatever it was, it's really taking me for a loop."

Ed took the coffee, handing over to Celica the retractable leash with Ozzie still at the end of it.

"You up for getting out of here?" Cecilia asked.

Ed took a sip of the coffee. "Not bad. Not bad at all."

"I'm happy you are enjoying the coffee. You ready to go?"

"Yeah," Ed put one hand up in surrender. "We can go."

"Good," Cecilia said triumphantly. "Because Ozzie has to go again."

Cecilia walked out of the room.

Ed chugged the rest of the coffee – it was that good – and walked after his wife and fur baby, tossing the empty paper cup into the closest receptacle like a responsible adult.

Ozzie pulled at the leash line and slid around, trying to dig his paws and claws into the floor. As he started to pant from fighting against the collar, Cecilia let out more line to keep him from coughing. Ozzie raced ahead as far as the leash would go before Cecilia could use the brake button.

Snap.

The line broke completely.

"Ozzie!" Cecilia chased after the tiny poodle. "Oz!"

Another wave of nausea hit Ed.

He gritted his teeth and chased after his family.

12

Steeplechase
Day Zero minus 4 – 2234 hours CST

Billy stood on the platform of the forklift outside the SCV doors, his fingers at the bridge of his nose and his eyes squinted closed. The lights inside that warehouse section had left him seeing bright stars in his vision.

Barking started up again and the yelling got louder. He opened his eyes to see a tiny black blur run past him and into the SCV.

"Shit!"

Billy had not closed the massive double doors after he had come out.

He hopped down, just as the driver's woman ran up.

"The mutt went inside," Billy said, pointing the way.

"Goddammit," the driver said as he caught up, his skin waxen and sweaty.

As the couple chased after the dog, Billy remembered the regulation that he himself hadn't bothered to follow. "You ain't supposed to be in there."

They either didn't hear him or decided to pay him no mind as they disappeared into the brilliant white.

13

Close Calls

Day Zero minus 4 – 2234 hours CST

Emerson stood behind the contoured office chairs in the main security office.

Three separate computer screens on the operators' desk monitored temperature tolerances, air quality, and security checkpoint lock statuses throughout the complex. The boards were green, except for in the SCV. The temperature in the chamber was increasing, but was still within safety limits. The air quality, though, was worsening... definitely outside the upper safety limits. The air contaminant was currently 1500 parts per million. A silent red flasher lit up on the far left screen.

Above the computer screens, the wall was filled with flat panel monitors. Each screen displayed a specific view of the warehouse or the perimeter fence line. Three of the monitors showed a small black dog running into the SCV. Two others showed the truck driver, his partner, and Billy in pursuit.

Where the hell was Bobby?

Those SCV doors should be closed.

And the damn exhaust system was acting up again.

Where was Regis? He knew how to handle these things.

Christ almighty.

The black and white closed circuit feed taped Billy pleading with the others to stay out of the restricted area, but they ran headlong into the SCV anyway.

The phone rang.

It was a hard line.

Shit.

Harvey picked up the receiver. "Farson Facility. Harvey Emerson."

"Please hold for New York," said a smooth female operator.

"Goddammit, Regis," Harvey cursed aloud.

"You have a situation," came a monotone male voice through the line without any warning or switchboard clicks.

"Sorry," Harvey stammered. "Minor restriction violation, sir."

"I am less concerned by the unauthorized access," the voice said with quiet authority, "and more concerned by the fact that the Special Containment Vault air quality has spiked outside its safety limits."

"We are monitoring that," Harvey replied. "Yes, sir."

"Where is Regis?"

"Offsite, sir," Harvey answered honestly. "Not sure where."

"Well," the commanding voice said from the east coast office, "it is time for you to make the hard decisions."

14
Bark at the Moon
Day Zero minus 4 – 2238 hours CST

Ozzie was found growling at the second steel shelf where the cylinder they delivered had just been put away. The poodle had urinated and defecated, obliviously standing in his own filth.

Cecilia went to scoop him up.

Ozzie bit her.

"What the hell, Ozzie!"

Ed came up alongside his wife and looked at the wound. Even though Ozzie was small, there was a fair amount of blood streaming from the edge of Cecilia's palm.

"Bad dog!" Ed yelled.

Ozzie did not react, still focusing on the cylinder on the upper rack location.

Billy lumbered up beside them. His eyes hurt from the vault's brilliant color.

The starkness of the red blood on the white epoxy floors made him queasy.

Visitors were not allowed in here.

Dog piss and shit were definitely not allowed here.

He would lose his job if he didn't get these people out of here.

Taking work gloves out of his back pocket, Billy put them on and reached for Ozzie.

Ozzie whipped his muzzle around and sunk his teeth into the leather. Billy scooped him up in his free hand, Ozzie thrashing and trying to squirm out of his grip.

"I'm sorry, son," Ed said.

Billy winched from at least two teeth pierced through the gloves. "Let's get you out of here, please."

"So sorry," Cecilia said, holding her bleeding hand now wrapped up in the bottom of her T-shirt.

"Forget about it," Billy replied. "Let's go."

Ozzie squirmed, digging his teeth deeper into Billy's gloved hand. He held the dog under his arm like he used to carry the pigskin thirty yards after breaking through the line of scrimmage on Friday nights. Those were the glory days.

The end of the aisle was twenty feet away.

One of the loose compressed gas lines Billy had swiped with the forklift popped off its white eight-foot capsule. Its end whipped violently through the other wiring and hoses. Several other lines were severed, all expelling their cold gases into the room. Sparks flew as wires were ripped from their connections and their raw ends bumped into each other.

"Goddammit!" Billy yelled.

He ducked as one of the hoses swung over his head.

It caught Cecilia straight in the nose.

"Ugh," was all she could muster.

Cecilia raised her bloody hand to her now bloody face. She staggered into one of the capsules with a dull thud, leaving a red handprint on the smooth white casing.

The capsule, no longer secured by the series of cables, thudded liked dominos into the ones next to it. Some wedged against each other. Two others spilled into the aisle in front of them, blocking the aisle for their most direct escape.

Something slapped against the inside of the view port.

"Watch out!" Billy sidestepped as another capsule crashed onto the one in the aisle.

The Plexiglas viewport popped off before the falling capsule finally skidded onto the floor.

A putrid gray-skinned hand reached out.

A second hand grabbed the edges of the shell.

A long-dead soldier of some forgotten war hoisted himself out through the viewport.

He snarled and sniffed the air, his neck twisting toward Cecilia.

His eyes were covered in cataracts, but he seemed to look directly at Cecilia as he struggled toward her.

The tan tattered sleeve on his left arm snagged on a bolt on the frame, making a loud tearing sound.

She backed up into Ed with her hand still to her nose.

The air was bitter cold with the nitrogen gas filling the room.

The hoses still whipped about, dislodging more cables and wires in their paths.

Another capsule fell over into the aisle, boxing them in.

With skin sloughing off his face, the escaped soldier lunged through the cold smoke at Cecilia.

She screamed.

Ed punched him in the face.

His jaw dislocated.

The skin on the soldier's cheek came off in chunks on Ed's fingers.

More skin was drooping on his face as his body acclimated to the higher room temperature.

The dead man lunged again at Cecilia, snapping at where he smelled warm blood.

Billy, still with Ozzie's jaws clamped down on his hand, slid over the second capsule to help the woman. The capsule rocked back to rest, its access door hissing open.

15
In Case of Emergency

Day Zero minus 4 – 2250 hours CST

Harvey stared at the monitors recording the scene in the SCV.

"Mr. Emerson," the voice stated through the receiver cradled between Harvey's shoulder and ear.

"Yeah," Harvey answered, still distracted. "Yeah."

"You have a situation, Mr. Emerson," the voice warned.

"Damn right we do," Harvey said as he stared at the monitors.

He saw Billy kick out the knee of one of the people coming out of some kind of suspended cryo-sleep. The capsules were opening one by one. Where there was one animated and attacking well-preserved corpse, there were four others climbing out of their white metal and carbon fiber tombs.

"Mr. Emerson," the voice said in its even tone. "Those subjects cannot exit the main facility. Do you understand that this situation needs to be contained with haste?"

"Yes," Harvey agreed.

On monitor seven, the truck driver punched several more of the walking dead before they tangled him up in their reaching arms. The driver's wife was already out of view under a mob of lunging bodies. Billy was still beating away at them with his feet. He had something in his arms keeping him from using one of his fists.

"Mr. Emerson, do you see the center computer monitor?"

The monitor referenced monitored the air quality, now at 20,000 parts per million.

"Yes," Harvey replied.

"Do you see the cursor prompt at the bottom left of the screen?"

A cursor blinked on a keyword entry field. "Yes."

"Excellent," the voice cooed. "Please type in Alpha-1-7-Delta-Zulu-Alpha-3-7-6."

Harvey did as he was told.

"Press the Enter key."

On monitor twelve, Billy had escaped the debris of the steel capsules. He was limping out from the aisle, still cradling something in the crook of his arm. Some of the capsule occupants were in slow pursuit.

"Okay," Harvey said. "The prompt field is empty. What now?"

"Enter the following, Tango-Foxtrot-1-9-9-Golf-Kilo-3-5-8."

"Done."

"Press the Enter key."

"Okay."

Alarms sounded.

Flashers high on the wall came into strobing life.

A countdown clock appeared on the main monitor, spinning down from 60 seconds.

On the monitor, Billy limped closer toward the vault doors.

The doors were slowly closing on him.

The undead were closing in on him.

"What happens now? Harvey asked.

All he got as an answer was several clicks and a droning dial tone.

16
Last Ditch Effort
Day Zero minus 4 – 2303 hours CST

Billy ran for his life, Ozzie's jaws still clamped hard into his hand.

Christ! Was this dog ever going to let go?

At least the animal had stopped thrashing about in his arms.

Those things still were after him.

They had ripped apart the truck driver and his wife.

Right in front of him!

He chanced a glance over his shoulder. Seven soldiers of the Red Communist Army staggered after him. He recognized the uniforms and insignias from his PlayStation games.

What the fuck?

The public service announcement speaker crackled into life.

"Get out of there, Billy." Harvey's voice was insistent... and scared.

Right there with ya, Unc.

Billy's thigh was bleeding from a gash or something, his pant leg wet all the way to his boots.

"Hurry up," his uncle's voice cried. "You have forty seconds to get out before those doors close."

Billy was running as fast as his throbbing leg would carry him.

He knew he would only need a few of those forty seconds to escape the vault.

The dead soldiers snarled and gurgled at him, following the scent of the trail of bloody boot prints he was leaving behind.

The massive steel vault doors were closing.

Billy sidestepped through just as the gap passed the point of him fitting through it.

The doors clamped down on one of the soldier's outreached arms, severing it with a burst of thick black goo.

The vault clicked closed and a whirring from inside the mechanism locked it into place.

Billy took a deep breath and let it out along with a fit of coughing.

The adrenaline bled off as he stared at the twitching fingers of the dismembered arm on the floor.

His leg was still bleeding.

Ozzie's ears perked up and he cocked his head in spite of the pain he was inflicting on Billy's hand. Soft beeps started to chime throughout the warehouse, repeating once a second.

"30 seconds," a mechanical female voice from the PSA system announced.

"Shit." Billy's heart raced as he dragged himself toward the loading bay.

"25 seconds," the voice reminded him.

Billy hadn't realized how far away the loading bay was.

Why were these aisles so long?

Why weren't there other emergency exits?

"20 seconds."

"Come on, sonofabitch," Billy cursed. "Come on."

"15 seconds."

The end of the aisle was a few feet away.

"10 seconds."

He stumbled across the receiving area and through the loading bay door, slamming the Quick Release Close plunger with his elbow on the way.

"5 sec–"

The metal doors rattled closed, cutting off the countdown.

Billy limped into the back of the semi-truck trailer.

He hooked one of the doors with his bleeding foot.

A silent warm whoosh lifted him off his feet and pushed him headlong deeper into the trailer.

17
Wanderlust
Day Zero minus 3 – 0118 hours CST

The series of carefully placed explosives had engulfed the entire facility in flames and ruin.

Harvey and any other personnel who had been inside were now dead. Ed and Cecilia, at ground zero, were vaporized from existence. All of the re-animated dead soldiers had their organs liquefied from the concussive blast wave before the Thermite flames found them.

The malfunctioning exhaust ports, the dampeners having switched to an open position a full two minutes before the blast, now vented columns of intense blue flames that ascended a hundred feet in the air.

The complex was now a hellish glowing dead zone.

Only Billy had managed to escape the fate of a fiery death.

He stared at the columns of flames rising from what formerly was a highly secured facility. Every so often, a popping noise startled him, most likely from a military-grade weapon or munitions that managed to survive the initial blast but couldn't escape the intense temperatures of the resulting fires.

With Ozzie' jaw still attached to his hand in a death grip, Billy limped out from the back of the trailer. He tripped in the gap between the trailer's steel deck and the loading dock, but maintained his balance well enough to make his way down the ramp to the driveway.

Fernandez saw Billy as he finished the call to the local fire department.

"Christ," Fernandez said in disbelief as he ran over. "You okay?"

Billy walked in a drunken bee-line toward him, shaking his head.

"What the hell is that? Is that a dog?"

Billy's leg was still seeping blood.

"We need to get that leg looked at," Fernandez said. "Let me get the first aid kit."

He turned toward the gatehouse.

Billy dropped his hands to his side, the singed and limp Ozzie still hanging on with his locked jaw.

He muttered something.

The guard turned back to him. "What?"

Billy looked up.

"What, Bill?"

Billy opened his mouth.

Fernandez leaned closer.

Billy bit his nose off.

Fernandez gurgled a scream as his hands went up to his face.

Billy lunged for another bite, Fernandez's hands too far away from his sidearm or his concealed knife to be effective.

18

Risk Assessment
Day Zero minus 3 – 0430 hours EST

The man in the black suit stood at the window of his executive office, looking down on the barren avenues of Manhattan Island. Sure, some cockroaches lived and thrived in the shadows of the concrete and steel canyons, serving a dark master that skittered back to the underground with the first warm rays of light, but most of the denizens had not truly awoken from their slumber.

The Powers That Be – not the Roanoke & Raleigh executives – had decided that his career trajectory was changing. The Fates had something different in mind for him.

The Farson facility was now a purified fiery crater.

Farson was gone.

He would still be expected to explain his decisions to the Board.

But how do you explain God's work to Neanderthals?

He would be able to spin this tragedy into something profitable, eventually. Sure, they had lost some of the earliest materials that had resulted in scores of genetic and military advancements, but that was archaic science and alchemy compared to his own achievements in the last twelve months.

He, alone, could shape the world into one created in his own image.

𝘒𝘈𝘈𝘈𝘈𝘈

ABOUT CHARLES INGERSOLL

The love of zombies was in my blood as soon as I watched George Romero's *Night of the Living Dead* at a far too young and inappropriate age. That feeling never faded, only taking 40 years to finally decide to write my own "Great American Zombie Novel". One story became two and...

I love my canine fur baby, comic cons, cosplay, movies and television, and the supernatural. I live on Long Island, New York, with my girlfriend and a certain dog named Holly - both straight off the Day Zero pages.

A special thank you to Judy, my partner in crime. Also, thanks to everyone who makes sure my zombie universe doesn't crumble.

The Day Zero series can be found on **Amazon.**

To find more information about Charles Ingersoll and Day Zero, please follow him on the social media sites below or **www.dayzerozombies.com**

facebook.com/dayzerozombies

twitter.com/dayzerozombies

instagram.com/dayzerozombies

TO THE HILLS

W here was I when the Zompoc started? Same place I always was, at work. I start work at 2:00 pm and by the time all the paperwork is done and my reports are sent, I get off around 1:00 am. I didn't know anything was going on until I glanced at the TV about 8:00 pm. The news was reporting explosions and flu-like bugs spreading across the country. Now, I'm not a big prepper or a doom and gloom kind of guy, but I am a camper and a hunter. I love getting out in the woods, I can tell you a little about some plants and I can start a fire seven different ways. I like my "toys", meaning my camping gear, guns, and tools. The back of my truck has a storage bin containing a backpack, an axe, a shovel, a hunting knife, water bottles, a couple backpacking meals, and a sleeping bag. That just makes sense in the winter, as too many people forget that winter can kill you. This bin lives in the back of my truck and the contents change as needed, or if I have a trip planned. My truck is a four-wheel drive GMC Sierra with big tires and a big engine.

So, back to the news blurbs from the local news station

based in Detroit. You get info from the city and the suburbs, nothing unusual there, but I guess every city is like that. What was unusual, though, was the scenes they were show-ing. During the day, about the time I headed into work, explosions rocked most major cities in the US. In Michigan, it was Detroit, Grand Rapids, and Saginaw. There had to be thousands of explosions across the country, but the funny thing was that they didn't take out buildings or dams or any of the infrastructure.

In Detroit, someone ran onto the field in the middle of a baseball game. The explosion shook the building and knocked some people to the ground, causing cuts and scrapes, but no fatalities out of the 40,000 people in atten-dance. Now, looking back, the bugs that had been spread by this explosion got almost everyone at the game. This means people from Ohio, Canada and all over Michigan were instantly infected. In Grand Rapids, the same thing happened at Fifth Third Field, infecting 11,000 people. Being at work had kept me away from any infection or infected. The people at the ball fields spread out like a covey of quail being flushed by a bird dog. Reports of the hospitals being inundated with people exhibiting flu-like symptoms escalated over the first twelve hours. Within the next twenty-four hours, reports of strange things happening started coming out. Reports of cannibals and mass murders, group hallucinations and bad trips, people eating other people.

Now, back to me. Everyone knows it's all about me. I left work at about 12:30 in the morning and drove home. My drive is pretty short, only about fifteen miles and it usually takes about twenty minutes. On the way home, I saw very few cars and I swear I saw people running at my truck as I went by at 60 mph.

The dog greeted me at the door as usual. I had a bite to

eat while throwing a ball for her in the backyard. My dog is one of my favorite people, and yeah, I know dogs aren't people. If you don't know what I mean, you won't get it. My dog is a well-trained animal that responds immediately to the proper commands, such as "dinner", "treat", "ball" and the always popular "*squirrel*". She's part Lab, part Staffordshire terrier and part chow-hound (Chow as in *food!*). Everything was nice and quiet in the backyard, and I was relaxed and happy. I wasn't thinking about the crazy stuff going on in the cities. My nice, quiet, little suburb wasn't going to be a target for terrorism. Little did I know! Sounds ominous, doesn't it?

I woke up the next morning and went to the kitchen to see my best friend. Oh, how I love that coffee pot! As my pot of morning elixir brewed, I kicked on the news. About that time my phones went off, and when I say phones, I mean phones. The personal cell, the work cell, and the landline (yes, I still have one of those). I grabbed the landline since it was closest and heard that there was no work until further notice,, allegedly due to the current health crisis. Health crisis? What health crisis? I remembered hospitals/news saying there was an outbreak of the flu. Well, looks like I have at least one day off, so I'm not going to complain.

When the morning go-juice was done and the proper amount of worship had been paid to the gods of caffeine, I went back to the news. Hospitals were inundated with the dead from this "Flu", only they weren't dead, or maybe they were undead. Either way, they attacked people.

I thought about it as I watched and realized that it was an apocalypse. Yes, my friends, a real honest to god, end-of-the-world scenario. Now, a lot of people would start freaking out, but not me. No, I'm a bit different, or so I've been told. I figured I better think about heading to the cabin and getting to my girls. My wife had taken a couple of days off and headed up there. The cabin sounded like a great idea. It was in the middle of nowhere with no people around, which hopefully meant no zombies. I hoped the girls hadn't decided to drive the fifty miles into town to go shopping. If they hadn't, it would mean I could just grab them, load up the truck, and head north, no problem.

The cabin was on a piece of land that had been my grandfather's. It was surrounded by *nothing*! All the land around it was owned by some power company that seemed to have forgotten about it. There was no electricity, no natural gas, no city water and no city sewer system. I like my creature comforts so I had to make a few changes when Gramps passed away, like a windmill for power, along with a couple solar panels and a hydroelectric generator (okay, it was an old truck generator but hydroelectric generator sounds cooler) in the creek.

The water situation was fixed by driving a pipe into the ground. After I dropped the pipe, I realized that water was only about 35 feet down. That was fun, I mean, have you ever tried threading two pieces of pipe together when the end of one is 15 feet in the ground and you can't hold it? Yep, that was a long and thirsty job. When the pipe was in place, I hooked a 12-volt pump to it and, to my surprise, it worked. My arms, hands, and shoulders hurt for a week after doing that.

After I had water and electricity, I installed lights. I got a great deal on some 12-volt lights that were LEDs. They worked nicely, didn't use much juice, and they put out some decent light. I even got a couple to put in the yard. Now, for heat, I had a double attack planned. Winters get damn cold. I found an old pot-belly wood stove on Craigslist for a hundred bucks. Then I got a propane furnace out of a motorhome at the junkyard.

I decided that a bathroom with indoor plumbing would be the next project. I found a toilet out of the same motorhome at the scrap yard. I put on my hazmat suit, drove to the junkyard, and removed it, along with the holding tank under it. Just like that, I ended up with indoor plumbing. All the doors and windows have heavy-duty steel-plate shutters on them, complete with gun ports. That's because some drunken guys on snowmobiles broke in one year. They smoked my cigars, drank my beer, and even emptied the liquor cabinet. At least they were kind enough to put cardboard over the window they broke. So I went whole-hog on proofing the place. Off to the junkyard I went again (I think they like my money), and my fortress of solitude ended up being pretty much idiot proof.

The only problem with my escape plan was 250 miles and hordes of the undead getting in my way. Why does this not sound good? By the time I had loaded the truck with everything I wanted, it was too late to hit the road. I turned on the news to find only one station operating. Pandemonium in the cities resulted in a mass exodus blocking all the expressways. Note to self, find a map and a route using back roads. Google maps would be down shortly, so either a dead tree version or, maybe, if I got lucky, the GPS would work. Oh, and dog food, I can't forget the dog food. I set my alarm for daybreak and figured it would be light by the time I got moving. Coffee, can't forget the coffee. It was midnight when I finally piled the last of my stuff into the truck in the garage. I was tired. It had been forty-eight hours since this all started and I had yet to kill one zombie. I saw lights on in the houses next door on both sides.

Earlier I saw my neighbor in black BDU's with a tricked-out rifle, which should be comforting, knowing an armed friend had my back, except it wasn't comforting. I hated that old SOB and he was, like, 95 years old. I'm surprised he didn't take a shot at me, all over one little pile of dog poop left in his yard. After that, I trained her, so when it was dark she went on the far side of his yard to take care of business.

He never did figure how Mrs. Johnson's Chihuahua could leave such a big pile. He never bitched at her, I think he's sweet on her, she is a younger woman at 85. Oh, Zompoc... escape... yeah, back to the story.

The next morning, I worshiped the coffee gods, then wrapped the pot in three layers of bubble wrap and boxed it twice. Then, I secured it in the passenger seat with the seat belt. Hey, you have to take coffee seriously. I had on jeans, an old sweatshirt and a battle harness. My weapons were ready. I had a Hemphill Bowie knife, an AR15, a Colt Commander .45, and the coolest machete. Inside the truck was my Louisville slugger, after all, what Zompoc is complete without a baseball bat? I'm sure some of my friends in the UK would argue that point. They actually think a cricket bat would work better (they've seen Shaun of the Dead too many times). A baseball bat gets so much better velocity.

I opened the garage door to see my 95 year-old neighbor standing there with his rifle hanging from a sling and his other arm all chewed up. His eyes were blood red. Wow, ZOMBIE, and as an added bonus I get to take out my hated neighbor. I raised my rifle but then thought "nah, not very sporting", so I pulled the Colt. Well, that just didn't feel right, so I went for the bat. Yeah, Louisville slugger all the way. I turned around to find that the old coot moved faster dead than he did alive. I couldn't get a good swing in, so I jabbed the end of the bat into his mouth, knocking him backwards, then double-tapped his head with the .45. Now taking out my first Zombie, for me, was a big deal. The fact that it was 95 years-old to start with was not something to brag about, but I was working my way up because, the next minute, Mrs. Johnson came at me. Another double-tap and done.

"Okay, I can handle this," I think. My hands started shaking, my knees felt weak and quivery. Quivery, is that even a word? I grabbed the rifle from my dead neighbor and sat in the truck shaking for a couple minutes when I realized that the dog was in the backyard. I went to get her and heard her barking. There were zombies leaning over the fence. I grabbed the dog and ran as the fence broke. My backyard now had a zombie infestation, so I ran faster.

I finally got to the damn truck and got on the road before anything else could slow me down. I turned onto the main road and after a couple blocks, I saw your stereotypical Zombie couple staggering down the middle of the road. I'm not usually into profiling, but, *dumb zombies*! I got closer and realized I knew them. Greg and Denise... great people, err Zombies. I swerved to go around them and they stepped towards me. End result? Truck-2, Zombies-0. Brush guard paid for itself. Then my I-pod shuffled to R.E.M. – It's the End of the World. It's all in the timing, my friends, all in the timing.

I started hitting the back roads, trying to avoid any cities that had more than two stoplights. Now that sounds easy but try it on a map, and throw in a couple rivers big enough for freighters. The bridges kind of limit your choices. You either go for a bridge on a major road or you go out of your way and head upstream until you find a smaller bridge. Well, I had to avoid the big cities and that meant slower travel and two-lane blacktop where ever possible. I had looked at the map last night and programmed a route into my handheld GPS.

I would go north, then turn west to avoid Flint, Saginaw, and Bay City. About halfway between Flint and Lansing, I'd cross the river and turn north. This put extra miles on the trip and extra time but it also avoided people and population centers. Once I headed north, from that point on, the only thing I'd see would be little one-horse towns that I could blow through at high speed. Oh yeah, I've got 200 miles to go, a full tank of gas, three cartons of smokes, it's high noon, and I'm wearing sunglasses. Always wanted to say that, but it just doesn't sound right. For those that don't know, that's a Blues Brothers reference.

A full tank would get me where I needed to go and I wasn't worried about stopping. Even if I needed gas, I had ten gallons in cans in the back. But again, that's if Mr. Murphy didn't put in an appearance.

So I was driving down the back roads at 45 mph and making good time, but I was getting a little nervous because it had been going pretty smooth since I left the house. Now I knew from the GPS that Grand Blanc was the next town I'd have to skirt. I knew I'd be making a turn soon and then it was a long, straight stretch going west to the river. Then, just before I made my turn, I swear I saw a flock of pink flamingoes in front of me. I drove closer to all that pink and realized it was the Breast Cancer 5K walk. I guess it was interrupted by a few Zombie attacks. I stopped and stared at all the people and, as I stared, I realized that I knew some of them.

Every year, they would try to get me to do that walk. Yep, Jamie, Sherri, Dan, Candice and the whole Girl's Breast Friend crew. Jamie looked like she had been in a cat fight, her clothes were torn and rumpled. A large bite mark on her neck stood out. If only she was alive, I'd be making hickey jokes. Sherri was in her fancy legging things, which were also torn and dirty. Her right arm was hanging with bites torn out of it. Dan and Candice were leaning on each other. Dan's head was leaning on Candice's shoulder because part of his neck was just gone. Well, sorry guys, but don't get in my way. I'm on a mission, you pink zombies.

Thank God, I didn't have to run through them. My turn came up and I took it. I don't know if that was the right thing to do or not. They were my friends. Do I leave them to wander and maybe hurt others or do I take them out? Could I even do that to my friends? It wouldn't help me if I got mobbed and killed, so I ran, but my heart was heavy over the loss of so many good people.

The next stretch of road passed quickly after I pushed it up to 65 mph on the long, straight flat section. When the river came up, I had to slow and turn before the bridge. At the bridge, I knew I was in trouble. Barricades had been set up on both sides of the bridge. There weren't any road construction signs, so it was either locals trying to keep people out or bandits. I started looking around and trying to back up, you know, using that power turn they use in the movies? But it doesn't work so well on a narrow road with a long-ass pickup truck. I dropped the rear tires off the blacktop and mashed the gas pedal to get back on the road. About that time, a shot shattered my back window. The dog was growling and snarling in the back seat. She gets a bit testy when you interrupt her naps. That also told me she saw a stranger that she didn't like. Everyone knows that animals are a better judge of people than humans. I had the truck floored and got the heck out of there as fast as I could. No more shots, no more problems and I get to live to fight another day.

I still had to get across the river, and if I went north I'd hit a small city. City = Trouble. Nope, not gonna do it, so I had to get creative. I went back to some railroad tracks that crossed the road and headed across the river. I figured if it could hold a train, it could hold my truck. Once I got across the river, I stopped and grabbed a shotgun out of the back of the truck. I loaded it with 3" magnums of #4 buck. Everyone talks about oo buck, #4 puts more shot into the air and will still mess you up. It may not kill you right off but a wound made by it during a Zompoc, with no medical care? It would do the job depending on the range. With all that lead flying in the air, it would make people duck.

Now, why was I doing this you ask? Well, I had to go north and those jerks at the bridge were there. I'd have to drive behind them. I rolled down the passenger window and stuck the barrel of that goose gun out the window, it was long enough that I could lean over and reach the trigger. I wasn't too concerned about aiming. The truck started rolling towards the bridge, the road running along the side of the river. When I saw the bridge, I stepped on it. Leaning against the barricades were four guys with guns in one hand and beer cans in the other. Hard to shoot a gun with a beer can in one hand, unless it's a handgun. When I was beside the bridge I cut loose and rattled off five rounds as fast as I could pull the trigger. That old long gun can crank 'em out. The beer drinkers either fell to the ground or dove over the barricade. I saw a 12-pack of beer explode, oh the inhumanity of it all, alcohol abuse.

The trip north from there was pretty mellow. When dog had to go, I stopped in the middle of nowhere. Since I was stopped, I figured it was a good time for a break myself. Now, a libation is required during a proper break. The making of camp coffee is a ritual all unto itself, which must be observed. My trusty tote in the back of the truck yielded some of the magic beans, roasted and ground to perfection. This was not your average coffee, no, I had this tucked away for just such an occasion (like I knew there was going to be a Zompoc). Black Hills Coffee – Roosevelt's Blend. I heated the water to a delicate boil and gently poured it into this neat little French press that I found for camping. I tucked everything back where it belonged and sat drinking my coffee out of a tin cup. Well, okay, I'll confess, I dosed it with a bit of bourbon, for my nerves. It was in the tote for snake bites, honest. Dog ate her lunch and had a last stretch before we hit the road again.

We hopped in the truck figuring three hours or so to get to the cabin. Again Mr. Murphy had other plans. We passed through this little burg in the middle of nowhere that had a one-pump gas station. One pump. Who the heck runs a gas station with one pump? Suddenly the steering wheel started pulling. A flat tire, just what I needed to make my day. I pulled off the road and started to change the tire. Kind of funny, but funny "hmmm", not funny "ha ha". I had roofing nails stuck in my tire. Dog started growling. I looked up and there had to be forty zombies walking down the road. They didn't see me, so now was either the time to run or the time to fight. No way was I going to get away in the truck and they would see me if I ran. Nope, it was time to fight, and nothing was keeping me from my girls.

I quickly climbed into the back of the truck as they saw me and started moving faster. Dog hopped into the back of the truck with me and whined. I was a little busy so I didn't really pay much attention to what she was whining about. I raised my rifle across the top of the truck's cab and proceeded to play shooting gallery. It is a lot harder to score head shots with moving, lurching, and staggering targets.

My rifle was zeroed in at an inch high at 100 yards and they were about 75 yards away, so I just aimed at the nose. High or low a bit didn't matter, it killed them. This group was a mixed bunch from who knows where. A short heavy-set African American with a shaved head lurched in the front. Sorry dude, you're done. Mechanics, housewives, and even a guy in a three-piece suit. After going through every magazine I had, there were only four or five left. I had burned through a lot of ammunition. That means lots of missed shots. The shaking hands might explain that.

One zombie really caught my eye. This lady had to be forty-ish, wearing nothing but a pair of underwear. Now, the middle of the Zompoc, with zombies closing in on you, is no time to be a pig. What can I say? I'm a guy. She was beautiful when she was alive, I'll bet. Seeing her like this reminded me that I hadn't sent my donation for breast cancer in yet this year. About that time, I saw Dog launch herself off the back of the truck. I was empty on the rifle so I swung around with my pistol just as I heard a man screaming. Dog was on top of someone, and I noticed a second guy swinging a rifle towards her. Hell no, you aren't shooting my dog. I sent three rounds towards him as I jumped out of the truck and ran to Dog.

My suspicions were confirmed by the sneak attack from behind, but I didn't have time to screw around. I put a bullet into his brain and got Dog back into the truck as the remaining shambling things approached...quickly. Now, in the movies you see these fantastic pistol shots from a hundred yards away. In real life, that could happen if you're a competitive shooter that goes through thousands of rounds weekly. Generally speaking though, it doesn't happen in real life. I've pulled off some sweet shots on stationary targets. I'd say I'm above average, which isn't all that great. But on moving, lurching zombies when it has to be a head shot? Not so easy.

I let them get 15 yards away and opened fire with the pistol. Before they got there, I changed magazines so I'd have a full one to start. Double tapped three of them as fast as I could and then missed the next zombie twice... not once, but twice. One round left and two to get rid of in no time at all. I holstered the pistol (okay, I dropped it but holstered sounds so much better) and pulled the machete. They bumped into each other trying to get at me and I took off a hand as it reached for me. I went for the kill when one of them fell over. The machete cut through that skull like it was a rotten watermelon. I looked down to make sure the other one wasn't going to chew on my ankle or leg.

Now I had to laugh. Dog was dragging this evil stinking zombie around by its pant leg, shaking her head like it was a chew toy. Every time it would reach for her when she stopped, she would walk backwards shaking her head. I walked over while changing magazines and ended this bizarre tug-of-war game.

The coast was clear so I reloaded all my magazines and got the tire changed. As I was changing the tire, it gave me time to think. I figured that the two guys were going to ambush me and feed me to the zombies. Roofing nails in my tires sounds like somebody's idea of a slick trick. I remember seeing some cars behind the one-horse gas station and I started to wonder what was at the station. Dog groaned from the back seat as I got into the truck. I had to stop messing with her naps.

The truck fired up and I headed for the shoulder on the opposite side of the road. I drove down into the ditch and followed it back towards the gas station. I looked and saw nails scattered here and there. Yep, someone was stirring the pot. I got out of the truck at the gas station, keeping the truck between me and the front windows. Behind the station, there were a dozen cars with flat tires. I did a quick sprint to the front and peeked in by sticking my head around the corner and pulling it back. I didn't get it shot off, so far so good. I stepped out holding my rifle against my shoulder and then I saw it... absolutely nothing. The place was empty.

Something didn't add up. There was a door leading back to the one work bay that was attached to the station, which was closed. When I slowly tried it, the knob refused to turn. Oh boy, I get to kick in a door! I've never done that and it always looked like fun. I pulled back my leg and stepped forward slamming all my weight and everything I had into the door. The door moved, maybe. My leg, on the other hand, decided my knee needed to be set on fire. I couldn't feel my foot and my ankle started screaming. Well, it could have been me screaming. To sum it up nicely, it hurt. I think I could have made a truck driver blush.

The really sad part was the fact that I didn't open it. Then I saw a set of keys hanging on a nail a couple of feet to the right of the door. When I opened the door, I found a treasure trove. Food, guns, and all kinds of gear. It was all loaded in a trailer with tarps and ropes laid out next to it. Someone was getting ready to leave soon. I quickly opened the bay door and backed the truck up to the trailer. Pulling the insert for my hitch out of the tote in the bed (told you I had all kinds of stuff in it), I hooked up to the trailer and took off. I wasn't slowing down in case they had some buddies running around. I was worried about getting a ticket because I didn't hook up the lights and it was starting to get darker. I didn't have too much further to go.

After about a half hour and twenty-five miles later, I

turned onto a dirt road that leads back to the two-tracks. For those of you who don't know what a two-track is, the easiest way to explain it is two tire tracks with grass, ferns, and who knows what growing up in between. Tree limbs scrape the side of your vehicle as you go down some of them and they don't get plowed in the winter. Mud puddles could be three feet deep and attached to creeks. After that, the going got a bit rougher. Turning off the two-track, I headed up a valley that was pretty narrow. The bottom of the valley was wide enough for one vehicle and the wheels were higher than the bottom. There was a two foot gap under the bottom of the truck that wasn't there before the valley. So I slowly made my way up the valley. I put the truck in four-wheel drive since I was dragging the trailer and the valley steadily climbed to a higher altitude. The path started to open up and my headlights lit up a jeep parked in the middle of the trail. Now, I didn't recognize the jeep and didn't know anyone that owned one. To top that off, there was blood on the door handle of the jeep. This had to be more trouble, thank you, Mr. Murphy. I couldn't just drive up to the front door, no...

I fumbled with the door handle and killed the truck. Dog woke up yawning and stretching as she climbed out of the back seat.

"Go home."

My command was met with indifference. "Want a treat?" Her ears perked up. "Then go home. Find your mother." She looked up the trail and slowly walked up it towards the cabin, her nose was working overtime and she started growling. She stopped and looked at me. Yep, bad guys around. I avoided the trail and headed a couple hundred yards up the valley, past the crest of the rise. The creek flowed down this side of the ridge and could be followed to the cabin. It was pretty dark but I knew this path like the back of my hand, or did, until I tripped and fell into the water.

Dog sat and laughed at me until we heard a gunshot, which was soon followed by another. I climbed out of the creek and hustled up to the clearing around the cabin. I saw one man on the ground and another standing next to him. The man standing yelled, "I want in that cabin, my friend is hurt and I'm going to take it, so just walk away and nobody gets hurt." Now that set my blood to boiling. As I moved closer for a shot, since it was so hard to see, I watched the form on the ground grab an ankle and proceed to chew his way up the leg nearest to him. He had turned and his friend didn't even realize it. While they were both distracted I aimed and started pulling the trigger. When the bolt locked back and I was out of ammo, I pulled the .45 and got close enough to end it for them.

Walking up to the cabin I shouted in my loudest voice.

"Honey I'm home!"

The door swung open and the most beautiful sight in the world stood before me. My wife and our two girls. They all fell to their knees and group hugged the dog. "Who's a brave girl?" "We missed you Moo cow." The lights lit up the white cow patch on her chest. My wife smiled at me as I got tackled by two little girls. Yep, I was home. It made the trip to the hills worthwhile.

ABOUT T.D. RICKETTS

T.D. Ricketts lives in Michigan. Married for 35 years, and his wife deserves a medal. Two beautiful daughters, a grandson and grand dog can be found running in and out of his home at any time. Hunting, fishing, motorcycles, camping and hanging out in the woods take up a lot of his time. A lifelong worker in various manufacturing and warehousing jobs, retirement figures prominently in his future.

T.D. will have seven short stories or more in various anthologies being released in fall of 2017.

Currently the plan is for his first novel to be released in Feb. of 2018.

Thanks to Tamra Crow for her editing skills.

Thanks to Valerie Lioudis for giving a new scribbler a chance. Michael Peirce for suggestions and reading rough drafts. Christopher Artinian for his kind words and encouragement.

T.D.'s first book "Release the Hounds: Dogging the Dead" will be out in 2018 via Amazon.

To find more information about T.D. Ricketts please follow him on the social media sites below.

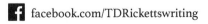 facebook.com/TDRickettswriting

14

THE FORT

A short story from the series: Legion of the Undead

"Sir, why don't they just attack?" One of the legionaries asked from up ahead. Decanus Marcus Crespo looked to see who had spoken. He thought it might have been Lepidus, but whoever it was had turned away to look ahead. The seven men around him were moving as fast as they could but the injured man was slowing them down. Sweat ran from inside Crespo's heavy helmet and down his neck as he jogged along. The Romans' sandaled feet kicked up dust on the hard dirt road. Even if the enemy weren't keeping them in sight, they wouldn't be hard to track.

"I don't know," he answered honestly. His men were almost as experienced as he was, and lying to them would do no good. "We keep moving, the fort is five miles ahead." It was all he could think to say.

The fort sat in the centre of the Gaulish province and had seen no trouble in years. The odd fight between the local tribes had to be settled from time to time, but nothing serious. In fact, the posting was considered to be one of the easier jobs in the legions. That was, until a few weeks ago.

News of the Risen had reached them before the actual undead themselves had. Word had been sent from Germania, which was rumoured to be the centre of the undead uprising. The men had laughed at first, sure the messenger had been part of an elaborate hoax. Then they had seen the first of the grey-skinned, dead-eyed monsters.

It had been a patrol, very much like this one, that had first encountered the Risen. Two of the creatures had attacked the eight-man contubernium while out in the forests around the camp. The creatures had been destroyed, but not before one of the men was bitten. The messages from Germania had warned them what would happen to the man, but no-one had come out and said he should be put to death. In the end, the legionary had turned and most of the men in the fort had seen their first Risen.

In the weeks since that first sighting, the local tribes had become more and more desperate. A couple had sent envoys to persuade the Romans to allow them shelter in the fort, but Tribune Avitus had refused. It wasn't a big fort and the Romans were there to keep the peace, not to protect the local tribes, he had argued. The chiefs had spread the word and Roman patrols had started to go missing. When men left the fort, it was now never in units of less than eight.

An arrow landed close to Crespo's feet. He glanced back and saw a group of approximately fifty tribesmen. They had halted in the road and a number of them had bows drawn but they weren't firing. A sick sense of dread started to form in Crespo's stomach. There was something up ahead that these men wanted them to reach, it was the only explanation he could think of for why they weren't attacking.

The remaining miles to the fort were a nightmare of harassment and intimidation. At random intervals, the tribesmen would appear at the side of the road, throwing stones and other non-lethal objects. From behind they would see horsemen, who would ride past close enough to knock legionaries off their feet, and then ride away laughing. All the while there was the constant presence of the large group behind them.

Finally, the fort had appeared over the crest of a hill. Crespo knew there was something wrong immediately. The gate was open. In normal, more peaceful times, the gate would never be left open. At times like this, it would have a double guard on duty at all times. There was no sign of life on the walls, either. Even from a distance, the camp should look full of life but to Crespo's eyes, it looked dead.

A full volley of arrows fell no more than six feet behind his heels. The message was clear. Go in. Crespo turned to his men and saw they were all thinking the same thing that he was, they were walking into a trap.

Galba, the injured man, tried to stifle a cry of pain but it escaped his gritted teeth. The arrow protruding from his shoulder made his pauldron stick up on that side, giving him a lopsided look. The sound made up Crespo's mind. They had little choice, it was either stay here and be killed or enter the fort and face whatever was waiting for them in there. They pushed the gate open wider and Crespo was the first inside.

Every man in the unit had seen battlefields. The blood and death never left you. The sounds and smells were, in many ways, worse than the sights. The screaming of men and horses, and the smell of the blood and shit of dying men. Nothing he had ever seen in war prepared Crespo for the sight that waited for him inside the fort.

Around the walls, more than a dozen legionaries had been hung with the stretched arms of crucifixion. They had been chained to the wall by their wrists, to suffocate under the weight of their own bodies. The air slowly forced out of their lungs, never to be drawn back in. Before it had happened, they must have been infected with the undead blood because it was Risen that hung there, not truly dead men. Dead men would have been much better. Each man was dressed in his uniform, in a parody meant to taunt whoever saw it.

"Someone close and bar the gate," he called over his shoulder. "I want two men on the walls. Put an end to those fucking things and cut them down," he said as the men began to move around him.

The two legionaries who carried Galba waited, while a third dragged over a table. They lifted the injured man and laid him down. He grunted with pain as his head lay back on the wood. One of the legionaries began slowly unbuckling Galba's armour so that they could get a better look at the wound.

From above his head, one of the men shouted down, "Sir, these chains won't come free." The soldier had removed the undead creature's helmet from above and had put an end to it with his sword. Now, he was trying to pull the chain from the wall. Crespo sighed and closed his eyes in exasperation.

"The man is dead, Julius. I'm sure he won't feel it if you cut his hands off."

Julius looked at him for a second, evidently trying to decide if his senior officer was being serious. Seeing no hint of humour in Crespo's eyes, he took up his sword once more and cut the hanging man's wrist with one stroke. The corpse dangled for a moment by one wrist before Julius stepped over and repeated the procedure.

Crespo turned to the remaining men, who were standing and watching this most gruesome of tasks. "Gather the bodies into the corner, I won't have them lying around the place." The legionaries started the gruesome work without hesitation. Crespo took the time to look around the fort. Every door he could see was closed, no need to guess what would be waiting behind every one of them. The patrol had been out for four days, plenty of time for the Gauls to prepare a number of surprises for their return. He wondered how many other patrols were still out and whether they would be allowed to return, or if was this a one time surprise that Crespo and his men had been lucky enough to stumble on?

It took the best part of half an hour to clear the men from the walls. The task was made harder by the fact that, if they looked closely, most of the corpses were known to the men doing the work. They learned not to look too closely. With the work done, Crespo stood the men down and told them to drink while he checked on Galba.

"How is he?" He asked of the men who tended him. Galba himself was either asleep or unconscious, a film of sweat coated his face.

"Not good, sir." The man answered. "He's reacting like he's been bitten and the arrow wound is starting to look necrotic. I think those bastards out there have been coating their arrows with Risen blood."

Crespo winced. "How long does he have?" He asked.

"Hard to tell. The arrowhead went straight through one side and out the other. The tip wasn't in him for more than a second. It's hard to tell how much of the poisoned blood was left in him. Either way, there is nothing we can do for him."

Crespo made a decision, an officer's decision. "Go join the other men, get a drink, and rest for a bit."

The legionary looked at Crespo, knowing what was going through the officer's mind. "Are you sure, sir?"

Crespo took the man's hand in the over and under grip of the legions. "You've done all you can for him, let me do the rest." He waited until he was alone with Galba before drawing his knife.

He looked at the blade. He had found it during the Jewish revolt. He'd been with Galba on that day as well. They had been dispatched under the command of soon-to-be Emperor Vespasian to put down an uprising in Judea, both of them fresh-faced legionaries, with ideas of wealth and glory. It had been a bloody campaign with whole towns destroyed and thousands of Jews put to death.

It had been after the sack of one of those cities, for the life of him he couldn't remember which one, that he had found the blade. He and Galba had been drunk and celebrating the fact that they were still alive. Galba had been in an alleyway, throwing up from too much drink, and Crespo had seen the glint of steel in the gutter. He'd bent to pick up a fine blade, with an ornate handle, that lay next to the hand of a dead Jew. He'd kept it with him every day from then until now. Today, it would be used to put his friend to death.

He leaned down towards Galba's ear. The flesh of his face gave off an unnatural heat.

"I don't know if you can hear me, my friend." He paused, hoping for an answe, but none came. "I hope you're satisfied with the life you've had, because you've lived it all the way from beginning to end. I'm proud to have shared it with you." He straightened back up and whispered a prayer his father had taught him, a prayer to Jupiter. When it was finished he said one more thing to Galba. "Wait a little while and I think we might all be joining you. Goodbye, friend."

With that done, he slid the blade deep into Galba's temple. He had killed hundreds of people in his career. Never had a blade hurt him when he had put it into someone else's flesh, but this one did. Galba arched up off the table for a moment then fell back dead. Crespo withdrew the blade and cleaned it on the hem of his own tunic. He looked once more at the dagger and then placed it on Galba's chest.

"Find something to cover his body," he said to his men without turning. He wasn't ashamed to let them see his tears, but for a moment longer, he wanted them to remain his own.

"They're still out there, sir. In fact, I think it might be the whole tribe. I'm sure I can make out women and children amongst them. I think we are being used as entertainment. They look like they've got cooking fires going," the lookout on the wall shouted down.

Crespo turned to the rest of his men. "I guess it's time we gave them what they want. We can't stay out here all night, we are going to have to see what's waiting for us in there." He pointed into the main building of the fort. There were smaller stone buildings that contained sleeping quarters but most of the fort was set in the one main block. The tribune's office, quartermaster's store, weapons stores, and most importantly, the Culina. Without the food stores, they would only last a matter of days.

"We go room to room. In the narrow space, we shouldn't have to worry about the jumping attack they do. We need to use our advantages, shields to block the corridors and spears over the top, I think. If anyone has any other ideas, speak up now."

He looked around at the faces of his men. They had been through a lot. Normally after a four-day patrol, the least they could expect would be good food, a decent night's sleep, and a day off. Not one of them spoke, so he nodded and stood up. The men followed him without a murmur of dissent.

The main door would be the easy one. Two men held shields, locked into the world's smallest shield wall. Crespo leaned in to turn the handle and throw open the door. The two men rushed forward and blocked the doorway, bracing themselves for an attack, but it never came. The corridor was empty. The Gauls must have been thinking the same as Crespo. It was a waste to have the Romans face the undead where they had plenty of room to retreat. The legionaries looked at each other, relief mixing with fear on their faces. Crespo didn't want them to lose heart and so he ordered them forward.

The next room was the Tribune's office, the smallest of the rooms along the corridor. The two shield men stood ready at the door. Again the door was opened, and again, nothing attacked them. The door seemed to stick against something and was only half open but nothing tried to get through the opening.

"Step back," he said to the shield wall. He drew his sword, then stepped through. As he did, he felt the pressure of a tripwire snap against his ankle. A shard of ice went through his heart as he saw a shadow above him. An undead had been attached to the ceiling in a feat of engineering that the Romans would have been proud of. By catching the tripwire, Crespo had set it falling onto him. He twisted to deflect the weight and managed to get out of the way of the worst of the attack.

He fell back against the Tribune's desk and kicked out at the Risen on the floor. By its clothes, Crespo knew it was the Tribune himself. The creature grabbed at his foot and there was a moment of panic when Crespo though it might get his flesh to its mouth.

As quickly as the fight started, it was over. Julius was standing over the still figure of the dead Tribune, with his sword in the back of the creature's head.

"I think I just shit myself," he said to the legionary.

"Me too, sir. Me too," Julius replied. There was a round of laughter that broke the tension among the men.

"Go down the corridor, doing the same thing in each room," he said to his men. "Take your time and do the job properly, not like I just did." There was another short round of laughter but tension was starting to grip the men again. Crespo waited until the men were out of sight before leaning back against the Tribune's desk. His heart was beating like a galley drum at charging speed. He breathed deeply and felt calmer.

The next three rooms were empty. The tension was beginning to grate on the men. The one thing a legionary couldn't stand, was an enemy that refused to fight. It was becoming obvious to Crespo what was happening and he had to admire the Gauls for their thinking. There was only one room in the fort that the Romans really needed, the food store. They could manage without everything else the fort could offer but without food and water, they were as good as dead.

"Come back outside," he ordered his men. The five legionaries in the corridor followed him into the sunshine. Crespo called up to the sixth man who was still watching on the wall.

"What news?"

"Sir, the bastards are actually having a party out there!" The guard, Lepidus, replied with disgust in his voice. "They're drinking and eating. I'm fairly sure they were singing a minute ago but it's hard to tell in that grunting language of theirs."

Crespo nodded. He had to admit, he wasn't shocked. The bitterness that had been growing in the tribes since that first Risen attack was bound to have spilled over eventually. They were hard men with a lot of pride. If they couldn't destroy the Risen, it stood to reason that they would try to destroy the Romans and take back a little of their dignity.

"It's the food store. That's where they all are, I would bet my year's wages on it. We have a hard choice to make now and I don't know the correct answer. Do we carry on the way we have been going or do we try to fight in the open?"

There was murmuring amongst the men before Julius asked, "How many do you think are in there, sir?"

Crespo thought out loud, "We have a century stationed here, that's eighty men. We just cut twelve off the walls and the Tribune, of course, that leaves sixty-seven. There are eight of us." *Actually, there are seven*, he thought, but didn't turn to look at the shape of Galba under the blanket. "I don't know how many men were outside the fort when those fuckers attacked but we have to assume we were the only ones. We could be facing fifty to sixty Risen in there, boys."

"Fuck!" Said Julius, it came out in a long slow sigh.

Balbus, a grizzled and scarred veteran, spoke up. "We can't fight that many in the corridors. The sheer weight of them will make holding the shields impossible."

The men nodded at this, and Crespo knew they were right. "Outside it is," he said. "Any ideas how to even the odds?"

It was Balbus who spoke next. His answer was, at the same time, both simple and obvious. So obvious that Crespo was a little ashamed not to have thought of it himself. The men actually seemed to lift their spirits as the old man spoke. The seven men discussed the plan, but in the end, there really wasn't much to discuss, the flesh was already on the bones. After the talk, the legionaries passed around the last of the rations they had taken on patrol and drank the last of their water.

It was as the last light still hung in the sky that Crespo stood on the wall, looking out over the grassy plain in front of the fort. The Gauls were in full voice, singing drunkenly and enjoying their food. It occurred to Crespo that there was a good chance they could slip out of the fort under the cover of darkness but the Gauls must have guards stationed around the fort. No, this plan would work and it would give the Romans a little satisfaction in the bargain.

He turned to his men, who rested, readying themselves for what was to come. He had told them they would need to draw lots to decide who would undertake the most vital role in the plan, an almost certain suicide mission. There wasn't a man among them who wouldn't give his life to save his brothers, but he wouldn't ask them to do that. He was their leader and he would be the one to risk his life. It wasn't heroics, it was the right thing to do.

He stood before his men, some he had known for over a

decade, others not so long. He looked down at them and smiled. "I'm going to do it," he said simply.

Julius spoke up from his place on the wall. "We knew you would, sir." It was a simple confirmation that his order had been accepted and a statement of thanks, wrapped up in five words.

Crespo turned to Balbus. He wasn't just the oldest, but also the most experienced of the legionaries in front of him. Crespo had never asked the man why he had never advanced through the ranks. It wasn't a question most veterans cared to answer. There were a thousand reasons why he might have been passed over and not all of them were bad.

"If I fall, you take over," Crespo said. Balbus nodded his agreement and the group lapsed into sullen silence.

"Fuck this," said Julius from the wall as he reached to the back of his belt. He produced a water flask and opened it. "I usually keep this for special occasions, injuries and such, but I figure this is one of those times. He took a mouthful of the drink, put the lid back, and threw it down to Crespo. The Decanus took a drink of a bitter tasting, hot spirit. It hit the back of his throat and burned like a glowing ember. He passed the bottle to Balbus and turned to look at Julius.

"Fuck me, that's got a kick, where did you get that?" He asked.

"Actually, sir, I bought it from those guys out there a couple of months ago. You get used to it after a while." The legionary smiled but there was sadness in his eyes.

The rest of the men took a drink before Crespo gave the order and everyone took their places. After taking a few seconds to settle, Crespo turned to look at the yard. No-one could be seen but everyone was in their places. Some had jobs and others were there as backup. If this failed, they would all die.

He walked down the corridor towards the food store. The room on the other side of this plain wooden door was easily big enough to hold sixty men. Crespo felt his legs get heavy as he approached it. His armour was lying outside under the table on which Galba grew cold. No need for it now, it would only slow him down. His sword was with his armour. If it came to a fight, they had already lost.

He lifted a hand and banged hard on the door. There was a sound of movement behind it. A lot of bodies were shuffling behind that door and they wore Roman armour. Anyone who had spent time on a battlefield knew what legionaries sounded like when they were packed together.

He braced himself and took hold of the door. One last prayer to any gods that might be listening passed his lips as he turned the door handle.

The door crashed against the corridor wall and Crespo saw a solitary, grey-skinned, face before he turned and ran like the Hounds of Hades were behind him. He heard the clash of armour and sandaled feet on the stone floor as the Risen gave pursuit.

He was out of the door at the end of the corridor and heading towards the gate with his hot breath drying his throat. He saw the two ropes attached to the gates draw tight and, just as he reached the entrance, they were pulled inwards to allow him out.

He dared not turn to look behind him as he left the fort. He imagined the breath of his pursuers on the back of his neck but they didn't breathe. One of them must have lost its footing in the chase because he heard it fall, a crash of armour in the growing dark.

He kept his eyes on the Gauls up ahead. Drunk as they

were, they were slow to react, so slow. No-one seemed to have seen his sprint towards them. Surely the sound of sixty running undead, in heavy armour, must alert them. It sounded like a cacophony in his own ears.

He counted his steps, a trick he had been taught by a man called Kane. It focused his mind and stopped his panic. Fifty long strides from the fort and the Gauls had no idea he was there. One hundred strides and he was more than halfway to the drunken tribesmen, still, the merriment and drunkenness masked the approach of one tiring Roman and sixty undead.

Crespo felt his legs turning to lead. Maybe he should have let one of the younger men do this thing. He forced every last part of his will into keeping his feet moving. The sound of Hades coming up behind him gave him the strength to push on.

He was so close to the Gauls when one of them finally saw what was happening, that they barely had time to react. Men sprang to their feet and grabbed at swords, shouting to those who were slower than they were. The drunken good cheer was ripped from them like flesh from a bone.

Crespo knew this was the moment of his death and met it gladly. The plan had worked, the men in the fort would be safe and the Gauls would feel the full revenge for the Romans they had slaughtered. To be cut down by a tribesman while bringing them death would be enough.

He slid into the feet of the nearest warrior as he reached him. A sword missed the top of his head, close enough to feel the whip of wind as it passed. He caught the tribesman low on his legs and felt the weight of the man pass over his head. There was the sound of bodies crashing together, almost at the same instant that Crespo passed underneath the tribesman's body. Had they really been that close?

He glanced around him, there were indeed children but no women in the group. The children were young boys, probably brought along to give them a taste for Roman blood, to let them see the tribal warriors killing the Roman invaders. It would make them men. Well, now it would make them food for the undead. Crespo thought back to Galba, lying on the table back at the fort and his heart hardened.

He got to his feet and, for the first time, risked a glance behind him. The tribesmen were in a fight to the death with, what seemed to be, all sixty Risen. The undead were all over the sword-wielding, painted warriors. Crespo saw one man dragged out of sight by a pair of rotting, grey hands that grabbed at his ankles and pulled him to the ground.

Crespo had no intention of fighting and dying with these savages. They had killed his friends and made sport of doing it. He pushed past a young warrior, who had eyes only for the fight happening behind Crespo. Chaos aided his escape from the Gaulish camp and he made his way into the almost total darkness beyond the campfire.

As he circled the fight, lost to both sides in the darkness, he watched the massacre unfold. The Gauls were dying in rivers of blood. The undead tore flesh from living bodies and in turn died, with tribal iron buried in their skulls. He breathed hard as he made his way back to the fort and his waiting men, the sound of screaming men filling his ears.

Julius was the first to see him as he reached the bottom of the fort's wall.

"If you cheer, I will throttle you," he called up as loudly as he dared. "Did they all follow me out?"

"Every one of them, sir. Like water out of a bottle," the young legionary replied.

"Are you going to throw down a ladder or do I have to scale the walls?" Crespo asked.

"I'm pretty sure you could if you tried, sir," came the reply, followed by a ladder.

As he climbed, Crespo took one more look back to the now smaller battle. The fighting continued but in the firelight, it was impossible to see who was coming out on top. The Romans would watch, wait, and be ready for whoever walked away from the fight.

ABOUT MICHAEL WHITEHEAD

Michael was born in Liverpool, UK. He is 43 years old and has two novels to his name. He tries to take his interest in history and add a horror twist. Romans and zombies seemed an interesting place to start.

I'd like to thank Tamra Crow for giving her time and expertise in editing this story.

The Legion of the Undead series can be found on **Amazon.**

To find more information about Michael Whitehead, please follow him on the social media sites below.

facebook.com/MichaelWhiteheadAuthor

twitter.com/gyp11111

15

ADAM

"When men have it all, they're grateful. When men lose it all, they're vengeful. And a vengeful man is truly no man at all."

In the south, there are two things that outshine everything else in life: football and God. Both are staples down here in Georgia and, for my family, both were big business. You see, my Pops is Greyson Rhodes, the former head coach for the UGA Bulldogs. So, football was life. My brothers played football, and Ma and I went to every game until she got sick. Come to think of it, when Mama got sick that's when everything kind of blew up.

Ma had cancer and the bills were piling up. I mean, Pops was a hard worker but his paychecks only went so far. So he came up with other ways to make some cash. He started throwing games for a few good old boys. Some Carrollton coke dealers that also handled sports bets would take the bets and give Pop's a call when the action got hot. Then he would call a lot of shitty plays and we would have a check to pay for another appointment. Everything was golden until the dealers got arrested and thought turning on Pops would get them a lighter jail sentence.

It didn't.

The judge didn't give two shits about rigged football games, but oh boy, did Georgia care. Pops got fired on the spot and no one would touch him after that. Times got hard, but remember when I said there were two things in the South? Well, when football stopped helping, God came to the rescue. Pops started doing this televangelist thing, Touchdown Jesus, he called it. It was to avoid some tax issues him and Ma fell into. Yet, when Pops told those people he gave himself over to the lord and started praying on tv, it was like all was forgiven. People started sending in checks just to help the church and to be forgiven for their sins. However, sinners can't forgive sinners; that's just not how it works.

"I'm telling you! We get one of those people on stage. Hit them with some holy water and bam! Everyone will be talking about how we prayed the evil out of that son of a bitch," Pops said. He nodded and laughed before saying into the phone, "Well not a real one, you fucker! I'm not flying someone in for that. We'll get Carol's kid to dress up like one. How's she doing anyway? I haven't seen her since the party." I listened from the living room as I watched people tear each other's throats out on television. There were people killing people and zombies killing people. The world was falling apart and here we were, in our big mansion; at times I'd look at my life and I'd feel sick inside.

"Turn the fucking channel. No one wants to watch this depressing shit!" His voice was deep and demanding of attention. I don't think there's a room on earth that my brother wouldn't leave in awe by his demigod-like size. We stared at each other for a moment, then Daniel's hand came flying into the back of my head. From my new spot on the floor I heard him say, "Keep disrespecting me and I'll pop your fucking grape, boy!"

"The war's over Sergeant. You can put your crazy back in its box," I said softly. I got to my feet to see Pops' smile drop.

"Ronnie! Ronnie? Hello!" Pops shouted. He held the cell phone up while walking towards the window, "The fucking call dropped again" he said.

"I told you this shit is getting real Pop! People keep pussyfooting around it, but when all the fucking Hajis start gassing us then-" Daniel's rant was cut short by my harmless question.

"Were you always racist or did the Marines make you this way?" I asked.

"Your face is racist, you little brat," he replied.

"It's not just your bars. The whole network is down." The voice of reasoning in our house pulled my attention away from the shell-shocked mountain man to my other brother, Matthew.

"Shit!" Pops shouted.

"It might come back," I said. The three of them stared at me until I saw my statement of hope for what it really was, a delusion. America got hit by the virus last. It was only in DC last I checked. Every other nation except for those south of the wall were reporting the same thing. People were dying, but they weren't staying dead. Small things like no hot water or no cell service were just an inconvenience before but now, they were signs of some bad stuff to come.

"Adam, can you check on Ma? Make sure all her equipment is working right," Matthew said. I looked over at Pops and he nodded slowly. So I made my way upstairs. Being sent away wasn't anything new to me, they used to do it all the time when they were dealing with those dealers.

Sending me off to get milk or Mama's medicine. I used to feel disrespected, but I guess they wanted to hide their dark sides from me. Although, the one thing I've learned in life is everyone has a dark side.

"Hey Ma," I said softly, although I didn't expect an answer. Long gone were the days where she would smile and ask me how I was doing. The doctor called it Primitive Neuroectodermal. I learned that word backwards and forwards, letter by letter. I thought I oughta know just what was killing my Mama. "Cell phones are down. So that's why your friends aren't inviting you out to dinner," I said with a smile. I walked over towards the window and softly said, "But I'm gonna fix you up something nice for dinner." She laid there with eyes fixed on the ceiling, never acknowledging my words or my presence. She was dying, but I was the one that felt like a ghost. Never seen and never heard. I went about checking all her equipment and decided to give her the meds just in case the power went out and I forgot. I spent a good hour talking with Ma, she never answered or looked at me, but she was the only one in the house that ever listened to me. "Mama things-" My words were cut short by the sound of pounding on our front door. Quick and frantic booms! One right after the other. I could hear Pops' name being shouted. My eyes went towards the window and I could see three shadows casting down the driveway; mixed in with the darkness of those shadows was blood, lots of blood.

"Mr. Rhodes!"

The banging got more intense to the point that Pops couldn't avoid it anymore. I heard the door open and voices battling back and forth.

"I think we have guest Ma," I said softly. She didn't even

blink. I liked to imagine she was playing a trick on me and when I closed the door she would pop up and smile.

"What the fuck is going on?!" Pops shouted. I liked to imagine we were all better than we truly were.

"We were at the studio and it got overrun by those things. We barely made it out," a male voice said. I listened to his story as I slowly came down the stairs. It was no different than any of the stories I'd seen on tv or read about on the internet. The only thing that set this tale apart from the rest was it was in our backyard.

"I fucking told you! I fucking told you guys! Those fucking ragheads-" Daniel got cut off as Matthew stepped in front of him and sighed.

"What are you doing here, William?" Matthew asked. The tone in his voice carried a hint of concern but I could tell it was more for us than our guest. William Mills was Pops' head stagehand at the studio. He made sure everything ran smoothly, always had everything organized right down to the letter. William was muscular, years of hanging stage lights can do that to you. His shaggy black hair tossed to the side as he rushed in with a hint of a smile that was framed by his pointed goatee. When I first met him I thought, 'This is what the devil would look like.' I'm not sure why I thought that. William had never been a wicked person, but then again, even the devil was an angel once. William was holding up a bloody mess of a man in his hands. The man's name was Travis. I had seen him around every now and then but never talked to him, and from the looks of him, I never would.

"Travis got hurt as we were trying to get out, he-" Matthew wasted no time listening to William's explanation as he jumped towards the question we were all wondering.

"Was he bitten?" Matthew asked. My brother's eyes were

fixed on William. They stared each other down like two lions battling for a gazelle. Just when I thought their eyes would cut each other in half, I heard her voice. The only Angel I had ever seen. Her name was Ruby, Ruby Mills. She was William's little sister, and even with blood covering her body, she still looked amazing.

"Would you two cut the shit! He was shot. A bullet clipped him when everyone went nuts," Ruby said. She released her hold on Travis and walked up to Matthew, "Now you gonna help us? Or you just gonna stand there like some fucking clown?" She asked softly.

Matthew's jaw tightened and he looked at William. "Put him on the dining room table. We'll call a doctor," he said softly.

"That's very kind of you, Matty Boy," Williams said.

"Yeah, you're a real saint," Ruby replied. She and William rushed Travis into the dining room. I stood there, looking at the blood trail through the open door. Then, Pops slammed it shut as hard as he could.

"It's fine," Matthew said.

"Don't tell me it's fucking fine! Make it fucking fine!" Pops hissed and pushed passed me as he made his way up the stairs.

"Where you goin!" Daniel shouted, but the only answer he got was another door slam that echoed through the house. "What the hell is that all about?" Daniel asked.

"I'll tell you later. For now, go see if you can help Travis," Matthew said softly.

"I can tell you right now I can't help him because I'm not a doctor, nor do I play one on tv," Daniel replied.

"Jesus Christ! Daniel, did the military teach you anything other than how to shoot a fucking-" Matthew was cut short by another one of my simple questions.

"Why did you tell them we'd call a doctor?" I asked. Matthew's head turned towards me and then he looked at the doorway leading to the dining room. Ruby was standing there with her arms crossed.

"I'll tell you later," Matthew replied.

Ruby's hazel eyes slowly gazed at each of us for a moment before she shoved her hands into her pockets and softly said, "We need some towels or something to stop the bleeding." There was a man bleeding to death on our table but panic or sorrow weren't the emotions that seemed to fill the air. I looked over at Ruby and she smiled at me.

"I'll get you some," I said softly. I was a sucker for Ruby's smile. All of Georgia knew that, especially Ruby. She nodded and turned around, walking back into the dining room, and I ran up the steps to retrieve her towels like the good lapdog I was. When I returned downstairs I saw my brothers and Pops whispering, no, plotting, in the office. My footsteps were light as I crept towards the doorway.

"Freaking out now isn't gonna make the problem go away," Matthew said softly.

"You shut the hell up with that 'calm breathing' bull-shit!" Pops snapped back.

"Lower your fucking voice," Matthew hissed as his head turned too fast for me to dodge his glare. He walked over and pulled me into the office by my arm and gently closed the door behind me.

"What the hell you pulling him in here for?" Daniel asked.

"Because like it or not he's a part of this," Matthew said. My head turned from side to side as I held the towels close to my chest.

"A part of what?" I asked.

Pops' finger shot out and he said, "Don't you fucking say another word."

"There wouldn't be anything to say if you listened for once," Matthew said.

"What the hell is going on!" I shouted as Daniel's massive arm came around my head and quickly pulled me down into a headlock, with very little protest from myself. I was trying to fight but my efforts versus his natural and synthetic strength were well wasted.

"Shut up," Daniel said softly as his bicep tightened around my neck, "or I'll make you shut up."

"Let him go, Daniel," Matthew said and the beast quickly released me from his grasp. Matthew leaned on our father's desk as he folded his arms over his chest. "We need to get them out of the house," Matthew said softly and pointed at the door.

"Who?" I asked, and once the words left my lips, we heard the office door slowly open to reveal William in the middle of the doorway. His eyes were scanning the room as he smiled.

"This is a real lovely home you got here, Mr. Rhodes. Real nice woodwork, built to last," William said.

He slowly walked past the mountain of a man, known as Daniel, and made his way towards my father's bookcase. He placed his green beer bottle on the stained mahogany wood as his finger ran along the spines of the books.

"I didn't take you for a Yuengling drinker, William," Pops said

William laughed as he pulled a black book off the bookcase. Slowly flipping through the pages he softly said, "I'm a 'what's available type drinker', Mr. Rhodes." Then he smiled closing the book. "I don't know many people that keep the Bible on their bookcase."

"I like the Lord close," Pops said.

William nodded. "Close, to me, is my nightstand, but then again I guess you're not in your bed much these days," William said.

"Excuse me?" Pops said.

"I mean a busy man like you, I bet you hardly sleep," William said. He tossed the book onto Pops' table and picked his beer up, smiling. After a long swig, he said, "That New Testament shit, with all due respect, Mr. Rhodes, I don't know how you can stand up there and spit all that soft crap." William turned his gaze towards me and pointed the neck of his beer my way and said, "The Old Testament, that's the true word of God. You know that because man fears it."

"The Lord forgave our sins with-" Pops' words were cut short by Williams's laughter.

"The Lord doesn't forgive shit! Men change their minds, not God. You think a being who's all knowing and powerful just woke up one morning and said 'Oh fuck, I was wrong?'" William shook his head, "Nope! Men got sick of paying for their sins, so they watered down the Lord's words, thinking that would help them escape judgment." The beer bottle went to his lips one last time and then came down, resting on Pops' desk, "No one escapes judgment." He looked over at Matthew and smiled. "When's that doctor getting here?" He asked.

"Soon," Matthew said softly.

William nodded his head and he walked passed me and my brothers. "Soon?" He said to himself as he walked off towards the dining room once again. I looked over at Matthew as his fingers ran through his wavy black hair.

"We need to do this now, Matthew," Pops said softly, and Matthew rolled his eyes.

"Just give me a fucking second to think," Matthew said. The cool head that ran our little family circus for years was showing an emotion that I only recalled seeing when Ma got sick.

Fear...

Lots and lots of fear.

"What's there to think about? Why is he here? Why was he at the studio?" Daniel slammed his hands on the desk. "Use your fucking head Matt, his up to something," he said.

"Why don't you just ask him?" I asked softly. Their heads turned my way and I felt as if I had just leaped into a burning spotlight. I cleared my throat and did my best to speak with more bass as I said, "You wanna know why he was at the studio, just ask him." The three of them stared at one another and then Matthew nodded. Before I could react, I was being pushed aside as Daniel started storming towards the dining room.

"William!" Daniel shouted. As if he were summoned from the gates of hell, William appeared with a smile on his face, leaning in the doorway.

"You bellowed, Danny Boy?" William asked, but this time his shit eating grin was bashed into submission by Daniel's massive right fist. I watched as William slammed into the floor. He stayed on his back, his eyes fixed on the ceiling for a moment. Then he did something none of us expected. His bloody lips parted and he smiled.

"Why the fuck were you at the studio?" Daniel shouted. Ruby took a step forward but William's hand went up.

"I'm fine, sis," William said. His hand went up to his lips and came back with dark red droplets. He laughed and sat up fully. "You got some power behind that rocket, Danny Boy." William slowly stood up and rolled his neck. The cracking sound sent a chill through me. I was slowly backing up without even knowing it. "But your form is shit," he said.

"Answer the fucking question!" Matthew shouted.

William's eyebrows went up. "What question was-" Daniel rushed towards William. They both moved faster than I expected. Daniel lifted William up in the air, then they both came crashing down into the floor. I was sure that was the end of it. But, Daniel wasn't getting up. I stepped closer to see Daniel's head locked under William's arm. He had my brother all tied up like a pretzel in a UFC cage.

"Let him go!" Pops shouted.

"Break his fucking neck." I heard Ruby whisper. I looked over at her and she winked at me. My body was far too confused at that moment to react. Thankfully Matthew's own wasn't. He came rushing over with Mama's lamp, but before he could strike, William's hands shot up and Daniel fell to the floor like a dumbbell after your last rep.

"Be cool. Be cool," William said with a smile, "He attacked me. I was just protecting myself." He slowly started pushing Daniel's body off.

"What were you doing at the studio?" Matthew asked.

"You mean why was I there after y'all fired me?" William laughed as he got to his feet. He started dusting himself off and softly said, "Why do you think I was there?"

"I don't fucking know," Matthew replied.

"He was cleaning out his locker, you fucking shit head!" Ruby shouted. Matthew looked over from Ruby to William and then back at Pops and me.

"We thought-" Matthew was cut off by William's laughter,

"You thought what? That I went over there to shoot up the studio? Go postal on Mr. Rhodes and y'all?" He asked and then his eyes scanned over us. "God damn! Why the fuck would I do that? Because y'all fired me?" William asked. The lamp slowly came down and Daniel started moving around on the floor.

"I'm sorry," Matthew said softly and looked over at Ruby. "I really am." Ruby glared at him and then rolled her eyes. She and William walked passed me. They got to the front door and William put up his finger.

With his back turned to us, he softly said, "There's only a handful of things worth killing over and a job ain't one of them." William's head turned to look at us over his shoulder, "Y'all get Travis some help. Whenever the phones come back on," he said. We all stared at one another, here we were accusing him of being dishonest and he knew we were lying the whole time.

"You don't have to leave," Pops said, and Ruby laughed as she pushed open the door. William quickly followed behind her.

My head turned towards Matthew, and I shouted, "What the hell was that about?"

"Maybe he doesn't know?" Matthew said to himself.

"There's nothing to know because nothing fucking happened!" Pops shouted. My eyes went back over to Matthew who was helping Daniel to his feet.

We stared at one another for a moment before he softly said, "Let it go, Adam."

So, I did. I stormed up the steps and slammed my door. Locking myself away from all the secrets. I rested my head on my pillow and the next thing I knew, I was asleep.

A loud crash jolted me awake. The moonlight was filling up my room and my clothes were soaked from the summer sweat. I sat still for a moment, pulling my head out of dreamland and into the real world. Banging and rustling could be heard coming from below. My white sneakers slid out of bed as I made my way to the door. My fingers went around the knob and I wondered what was I walking into? Was it Matthew and Pops finally having it out about their lies? Did William return for round two with Daniel? Or maybe it was sweet, beautiful Ruby, here to burn our house down. I wasn't sure what was below, but I pulled the door open anyway. It made a loud creaking sound that took over the darkness of the upstairs. Then the rustling stopped. Whatever it was heard me, just as I heard it.

"Matt?" I said softly. My rubber soles lightly pressed into the wooden floor as I did my best to creep towards the staircase. "Pops?" I said softly. A loud bang rattled me and I jumped back.

"What the fuck, shit brick!" Daniel's deep voice came from behind me before he pushed me forward towards the staircase. I grabbed the railing in hopes of saving my life. When I turned around I saw all three of them looking at me.

"What you push me for?" I asked.

"You stepped on me," Daniel said.

"Well, that's a justifiable reason to toss someone down the stairs. You sure your steroid dosage isn't too high?" I replied. Matthew laughed but Pops didn't. His attention was on the situation that was coming from below,

"Daniel, go get my gun," Pops said softly.

"Your gun's in your office," Daniel replied.

"I know that," Pops said.

"So why the hell would he go downstairs, risk getting shot just to come back upstairs, old man," Matthew hissed.

"Shot!" I shouted. My hand slapped over my mouth, it was a reaction. A very, very bad time for that kind of a reaction. But a reaction nonetheless. Daniel went to grab me, but I quickly backed up, another reaction that came at a very, very bad time. We all watched Daniel's two hundred and sixty pounds of muscle tumble down the wooden stair-case; every step sounding off with a chilling thump against his body.

"Danny!" I shouted and the three of us went racing down the steps. Daniel was passed out on the floor for the second time today. This time there was blood, gushing from the side of his head.

"Fuck," Matthew said softly as he started to check for life in our older brother. "He's breathing, so that's-"

Matthew's words were overshadowed by a frantic whisper, "Matthew," Pops said.

"What?" Matthew replied. When his eyes came up, I'm sure he saw dropped jaws and bugged out eyes from Pops and I. We pointed towards the kitchen and Matthew slowly turned around to see it standing in the middle of the doorway. "Travis?" Matthew said puzzled.

Travis' head snapped towards us and we could see his jaw slowly grinding along on something; he was chewing. When his mouth opened wide and a chunk of his tongue fell to the floor we knew, Travis was dead and in his place stood a zombie.

"Oh fuck," Matthew said softly. But the whisper was enough to send the monster into a rage. It moved faster than I thought it would. In seconds, it was upon us. Matthew was doing his best to hold it back. Pushing against its snapping jaws with one hand and cuffing Travis' wrist with the other. It was a position that could only hold long enough for help to arrive. Unfortunately for Matthew, his only saviors were Pops and me. Pops had run to the front door just as quickly as the zombie had moved towards us. As for me, I was frozen in fear.

"What the fuck? The door's locked!" Pops shouted as his fist pounded on the front door.

"Dad!" Matthew screamed. Pops looked over at us and started backing up, then he took off towards the kitchen. "You son of a bitch!" Matthew shouted. My head spun towards Matthew and, by the grace of God, I found it in me to get up and run. "You too, Adam!" I heard Matthew scream from behind me, but I didn't turn around. I was on a mission.

"Where's the gun!" I shouted. I turned to see the zombie's bloody teeth just inches away from Matthew's face. "Jesus!" I shouted. I rushed over with the first thing I could get my hands on. My body tilted to the side. My hands came racing forward. I don't know if it was the adrenaline, luck, or the Lord, but I connected with that Bible right into the open mouth of Travis; we both tumbled over onto the ground.

"Shit," Matthew said softly.

I rolled around with the corpse for a moment. It was strong, stronger than the television let on. But, with a quick twist of my hips, I was on top, pressing the Bible deeper into its mouth. I watched as it's bloody teeth carved into the black cover.

My head turned and I shouted, "Run!"

Matthew wasted no time, he dragged Daniel towards the basement door. Travis gave up biting through the book and did its best to claw at me. I had no plan beyond getting it away from Matthew. I never had a plan beyond helping my family.

"Pops! Help Adam!" Matthew screamed from the basement steps. My head came up to see Pops standing at the basement door. As he crept towards me, I could see the internal battle he was having. His forehead wrinkled and his jaw tightened. Travis' hand shot up, blocking my view and then I heard it.

"Fuck this!" Pops shouted, the battle cry of a coward, as

he took off down the basement steps. I wasn't an angry person. I believed in turning the other cheek, but in that moment, I wanted nothing more than to get my hands around that old man's neck. I took a deep breath, released the blood-soaked book and sprinted towards the basement door. Frantic footsteps shadowed my every movement. When I made it through the door frame I spun around and grabbed the door handle. As I pulled the wood towards me, Travis' ghostly pale hand slapped onto the door.

"Oh my God!" I shouted. My heart was pounding out my chest. I was so focused on the crazed eyes that were staring me down that I didn't hear Matthew coming up from behind,

"Eat shit, motherfucker!" Matthew shouted. He rammed a flaming mini Christmas tree into Travis' face and I watched as the zombie stumbled back far enough for us to pull the door closed and latch it. Matthew's sweaty head rested on my shoulder and mine rested on the door. "You did good kid," he said softly.

The door started to frantically shake as Travis slammed back and forth between the basement door and the wall. The scent of burning flesh started to take over my senses. I covered my face as black smoke pushed under the door. Matthew and I ran down the steps to find Pops kneeling over Daniel.

"You son of a bitch!" Matthew shouted. He started rushing towards Pops, but I wrapped my arms around him and did my best to pull him back.

"He's not worth it!" I shouted. Pops laughed and shook his head.

"Something funny old man?" Matthew asked.

"Yeah, you two little clowns are funny," Pops said softly. His eyes cut over to us. "What did you want me to do? Bear hug it?" He rolled his eyes and stood up slowly. "One bite! One scratch and you're done! We've seen this on the news. Now isn't the time to play hero..." Pops stared at us and then his lips turned upward into a shitty, crooked smile as he said, "but you two know that, because I ain't see you boys running upstairs with your capes." My eyes went over to Matthew and then we both looked back at the basement door. In our panicked and fearful state, we forgot that the most helpless member of our family was lying upstairs, blissfully clueless to the horrors that were going on below her.

"Ma," I said softly and then took off toward the steps. This time it was Matthew's arms that wrapped around me, trying to keep me back.

"Adam! Don't be fucking crazy!" He shouted.

"Ma!" I screamed.

"Adam! Calm the fuc-" Matthew's words and everyone's hearts for that matter, were stopped cold by one loud chilling sound. A sound we never expected to hear in that moment.

The sound of a gunshot.

"Ma!" I screamed. The gunshot was followed by some light drilling sounds. I stood there staring up at the door as Matthew cautiously started making his way up the steps.

"Matthew! Get your ass down here!" Pops hissed. But Matt continued up the steps, one cautious footstep at a time. "Matthew!" Pops shouted.

"Listen to your daddy, Matty Boy!" A cold southern twang came from beyond the door. Then the laughter started. Two sets of it, a man and a woman.

"Yeah, I wouldn't get too close. I would hate for a bullet to mess up that pretty face of yours," the woman said.

"William? Ruby?" Matthew said softly. Matt's fingers

pulled back on the latch, but when he pushed the door it didn't move. "William the door's stuck, buddy," Matthew said with a laugh. "You mind-"

"Boy, I ain't your God damn buddy! I ain't your pal! I ain't your fucking friend!" William hollered.

The female voice, which I knew from anywhere, laughed, "All the doors and windows are bolted from the outside. We did a little DIY while y'all were sleeping," Ruby said.

Matthew's fist started beating on the door. "Open the fucking door! You Bitch!" Matthew shouted.

"Oh, Matthew! That's a dirty, dirty mouth you got. Your Mama ain't teach you how to talk to a lady?" Ruby asked.

"Sis, that's a job for a daddy," William replied.

"I hope not, because then the whole lot of them are fucked," Ruby said and started to laugh.

"Mr. Rhodes!" William shouted. "Can you hear me well enough down there?" Our eyes darted towards Pops. He stood next to me at the bottom step.

I elbowed him and he rolled his eyes as he said, "Yeah."

"Good," William said softly. "You know I woke up this morning and I had no plans on ever seeing your shitshow of a family again. I said to myself 'Self! You are a man with many gifts. Many skills. You can do wonders.' I wanted to believe y'all firing me was a sign from God to move on and rebuild elsewhere," William said.

"So, why didn't you?!" Matthew shouted.

"Because when I went to check on my little sister, to let her know that none of this was her fault, that we were given an opportunity to escape your family's prison of a life, I found her looping a bed sheet around her neck," William replied. There's very little in this world that shuts Matthew up, but that statement sure enough did. I don't know exactly what it did to me. My heart wasn't racing but it wasn't still. The only way I can describe it is how a deer must feel after a hunter shoots it and it's watching those camo pants coming closer, but it can't move. Then it sees that buck knife and all it wants to do is turn tail and run. All it wants is to be free of that moment. However a deer's heart feels in that moment, mine felt like that on cocaine.

"Ruby? I...I had no-" My words were cut short by the sound of a gunshot. Matthew bolted down the steps towards Pops and me.

"Don't you ever fucking talk to her again!" William shouted and the boy in me wanted to run and hide. If I'm honest, the man in me had the same idea. "Not you, not your shithead brothers, and for damn sure not that fucking old man down there!" We all stood there in silence. Because no matter what any of us wanted to do, in that moment we knew William was running the show now. "I begged her to come down off that chair. Hell, I threatened her! Told her I could knock her ass into the ER before she could even think of stepping off that chair!" William shouted. Then we heard his voice soften as he said, "It was all talk. I was scared out my mind. I didn't want that moment to be our last moment. I didn't wanna..." All men cry. Bad men, good men, weak men, strong men. We all do it. So I wasn't gonna judge William when he did it. Yet, while Matthew and I are brothers, we are not the same. The laughter started light at first and then it wasn't light anymore. "You laughing at me?" William asked.

I pushed Matthew and he pushed me back. "No. No one's laughing at you William," I replied. Only because I felt anyone else's voice would have brought William down those steps, guns blazing.

"Nothing I said would make her come down. She was

hell bent on killing herself, until..." William stopped talking. As much as his words were scaring the hell out of me, him not talking scared me even more.

"Until what?" Matthew asked and I was sure that door was gonna fly open and bullets were gonna tear us in two, but you don't always need a weapon to tear someone in half.

Ruby knew that and she taught me that. "Until he said, we can kill them all, Ruby," she said, ever so sweetly.

"And that's what we aim to do," William said.

"You two are fucking crazy!" Pops shouted.

"No! Crazy is thinking you could fuck someone's world up and then toss them aside like a used condom," William said. I looked over at Pops and he couldn't even look at me. His eyes were locked on the bottom step, like it was gonna come alive and save him from all this. "This, well it's just a good old family bond. I'm sure you understand what someone will do to protect their family. Some people lie. Some people steal. Me, I'm part of a rare breed, that will kill and die for my blood," William said and then we heard the door unlatch. It slowly came open to show William and Ruby standing at the top of the steps in full tactical gear. Bulletproof vest, magazine pouches, knee pads; they came dressed for war. William's M4 pointed down at Pops and a red dot appeared on his chest. "The question is what breed are you, Mr. Rhodes?" William asked. Ruby's M4 came up and her red dot landed right in the middle of Matthew's head. "Because maybe if you were willing to die first, I might let your boys go," William said.

"If he dies, you'll let us go?" Matthew asked.

"He said maybe," Ruby replied. William laughed and then the two of them took slow steps back before closing the door.

"Someone has to pay for the sins of this family! I want

an answer by the morning," William said.

"Tic Toc!" Ruby shouted. With that, we heard footsteps, laughter, and then nothing.

"You son of a bitch! I'll fucking kill you for this! You hear me! I'll fucking killing you!" Matthew shouted.

"Calm down, Matt," Pops said softly, and then Matthew's cannon of rage found a whole new target. I was, once again, the only thing between Pops and a painful moment of picking his teeth up off the floor.

"Calm down! Calm down! None of this would have happened if you fucking listened to me," Matthew shouted. He tossed me to the side and I slammed my elbow onto the claw end of an old hammer. They were arguing back and forth, but their words didn't seem to resonate with me. They were just empty shells as my mind focused on one thought.

One that echoed throughout my soul until my lips softly released it. "What did you do?" I asked. My words were ignored by the pissing contest that they were knees deep in. I was always ignored. Always thought of as this second-class citizen who didn't need to know anything more than what he was told. Always taught to never have a voice, so I decided to raise it for once in my life. "What did you do!" I shouted and before they could react I sent that hammer sailing through the air. The blood came quickly. Then came the screaming. I watched as he crumbled down to the floor holding his face. I took a step forward and felt Matthew's hand go on my chest. The cursing never stopped. It went well on into the night, but we never checked on him. I just sat there staring at the blood rushing from his face.

† † † † † †

"She came into my office a month ago," Matthew whispered.

It had been close to five or so hours since anyone said anything. Pops had stopped crying and was passed out on the floor next to Daniel. I wanted to check on Danny, but I couldn't get over my rage enough to even make a motion towards Pops. I looked at Matthew and he let out a sigh as he said, "Ruby said that the old man got a little fresh one night after drinking." Matthew laughed and shook his head. "She was telling me my father was a monster and all I was thinking about was what kind of damage control this was gonna take."

"Did he...Did he..." I couldn't even bring myself to say the words.

"You know there's no reasoning with him when he's drunk. I'm sure she did her best to fight him off; knowing Ruby, I know she fought the whole time," he said. He tussled his hair with his fingers before softly saying, "I thought looking out for the family was the right thing to do. So, I offered her some cash, but she declined and said she was gonna tell everyone. So, we fired her and William before she could."

"So that's the sin? That's what all the whispering has been about?" I asked and Matthew nodded before resting his head on the wall. "And your damage control was hoping they would just forget about it?" I asked.

"It was better than Pops' plan," he said. I didn't ask what that plan was, because I already knew. However, as I sat on that cold basement floor facing another long hour in our billion-dollar prison, I thought maybe Pops' plan wasn't that bad. I know God is always watching, but I hoped he wasn't in that moment, because I truly believed anything would have been better than letting William live.

"I'm hungry," I said softly.

"I'm starving." The faint words came from the bloody

corner of the basement where Pops and Daniel lay.

"Danny?" Matthew said and we both rushed to his side. The mountain man didn't move. His body was still as he stared up at the light of the basement. My face came into to his view and he closed his eyes.

"I'm gonna kill you shit brick," Daniel said softly.

"You're gonna have to sit up first," I said.

We all laughed and then Daniel's eyes went over towards Pops, he looked back over at Matthew as he said, "What's up with the old man?"

"He got his nose smashed in by a hammer," Matthew whispered.

"No shit! By who?" Daniel asked and I raised my hand slowly. "Is no one safe from your terror?" he asked and I sighed shaking my head.

"I think we should do it." Matthew said.

"Do what?" I asked. Matthew's eyes came upon me and no words needed to be spoken. I shook my head and got to my feet. "No, we're not doing that," I said.

Matthew shot to his feet and shouted, "What other choice do we have? You heard William, he might let us go!" I rolled my eyes and looked over at Pops. Matthew started walking towards him and I stood in his way once again. "It's him or us," Matthew said softly. I heard Pops shuffling behind me and then Daniel slowly sat up for the first time in hours.

I took a step back and shook my head as I softly said, "We're family."

Before I got the chance to see the reaction on Matthew's face, the basement door opened and he took off, speeding up the steps. I ran after him, but came to a stop when I saw the barrel of William's M4 rifle being pointed down at us. The red dot found a nice home on Matthew's chest.

"Back the fuck up, Matty Boy," William said softly. The door opened up wider and Ruby came into view with a large pot in her hands. "Unless you're coming up to be the first to die?" he asked.

"I wish," Ruby said. She looked down at me and smiled. "Adam, I made you boys some stew."

"I'll take it," Matthew said softly as he put out his hands.

Ruby stared at his palms for a moment before looking back up into his eyes, "It's Adam or none of you little shits eat!" She screamed. I've loved Ruby pretty much all my life. I knew her favorite color, her zodiac sign, even her shoe size. But I missed the moment when my beautiful angel fell from grace. I wondered how long she was crying out for help with no one answering her? I wondered how many studio sessions she had wished she could avoid. How many fake smiles did she have to put on? I slowly started making my way up the steps past Matthew. I came up to the top and Ruby placed the pot in my hands. Then she put a set of spoons on the lid. "I did the best I could with what I had," she said. I stared down at the lid for an awkward moment trying to think of something to say.

"I'm sorry for what they did," I said softly. Ruby's hand rested on mine and she leaned in. As her body came closer I saw the barrel of William's M4 slowly turn towards me. With one jerk of a finger he could end my life and part of me wished he would, but instead of a bullet in my chest, I got a soft whisper in my ear.

"All we want is him," Ruby whispered. She leaned back and her soft pink lips brushed along my cheek and sent a chill through me. I was in such a trance that I didn't even notice when they closed the door and locked it. I was standing there staring at the lid of the pot.

"Umm dipshit! You mind bringing the food down?"

Daniel shouted. I turned slowly on my heels and then started down the steps thinking about Ruby's soft words. She and Matthew seemed to be on the same dark page. They started digging into the sweet brown stew, but I wrestled with thoughts in my head. The world was changing, it was getting colder, but that didn't mean we had to get colder with it. We could stand our ground and figure something out, or we could stumble in the dark with the rest of the world. I watched as my father took a bite of a large chunk of meat, his eyes didn't dare meet any of ours. We were family, we could make it through this. That's what I wanted to tell myself. But even if we could, Ma couldn't. Ruby and William had no idea when she needed her shots, or when it was time to change her bags. The longer we stayed down here, the more likely she was to die up there. With that one thought, I stepped into the darkness.

"Ruby says all they want is Pops," I said softly. The spoons stopped their frantic shoveling of stew and everyone's eyes fell onto me. Everyone but Pops who kept his gaze on the floor. "We give them Pops and they'll let us go," I said. There were no words, just empty stares at one another. I don't know how you could form words for that kind of moment. Pops slowly started to get to his feet and Matthew did the same.

"So, that's how it's gonna be?" Pops asked softly. He looked at Matt and he took a step back and shook his head. "No! No! That's not happening! Not after all I've done for you! For all of you!" He shouted.

Matthew looked at me and I shifted my jaw for a moment before I looked at Pops' bloody face and softly said, "It's your sin, you should answer for it."

With that, Matthew and I rushed forward towards Pops. He backed up as far as he could until his back was against the wall and, like any cornered animal, he fought. I took the first hit to the jaw and went down fast. Matthew took one to the arm but he fired back with a blow to Pops' gut. I watched as Matthew unloaded fist after fist on the old man. Years of resentment and anger finally finding a way free from his body. There's no telling how many things he had to cover up, how many lies he had to tell to keep Pops above water. For years, the old man was drowning in his sins and he was pulling Matthew down right along with him. I got to my feet and joined in. Daniel didn't say a word as my white sneakers started to turn red from the blood. I sent each kick flying into his already pummeled face. Bones cracked. Screams were heard. Tears were shed from all sides. I turned and picked up the hammer off the ground but then Matthew's hand came out towards me.

"That's enough," Matthew said. I dropped the hammer and listened to the metal echo through the basement as the head hit the floor. We got down low and lifted our bloody mess of a father off of the ground. One shaky step after another we made our way up to the basement door. "Just sit him up," Matthew said softly, and we did.

I stared at the red balloon that was once his right eye socket and I bit my lip as I said, "I'm sorry, Pops." I heard a gurgle come from his mouth as a stream of blood gushed from his lips. I stood up and pounded on the door. Then, Pops' hand shot up grabbing a hold of my neck. My eyes came down to see just a small bit of hazel staring back at me. His fingers tightened around my neck. I could feel his nails breaking into my skin. My Adam's apple had no room to move. I was being choked. The last bit of energy he had in him, he was using it to kill me. I felt a sudden rush of pain in the back of my eyeballs as my head started to fall back. Just when I thought I was a goner the basement door opened up and William slammed the butt of his rifle into Pops' head. His hand fell and I went tumbling back into Matthew's open arms. We watched as they dragged Pops into the house and slammed the door, locking it once again.

"You alright?" Matthew asked. My hand rubbed along my neck and I nodded. But I wasn't alright, who could be. I had just turned over my father to a pair of psychos in hopes of saving my own life. I beat my father until he couldn't stand and his last memory of me would be of him wanting to kill me.

I turned around and started down the steps as I softly said, "I'm alright."

We all sat around the stew and started eating once again.

✦✦✦✦✦✦

It had been a few hours since we last saw Pops or anyone from the other side of that door. While a few hours isn't much time in the normal world, we were far past normal at that point. We gave up Pops in hopes that William's 'maybe' was closer to a yes than a no.

"They're not gonna let us out," Matthew said softly.

"No, they have no reason to keep us down here," I replied.

"They got twenty to twenty-five years of reasons shit brick. They don't want to go to jail over this," Daniel said.

"There aren't any more jails," I said.

"Why? Because we saw one fucking zombie? For all we know, they took care of the outbreak and the world is moving on just like it always does," Daniel said.

"So why keep us down here? Why keep us alive at all?" I asked. Matthew shrugged and rested his head on the wall.

We all sat in silence for a moment before I softly said, "I wonder how Ma's doing."

Matthew's eyes came over to me and he placed his hand on my shoulder, "I'm sure she's fine," Matthew said softly. He coughed and then I coughed. My throat felt tight and itchy. I looked over at Daniel who had started coughing as well. It was then I noticed how grey the air looked. I walked closer to the steps and I could smell the smoke. I made my way up the wooden steps. I was face to face with the door.

I took a moment and then I started pounding on it, "William! Ruby!" I shouted. My hand continued to pound on the door. "William! Open up!" I shouted. I could hear Matthew and Daniel quickly coming up behind me. We all started coughing as the smoke seemed to be pushing faster into the room. "William!" I shouted. Matthew pulled me aside as he started slamming his hands into the door.

"Ruby! Open this fucking door!" Matthew shouted. Yet, there was no answer, no sound whatsoever. All that could be heard were our heartbeats and the door as it shook under Matthew's fist. "Open the fucking door!"

"Move," Daniel said softly. With those words, Matthew and I took a step back and allowed the mountain that was our older brother, to make his way towards the door. His hand took hold of the doorknob and he shook it for a moment. "It's warm," he said. Then he took a step back and lowered his shoulder. I watched as his shoulder went slamming into the thick wooden door. One violent ram after another was sent by Daniel. We all knew what this moment meant. If they weren't responding to this, then they were gone. We heard the wood start to split and then Matthew joined in on the attack. One giant ram later and the door went flying open. Daniel and Matthew hit the floor just as fast as the black smoke hit our nostrils. It was filling the house, but it was clear that the fire was upstairs. I stepped over them and started towards the staircase.

"Where the hell are you going!" Daniel shouted.

"I'm gonna go get Ma!" I shouted.

"Don't be dumb!" He shouted. I heard both my brothers calling my name, but I continued on. I closed my eyes slightly because the heat and the smoke were causing them to burn. I felt my way to Mama's room and when my hand hit the doorknob, I quickly pulled it back. The metal was burning hot.

"Ma!" I shouted. I started to kick the door. I didn't know what to expect. I wasn't even sure what I was doing. I just knew she needed me. I kicked the door one more time and it pushed open, then my heart stopped. The bed was engulfed in flames and the room was quickly following behind it.

"Adam!" Matthew shouted. He grabbed a hold of me as I fought to run into the room.

"Ma!" I screamed. Sweat poured down my face as the flames made their way towards the door. Matthew kept dragging me back, pulling me down the hall. It was a back and forth fight until Daniel came and tossed me over his shoulder. I kept screaming, "Ma!" all the way down the steps. We made it to the front door but it wouldn't move. It was bolted shut from the other side like Ruby said.

"What the fuck are we gonna do?" Matthew asked. Daniel tossed me down on the floor and he bashed his elbow through the window, knocking out the glass. He started pushing the shards of glass onto the floor. He turned around to look at us.

Blood was running down his arm as he shouted, "Move your fucking asses." We all went through the window one by one. I was last and as I coughed and stared at the staircase I honestly thought of just staying there and letting the flames take me, too. My eyes went towards the kitchen and I could see a pool of blood with two bodies lying among the red. One was Zombie Travis, all burned and freakish looking. The other body was Pops. I could tell from the gold watch that was still on his wrist. They might have done the deed but it was us, his sons that truly killed him. I turned and hopped through the window. When I came through on the other side, I saw Matthew and Daniel standing there staring out at the driveway. I took a step closer and I could see them. Ruby and William sitting on the hood of Pops' Mustang, with a front row seat to watch our home burn.

"Damn. Y'all got out faster than I thought," William said before pointing his weapon at us. "Maybe you were right, Sis. Maybe we should have started the fire on the first floor."

"Told you," she said softly.

I pushed passed my brothers and I pointed at her. "How could you do that? To her! Someone who ain't never did a damn bad thing in her life! How could you Ruby?" I shouted. She stared at me and rolled her eyes before sliding off the hood of the car.

"You're cute. Real sweet, I mean. I just like how you think the world works," she said. Matthew took a step forward and Ruby sighed. "Thinking you could just walk around here, like a gift. Without letting me take a peek inside."

"What the hell are you going on about?" Daniel shouted.

"You three been down there for damn near a day, he didn't tell you the juicy details about what he did? All the shit he said before he raped me!" Ruby shouted.

"I'm sorry for what Pops did to you, but we...but Ma! She didn't have anything to do with that!" I shouted.

"Pops?" William said.

"Your Daddy was a snake, who thought he could pay me to keep my mouth shut," Ruby said. William started walking towards us with his M4 aimed. "He thought because y'all had money that it was gonna solve everything. Like it could give back what you took from me!" Ruby screamed. Then I heard it. It wasn't a whisper, more like a dirty cat call you heard in the middle of the night from some drunk frat boys.

"You know you liked it," Matthew said, and I took a step back.

"What?" I said softly and Matthew looked at me. There was a small smile on his face and then he looked back at Ruby.

"You loved it, Ruby. I don't know what all this is really about, but it ain't about that," Matthew said and then we watched as the red dot moved to the middle of Matthew's chest.

"You raped me!" Ruby screamed.

"And now you're gonna pay!" William shouted. A loud blast was heard but it wasn't the one I expected. Mama's window exploded, sending glass flying. It was only a small moment, but it delayed William's reaction by a second. That was all Daniel needed as he rushed William, picking him up into the air and slamming him down onto the ground. The two of them rolled back and forth on the ground.

"Get off him!" Ruby shouted. I looked over at Pops' car to see the handle of her M4 sticking up from the passenger seat. Ruby's hazel eyes fell on me, then they darted over to the car. Next thing I knew we were both racing towards it. I was just a second faster as I pulled out the rifle and pointed it at her.

"Back the hell up!" I shouted. Ruby's hands went up and she slowly started taking steps backwards. I turned the muzzle of the gun towards William and Daniel. "Alright! That's enough!" I shouted but they kept rolling, so I fired a warning shot into the air and the pair came to a quick stop.

Matthew walked over to them, picking up William's M4. "Get over there by your brother," I said softly.

"You alright?" Matthew asked.

"Yeah," Daniel said. They both walked over towards me. I kept my red dot on Ruby, and Matthew kept his on William.

"You don't have to do this. I told you all we want is him," Ruby said. I looked over at Matthew and then looked back at Ruby,

"Well, you can't have him," I said. I felt Matthew's eyes on me. Was he proud? Was he happy that his little brother was standing up for him? I don't know, I don't think I'll ever know what goes on inside his head. "You killed my father and my mother," I said softly. "And now you gotta pay for your sins."

"Any last words?" Matthew asked. William's hands were up along with Ruby's.

He smiled and nodded, "Yeah, just one. How did that stew taste?" William asked. Ruby's head turned to look at him. "Was it sweet? Maybe something Mama would make?" William said as he started laughing.

"What the fuck are you laughing at?" Daniel yelled.

"You ate your Mama!" William shouted. "You ate your Mama!"

His words still wake me up in the middle of the night, that crazed scream. I can't get it out of my mind. Matthew pulled the trigger and sent a bullet flying into William's head. Ruby jumped and looked over at me.

"Please, Adam. Please!" She cried as I pulled the trigger. I loved that woman with all my heart, and I pulled the trigger. I watched her body fly back and she tumbled over onto the ground. I should have turned my rifle on him or myself. If I was a real man, I would have done that a long time ago, but I'm more like my dad than I like to admit. I'm a coward who just wants to do right by his family. Daniel said I ain't been right since then, he said I'm broken, and maybe I am. We loaded up in the car and drove. Just took off. Daniel said he had some buddies down by Ft. Gordon that could help us out, but the car crapped out on us before then. We ended up coming across this nice traveling circus. They took us in. Might be why we still keep them around.

I think about putting a bullet in them, but then I see all those people who saw three lost men and took pity on them. They didn't have to do that, so I just can't. Daniel doesn't do it because Matthew tells him not to. Matt says they come in handy. He says they're good at scaring people. Girls, they're good at scaring girls and Matt, well he likes the fear.

I'm sorry, I'm going on and on. I'm sure you three just wanna know why you're hanging upside down over these buckets. I wish I could tell you it's a joke. That this is all to scare you and you'll be okay. Y'all must feel like a deer right now, wanting to turn tail and run. But you can't, because I won't let you. I'm the only thing stopping you, so in a way, I'm like the hunter's bullet. Y'all are gonna die here. It's gonna be painful and bloody. They're gonna do some really bad things to y'all. So, I just thought instead of hanging here and wondering what's gonna happen next. I'd keep you entertained with some stories.

What was that? No, I'm sorry I can't remove your gag. Matthew would be really mad at me. He runs the show now, he's The Ringmaster.

ABOUT SYLVESTER BARZEY

Sylvester Barzey is a family man, a soldier, and an "Anything Goes HORROR" writer. What does "Anything Goes HORROR" entail? Missing Children, Deadly Wives, Haunted Baby Rattles, A LOT OF DEAD BODIES! Vampires That Don't Sparkle & Don't Believe In Dating Their Food Source! Would You Date A Cow? Werewolves, Zombies (A Whole Lot Of F#@king Zombies).

Oh & Some Bad Words. He writes what he wants and does what he likes and what he likes is HORRIFYING! Pick up one of his books today & step into his wicked world at **www.sylvesterbarzey.com.**

Planet Dead is available on **Amazon.**

To find more information about Sylvester Barzey follow him on the social media sites below.

facebook.com/sbarzeyauthor

16

ON THE ROCKS

Marcie Tisdale chose to ride out the end of the world in the comfort and safety of her high-rise apartment, far above the people running on the streets below. The latest chapter of her life began as a love story there, and had an uncertain middle, though she clung to the hope it could still end with a happily ever after.

Marcie had spent all of the morning and much of the afternoon staring blankly at the two empty glass tumblers on her living room coffee table. From time to time she'd notice the gunshots outside; they were most remarkable when they dwindled to only a few per minute. She kept the balcony door and windows tightly shut—blinds down—in her effort to ignore the end of everything out there. It was easier and far more satisfying to stare at those glasses.

Last night they were full of mixed drinks and attached to happy company. Her new friend had come over. Scratch that. She'd known her friend for several years, but Marcie had only just summoned the courage to invite him up to her apartment, socially. They had a few laughs, despite—or possibly because of—the unraveling of society. Even the gunshots and concrete-rattling explosions from the city beyond couldn't ruin their night.

Brian lived in a condo upstairs on the 20th floor of their downtown building. Somewhere between swanky and retro, the old tower was restored to attract young, successful, and creative-type tenants. Marcie was financially independent but chose to work at a small bistro and coffee shop in the building's lobby. It helped her make friends, including the attractive architect she'd chatted up almost every day for two years. Last night was the culmination of that friendship. Instead of coffee, the beverages she served were warm Jack and Coke's. The night ended in a tipsy blur, but when she woke up, he was still there. It wasn't a dream.

"Do you want one more, on the rocks, Brian?"

"Oh, you are a sly devil. Are you trying to keep me here against my will?" With a coy smile, Brian added, "I would stay forever if you had ice."

"I'd never think of that." It was exactly her plan. The smell of his cologne reminded her of the weeks, months, and years of the pursuit. "But I don't want you to go, even for five minutes."

"I don't either, but I won't be gone long," Brian said, suddenly serious. "I'll grab some clothes and a little food, and I'll be right back down. It will be good to share your condo until this thing blows over. Neither of us wants to be alone, and most of the people on my floor are already gone. There's safety in numbers."

They shared a brief moment of passion. When he opened the door to leave, the sound of gunfire tried to rush in. It fell back when the heavy door slammed, but kept watch over her, like a stalking predator.

That was six hours ago.

Now, only the glasses remained.

Why did I let him get away?

With the failure of the power grid and no mobile phone service, there was no way to call Brian. She would have to walk out of her safe space, go up the dark steps, and knock on his door to check on him.

She wanted to believe she could do it. Be the hero. Hell, just be a friend. But the cups on her table insisted she play it safe. They were relics of the happier story she so desired.

At that moment, the balcony door exploded with a gunshot. The painful burst of noise stopped her heart in fright. A bullet came through the glass pane and chewed a ragged swath through her voluminous record collection along the wall. Black vinyl fragments rained down, some tainting the perfection of the clear empty glasses.

Without the hurricane door to dampen the sound, the bedlam of gunfire finally had the run of the place. She could no longer tune it out.

Standing up, she moved to the balcony. A light breeze and the smells of death embraced her.

She lived in this condo because it overlooked prime real estate in downtown St. Louis. Her parents had a bigger condo on Columbus Circle in New York City, but she thought her view was more spectacular. The glimmering stainless steel of the Gateway Arch towered above. Below it, a beautiful park stretched from the foot of her building to the riverfront where the verdant green met the earthy brown of the Mississippi River. Every morning she stood in amazement on this very spot, marveling at the picturesque landscape.

Now, she swayed and nearly fainted in despair. A seething mass of humanity milled around the bases of the Arch. People huddled together in every open spot as far as she could see. Healthy refugees of the apocalyptic plague ravaging the country. A noisy cordon of soldiers and police guarded the outer edge of the park and shot at the crazies on the outside. Right now, the wave of plague victims ran and jumped toward the cordon only to be sliced to pieces by the weapons of war. The piles of dead lying in the streets formed a reef around the park and illustrated the steep price the zombies had paid, but more kept coming.

I called them zombies. Mom always said I had a vivid imagination.

Marcie backed away from the edge and returned to the glasses. She was compelled to get the black speckles out; make them clean again. That would bring Brian back. As she picked away the pieces, her attention drifted to the fond memories of last night. Most of the night, anyway. She felt deep regret she couldn't remember how that fade-to-black scene ended. The glasses were guilty of erasing those final hours. Only the rumpled sheets of the bed provided proof of a delightful tussle. Still, the sense of having those memories stolen gnawed at her soul as the afternoon bled away.

When darkness fell, she caught a whiff of Brian's scent. Like a bolt of lightning at midnight, she instantly knew where he'd gone. It was her opportunity to make it all right.

It demanded all her courage as she went to the front door. Looking once more into her dark apartment, some light from below lit up those glasses. They finally helped her recall one perfect memory with the brainy architect; a pleasurable passage from her life's lost chapter. She wanted him. Needed him.

Out the door she went, drawn by an insatiable longing to find her friend. Soon she was in the deepest darkness of the building's stairwell, descending. Her teeth chattered from fear.

If this were a TV show, a zombie would have bitten me in the darkness.

Why did I just think that?

She reached the last illuminated exit sign on the ground floor. It draped a soft red glow over all the strange shapes piled at the bottom of the stairwell. There was only enough light to see how they died. She stumbled over the burned corpses, doing her best to ignore what they represented. Nervous sweat soaked through her hot-pink nightgown.

If this were a book, I would be the zombie.

Haha. Another stupid thought. Just stop thinking!

The exit door was off its hinges so getting outside was easy. The manic gunfire was very close now. Concussive waves blew her long bangs back and forth. Marcie tried to focus, but her brain wouldn't cooperate. It helped a little to put her hands over her ears as pages and pages of her story-book life were stolen from her.

Memories.

Dreams.

Hopes.

Looking up in fear, she saw people running toward the lights of those men and women at the Arch. She could see them, too. A million tiny lighthouses guided everyone to the last island of safety. Something wasn't right about the comparison, but she was certain that's where she needed to go. She felt another wave of confusion and thought only of simple things this time.

Safety.

Loss.

Desire.

Focus, girl. Brian is in the light.

Marcie started her run. Slow at first; it took a few paces to hit her stride. As she matched speed with the others, a seductive siren song beckoned from the lights. Brian's primal cologne lured her forward.

If this were a movie, the lights would be flashes of gunfire.

That's stupid. Movies need happy endings.

She sensed the lights were somehow harsh, violent, and angry.

But they wavered at the last moment.

Frightened companions fell on each side of her, but she was committed. Plunging into the turbulence, and slamming onto the rocks of that perilous reef, Marcie found her lost friend.

Brian? I got ya. I'm never letting go.

The pair embraced as the lights went out.

See? A happy ending...

ABOUT EE ISHERWOOD

E.E. Isherwood is the New York Times and USA Today best-selling author of the Sirens of the Zombie Apocalypse series. His long-time fascination with the end of the world blossomed decades ago after reading the 1949 classic Earth Abides. Zombies allow him to observe how society breaks down in the face of such withering calamity.

Isherwood lives in St. Louis, Missouri with his wife and family. He stays deep in a bunker with steepled fingers, always awaiting the arrival of the first wave of zombies.

To find more information about E.E Isherwood please follow him on the social media sites below or **www.zombiebooks.net.**

facebook.com/sincethesirens

twitter.com/eeisherwood

17

MORNING OF THE LIVING DEAD

A Zombie Park Short Story

Marvin Weaver wasn't a morning person. The sound of his alarm ringing in the new day was the morning routine he dreaded. He looked over at his wife's spot on their queen-sized bed and saw she wasn't lying there like most mornings. He stretched and looked around the room to see if the bathroom door was closed, but it was wide open. He slowly stood up and made his way over to the closed bedroom door and opened it.

From down the hall, he could hear somebody in the kitchen having a conversation. He made his way down the hall until he reached the kitchen and found his wife sitting at the kitchen table having a conversation with someone on her cell phone. She looked concerned. She looked at him as he entered the kitchen and stood staring at her. She waved him away and continued with her conversation.

He poured himself a cup of coffee as he heard his wife say something about the Zombie Park that had recently opened near the city. He could tell something had happened, but from the one-sided conversation, he couldn't tell what it was. He knew he would have to wait until she hung up before he would get all the details. He made his way back down the hallway heading toward the bathroom when his nine-year-old daughter, Haley, one of his two daughters, came out of her bedroom. She stood rubbing her eyes. "Is breakfast ready?" she asked in a low voice.

"Not yet. Your mother is on the phone right now. Is your sister up yet?"

"Sabrina was up about an hour ago. Isn't she in the kitchen with mommy?"

"I didn't see her." He paused for a moment. "Maybe she was. I really didn't pay that much attention while I was in there. Why don't you get dressed and meet me in the kitchen? I'm sure breakfast will be started soon." He left his daughter and went into his bedroom. He glanced out his bedroom window to see what kind of a morning it was before taking a shower and getting ready for the day.

He saw Sabrina on the front lawn looking at something. It looked like a white cat licking something off of its fur. He took another look. He couldn't be sure, but it looked as though the cat was covered in blood. "Sabrina, get back in the house!" he screamed, but he knew she couldn't hear him. He raced out of his bedroom to the front door and ran outside screaming for her to get away from the cat. All of the excitement caught the cat's attention and it turned to look at him as he ran across the yard toward them.

Marvin's eyes widened when he saw the cat's eyes were milky-white and clouded over. The first thing that ran through his mind was the cat was diseased. "Come to me, Sabrina!" He kept running toward them but the cat kept its gaze on him as he drew nearer. He had a sickening feeling something bad was going to happen to his daughter. He reached them and snatched his daughter and pushed her hard behind him.

All he could think about was getting in between her and the diseased cat. The cat growled, and before he had a chance to react, leaped onto his arm and ripped off a hairy hunk of it. He painfully watched as it closed its eyes and chewed noisily on his ripped flesh. He covered his wound and turned to push his daughter with his leg. "Get back to the house now!"

His wife was standing at the front door as they both reached it. She immediately saw the open wound on her husband's arm. "Marvin, what the hell happen to you?"

"That damn cat took a hunk of flesh out of my arm, Sheila! I need to get it covered, and then I need to get to the hospital!"

"Go bandage it. The first aid kit is in the bathroom closet. I'll get the kids ready!"

He ran into the bathroom and found the first aid kit and grabbed the gauze, and then did his best to cover the wound. He felt lightheaded. He was losing a lot of blood. He knew if he didn't get to the hospital soon he was going to be in major trouble. He looked back outside from his bedroom window to see if the cat was still there. To his relief, the cat was no longer in view. He reached for a bottle of aspirin from the nightstand and poured out two pills and popped them into his mouth and swallowed. He hoped they worked fast because he didn't know how much longer he would be able to take the pain. His wife came into the room looking concerned.

"How are you feeling? Will you need me to drive?"

"I feel like a cat took a hunk of my arm! And to answer your question, I think I can manage driving to the hospital. I will let you know if it's too difficult for me to drive.

Go get the girls into the car. I'll be out in the garage in a minute."

His wife hurried to the bedroom door and then abruptly stopped. "It was Cindy Hodgins on the phone. She said there was a problem at the Zombie Park." She turned to look fearfully at her husband. "She said some of the zombies have escaped."

"What!?"

"I didn't believe her. I thought she was trying to scare me. You know how she is with her horror movies. She's always trying to scare me. What if she is telling the truth?"

"Look at my arm, Sheila! I'm sure she's telling the truth!" He looked outside once again. He still didn't see any sign of the cat or anybody else. He turned to look at his wife. "We need to go now. If the zombies have escaped the park, it won't take them long to reach here." He stopped to think for a moment. "What if that cat was a zombie?"

"Don't say it, Marvin. You're not going to turn into a zombie. You can't. Do you hear me? You can't turn into a zombie."

"Is daddy going to turn into a zombie?" asked Haley.

"No, I'm not going to turn into a zombie." He looked at his daughter while trying hard to conceal the excruciating pain he was experiencing. "Haley, could you please leave the room so I can talk to your mother alone?" Once she had left the room, he steadied himself against the nightstand near the window. "I know this is going to sound strange, but my blood feels as though it is boiling. Also, my vision is becoming blurry."

"You better stop that right now!" ordered his wife. "We need you right now. Try to resist it."

"Resist what?" He turned to look at Sabrina standing in the doorway. "What, Sabrina!"

"Haley said you're turning into a zombie. I don't want you to turn into a zombie."

"You go tell your sister to quit spreading rumors. Listen, Sabrina, I'm not turning into a zombie. I just feel under the weather. I will be fine. Go get your sister and get in the car. We'll be there in a moment." He waited until she left before continuing the conversation with his wife. "We need to leave now! We'll stop by the hospital along the way. Once they get me fixed up, we'll leave and head to Chicago. We can stay at my brother's condo."

"I agree. Let's get going before the girls lose their minds."

They quickly left the room and headed toward the garage. Marvin fumbled with the door handle as he lost sensation in his hands. He looked at his wife. "Can you open the door for me?" He waited impatiently as his wife fumbled with the door handle, and then opened it. He managed to make it over to their Ford Escape after fighting the urge to pass out in the middle of the garage.

He got in behind the wheel and placed his head on it as he felt his blood continue to boil. He knew he was in trouble, but he was trying to stay strong for his family. He knew if they knew how bad he was feeling, they would panic worse than they already had. He was rapidly fading in and out of consciousness. He slowly lifted his head and turned to look at his worried wife.

"I think you better drive. I don't know what I was thinking."

Sheila looked worried, but she stayed silent as she switched seats with her husband. She sat behind the wheel looking in the rearview mirror to see what Haley and Sabrina were doing. They both sat there staring back at her as if they were in shock. She felt helpless. There weren't any comforting words she could say to them to make the situation better.

She knew she had to be the strong one if her family was going to survive the ordeal. She peered over at her husband who was looking worse. His skin was pale, and blood was trickling from the side of his mouth. He was in dire need of medical attention, and she was sure he couldn't wait much longer.

"Everybody buckle your seat belts." She reached for the remote to open the garage door. She pushed a button and waited as the door slowly made its journey upward. She sat impatiently as it seemed to take forever to reach its final destination. As it continued upward, her eyes widened as a large black panther with milky-white eyes stood <u>watching</u> them from outside. The creature's mouth was gaped wide, eager to devour. Sheila screamed without thinking about the consequences.

As the garage door reached the top, she pushed the button once again to close it before the creature had a chance to react. As the door made its descent, she kept her eye on the creature hoping it wouldn't try to jump inside before the door had a chance to put a barrier between them. She tried to remain calm, but the horror was too much for her and she shut her eyes.

She imagined what it would be like to be ripped open by the creature and then devoured vein by vein, blood spraying in all directions. Her thoughts were vivid. She could see the creature standing in front of her salivating at the thought of its feast. She watched frightfully as it moved forward on its paws as if it were stalking its prey. There wasn't anything she could do to protect herself.

There was nowhere to run or hide from it. Without warning, it <u>leapt</u> toward her right as the garage door closed separating them. She stared at the door as she snapped out of her trance. She breathed a sigh of relief, but her relief was short-lived. Something crashed hard against the garage door. Her relief turned to anger.

The creature had them trapped inside their garage and was now trying to get inside with them. She stole a glance toward her husband. He was still with them, but his breathing was erratic and sounded labored. She knew he was running out of time, but there wasn't anything she could do to help him. The panther was standing in their way of getting to the hospital. She thought hard about what course of action she should take next.

Once again her concentration was interrupted by the sound of the creature crashing into the garage door, and this time with much more force. Her heart felt as though it was going to leap out of her chest. She swiftly turned in her seat to look at her daughters. "Back in the house. Don't ask questions– just do it now!" She turned her attention back to her husband. "Marvin, we need to get back in the house."

She stared at him hoping he was listening to her. He slowly reached for her arm and held it. She looked at his eyes. They were glassy. "Come on, Marvin, I'll help you inside and get you to the couch while I figure out what I'm going to do about getting you to a hospital."

After having struggled to get her husband inside and situated on the couch in the living room, she looked around trying to come up with some sort of plan. Haley and Sabrina stood in front of her worried their father was going to turn into a zombie. She didn't have time to console them. Her husband didn't have much time left. She walked into the kitchen and saw her cell phone on top of the kitchen table.

She knew instantly what to do. She would call Cindy Hodgins to see if she could come pick them up, or at least divert the panther away from the garage door so she could drive out of the garage. She snatched her phone and called her. Cindy answered in a shaky voice. She explained the situation to her in a calm voice, but her emotions got the best of her. She listened as Cindy explained to her that her husband, Bob, had gone outside to help a neighbor who was attacked by a raven in the front yard.

In the process, he was killed by a lion. She said she had stood horrified as its claws dug bloody furrows into her husband's chest. Sheila didn't have comforting words for her. Instead, she tried to convince her friend to come get her and take them to the hospital, but she refused. She listened as her friend screamed at her about being selfish. Then the line went dead. She knew her friend had disconnected the call. She was frustrated.

She suddenly heard both Haley and Sabrina screaming. She ran back into the living room and saw them standing behind the curtain, staring at something through the window. She quickly made her way to the window to see what had them so excited. Her eyes widened in terror. A patrol car was in the middle of the street with its door open. She looked to the right of the door and saw the panther ripping shreds of flesh from a police officer's abdomen.

Blood showered the side of the patrol car. She pushed her daughters away from the window and closed the curtain. She ushered them into the kitchen and made them sit at the kitchen table. She held back tears of grief. She didn't want to be in the position she was in. Usually, her husband was the one who took charge of things, but now she was forced to do so.

She went back into the living room to check on her husband. He was lying on the couch with his eyes closed. She didn't know if it was a good thing or not. He could either be sleeping, or he could be dead. She wasn't sure she wanted to find out. She slowly made her way over to the couch and bent over to see if he was still breathing. It looked like he was, but she couldn't tell for sure. Her emotions were bottled up inside her, and she knew she was going to lose it at any given moment.

She stared at her husband's chest hoping she would see it move, but she still couldn't tell. She reached for one of his arms and lifted it. The only way she was going to know for sure was to check for a pulse. She placed two of her fingers on the inside of his wrist. To her relief, she felt his pulse.

She lowered his arm and turned to head back to the kitchen, but her husband grabbed her arm before she had a chance to leave his side. Startled, she turned to face him. He tried to speak, but his words were muffled, and she couldn't understand what he was saying. He spoke again. Still, she had trouble understanding him.

"Are you asking for a glass of water?" she asked, thinking it was what he was saying. She watched as he managed to nod his head. "I'll be right back." She made her way back to the kitchen where she found her daughters sitting next to each other holding hands.

"Is daddy going to be all right?" asked Haley.

"Is he turning into a zombie?" asked Sabrina.

Sheila went over to the sink and retrieved a glass and filled it with water, and then turned to face them. "Your father is going to be fine. He just needs some water. I'm sure he'll feel better after drinking this."

Neither Sabrina nor Haley believed what their mother was telling them. They witnessed for themselves how their father had looked when they came back into the house. They both knew he needed medical attention, and they were afraid for him. Even though their mom was denying it, they knew he was going to turn into a zombie.

They knew it because the news on TV said getting bit by a zombie meant you would turn into a zombie. When the construction of the zombie park was first announced on TV, they said the zombies could escape. They were right. The zombies had escaped and now their father had been bitten.

They looked at each other with tears streaming down their cheeks. They both wished there was something they could do to help, but they were both too young to do anything. As they sat there, their mother came back into the kitchen to get another glass of water.

Sheila made her way to the sink and filled the glass. She had spilt half of the previous glass of water on the floor trying to help her husband drink it. He had been thirstier than she anticipated. Deep down, she knew she was losing her husband.

His skin was turning gray as if he were dying. She wanted to take the glass of water she was holding and throw it across the room. She looked at her daughters. They were the only reason she didn't. She didn't want to lose it in front of them. She knew they were worried enough without adding any extra stress to the situation.

She went back to the living room and checked on her husband. He was asleep. She stood over him trying to remember what was said about people turning into zombies on the nightly news. They had said that if someone was bitten, it could take from minutes to hours for the infected to turn into a zombie. There were several variables that came into play. She thought about the possibility of her husband turning into a zombie.

What can I possibly do to protect myself and my children against my husband? She looked at him once again.

You wouldn't eat me or your children, would you? The prospect of something like that happening frightened her. She looked around the room. She needed to find something she could use as a weapon. She looked at the fireplace and saw the fire poker. It would make the perfect weapon.

She put down the glass of water and went over to it and snatched it. It was heavy. She held it firmly in her hand imagining hitting her husband in the head if he turned. It wasn't what she wanted to imagine, but if it came down to it, she wouldn't have a choice. She carried the fire poker to the window and drew the curtain back. She wanted to know if the zombie animals were still out there.

The patrol car was still there with its door open. On the ground near it was a large pool of blood, but the fallen police officer was missing. She saw smear marks and several footprints leading away from the blood. The only thing she could think of was somebody or something had dragged his body away from the scene. She then turned her attention to the surrounding area.

She didn't see any sign of any zombies in the immediate area. She wanted to believe her family was safe now, but she knew just because you couldn't see them, didn't mean they weren't there. With her daughters in mind, she knew it wasn't worth the risk of trying to leave the house. She heard her husband groan and quickly turned to see if he had turned.

She held the fire poker outward expecting him to rise at any moment and come for her. She wasn't going to let him get anywhere near her. She watched him for several painstaking moments before realizing he hadn't turned. She stood frozen trying to decide what to do next. She was afraid to leave the living room in fear her husband would turn while she was out of the room.

On the other hand, she was worried about her daughters. She didn't want to leave them alone for long. She was worried they would panic if she left them alone for too long. She looked toward the kitchen, and then back at her husband. She wished she knew what to do. She thought about bringing her daughters into the living room so she could watch everybody at one time, but she knew it probably wasn't a good idea.

If her husband did turn, she didn't want her daughters to have to witness it. She didn't want them to have to remember him that way. The best thing she could do for them was to keep them in the kitchen. She made up her mind and then made her way into the kitchen. She thought that if she only stayed with them briefly, everything would be fine.

Once again, she found her daughters at the kitchen table still holding hands. They still looked frightened. She wondered if she looked as frightened as they did. If she did, she had every right to. Anybody would be frightened if they were put in her situation. She went over to the kitchen table and sat in a chair opposite her daughters. She looked at them lovingly.

"How are you two holding up?" she asked, realizing it was a dumb question to ask. She already knew how they were holding up. She hit her head on the table and then looked at her daughters. She was losing it.

"I'm scared," Haley finally said after watching her mother hit her head on the table.

"I am, too." She paused for a moment. "I'm sorry you had to see me hit my head on the table. I hope you can forgive me."

Neither Haley nor Sabrina said a word. They both knew

their mother was worried. They just quietly sat at the table watching their mother rubbing her head.

Sheila stared at her daughters while trying to fight back the tears. She had to regain her composure and go back to the living room. She wasn't being productive by being in the kitchen. Her real worry was in the living room. She picked up the fire poker and stood up. "I'll be back in a moment. I need to go check on your father."

She looked lovingly at them for a brief moment, and then went back to the living room. To her relief, her husband was still asleep. She now had to figure out exactly what she was going to do once her husband turned. She looked at the fire poker she was holding. It was going to be the only thing standing between her and her husband. She hoped she would be able to kill him.

Even as a zombie, it would still be her husband. Zombie would be the one word she would have to remember. He would be a zombie who wanted to do harm to both her and her daughters. If she could remember that, she knew she would be able to kill the zombie version of her husband. Her concentration was interrupted by a sound coming from the fireplace. Now what? She stared at the fireplace wondering what the sound was. She heard it once again.

She still couldn't figure out what it was, but she thought it sounded like flapping wings. If it was, it could mean a bird had got into the chimney and was making its way down. She thought about the possibility, and then she realized what it could mean. If it were a zombie bird, it could get inside the house with them. She couldn't let it happen, not with her children in the kitchen in harm's way.

She tried to remember if the damper was closed. If it had been left open, then she knew whatever was inside the chimney was going to get inside the house. The only way she would know for sure was to physically check it herself. The idea of accomplishing it scared her. She could get attacked while checking! She wasn't sure what to do. She suddenly heard Sabrina discussing something with Haley in the kitchen.

Whether she wanted to or not, she had to check for the sake of her children. She slowly made her way over to the fireplace and stood in front of it listening. She could still hear the sound, and it sounded as though it was making its way down the chimney. She got down on her knees and tried to summon enough courage to look up the chimney to see if the damper had been closed.

Fighting the urge to stand back up and forget about it, she checked to see if it was closed. To her surprise, the damper was wide open and she could see something coming down the fireplace in a hurry. Fear drained the blood from her face. Without thinking, she reached for the chain to close the damper, but it wouldn't budge. She frightfully looked at the thing coming down the chimney rapidly.

She had a better view of it and could see it was a blackbird. It was staring at her with milky-white eyes. Her heart raced in her chest as she pulled on the chain trying to get it to move. Still, it refused to move. The bird was now nearly upon her, and she knew it would be the end if she couldn't get the damper closed.

She closed her eyes and said a silent prayer. She needed all the help she could get. She opened her eyes, and with all the strength she could muster, yanked hard on the chain. It gave way and the damper closed right before the bird reached her. She heard it crash into the damper, and then all went silent. She pushed herself away from the fireplace and fought back the urge to let the tears flow.

She glanced back toward her husband. He was still

sleeping. She stood up and went back to the window. The patrol car was still there, but it was all she could see from her vantage point. The area seemed to be void of any zombies. She knew it didn't mean they weren't there hiding somewhere. She thought about turning on the TV to see if there was any news on what was happening, but she was afraid of what she would find out, so she decided against it.

She knew it was a foolish thing to do, but if she heard anything about zombies escaping the park, she would completely lose it. She refused to believe her husband was slowly turning into one of them, but she didn't know for sure. She wasn't an expert on zombies, and she didn't know anybody who was.

She also knew she couldn't call anybody for help. The patrol car in front of her house was proof of it. She wondered if the same thing was happening at the hospital. If it was, then what was the sense of taking her husband there for help? It would only put her children at risk then. There had to be something else she could do, but what? The only reasonable thing she could do was to get her family to the car and to get them away from the area. If she could drive them to Illinois, she could get them away from the zombie park.

She didn't believe the zombies could reach another state, but once again, she wasn't an expert on zombies, so she couldn't know for sure. The one thing she did know for sure was she needed to check around the house to see if the house was surrounded by zombies of any type. The only way she could accomplish it was to go from room to room and look out the windows.

That posed a significant problem. She couldn't leave her children unattended in the kitchen. She would have to take them with her while she went from room to room. She went to the kitchen and went over to the kitchen table. She stood looking at her frightened children. She knew they wanted to ask more questions, but she didn't have time to answer them.

"Listen, I need you to remain silent and follow me. Don't ask any questions about daddy. He's going to be fine. I need to go inside every room in the house and look out the windows. I need to see if there are any problems out there I need to know about. Once we're done with that, I'll answer your questions. Do you understand?"

Both Sabrina and Haley nodded their heads to let her know they knew what she wanted of them. They both stood up and followed her out of the kitchen and down the hall to the first room on the right. They followed her and waited as she went over to the window to glance outside. Nothing had changed since she looked out the living room window earlier.

The patrol car was still there, and there still wasn't any sign of zombies. She was satisfied that side of the house was clear. She left the room and crossed the hall to another room and went straight to the window. It was the side of the house she was more interested in at the moment. She hoped she wouldn't see any zombies in the backyard. If she didn't see any, she thought she could get her family back to the car and try to leave the area as quickly as she could.

She drew the curtain back and scanned the backyard for any sign of trouble. At first, everything looked normal, and then something caught her eye. Something black had vanished behind one of her bushes near the back corner of her yard. She kept her attention focused on the bush waiting for it to reappear, but it didn't. Thinking she was imagining things, she rubbed her eyes, and then took another look.

Still, nothing had emerged from the bush. I'm just seeing things. She turned her attention away from the bush and continued to scan the area for anything out of the ordinary, but nothing else caught her attention. She decided the next thing she needed to do was to go to the garage and open the door.

Once it was opened, she could wait by the kitchen door to see if anything came into the garage. If it did, she could close the garage door and have whatever came inside trapped. Then she thought about her plan. It would mean she couldn't get to the car so they could escape. She was about to abandon the plan when she remembered the patrol car outside her house. The keys were most likely inside it. She could use it to escape the area.

She looked at her daughters. "We need to go back to the kitchen."

Sabrina and Haley followed their mother back to the kitchen and watched her as she opened the door leading to the garage, and then push the remote mounted to the wall to open the garage door. They heard the door begin to open.

Sheila watched impatiently as the door slowly made its way upward, exposing the morning light on the other side. She stood watching, praying nothing would come inside, but then she saw something big and black. She immediately knew what it was. It was the panther they had encountered earlier.

This time it wasn't going to be fooled. It leapt inside the garage before she had a chance to close the garage door. Her heart sank. She pushed the remote once again and quickly closed the door leading to the kitchen and locked it. She looked at her daughters as she felt the panther crash hard into the door. Her daughters screamed in unison.

"It's going to be all right. We need to get your father and

get him outside to the patrol car. Just give me a minute to check on him."

She left them in the kitchen and hurried into the living room. Her husband was no longer lying on the couch. Fear flashed through her mind. She immediately turned to look toward the hallway. He wasn't there. She didn't know if he had turned or if he was still human. She needed a weapon to protect her and her daughters, but she remembered leaving the fire poker in the back bedroom when she was looking out the window.

Knowing she could be heading into a trap, she made her way down the hall to retrieve it. She pushed her fear aside as she cautiously made her way to the bedroom. She peered inside. Her husband wasn't inside the room. She quickly went over to the bed and snatched the fire poker and turned to leave.

She half expected to see her husband standing there waiting for her, but there wasn't any sign of him. She quickly made her way back to the living room and saw Haley standing there pointing at the front door.

"The front door is open," she said in a frightened voice.

Sheila turned her attention to the front door. She knew it had been closed and locked moments ago. The only reasonable explanation for it was her husband had opened it and left the house. She wondered which husband it was who left. There were only two options. She looked at her daughters. "Come on. We have to get to the patrol car before it's too late."

She opened the door the rest of the way and looked outside to see if she could locate her husband. If he had turned into a zombie, she didn't want him surprising them. To her relief, she didn't see any sign of him. "Come on!" She rushed out of the house with the fire poker raised, ready to strike at anything that got too close to them.

The toxin of terror blazed through her veins, but she couldn't let it hamper her. She had to get to the patrol car and get her daughters inside before anything could happen to them. From the corner of her eye, she saw something large coming quickly toward them. She turned to look and screamed causing her daughters to crash into one another.

They both tumbled to the ground as they saw what their mother was looking at. A large lion was charging at them at full speed with its mouth wide-open, promising death. Sheila knew it could be the end, but she still needed to protect her daughters. She raised the fire poker and waited for it to attack.

If she could stand her ground, she might have a chance to kill the creature before it killed her. She doubted her chance of survival, but she had to try to survive. If the lion killed her, it would definitely kill her daughters. "Come on!" she screamed as it was almost upon her. She tightened her grip on the fire poker and waited, trying to mask the fear she felt.

Without warning, something leapt on the back of the lion and was gouging its eyes. Sheila couldn't believe what she was witnessing. Her husband was on top of the lion trying to bring it down. He looked at her and in an unrecognizable voice screamed, "Get out of here! Get our daughters to safety!"

Blinded by tears, she helped her daughters up and dragged them to the patrol car and helped them into the front seat. It was a tight fit, but she managed to get them around the computer inside the car. She turned to look at her husband. He was lying on the ground with the lion on top of him. It was ripping shreds of flesh from his face.

She fought the urge to scream and jumped into the car next to her daughters. She looked at them. "Mommy is going to get you out of here? I know you're going to ask about your father. He won't be coming with us, so please keep it together so I can get us to safety."

She looked at the ignition. The keys were dangling from it. She smiled briefly and brought the car to life. She wanted to take one last look at her husband, but she didn't. She couldn't do it. She put the car into gear and hit the accelerator. She swiftly made her way down the street. Her eyes welled with tears as she thought about her husband saving them.

Even as he turned into a zombie, he put his family first. She pushed on the accelerator and wiped away the tears streaming down her face. She watched as several people were brought to the ground by several zombies. She wasn't going to let that happen to the rest of her family. Her husband had saved them, and now she had to honor his death by making sure they survived.

She managed to leave the city limits and reach the expressway. She looked at the large sign informing her which way Chicago was located. She smiled. Chicago was exactly where she wanted to go.

ABOUT MARK CUSCO AILES

Mark Cusco Ailes is the author of several novels, including *The Day the Earth Cried* and *Zombie Park*. He currently resides in Valparaiso, Indiana and often mentions his hometown in his books. His hobbies include meeting celebrities at conventions, reading, writing, and acting. He was the drummer for the 80s heavy metal band Latem. He was an extra in the movie *Moon 44*, and he has been in several stage plays. In the eighties he designed haunted houses in Stuttgart, West Germany three years in a row and won two awards for best design. He also has done several radio and television commercials.

The Z-Day series can be found on **Amazon**.

To find more information about Mark Cusco Ailes please follow him on the social media sites below.

facebook.com/Mark-Cusco-Ailes-227676090602767

twitter.com/MarkCuscoAiles

18

BRAIN WAVES

89 Wisteria Lake Drive,
REC Games Testing and Development

Dave walked into his cubicle, reclined in his chair and grabbed the virtual reality glasses from his desk. He took the strap and looped it around his head. He was about to put the glasses over his eyes when he heard Lance's voice from behind him.

"Hey, buddy. I didn't see you come in. Are you still— wow, what happened to you?"

"I...um," Dave said, rubbing his eyes with the palms of his hands, "I was up all night talking to the cops and making a report."

"What? Why?"

"Someone broke into the house, while I was *here* last night, working late."

"Holy shit. What'd they take?"

"I don't...they just trashed the place but left the TV and the computers. They emptied my filing cabinet on the floor and basically ransacked the place. I just spent all night and all morning giving a report to the cops and cleaning up after. I'm running on caffeine fumes, pretty much."

"Wow, do you want to head to Tracy's to get a bite?"

"Nah, I have to keep working on this Kirken model before the end of the day, so I'll probably cram this thing and head home early."

"Alright, man. See ya."

"Later."

Dave felt his eyes being pushed out of his skull as if two little linebackers inside his head pushed out from the inside. He liked his job for the most part, but today he couldn't wait to leave. He pulled the VR glasses over his eyes and was thrust into a large room with bay windows which overlooked large planets with nearby hovering behemoth spacecrafts of composite steel. In front of Dave was a hovering translucent diamond. He lifted his hand and pushed on it. A section of the diamond opened and offered a selection menu.

Dave had been working for months on the Kirken project. He was part of a team which had to model a spaceship inside a game called Tesseract. His job was to model a real-world spaceship which could accommodate 12,000 colonists and crew members. Dave went through the motions and started building.

Virtual reality had catapulted the video game industry and allowed 3-D modelers to create vastly greater worlds in a fraction of the time. Dave walked through the levels on his spaceship and occasionally looked out the windows to admire the Tesseract star system—a large white dwarf in the middle with seven planets orbiting it. Dave continued down the corridor and saw something to his right that caught his eye. A large screen was posted up on the wall. *Did I model that? I'm pretty sure I didn't. Why is it even there? It serves no purpose unless Derrick put it there for some reason.*

Dave approached it, and the screen flickered on. Bright orange and yellow lights started flashing blindingly, and before Dave had a chance to remove his VR glasses, the lights turned even brighter and seemed to paralyze his movements.

Violent colors. Patterns. Smoke. Helicopter blades whirring. Deafening blasts. Casings falling to the floor. Red tissue turning inside out. Red soaked innards. Wind chimes. Visions of people running in the streets.

Dave was powerless as he watched and became aware of only what was on the screen. It was somehow meditative, like thinking of nothing else but what was being shown to him. Then he was aware of himself again as pain filled Dave's temples, and he regained his limbs and thrust the glasses off him, ripping the head strap. The headgear fell onto his desk, with bluish electrical smoke emanating from the circuits inside. Dave backed his chair up, rubbing his temples. His ears still rang from the loud wind chimes or whatever that noise was. *What the hell was that?*

"What the?"

Dave was startled again at siren noises up above—the fire alarms. A loud, bawling wail. He winced at the red strobing lights. The fluorescent lights above turned off with a mechanical jolt, prompting the emergency lights to illuminate a red ring of lights around the perimeter of the office.

"Really?" he said, dubiously.

He turned to the entrance of his cubical and saw a couple of his coworkers run across. Dave pushed himself up from his chair and caught one of his project managers by the arm.

"Jerr, what is going on? My headgear just exploded while I was working on the Kirken proj—"

"I think there was a power surge in bank three and four, I don't know, there's a fire in one of the breaker rooms. I have to deal with this," he said while backing up.

Dave looked around and saw heads popping up and down from cubicles like a whack-a-mole game. Dave looked for Lance's head, but there was none. He walked a few paces to where Lance's workstation was—Lance lay sidelong on the floor, his VR glasses still over his eyes, he twitched and convulsed on the ground.

"Lance!"

Dave threw himself on the floor—and was about to remove the VR glasses—when he noticed blood oozing from between the glasses and the skin under his eyes. Dave violently ripped off the glasses from Lance's charred face. The skin around his eyes was burnt and blistered.

"Lance...Someone help me!"

Managers and other staff rushed in Lance's cubicle, pushing Dave aside. Dave side-stepped out of the cubicle and rubbed the back of his neck. The ringing in his ears was like a thousand mosquitos buzzing around his head. The alarms didn't help either.

"Are you OK," someone said, putting their hand on his shoulder.

Dave looked up and saw another manager staring at him.

"Yeah, I'm fine. I saw some corrupted files in the Tesseract game, and then my headset blew up on me. I took it off just in time. Did someone call an ambulance for Lance?"

"They're on the way. I want someone to look at you before you go anywhere, do you understand me?"

The ringing in Dave's ear intensified, and he could barely hear what his manager was saying, "Is everyone OK?" Dave asked.

"Listen to me. Stay here. Stay here," the manager said, pointing with both his index fingers to the ground.

Dave nodded his head and sat down in a chair against a partition wall. He noticed his right leg start to fall asleep almost instantly. He lifted it slightly and kneaded his thigh until the prickling went away. He watched as paramedics and firefighters flooded the office. They brought Lance out on a stretcher. He still wasn't conscious. A paramedic approached Dave and checked his vitals and asked a myriad of questions. Dave's headache had gone down, but he still refused to go to the hospital.

Several people went to the hospital, ailments ranging from headaches to nausea to severe visual disturbances, some just shirking their duties from work. Dave opted to go home early. Outside, in the hot parking lot, Dave stopped for a second to let his body adjust to the painful sunlight hitting his eyes. He looked down at the pavement and saw only wavering hues of gray and black. He dug his hand in his jacket pocket and pulled out his sunglasses. *Well, that didn't do anything.* The temperature was in the hundreds. He could feel his shirt was soaking through. He walked slowly to his car, only lifting his head up a few times to see where he was going. Sirens wailed in the distance, the frequencies moving from high to low. They were moving away.

The car wasn't any better. He quickly turned the ignition and hot air blew directly into his face, making him instantly dizzy. Once on the freeway, the dizziness turned into almost unconsciousness. Flashing images superimposed into his vision—strange symbols he couldn't decipher, weird color gradients. *Am I tripping on acid or what?* A nervous laugh. He startled at a car honking beside him as a motorist noticed he was veering off the road. Dave grew angry at his predicament and slapped himself in the face twice, willing himself back to the real world. Dave drifted off to sleep again and woke up to a tapping on his window. A police officer. His car had gone off the road. Dave immediately noticed the automatic pistol in his holster.

34 Transection Boulevard, PosiLabs Data Center, Terra Business District

André walked to the entrance door with a knowing smile on his face. He swung open the door and greeted everyone he passed, as if he were walking out on a Friday afternoon. He was also carrying a large box in front of him. Inside the building, he pushed the button for the elevator with his free index and then decided to take the stairs, out of sheer excitement. On the second floor, he walked into the hallway. The first floor housed the thousands of servers that provided Positron Labs—the corporate giant that manufactured and designed infection deterrent equipment—their data storage, backups, and email servers. A server farm.

The second-floor housed offices that were homier and didn't have impersonal concrete walls at every corner. André smiled as his assistant approached him.

"OK, we have a problem, half our servers are updating the new firmware and the other half are picking up the slack and the temp sensors are dangerously—" she stopped in her tracks. "What's with the smile?"

"Who? Me? Just happy to be here, that's all."

"What's in the box?"

"Get the door for me will ya, Diane?"

"Sure."

She followed in behind him as he carefully put the box down on his desk.

Diane eyed the box with a crooked smile on her face, "If that's for Isaac, he's not gonna be happy. His birthday is next week, by the way."

"It's not for Isaac, it's for Larry. And his birthday is tomorrow. Keep your voice down."

"Why?" She asked, even louder. "That's a big cake," she said opening the lid. "There's not even any candles on it."

"Shhh, don't—"

As they were arguing, Larry swung the door opened and André and Diane both crowded together to hide the cake.

"Hey, Dre, there's a problem with the—"

Larry stopped mid-stream and stared at their closeness, wondering if maybe he had interrupted something.

"A problem, Larry?" André picked up where he left off.

"I...was...just saying that servers one through fourteen are really running too hot and we should adjust the cooling temp limits. Just to be sure."

"Absolutely. I'll be down there in a sec, bud."

Larry looked at them both, lowered his head and then retreated, "Yup, no problem."

The door closed.

"Well, that's great! Now he thinks were the office fuck buddies!" André said.

Diane burst out laughing.

"It's not funny, Diane," he said, laughing himself. "Keep it up, Sir Laughs-a-lot. Come and help me set this up in the conference room, please? I want to wish this son of a bitch a happy birthday."

"Wait, if this is what I think it is...do we have to do this this morning?"

André had known Larry for twenty years. They had known each other since they were kids. They had an on and off again ritual of playing pranks on each other. They had been infantrymen in the Atlas Wars and helped push back the infected masses that had almost taken out the entire world, all the while swapping each other's magazines with fake ammo and throwing flashbangs in each other's tents.

"Yes. We. Do."

They headed for the conference room, which was further down a maze of furry dull gray hallways. Diane led the way. She checked her phone, "There's an active contagion protocol going on at Anderson Heights General. That's like...ten blocks from here."

"Really?" André said, distractedly. "Hey, Susan, could you gather everyone in the conference room, please?" He asked as they passed Susan's desk.

Susan barely turned to acknowledge him, just waved her arm. Her eyes were glued to the TV mounted on the wall. Diane and André walked into the conference room and were surprised to see several staff members already there. André was the senior supervisor on duty today and was taken aback to see so many people in the room—security guards, building engineers, even the gardener was there. André put the box on the conference table and approached the crowd. They were all gathered around a large screen.

André could hear it before he saw the news anchor:

"...is on site with more. Shelly, I'm about half a block away from Anderson Heights General Hospital and police have cordoned off the area, we believe because of an MR-35 outbreak at the hospital. We have reports that several people were brought in

by ambulance from REC Games around 7:45 this morning with illnesses ranging from headaches to nausea. The hospital has very strict protocols in place for a potential viral outbreak..."

"Wow, I hope it's just a false alarm," André heard someone say.

"...ever since the San Delgado incident a year ago...there have been very strict implementations of MR-35 protocols and equipment...If you remember, Holly, the last incident was in San Galleria, and the ehhh...version of the MR-35 virus caused the...hosts... to be unaffected by trauma to the head or via gunshot. So far, this is an isolated incident with no other reports of infected in the area, but please be vigilant..."

A loud bang. Screams. The noise made everyone jump and pivot toward the noise. Larry was at the cake box André had brought in earlier.

Susan walked inside the conference room, "What in the world? Larry, why are you covered in frosting?"

Larry turned and looked at her. His eyes wide. After a few seconds, he laughed. "I don't know. I just took a knife and started cutting myself a piece and—"

André and Diane laughed. Larry noticed and started laughing with them.

Then another loud shot rang out, this time further away, but in the area.

Susan turned, "Now, what the hell was that?"

Another shot, this time close.

"That sounded like an M-80...or a gunshot," André said.

Then, mass screams emanated from below, and more loud shots.

Something inside André told him to look out the large window of the conference room. Maybe it was the way the wind pushed and pulled on the blinds, maybe the dank smell emanating from the slight breeze, maybe the way ethereal shadows glided over the glass. He pulled on the blinds and looked down, over the front courtyard—lumbering figures, dragging their feet, fifteen or sixteen that he could see.

André turned and immediately went into boss mode, "OK, I want everyone to go find a place to hide and stay there until I give the all clear, but don't rush. Susan, Diane, Larry, let's get the kit out and start handing out the gear. Jerry lock all the entrances to the front and back, please."

Everyone scrambled out of the conference room, and André rushed out to a maintenance closet down the hall. He opened the door and pulled out the Infection Emergency Kit and laid it on the floor, spilling out its contents. Susan, Larry, and Diane helped take everything out.

"Here, Susan, take these and hand them around," André said, handing out what looked like bracelets and straps. André also handed out devices called a Pendulix, which looked like a VR headset; its main purpose was to reverse the infection completely and bring the patient back to his normal sedate self. The bracelets and straps were to stop the infection from spreading if any extremities were bitten.

Diane had her phone over her ear. Her hand shook and threatened to throw the phone to the ground. "Hi, I'm calling from 34 Transection Boulevard, at the PosiLabs, there's shooting going on downstairs, please—"

More shots, this time closer, made her stop and scream, "Please help us we're on the second floor."

More shots rang out, and André felt beads of sweat on his forehead. André was part of the Emergency Preparedness Committee and still felt like this wasn't real. Maybe it was a prank. A bad one, but still a prank. Or a mock active shooter scenario. Since there was a contagion outbreak at a nearby hospital, it could have spread here. He took out all the infection garments that were used to stop the infection if anyone was bitten. He also took out a pistol and checked that it was loaded. He pulled the hammer back and made sure the safety was off.

Another shot, and Susan screamed again. It sounded closer, maybe in the stairwell. André looked down the hallway. People were scurrying left and right across the hallways.

Jessica, another employee, came running toward them, "There's more shooting coming from the rear entrance," she said, her voice quivering.

"Let's get to an office," he told Larry and Diane.

Inside the office, Diane fell to the ground, her breathing fast and uncontrolled.

André leaned toward her, "Hey, hey, hey, it's OK, they're slow and stupid, OK? We're gonna get through this. I have a gun, and Larry and I have been in this situation before. It's OK. Look at me, we're gonna be OK."

Diane managed to look up at him, her eyes running because of her makeup, "OK," she said, taking in a deep breath, "OK."

André turned to Larry, who looked through the blinds at the hallway.

"What's it like out there, Larry?"

"You're not gonna believe this one, bud," Larry said. "See for yourself."

André approached the window and parted the blinds— an infected was staggering twenty feet down the hallway, leaning against the wall, billboards and water coolers falling and trailing behind his wake, he also had a pistol in his hand. André also saw Susan standing around the corner from the infected man.

"Is that what I think it is?" André said.

"Yup, sure is," Larry replied, dabs of frosting still clinging to his chin.

Susan had her back to the wall and was sidestepping closer to the infected, who was just around the corner from her, unable to see her yet. In her arms, she held out a large obsolete piece of infected-curbing electronics equipment. It looked like a football helmet but with circuit boards attached to it and wires dangling from the sides. The device was meant to position on top of the infected's head. Two titanium plates would squeeze together due to a magnetic field and presto!

"What the hell does she think she's doing?" Larry wondered.

They watched as Susan strained from the weight of the helmet, turned the corner and, with admirable strength, managed to lift the device onto the infected's head. Susan's arms were shaking as she held up the device. A shot rang out from the gun as both Susan and the infected both fell backwards—Susan with a bullet in her stomach and the infected with grey matter spraying outwards from the helmet.

André jumped as the gunshot went off, then, he turned to Larry, "Listen, I'm gonna get Susan and bring her back here," André said.

André opened the door slightly, the sweat on his forehead stinging his eyes, and walked low into the hall only to be cut off by another infected. André's gun slid away from them as they fell to the floor. The infected wasn't rotting yet, but his eyes had a pale grey obscuring his irises. André grabbed the infected's neck and pushed up, reaching into his bag to retrieve a Pendulix—a beautiful piece of solid-state components capable of reversing the infection process in the brain. André hit the green "ON" button and placed the headset over the infected's eyes. Small, steel and coarse-threaded screws whined and drilled into the infected's temples. Electrons and positrons flowed through its metal traces like a turbulent river. The infected's eyes acted like opening floodgates, letting in powerful electricity that short-circuited the infected neurons in the host's brain.

The infected soon lost its strength and rolled off André, clutching at the entrenched headset, screaming an almost humanlike howling. The noise made André shudder. He could hear more sirens, getting closer. Infected tactical teams on the way. *About fucking time.* André heaved himself up, panting.

Susan suddenly came to mind. He approached her carefully while looking for anymore infected. She was lying on her side, facing the wall.

"Hey, Susan," he whispered.

André pulled her cautiously toward him, her mauve blouse was soaked in red.

"Oh...André...you got two messages, one's from.... —" she said, her watery eyes looking at the ceiling, avoiding looking at the blood, her words coming out quivering.

"Shhh. It's OK, I'll call them back later."

"Please take this off me!" A slurred voice shouted next to them. They both looked and saw the infected man trying, with little success, to pull off the Pendulix, blood oozing from the screws buried into his temples.

André grabbed Susan under the legs and back and carried her back to the office, being careful not to step onto painted bodies littering the floor. Sirens wailed in the background—they were here, finally.

After the infected tactical team took out the rest of the stragglers, the medical teams took Susan out on a stretcher in a black, thick plastic bag. André stood in the hallway a long time looking at nothing, then he walked up to the infected that Susan had used the skull crusher on. His nametag said VR Specialist, Dave Derickson, REC Games Developer.

ABOUT JULIEN SAINDON

Julien Saindon is a Canadian author whose debut novel, "Electronics of the Dead", was created after studying two years as an Electronics Engineering Technologist and not getting a job.

He is also a full-time paramedic who occasionally saves some folks.

Electronics of the Dead is on **Amazon**.

To find more information about Julien Saindon follow him on Facebook.

19

THE HORROR AT ROSWELL MILLS

The situation, fighting to hold North Atlanta...

P ublic Safety Director Stephan Harper had taken personal command of the North Atlanta Battle Zone. He had directed 'Captain Alice' as she was now, officially, to relocate her reinforced company to the Barrington Plantation near the Roswell Mills in Historic Roswell near the river. Harper had made his personal HQ at St. Andrews on the river, in between the two bridges. The Posse was positioned so it could reach out in several almost equidistant directions as Harper's mobile reserve.

The fight had been raging along the Chattahoochee River line and those two bottlenecks, the bridges at Highways 9 and 400.

The Georgia forces had hurriedly fortified the north shore of the 'Hootch, working well into the night. The director could hear the shooting and hollering coming from south Atlanta and it seemed the Zs were attacking in much greater numbers than had been anticipated. They were already swarming across the 285 beltway in places near the big hospital complex, and would soon be in Sandy Springs, right across the river from Roswell.

Stephan Harper meant to hold that river line and he was ruthless at a level even the Zs couldn't match. That bothered him sometimes because, otherwise, he liked to think he was a pretty nice fellow. He may have been, but he was also a fearsome warrior. Stephan Harper played for keeps.

Then, as the Zs massed on the southern side of the 'Hootch, Harper quietly asked God to forgive him, there would be no zombies, nor living humans, either on the south shore after this. He hit the clackers that detonated the Claymore directional mines on the south shore of the Chattahoochee.

Embedded as the Claymores were on wooden or metal stakes and mounted at head level, Harper had initiated the battle as soon as the creatures massed up enough to be considered a high value target. The Zs were cut to pieces but there were more, many more. Howling and raving as they raced to the river, trampling indifferently over the remains of the creatures slaughtered by the directional mines, over the anatomical mess that was their undead predecessors. The battle was on.

The director would soon need his reserves. Zombies were leaking past the defenders, moving across the river and up towards the Roswell Mills area. Many were following the Vickery nature trail, while others were pounding their fists against trees or bits of fencing that impeded them, raving insanely. They knew only hate and rage. They were monsters, but they were not heavy thinkers. They were impatient; they wanted to kill human beings.

Some of the Zs had made their way past the defenders at the 400 bridge, slaughtering human beings, some of whom reanimated. They made their way, inevitably, toward the courthouse.

These monsters would approach from the woods above Riverside Drive and then east of the Mills and waterfalls. Some of them would be wearing the uniforms of the defenders, their corpses reanimated and full of rage, shaking their fists at the heavens.

A young soldier named Evan Carlson was eviscerated by two of the infiltrators who'd made it across the 'Hootch and who howled their triumph at the sky, a dark challenge. They tore at him with their hands and teeth, and pounded him with their fists...they threw bits of him around in dark triumph. Carlson's body was destroyed to the extent that he couldn't reanimate. The bridge was held, but Carlson and his mates paid the price.

They accepted the price, even when it was their lives, and the ones that survived held that 400 Bridge.

Zombies

So where had all those leakers, those zombies, come from? Had they all come across the Chattahoochee? It seemed unlikely since that battle was still going on. But some were certainly coming across, their awkward gait and constant agonized wailing signaling their presence.

There just seemed to be too many of them...

Zombies existed in a fiery and dreadful universe of agonizing pain that no doubt contributed to their constant state of homicidal frenzy. Scripture calls it "...the agony of death." It was learned subsequently that Zs could only encompass three states of existence: murderous rage, migration, and a sort of stasis. They were later discovered to mass in dark caverns, moaning softly and maliciously, as if eagerly awaiting their chance to rend and tear the bodies of those with life still in them. It was never clear what the triggers were for these states but the boffins were certainly looking into it.

They moaned and screeched most of the time, because no matter what they were doing, it hurt. A lot.

Some were infiltrating through the wooded areas behind Riverside drive, but many of them were shot down in that sector. The humans couldn't defend it all. It was a park, and there had been simply too much foliage to clear it all. Where there were no fire lanes, many of the reanimated corpses got through undetected. Crashing through the bushes and trees made very little noise compared to the noise of all the guns and mortars.

There were Zs that had already broken through near the lower mill by the covered bridge and were headed towards the Court House where the governor had her headquarters. Nobody had thought they'd come that way.

Iraq Flashback

Several years previously, then Colonel Stephan Harper's 11th Georgia National Guard Engineers had encountered a horror in Iraq, fifty-seven kilometers from nowhere. It was often remembered by those that had seen it as the Black Asylum. Where the dead raged and shrieked in the hallways. They'd recorded what they'd seen and then blasted that obscenity into oblivion. They were, after all, engineers, and they knew how to take a building apart. They just doubled what they'd have normally used.

Sergeant Major Pete Norvel had been a special ops

regular leading a team sent to assist Harper's engineer battalion which had been out of communication for too long. Norvel was quick. He got the picture and wished he'd never been there.

Sweltering in MOPP IV gear, Norvel colluded with Harper and his second in command, Major 'Enrique Dave' Martinez to report it as a biological warfare event and quietly keep copies of the video tapes. They'd seen the dead bodies howling and screeching in that asylum. They tried to phrase it in a way that made it sound like they were not raving maniacs.

It was their duty to forward reports up the chain of command. They knew this report could come to a bad end in the obscurity land where uniformed perfumed princes cavorted obscenely with people in business suits. And so it was, the report came to a bad end, sinking into the morass of 'classified' information that is never acted upon. And that was despite the very real evidence presented in the videos and the signatures of many officers in the battalion. The Administration characterized all that as a 'Health Care Crisis, with Civil Rights Implications.'

Public Safety Director (and former Colonel) Stephan Harper liked working with people he could trust, motivated people, professionals. If they couldn't save the United States, these were people who reckoned that they were at least going to try to save the state of Georgia. That they had to because nobody else was going to do it. With Governor Vera Selvedge at the helm, a working group of dedicated individuals set out to do just that.

They could only assume that this terrible horror they'd seen in Iraq would ultimately get loose and make its way to Georgia. They were engineers and they understood just what planning for 'worst case' means.

Alice's Posse

'Captain Alice' McBride was the daughter of an officer who'd been with the 11th Engineers in Iraq. He'd briefed her thoroughly when she turned fourteen, and taught her how to use weapons and communications gear, and expect the worst. She'd been in her late teens when her father had been torn to pieces by her late grandmother, who'd died and reanimated while Alice was at the Publix supermarket. The revenant had never been seen again. Nor had Alice's mother.

Alice had formed her posse and combated the Zs where ever she could find them. She recruited much of the Posse from friends at the Roswell Academy. Others were survivors of a zombie incident, identified and contacted by her Spooks Platoon. When the newly formed Combined Ops South took a long look at her operations, she was invited to join the State Defense Forces.

'Captain Alice' had worked rigorously to integrate her "Alice's Posse" vigilante group into the Georgia State Defense Force. She was quick on her feet so the Posse was being re-branded as a fast recon company with better weaponry, better comms and an additional 'gunfighter' platoon, as Alice called her tactical guys.

She also had an escort platoon with improved comms, some engineers, and some heavy machine guns. The Spooks Platoon was smaller than the others but handled encrypted comms, intel, computers, and cyber recon.

They would henceforth be E (Recon) Company, 1st State Defense Force Battalion, Whispering Death. As commander of E Company, Alice's callsign was One Echo Six but she would soon be awarded an Honor Callsign, Vigilante Six.

They'd put the reorganization together at the Roswell Police Station across from the Court House / City Hall. That's where Sgt Major Jean-Pierre 'Pete' Norvel had joined them. He'd been directly assigned to help the Posse make the transition to the more conventional military by Public Safety Director, Stephan Harper.

They'd re-assembled at Barrington Hall but there was no rest for the weary, because Captain Alice had insisted upon numerous 'just in case' drills. She made sure the Posse could move in quickly in whole or part if required to do so and wanted them to be able to do it in the dark.

Larry Miller and some of the SDF people who recently transferred in showed the machine gun teams how to set up and map their fire lanes to set the guns to work in the dark. The Posse hadn't had any machine guns until they more or less "went legit" several weeks previously.

She'd had the Posse practice moving troops rapidly to the Roswell Mills, the Highway 9 Bridge, and the Court House. Alice knew she needed to be able to plug any gap, however unlikely.

Additionally, other State Defense Force troops had positioned two .50 caliber machine guns on the balcony at the Presbyterian Church on Atlanta Street, Highway Nine. Just above the bridge, interdicting anything or anyone coming north on Atlanta Street. That sort of fire would keep the Zs off the road but push them back towards the twisted path that led inevitably to the Roswell Mills and, ultimately, the Court House.

The Zs weren't sentient by any means, but even the undead don't like being hit by the big .50s. It's not just that it breaks them into meaty chunks, they don't understand that. It's the sounds, the tracers, the ricochets...they are wanting to kill human beings, not deal with a metallic light show that added to their pain.

At Barrington Hall

The Posse, more properly Echo (Recon) Company, 1st SDF Whispering Death, were on full stand to. They could hear and see much of the battle raging along the river line. There had been that ear-splitting bang when Director Harper tripped the Claymores, that got everyone's attention.

The bangs from the mortars and big guns told them how serious the battle had become. The star shells, flares, and spotlights were crisscrossed by tracer rounds as the machine guns opened fire. The night was lit up like a macabre Fourth of July spectacular, produced by Hammer Films. With sound effects...the continuous bangs were bad enough, but the howling...

The troopers were exhausted from relocating to Barrington Hall and then running through Alice's training exercises over and over until she felt they had a chance when it came down. The Posse could respond to break-throughs quickly in several directions and were admirably placed to do so.

Lack of sleep was weighing on everyone. They'd been up jumping around since well before daybreak and it was past midnight. But nobody could sleep with hundreds of enraged zombies racing awkwardly through the night, screaming for blood. In the dark.

Captain Alice knew that her Posse were the most experienced Z-fighters in the state at this point. People were counting on them. She hoped her troopers were not as frightened as she was...

Alice had been briefing her subordinate officers and senior NCOs, encouraging them to keep the young troopers cool. Reminding everyone of the drills they had done, to move in whatever direction they had to.

They all knew they'd be going into action soon.

Previously she'd been ordered to release any members of the Posse who were under sixteen, but she couldn't bring herself to do it if they wanted to stay. Those kids had been with her when it counted despite their youth. Alice interviewed each one and gave them the option to stand down. None chose to accept that offer. They may have been young but they knew what the stakes were in this war.

This would be a transition fight from skirmish to full-scale battle. She had felt that they deserved to have an opportunity to matter that much. Now listening to the howling, she wondered if she had made the right decision.

Captain Alice broke up her impromptu briefing and they spread out, reassuring the young troopers and keeping it upbeat. As upbeat as they could, anyway. There is nothing like going into battle against raving undead creatures in the dark to keep the happy feelings from really kicking in...

The boys and girls of Alice's Posse were feeling like their stomachs were tied up in knots. Several had actually vomited. They'd all been in small fights and skirmishes with the Zs, which were terrifying enough. But nothing like this. Everyone seemed to have to urinate, constantly. One young trooper actually sliced a hole in the leg of his black coveralls to facilitate that. Everyone seemed to pace back and forth; they checked and re-checked their weapons, some prayed...

Just a little nervous...

The tracer bullets, explosions, and flares at the river line were bad enough. Then a bright light erupted, right over head it seemed.

"What the hell was that?"

A thin voice answered, "Not a nuke or we'd be dead."

Another responded, "I'm guessing alien spacecraft, zooming in to attack the earth fighters. Or something..."

A female voice replied, "I guess all we can count on is that it sucked for us in some way!" Science fiction was big with the kids in Alice's Posse.

A heavyset young sergeant called Neatfreak walked up behind them and said, "Cut that shit out, you guys...it ain't aliens...it's bad enough without you all trying to do something you're obviously not qualified to do, which is heavy thinking! It was a flare for God's sake!"

Several blasts and more flares from the river line lit up the night. Neatfreak glared at the young trooper holding the flare gun and looking guilty.

The whole squad burst out laughing, not for long, but the spell was broken. They were back to being elite troops.

Neatfreak said, "OK, now saddle up, I'm guessing we'll be headin' down to the Mills just like we practiced, and we're fixin' to win us a battle."

The Call to Action

The calls came in from Director Harper and then Norvel. It was game on. Captain Alice issued orders to the commander of her 'Gunfighter One' platoon, Lieutenant Larry Miller. "Larry I just talked to Director Harper. I need you to get down to the Mill, kick any Zs out of there, and hold it no matter what. Don't let any more come through that mill area. Own it! We practiced that, but I'd figured we'd have the whole Posse... it just didn't seem likely we'd fight there given the terrain, but it looks like we will after all..."

Miller replied, "What forces do I have?" All the State Defense Force companies were beefed up with the militia that night and the 'odds and sods' showing up as the night wore on.

Captain Alice continued, "Take your Gunfighters and two squads of the new guys and some of my escort platoon for heavy weapons. There is a squad of roughly ten Roswell cops who know the area. Larry, this is Bobbi Hammond from the Roswell Police Department." Miller shook hands with a rather rough looking female police sergeant.

Sgt Hammond grinned at him and said, "Don't sweat it, tough guy. Some of us dames know how to get it done, just so you know."

They bumped fists.

Captain Alice continued, "You'll also have about fifty Armed Citizens, I'm not sure about their CO, seems like a blowhard, take him out if you must..."

Sgt Hammond wondered just what "take him out" might mean, glanced around at the others and got the picture. She looked carefully at Alice, "Are you sure? That's really playing hardball. But it's your call tonight."

Alice replied, "This is too serious to play games."

She turned to Miller, "Larry, I may not be able to reinforce you if you get in a fix...Uncle Jean says they're in big trouble at the Court House...The governor's HQ is at risk and he is making a stand there with a woman called Jane something...You've got to make it stop, Larry. We can't let any more get through or they will overrun the courthouse and the whole thing will fall apart. I'm counting on you."

Her 'Uncle Jean' was Sergeant Major Jean-Pierre 'Pete' Norvel. She was the only one who called him that.

She added, "If you can stop them getting past the Mill, I'll take care of the rest of them. I'm grabbing everything else and attacking in the direction of the Court House. I've got to rescue Uncle Jean. Hold tight...please don't get killed, and God bless you, Larry!" She hugged him briefly, and then chambered a round into her MP5 machine pistol.

Miller replied soberly, "Thank you, Alice. I'll hold that place until the devil gets tired of messing with me. You go on, now. And you should probably rescue the governor while you're at it!"

Alice shouted over her shoulder, "Don't worry, I will," and jumped into her Humvee.

𝄞𝄞𝄞𝄞

The Roswell Mills.

The Roswell Mills was a place of old now-renovated factory buildings that were very defensible if the attack came from the low ground, from the south. There were steep cliffs, the fast running waters of Vickery Creek below them, and excellent fields of fire.

There was a scenic nature walk culminating in a covered bridge, and next to it, the lowest level Mill building, a three-story abandoned structure with a smaller former blacksmith shop next to it. The covered bridge that was connected to the hiking trail next to the Mill structure led hikers right back to the Chattahoochee River.

To get across the fast-moving water below the Mills was not trivial although it wasn't very deep. There were several small bridges for hikers walking the scenic trails. Besides that, they'd have to come through the waters, or at the falls. Surely, they couldn't do that?

Above it all, not far from Atlanta Street (Highway 9) there was a small, trendy strip mall. And there were the construction sites where foundations were being poured for pricey new Condos...Miller's people would soon be there, putting enfilading fire on the Zs.

The Howling...

It was said that the souls of some of the mill workers haunted a sub-basement of one of the factory buildings, the one closest to the water level. It was rumored that sometimes they could be heard at night, howling and screeching for justice. The story was that they'd hidden from the Yankees but suffocated when those vandals had set fire to the mill. Others said the Yankees had merely abducted them, taking them up North. Regardless, they were never seen again.

It was fun to include the 'howling sub-basement' on the "Haunted Roswell" tour. Nobody really believed there was such a sub-basement since it had never been found. No one had ever been able to get a decent tape of the howling, but it was all in good fun. Right?

Most thought it to be the breeze amplified by some pipes or cavities in the brick work. Although there were some who noted that the howling began about the time the first Zs were engaged in Georgia. One of those who picked up on that was Sergeant Bobbi Hammond of the Roswell Police. Her superiors advised her to keep quiet about it but to watch the Mill carefully for threats.

*They had been there so long...they'd gradually melted into each
other, dead and together.*

They'd tried to elude the Yankees, by hiding in the sub-
basement. It was almost airtight and no light made its way
into that vaulted chamber. It was impossible to stand
upright in that noxious, cobwebbed space. They'd been
careful to make no sound. Most people had forgotten about
the sub-basement because it wasn't really used much by
then but one foreman knew it was there and the invaders
never noticed.

The Yankees burned the Mills and carried off all the
men and women who worked there, everyone they could
find, into a dark captivity from which many never returned.
It wasn't until the next century that anyone tried to track the
people in the sub-basement. Could they all have died in
captivity? Wouldn't their names have been noted somewhere? They were simply listed as missing. Considering the
thousands who perished in the battles for Atlanta, this was
not considered a huge deal. Not until much later.

The thirty or so human beings in the sub-basement
were killed partly by smoke inhalation. There wasn't much
oxygen in there but, after most had died, there was just
enough left for the others. The upper part of the mill had
collapsed in the fire so there was no way out. Those few who
survived the smoke starved to death in the total darkness.
Or at least, that was the assumption, though some suspected
they'd found other food...

In the end, no matter how they prolonged it, starvation
was a hard way to die. They, like the others, had slowly, very
slowly, decomposed in the almost airtight chamber. The
decompositional fluids ran into each other until it was as if

the sub-basement contained but one corpse, a blasphemous mingling of tightly packed dead bodies and body parts that had been partially consumed in the darkness...

There were rats there, too, joined in the end, to the dreadful amalgamation of the dead.

Then one terrible day, the dead rose everywhere and challenged the living for mastery of the planet. The nasty mess in the sub-basement had stirred before, but now it began to shriek, the many voices echoing off the stone walls. Whatever it had become, it was in agony, it was angry and it was hungry.

The thing in the sub-basement was quite insane, raving and howling. The sound of all the gunfire had set it into a frenzy while drowning out most of the shrieking in the sub-basement. This thing or things...their murderous desires almost destroyed them. They smashed and broke their hands and sometimes their heads trying to break through the stairwell, the stairwell that had been blocked for so many years.

Larry Miller takes command of the fighting group.

Lieutenant Larry Miller was a cocky young officer, and he backed it up with an instinctive competence. Handling troops seemed second nature to him. Miller was one of those naturals, he had an eye for terrain and he always seemed to mass his forces where the main threat was. He actually liked to fight. He dressed the part, instead of black coveralls he wore black jeans and a dark blue cavalry shirt with a double row of buttons. He sported a red kerchief around his neck but tied it around his blond hair in battle so his people could recognize him instantly.

Miller routinely wore his issue forage cap at a jaunty angle and swaggered a bit. He understood that somehow his gunfighter platoon appreciated that. This fight was too serious for officers who were not one hundred percent convinced they could get it done. The boys and girls in his Gunfighter One platoon knew that "Hollywood Larry" would get it done. This was to be the night he was put to his greatest test.

So far in his fights against the zombies, Miller had seen only two of his own people die in the fighting. It had nearly destroyed him. He'd had to put one of his people down as she started to reanimate.

Miller sucked it up, barely. That was when he and Captain Alice had bonded at a personal level, not as he had originally wished, as lovers, but as brother and sister. Somehow, she handled casualties better than he did. Alice taught him to deal with it.

She never told him how she stored it up for later, and then fell apart...

The Briefing

Lieutenant Larry Miller of the reinforced Gunfighter One Platoon gathered his squad leaders for a quick briefing. There were two squads from the new Gunfighter Three platoon that Harper had assigned to them.

He prudently included Dasher Samuels of the Armed Citizens and Bobbi Hammonds of the Roswell Police Department. Even combined with a small group from Captain Alice's HQ escort, Miller didn't really have close to enough people to hold the whole Roswell Mills bottleneck. At least, not in theory.

Miller looked at it realistically. He reckoned his reinforced platoon was the size of a small company, but that wasn't enough troops to defend the Mills the way he'd like to or how the book said he ought to.

So the alternative was to defend the Mills the way that seemed best to him with what he had. The fact that Miller had an almost magical gift for putting his people where they could do the most good was one of the reasons he was on a fast track for promotion.

But first, they'd have to destroy the zombies that had made the climb to the top, or found the path. He told them how he wanted it done.

𝕂𝕩𝕩𝕩𝕩𝕩

The Armed Citizens Militia Company under Dasher Samuels.

They were mostly in civvy dress or hunter camo with military harness, the khaki battle jackets would come later. These were the men and women of the Armed Citizens Militia. Their company commander, Dasher Samuels, was already in a bad mood. Larry Miller, the battle group commander, had scattered his men, marrying them to the much overrated (in Samuels's mind) Posse. He'd expected to be working directly with the well-known Captain Alice, but no. She assigned his Armed Citizens Company to report to a young blond-haired officer who looked like a child to Samuels.

His first words to Miller were, "Why are you wearing that ridiculous costume instead of a uniform?" Larry Miller affected a dark blue cavalry shirt with two rows of silver buttons. For those who had worked with him before the red scarf tied around his head said that Miller was in battle mode.

Dasher Samuels didn't know it yet, but Larry Miller was the most dangerous man he'd ever met. Miller looked him in the eye and said quietly, "Don't you even consider fucking with me. Ever..."

Dasher felt like someone had walked over his grave. He thought, "Alright, for now...but we'll talk again."

Samuels had a single platoon of his people with him. His other two platoons, much to his chagrin, were backing up the State Defense Force and police in locations designated by Lieutenant Miller. It didn't dawn on him that Miller was spacing them around his machine guns and more experienced troopers for their sake as much as for the defense. Fighting zombies in the dark can be traumatic, particularly the first time around.

As he put together the enfilading fire the way he wanted, Miller knew he could hold the Mills against anything the Zs were apt to throw at him. Alice had given him two squads of the new troopers from the State Defense Force. They were experienced in using machine guns, unlike most of the Posse. Miller had an eye for it; he put them where they could do the most good.

Dasher Samuels, however, reckoned Miller was a pipsqueak and he'd have to take over when the young officer got hysterical. The guy was a bit creepy though...he remembered Miller's wide, almost hopeful eyes, when he'd issued his threat.

Dasher fancied himself as a historian of the Roswell area. There are many useful records and documents to research, and the Roswell Courthouse was the place to go for that. After going over the original blueprints for all the long factory looking buildings usually just called 'the Mills,' he began to believe there was a sub-basement in one of them, and that he would find it.

It had started with a yellowing letter found in an old box in his attic. His ancestor, Edwin Dasher had mentioned something almost illegible about a sub-basement in the lower mill building near the water line, where the workshops had been located. Apparently, they'd kept spare belts for the machines there.

It would have to be in the Mill closest to the water, the first in the contour that went up two more levels, and yet another to the upscale strip mall next to Atlanta Street. Prior to the dead rising, Dasher Samuels had been certain he'd become a well-known historian if he could just expose the sub-basement, and whatever might be in it. He'd begun to suspect there might be a cover up of some kind.

The truth was, the sub-basement was already part of the 'Haunted Roswell' tour. He'd somehow missed that, yet thought himself a clever fellow. If he had actually been as clever as he thought he was, he might have asked himself why nobody ever got around to opening that sub-basement, to find out what caused the howling.

And that lower Mill building was just where that self-important boy lieutenant had sent him and a squad of Alice's Posse, the State Defense Force people. And some cops...What was worse, he was supposed to let some weirdo called Neatfreak have tactical command, yet the guy was only a sergeant! They apparently had no concept of seniority in the Posse.

🏃🏃🏃🏃🏃🏃

Neatfreak.

Miller, as the senior lieutenant under Alice, had as his platoon sergeant a rather strange sort of young fellow named Albert Nolan. Everyone called him 'Neatfreak', despite the fact that he was neither obsessively neat nor particularly sloppy. It happened, that's all anyone knew.

Sergeant Nolan had been a student at the same private academy as many of the Posse. His father, like theirs, had been with the 11th Engineers in Iraq. His dad had been a sergeant and, like his dad, the younger Nolan was a bit more deep south than the rest. He had broad shoulders and kept himself fit but he was something of a geek in jock's clothing. On wireless transmissions, he sounded like an air traffic controller, all of whom, worldwide, are apparently required to speak in a lazy southern drawl.

He was a Georgia boy but when not hunting or shooting with his Dad, Nolan had spent a lot of time staring at computer screens. Because of that, he'd narrowly avoided being assigned to the 'Spooks' platoon. Alice once described him as a 'warrior nerd.'

Nolan had been in many of the early fights, when the Posse was still a vigilante gang. People seemed to respect him and gravitate toward him in battle, but even in the early days he was considered just a bit 'off.' He was a fighter though, and there is a season for that, which was why he was a sergeant now, leading Miller's most important fighting group.

He'd be the point of the spear since he'd have to drive his troops, which included attached militia and police, right down the middle to break through the Zs on the Heights and the Mill Complex. Neatfreak was told then to keep moving and make his way down to the lowest level mill structure and put fire right in their faces.

Sergeant Nolan was offbeat but he took a perverse satisfaction in fighting the Zs. He liked these orders. He knew he'd been chosen to lead the attack because he was Miller's most aggressive fighter and he took pride in that. His eyes were wide, maybe too wide, and the look on his face was chilling. "I'll do that; I'll shoot their faces right off!" Neatfreak snickered inappropriately, and noticing the strange look on Miller's face, said, "It's OK Larry...I'll get it done."

Larry often suspected that fighting Zs had weirded the guy out or tipped him over some edge where he now lived in his own dark reality.

Miller nodded but thought of an old movie, a Dracula flick with a maniac called Renfield...well *his* Renfield could motivate soldiers and shoot like a pro and that was enough for Larry Miller tonight. It had to be.

Miller told him to occupy and defend the Mill building and take the foot bridge back from the Zs. He assigned two engineers from Alice's HQ group to blow it up as soon as they could. The Posse still lacked a lot of the fancy gear they'd have later, but the engineers did have C4 explosives and Det Cord.

Neatfreak looked up at Larry Miller whose face reflected his concern, then laughed again, a sly sort of chuckle as if he knew something nobody else could know. Miller caught an unusual hint of sadness in Neatfreak, and then it was gone.

Neatfreak led his people to the jump off positions. Miller's other fighting groups covered the flanks and began to move, as Neatfreak led his people down toward the factory buildings and, later, the basements and the three stories of the Mill closest to the water. He looked up over his shoulder at Miller, "I'll take care of it, Larry...no worries." His people moved off with rifles tucked into the shoulders

Miller knew he could trust Neatfreak in a fight, but he was under no illusions that the fellow was sane. In the days of the Z-War, sanity was considered 'nice to have' for leaders but not an absolute requirement in most cases.

It got really crazy later on.

Storming the Roswell Mills.

Lieutenant Miller's violent attack reclaimed the Mills for humanity. It cost him several of his command and one had to be put down. He stored that information somewhere out of sight, he couldn't consider that with troopers that were still alive counting on him. He knew most of his people and that just made it harder.

His troopers exterminated the zombies that had climbed the cliffs to the Mills, in a series of terrifying encounters with the monsters in the darkness. Twice it had come to close combat and both times the humans were torn to pieces. Knives, tomahawks, it just wasn't enough to stop them. The Zs were so frantic, so strong, that even a few stragglers were a serious threat. Nobody wanted to face the Zs up close and personal.

The State Defense Force people from Alice's Posse soon put an end to the last few zombies on the Heights. They had devised a shooting drill that was already being taught to new recruits called 'destructive decapitation.' These were not movie zombies, they took a lot of killing; shooting their heads to bits worked consistently.

The SDF used the locally produced Kalashnikov knock off called the GK-47 rifle which had a very useful double tap capability, thanks to some Polish engineers. Two or three pulls of the trigger would put twice that many properly aimed shots into the thing's head. One more pull as you run past it and the head is pretty much gone. An advantage of this technique was that it resolved any doubts your comrades might have upon seeing the neutralized zombie.

Not that many zombies had climbed to the Heights but they took some killing. Neatfreak's fighting group tore through the center of the Mills, with the other teams coming in from the left and right. They cleared the factory buildings and rapidly turned the complex into a fortress.

𝕶𝕴𝕶𝕴𝕴𝕴𝕴

The fight for the lower Mill and covered bridge.

While Miller was turning the Mills on the Heights into a fortress, Neatfreak continued his advance and took possession of the lowest level buildings and the covered bridge at Vickery Creek below the Mills. Sgt Bobbi Hammond's Roswell Police were shared out among his fire teams as guides.

Hammond herself commanded the mixed fire team that cleared the Blacksmith's shop where a fast zombie jumped one of her men and slaughtered him. The other Z coming at them was crippled apparently, weaving back and forth, staggering but still screaming for blood. Hammond's troopers put them both down, sorrowfully adding a bullet in the head for their own man. They prepared to defend Neatfreak's left flank.

The fight for the covered bridge was short and dreadful. The humans won, if that mess on the bridge could be called winning.

One of the kids from the original posse lost her nerve and fled. Her friend Lilly had raced onto the bridge, firing from the hip. She'd been butchered so fast that none of them could even aim their weapons and get a shot off in time to help her.

From eighteen-year-old Gwen's surprisingly literate written court-martial testimony:

"It seemed like there was a brief pause in the fighting that seemed to stretch out in time. This reeking, stinking creature took

a long horrible look at me. Like it was figuring out the best way to
kill me. It seemed to sniff the air, as if its stench hadn't already
overwhelmed the smells of springtime in Roswell Georgia. I
couldn't smell anything but death. It glanced down at Lilly who
had begun to reanimate then looked back at me and seemed to
force its lips into this wicked, awful grin.

   That was more than I could take.

   I was young and fit. It hadn't eaten any of my body or even
bit me, yet the blood around its mouth...the sheer ferocity of its
presence. It had consumed my courage; it dined on the parts of me
that mattered. There was nothing left.

   I threw my gun at the thing and ran like hell! I ran away and
abandoned my friends..."

   She was one of the first, but certainly not the last, of the
psychiatric casualties that were to almost overwhelm the
Georgia medical resources. Her name was Gwen Lipton and
she was treated leniently and medicated heavily. She'd
hoped she'd be executed for desertion...she was eaten up
with guilt. No one condemned her so she killed herself
several weeks later. She'd obtained a grenade, armed it, and
put up beside her head to blast out the bad memories.

   Slightly east of the bridge was a three-story brick Mill
building which was quickly occupied and turned into a
strong point. There were troopers, cops, and militia with
assault rifles, all the Mill shutters were kicked open without
ceremony. They believed they could hold this building.

   The soldiers didn't know about the sub-basement but
Dasher Samuels did.

Holding the Heights.

   As Neatfreak's people made their way down to the

covered bridge, Miller's other groups positioned themselves on the Heights and in the factory buildings that had composed most of the original Roswell Mills. The place was a natural fortress. They began shooting at the tangled masses of Zs loping along far below them in their jerky, malicious haste.

Larry Miller had vowed that no more zombies would come through the bottleneck that was the area of the Roswell Mills and he'd planned his defensives appropriately.

Once he had his people positioned the way he wanted, Miller unleashed hell on the zombies below them, exploiting the cliff-like terrain. He didn't have any mortars so he improvised, first with a volley of grenades, thirty of them all at once. Then his troopers shot flares into the night sky and his machine guns began to rip the darkness, punching tracer rounds into the startled creatures, taking them down, tearing them apart.

'Hollywood Larry' had held the Mills, and stymied the advance of any more Zs towards the Court House from there. He had somehow set up a fortress where the cliffs dominated but curved back to the north following the water line. So he had multiple enfilading fires going on from well-placed but often panicked shooters. Miller lucked out, only two friendly fire casualties so far and one of those had managed to shoot himself in the foot. Neither were fatal.

It wasn't over, though, as more zombies were making their way toward the Mills and the areas east of the Mills as well. Miller got busy assuring his troopers and the attached militia were re-supplied with ammo. His machine guns fired short bursts where the Zs blundered into each other or stumbled around the water's edge, trying to get at the humans who were putting all that fire on them. It just went on and on.

⚔⚔⚔⚔⚔⚔

Opening the Cellar.

Once Miller's hail of enfilading fire had ensured the initial threat had been repulsed, Sergeant Albert Nolan (Neatfreak) had left his post on the second floor of the Mill where he'd been directing fires. He'd gone outside the building to inspect the troopers and militia screening the three-story brick edifice and the nearby blacksmith shop. He checked the fields of fire of his two machines guns and made sure the gunners were chilled out enough to continue and ready to keep getting it done. Neatfreak and his men were on edge, they could hear the Zs howling as they approached the Mills.

They'd cleared the covered bridge and then blown it up keeping the Zs from massing below the Mills under cover of the cliffs. But they knew the waters were not really all that deep.

⚔⚔⚔⚔⚔⚔

Searching for the cellar of madness.

Somehow Dasher Samuels was able to corral the two young engineers who had taken down the bridge and gave them orders. He was a captain in the Citizens Militia and 40 years old. They were under aged troopers from Alice's Posse. So when he told them where to place the charges they did what he demanded.

"Sir, you need to evacuate the building before we set this off." Most of the troopers, some of the militia and one of the engineers on the first floor were already leaving in a hurry.

"Shut up and do as you're told, damn you!"

Neatfreak heard a sharp blast and felt the concussion slam up into his boots. A lot of dust and fragments blew out the windows of the Mill nearest to where the footbridge had been.

Then he heard a bestial shriek coming from that very factory building near the water. There was an undertone that sounded almost like a series of roars, of guttural off-key attempts to howl. The ground seemed to shake, like a big truck was pounding the pavement with a full load on.

Bobbi Hammonds came running up with two of her policemen. They were carrying AR style carbines; she had come with a squad of ten from North Atlanta Tactical, to stiffen the militia. Hammonds was well known for having nerves of steel but at that moment she looked terrified, she murmured, "No...what have they done?"

They heard a series of screams, then a couple dozen disheveled young soldiers ran out of the Mill. Many had lost their weapons and were hollering and throwing away their equipment, the better to run.

🏃🏃🏃

Confrontation with horror.

In the sub-basement, the thing was in a frenzy, all the shooting, the live human beings so near...it tore itself into several components, the largest attacking the stairwell exit in a self-destructive rage, breaking off parts of itself, smashing at the masonry and roaring at the humans above.

Then, the world exploded. The stairwell entrance and much of the surrounding stone flooring was blasted into jagged pieces that shot downward and obliterated the creature that had been trying to break in. Fragments struck the other horrors but only enraged them that much more. A militia man had fallen through the floor and they savaged him. His was a dreadful death, but mercifully quick. There was nowhere near enough left of him to reanimate.

Several more militia men were injured by the explosion but Dasher Samuels seemed invulnerable and stood in front of the blasted stairwell in mad triumph. Part of the creature came staggering up the rubble-strewn stairwell, apparently composed of elements of at least four partly decomposed human bodies and a rat. One of the bodies appeared to have been partially consumed, one of the heads was pointed in the wrong direction yet it howled in its rage. Greasy bits of it were sloughing off, the organic connections between the corpses was thin in places. It was growling and one head was angrily making hooting noises. The rat screeched angrily.

The thing slammed Samuels out of the way with a casual sweep of one of its many arms, then fell upon one of the injured soldiers, tearing him into pieces quickly with its numerous arms and mouths. The other soldier was desperately crawling away, trying to ignore his broken legs in his fear.

More soldiers were streaming down from the upper floors and the creature tore through them like a threshing machine. The second monster began to clumsily attempt to climb the stairs, its legs were backwards, pointing in several directions, but its rage was very real, and it shrieked in several voices. It kept stumbling and falling back down the stairway.

Dasher Samuels crawled to an open window and threw himself out, into the night. He didn't run far before he bumped straight into Neatfreak and Bobbi Hammond, both of whom seemed all too glad to see him. He quickly realized that was not a good thing.

Neatfreak said, "There are still men in there. Get moving."

Samuels replied, "No you don't, that's my redemption in there. Proof of a monstrous cover up."

Bobbi Hammond interjected, "You asshole, of course, we knew about this. We just kept it quiet because there were already enough threats. But you had to go and open it up." She swung her rifle into his face expertly and broke his nose, driving him to his knees.

Neatfreak grabbed him by the back of his neck and shouted, "Now we're going to go talk to your favorite monster!" He pushed Samuels back into the first floor of the Mill where the creature was ripping the bodies apart in a crazed search for what it could never have.

He kicked Samuels, who fell in front of the creature. Samuels looked up, beseechingly, and begged, "Don't hurt me! I freed you! You can have all of these..." He waved he arm around.

The monster rapidly dismembered him, pieces flying in all directions. Justice had been served, it was time to fight.

Neatfreak quickly emptied his GK into the thing while Hammond and her two pals dumped a magazine each from their ARs. Then Neatfreak screamed, "Not tonight, bastard!" and went after the freak with his bayonet, stabbing first this body, then that head, stabbing in a frenzy until the thing stopped squirming.

Sgt Bobbi Hammond walked over to the gore stained Neatfreak and said quietly, "Albert, I've never seen anything like that."

He looked at her sadly, and just couldn't think of anything to say.

One of the engineers came running up, "I've still got some C4, maybe we can get it down there and end this."

Neatfreak told him, "Make a package, think World War II bunker buster."

Hammond told her two guys to keep shooting up the thing on the stairs, then pulled over Neatfreak and said quietly, "It got you, didn't it?"

He looked at her carefully and said, "Yeah...yeah, it did. So I'll take that bomb down there and put it in their lap. I hope you understand, I think you do, and that matters to me."

She hugged him and said, "Yeah. I get it, you big lug. *Vaya con Dios,* my friend. We'll make it count."

Four of them expended full magazines, chopping up the creature on the steps and driving it to the floor of the subbasement. Neatfreak used it as a cushion and jumped on it and fell greasily into the still squirming monster. He tossed the bomb into the center of the room and waited as the other creature made its way toward him, slobbering expectantly and making disgusting grunting sounds. He could feel dead fingers groping at him. Then the bomb went off.

Sgt Hammond took command and was reorganizing the defense when a young officer with a red scarf tied around his head approached and demanded, "My God Bobbi, what happened here?"

She looked around at Lieutenant Miller and said, "I fucked up. I should have shot that son of a bitch the first time he opened his mouth..."

Captain Alice, with the rest of the Posse, caught the Zs that were swarming over the Court House and put them down. The governor had been injured by shrapnel from ricochets hitting the marble railings but would be all right.

Alice saw her Uncle Jean with a smoking gun in one hand and his other arm around a slender woman in civilian clothes who was holding an assault rifle and leaning into him. She looked like she was trying to hold off going into shock.

North Atlanta would hold. The war would go on.

The new reality was this: The zombies had only to win once. Humanity had to win every time.

ABOUT MICHAEL PEIRCE

Mike has been a musician and songwriter as well as a soldier in an African War and private security agent. His "Red Dirt Zombies" trilogy started life as a musical and draws on his experiences in those other areas. The TV show "The Walking Dead" shows the consequences of losing the war against the Zs. Peirce's books focus on the consequences of winning.

The Red Dirt Zombies series can be found at **Amazon**

To find more information about Michael Peirce please follow him on the social media sites below.

 facebook.com/MikePeirceAuthor
twitter.com/MPeirceAuthor

20

THE FESTIVAL

Fredrick
October 31st 2070
Reykjavík, Iceland.

Recoiling back from the sharpening stone, Fredrick puts his finger in his mouth. A droplet of crimson thick blood drips from his finger onto his black Motorhead t-shirt as he lifts his left hand to his face. A sigh of fatigued frustration escapes his nose as his shoulders sag with the weight of all his problems continuing to mount upon him. His heart was not in it this Hallow's Eve. It is merely three hours until the ritual siren is sounded, and then after that, an hour until Halloween festival officially begins. He hasn't even got his blades sharpened. This year was to be a year of broken records. He had planned out his route and his tactics the morning after the festival last year. Printed on A3 card, it was pinned to the cork board in his workshop. The planned route through the streets were in blue, plotting the most concentrated points, he could circle from behind, taking out as many rotters as he could without drawing attention. The red plot was the backup or alternative route. There were more red lines on the map than blue, because he had taken almost every scenario for variation and anomalies in the plan into consideration. He knew that any shift in the numbers could throw a plan off kilter, so planning for the worst was the best sort of strategy. He decided to go for blades this year instead of firearms for more points! He had lost out last year in his regional group scoreboard because of lack of proximity. Fredrick was convinced that bunkering from the vantage point of height would give him more visibility, and therefore allow him to make much more kills, without the threat of moving or attack. Unfortunately, the number of kills did not outweigh the penalties he incurred, thus averaging his score to much less than predicted. He incurred penalties and handicaps for using firearms, for killing from under the distance considered "sniping." Other penalties were for the lack of movement, lack of risk factor, use of "safe zone" and lack of originality. He was not going to make the same mistake this year. He had been training hard, every evening and most of each weekend, in hand to hand combat, Jujitsu, aikido, boxing and mixed martial arts. He had practiced with polearms, staves, swords, and even axes. He had devoted himself to the festival, so much so that he had neglected the other important part of his life.

Marta.

They were supposed to celebrate their three-year anniversary after the festival. They met while part of a murder bus tour. Both of them sat on the back seat, using the assault rifles, taking turns to dispose of the things that moved after the festival had ended. It was love at first sight. Both were avid campaigners for the festival, championing its effectiveness for the Icelandic culture, helping to keep crime to its lowest level in history. Boosting the economy with the thanks of tourism, weapon sales, and the advantages towards the rehabilitation laws, by allowing prisoner involvement.

Fredrick had based the plan on a two-man strategy. They would tackle the festival as a couple, side by side! What could be more romantic than slaying zombies together, side by side, on the country's greatest evening? The plan was now revised to a solo one. His obsession had overtaken his life. Marta called his desire to win "an illness". Fredrick knew she was wrong so he continued on with his plan. As much as he loved her, choosing between Marta and the Festival was an easy decision. Maybe he was sick? Maybe this was an unhealthy obsession? Who knows, who fucking cares! This was the greatest thing to happen to him. He was the 2nd generation of survivors, the Generation of Recovery they called it, the second baby boomer wave.

Fifty years ago, an altered and mutated infection spread. Global population plummeted by 60% in the first week, by various sources. Even more the week after. War against each other was put aside and a united front was established against the enemy. The mainland was wiped clean first. Overpopulation and lack of resources and defenses were the fuel to the fire. Island countries managed to survive without effect for a long while. Iceland being the best case.

After the war of the dead had been declared a victory, the rebuild began. Countries banded together to help each other, a united nation was in effect. Public holidays were no longer a thing, however. People no longer felt the need to celebrate public holidays that reminded them of the world that no longer existed. Even more so, religious holidays were discarded. Christmas, Hanukkah, Ramadan, Easter, all were done away with. Except for Halloween. A holiday that was reimagined as a celebration, a day of victory. The war was officially declared over on October 31st. So each year, Iceland, who had emerged as the global superpower, celebrate Halloween and Z-Day with "The Ritual and the Festival."

The Ritual is a time of reflection. Both for mourning and celebrating the lives of those about to give their last gift. When the body dies, it re-animates, no matter the cause of death, unless decapitation occurs. Therefore, when someone dies, instead of organ donation, which is no longer possible, people sign over body donations to the festival. The newly raised corpse is kept in storage until the festival, when they are released into the streets of a fortified Reykjavik on Halloween evening. The Ritual is the time the competitors and the families thank the deceased for their sacrifice and gift. The people's lives are celebrated. The deceased are fondly remembered before they are slaughtered for public amusement. During the Ritual, families share fond memories of their deceased loved ones, pictures, videos, stories, artwork, whatever. People come together and give the dead a final send-off. Before the ultimate, permanent send-off.

After the Icelandic prime minister gives her speech, the Festival horn is sounded and the competitors leave the church on the hill to make their way down into the city itself. Most people enjoy the sprint from the top of the hill to the safe zone at the bottom, where highlights are shown on projector screens, along with food stalls, entertainers and a final firework show to signal the end of the Festival. The other participants compete in a point-scoring system. All things are allowed to dispose of the dead, apart from explosives or intentional damage to buildings in the area. Drones record the entire event for spectators all around the world and for the lucky few who have tickets to attend the fan zone stands. A series of glass-bottomed zeppelins circle the city at a low altitude.

Points are awarded for originality, proximity, and brutality. Fredrick's brother, Hans, was once awarded the Brutality medal after he accumulated a personal best of 25 kills with modified electric sledgehammers. Wielding one in each hand, he crushed the skulls of a small berserks pack he was cornered by early on in the evening. Fredrick desired nothing more than winning the Holy Trinity, a special award for showing outstanding skill in each of the three categories.

Snori
October 31st 2070
Keflavik, Iceland.

Snori wrapped his gloved fingers around the icy and frozen door of the armoured, reinforced Ford transit van. The rear door cracked open and creaked as the old rusted hinges slid against an equally eroded door. The sound awoke the cattle inside the inner cage. The moans and splutters grew loud and acted in a form of call and response as the fresh and new deadstock moaned and called in guttural chokes. The Ketch-All pole that Snori gripped tightly with his other hand slid into a lock on the door's interior, securing the recently deceased in place. Pulling another shorter baton from the toolbox in front of the interior iron grating, Snori pressed on the middle button and watched the blue sparks zap and crack from the tip. He knocked the side of the cage, getting the attention of the once human cattle inside. Once they had locked eyes on him, he gave the button another squeeze. The blue sparks cracked and snapped in front of his face for a short time, then he pressed them into a coil of wire.

The coil conducted the electric spike through the line, causing an immediate yell from the vans current unhappy, yet now docile, occupants. An eerie silence fell as Snori touched the end of the cattle prod to the wire once more. The deadstock all fell silent before the spark touched. Snore nodded his head with pride and power, acknowledging to the infected that this was the correct response and that they had behaved, meaning no shock would be administered. He viewed them like trained rats or dogs.

The newly acquired infected woman still stood, attached to the Ketch-All pole. The wire was tight around her neck, holding her in position, as the pole itself was locked in place. She was once an 85 year-old woman, a mother of five, grandmother of twelve children, and great-grandmother to another eleven. Her husband had passed away the year before and, like him, she had signed her body over to the festival upon her death. The sum received in return would cover both a funeral cost and help substantially toward other financial requirements of her family.

The Icelandic government had signed a trade agreement with Skogarcorp, giving all control of the festival to them. This included preparation, acquisition, sponsorship, and clean-up. This resulted in aiding the Icelandic tourism trade from the other major cities left in the new world and also generating extra revenue for Iceland, without any cost to the people. Snori was one of the original Skogarcorp employees. His pest control business was bought out by them nearly 10 years ago. The pay-out was substantial enough to retire in his sixties, but Snori enjoyed his work, even more so since the infection had spread. The pandemic was big business for him.

Before Skogarcorp had risen to power and helped develop vaccines and anti-venoms for the virus, people did not understand why those who died from infection were reanimating and walking again. The fear was that the virus was spread by vermin, similar to the black death plague hundreds of years before. This, of course, was Snori's meal ticket, his open doorway to fortune, wealth, and value. No longer a low paid exterminator, he became a leader in his field, called upon for advice, services, and contracted every day of the week. Once the infection had spread, the virus reached the shores of Iceland. Thanks to pre-emptive measures, it was quickly quelled. Snori's company was leading the charge in safeguarding the citizens. Once the dead began to rise, however, the game had changed. Skogarcorp bought Snori's company and Snori went into the people business. Initially implementing methods that were used to kill rabid and feral animals, this cleared buildings and outbreak zones effectively. However, after the Festival was pitched at a Skogarcorp board meeting and accepted by the Icelandic government, Snori's tactics had to change. The aim was no longer to kill and dispose of the undead, but to capture them instead.

The first few years were difficult, reacting to quick response calls from a designated emergency line. Snori used to joke that he felt like the Ghostbusters, he just needed silly uniforms and Bill Murray.

The daily grind got a lot easier as time went on. Another government sponsored initiative was introduced, "The Death Contract." The arrangement was similar to an organ or blood donor card. The body of the deceased would be taken by Skogarcorp and contained until the annual festival season. The donor's family would receive a large financial payout upon delivery of the body. Certain safety measures were taken and, once the donor neared the end of their life, they were placed into a straitjacket-like apparatus and euthanasia was performed. This consisted of a cocktail of fatal drugs and tranquilizers to aid the capture and removal of the body after reanimation. Snori liked to stay on the front lines. He was good at his job, very good. So much so that he had been training new recruits in the art of acquisition. Today was a call out like any other, but he would let the apprentice take a shot at the caging.

Fredrick
Reykyvick
31st October

His personal best stood at only 12 so far, but he was aiming for 50 this evening. He had all his gear sorted. His armour was modified Kevlar with arm, shin, thigh and shoulder guards. His mask was fashioned to resemble a fencing guard from the Olympics, with the mesh grill on the front spray-painted with the Icelandic flag. His weapon design was something of beauty, he thought. He had dismantled a circular saw, and modified the blade to be a serrated disk. The motor from the saw was mounted on a backpack which held a battery generator with six hours of turning power. He had created a frame that wrapped around his right arm, wires and coils tucked on the inside of the skeletal structure out of harm's way. The trigger was a simple squeeze trigger. Once he tightened his fist, the circular blade would turn at blistering speed.

His right arm had a similar structure, an exoskeleton encasing his arm up to his wrist. Instead of a saw on his hand, however, he had a simple metal spike taken from a jackhammer, the type used for cracking concrete. Like the saw, he had attached the motor to the backpack he carried. This was an invention Fredrick was particularly proud of. The motor had been modified and overclocked to work at three times its speed. The piston coils had been stretched and extended so that instead of vibrating forward and back a matter of inches, it now extended fully, a total of two feet, when the trigger was pulled. It was this that he was just finishing on the sharpening stone when he cut himself.

Lifting the backpack up, he shuffled it onto his shoulder. Slipping his arm into the armoured cage, he reached towards the trigger. It was heavier than he had planned but he could still move around without too much trouble. He would not be running anywhere but he could still move, which is important.

Moving over to the practice dummy manikin, Fredrick held his fist out towards the dummy's head, about two feet away from it, and pressed down on the red button. The chisel style pointed blade shot out in front of him with the force of a shotgun, kicking his shoulder back, but he remained on his feet. The metallic stake had not only exploded the head but had imbedded itself into the wall behind it.

Taking his finger off the button, the spike did not return until he put on foot on the wall, pushed back and finally freed it. It had worked! Fredrick screamed with joy! Dancing and jumping with pure excitement and glee, he called to Marta over and over before the reality returned. She was gone. She had left him weeks ago. Without a word, just a note. The air of ecstasy was quickly drowned by a feeling of loss. He still set two places at the table, lifted out two mugs for coffee in the morning, made sure the toilet seat was down, and no hair was in the shower plug hole. Force of habit.

Marta had simply tired of his obsessing, he thought. He had felt that she was distant for a few months before she left. She was always an upbeat eccentric, singing and laughing and joking and cuddling and kissing. In the last month or so before she was gone, all of that had stopped, except the kissing and snuggling oddly. She no longer sang, ever. She wore her makeup less and less. She had no appetite or energy. In hindsight now, Fredrick put it down to a depression she never spoke about. In his mind's eye, he saw her stepping backwards while he continued to move forwards. He continued to bring her flowers every Monday, a tradition he had kept up since they first made it official that they were a couple all those years ago. Most of all Fredrick blamed himself for her departure, not just the neglect he now realized he had forced on her, but also for the way he involved her in all of the preparation. He thought she had enjoyed it, liked being part of it. She had even wanted to spend evenings planning and attending self-defense classes with him. Maybe she didn't? Perhaps she wanted out for a long time and he had just missed the signs? Furthermore, Fredrick knew, in a dark part of his heart that he never accessed (like knowing someone is watching you but refusing to look back) it was because of the baby. Marta had always spoken about starting a family. Fredrick was excited by the prospect and did not want to delay. They had been trying unsuccessfully for a year. Marta had gone to see her doctor one afternoon, Fredrick remembered. She kissed him goodbye as he lay on in bed. She was singing as she left, even tapping her keys to the song in her head. She had gone, he assumed, to the fertility doctor. That evening she returned dejected, heavy, and quiet. She sang no more after that, until eventually, she left. He knew now that it was because he could not have children. She had been tested months ago and all was well. Fredrick's heart broke over and over, realizing Marta had left to have a child with another man. It was the only explanation. He hated her to the core sometimes, but still, and always would, loved her and understood why.

Snori
Keflavik
31st October

The door at the driver's side of the van creaked open and slammed shut again. Ivan made his way to the rear of the Transit, blowing on his hands and rubbing warmth into them as he slipped on his thermal and armoured gloves.

Ivan was a relatively new recruit. He had worked for Snori for a year now, and in the pickup crew with Snori for three months. It was no surprise around the workroom that these two did not like each other. Snori thought Ivan to be no cocky, reckless, and undisciplined, whereas the other workers and staff enjoyed Ivan's stories, his banter, and his sense of humour, and were drawn to his charismatic personality. No one could really understand why Snori was so hard on Ivan, always giving him the worst jobs and silly tasks below Ivan's pay grade.

Ivan was obsessed with the Festival and had entered this year's competition, preparing for months. Everyone in the workplace knew it. The surprise came when Snori changed the rotation at the last minute to put Ivan on a late shift, the final collection route before the festival. Ensuring that Ivan would be late, and possibly even miss the tournament altogether. Snori cemented the insult more by insisting that he came along with Ivan, ensuring that no one could swap a shift with him, as he was sure any of the staff would. Ivan gave little resistance when he was informed of the change but Snori had heard talk from the staff room of Ivan's hope to clear up quickly and still make it to the Festival in time. He was even going to incorporate his uniform into his battle gear. His armoured gloves were a vital part of his defensive gear now.

The gloves fingers were thick iron and did not move like normal gloves. This reason was evident once Ivan sprang into action. He nodded to Snori as he walked around the new acquisition.

"She is an old one, eh?" He joked.

"Aye, not too much strength left in the old body, but numbers are numbers. She's the last one of the evening so don't be taking any chances. Follow the rules, do as I showed you, and all will be fine. Are you ready?" Snori asked, all form of humour gone from his voice. Ivan knew he was serious when this happened. "There is no room for joking when the lifting needs done." Snori always said this, Ivan lip-synced along with the motto as he used his teeth to pull the second glove onto his hand.

"Ok, here goes," Ivan said as he moved towards the corpse. He had watched Snori do this more than a hundred times over the last few months, but this was his first time handling the undead by himself. His heart raced and pounded in his chest, his breath was visible in the cold night air, his breathing becoming faster and shallower. Snori tapped his hand on Ivan's back.

"Take it easy. One deep breath, then go," he advised.

Ivan took a breath, placed one hand on the Ketch-All pole, and pulled it from the side of the door. Moving the corpse backwards. Once he was a few feet back, he retracted the pole, bringing the infected only inches from his face. The body shot its neck forward, snapping its teeth in Ivan's face. Unfazed, Ivan raised his other hand, the glove with the metal plated fingers, and shoved them into the deceased's mouth. The teeth clamped down and tried to bite into the metal, but to no avail.

"Good, you have a grip of her now. Push her back to the cage and I will swivel her in," Snori called. During the excitement and the movement, the dead in the van started to groan and moan again but were quickly silenced by a short snap of the cattle prod in Snori's hand.

Ivan pushed the woman back to the side of the van's cage, the Ketch-All pole still around her neck and his hand holding her in place with her mouth. This was Snori's idea. He always told them that if you had your hand in their mouth then you always knew where it was. No chance of it biting you if you held and controlled its jaw.

Releasing the pole, Ivan reached to the side of the cage, wrapped another copper wire around the dead's neck, and tightened it like a cable tie. With a quick flick of the pole, the first wire loosened and fell to the ground. Now the dead was held by both the wire choker and Ivan's glove.

The sudden slack of the choker must have given the dead a sense of freedom. She lashed out with her arms, both bound at the wrist with thick industrial cable ties. She managed to give Ivan a substantial blow to the chin, knocking him back slightly. As Ivan tried to place his feet in response to the blow, he foolishly tripped over his own legs. Falling back, his glove slipped from the jaws of the infected, cracking many of the old, rotten, yellow teeth free from the dark grey gums. He landed in a lump below the dead and the van, like a fallen tree, blown to the ground from root rot. The thump brought excitement to all of the van's occupants once more. Ivan struggled to get up from his back. His body armour and tool belt made this extremely awkward, like a turtle on its shell in the cold, with lip-licking predators staring down at their supper. With pure instinct, Ivan lifted his free hand to stop the infected woman from landing on him and locking her jaws on flesh instead of iron fingers. His hand pushed out onto her chest, holding her in position. Ivan may have been quite young but he was strong. You would guess by looking at him that he had a bit of strength behind his weight but he was surprisingly sturdy, durable, and solid.

While holding the dead in place, he reached out with his free arm to the cable on the door. The managed to wrap the frayed ends of a red and blue rope around his wrist and pull with all his might. This was the end of the choker cable, which he used to yank the dead up and back into position against the cage in the van. Using the tightrope as leverage, Ivan got to his feet. He took one look at the dead, who was now biting the air in his direction, obviously disappointed and angered by narrowly missing out on an evening meal, and punched the woman so hard in the face that he heard the crack of her skull under his iron glove. The vibrations in the iron fingers tingled as the body went limp. Ivan spat on the moving corpse as he brushed the grit and salt from the freshly treated streets from his overalls. Snori, without a word, swung the gate open. Ivan simply lifted the feet of the deceased and threw the body back into the van. The rope still around her neck, he pulled on the tug end once more, bringing her body to the side of the cage. He then tied it onto the inside lock, holding her in place. Snori did not even look at Ivan until the cage was locked and the rear door was secured shut. Before he had any time to discuss with Ivan what had happened, he was pinned up against the side of the van. Ivan had his forearm over his chest and neck, applying so much pressure upward that Snori's feet were only just touching the ground. He was pressed into the side of the van with so much force that the exterior metal bent under his weight. He could feel the heat of Ivan's breath on his face as he screamed at him.

"What the fuck was that, old man!" Ivan spat with pure anger, pushing the age difference once again in Snori's face. "You saw that she was coming down on me, you knew my fucking hand slipped, and you did nothing, you old fool! Did you want her to get me?"

Snori felt his face going purple, the airways being even more restricted, as Ivan continued his barrage of insults.

"This isn't the first time! I've fucking had it with you, Snori! Yesterday when you opened the cage without warning, then last week you called 'clear' on a room which held the dead. I don't know if you're going fucking blind or senile, but you are too old for this shit now, and I am not going to suffer because of you and your stubbornness. We both know you should have retired a long time ago!"

That one hurt Snori more than most. He knew that everyone talked about when his last year would be. He had seen the secret bets in the workroom on the year he would be killed on the job. Retirement was his biggest fear, more than the dead, because he would no longer be useful. Snori's fear, above most things, was being forgotten. Just as his head was becoming heavy and his body limp, he felt the tug of gravity as he fell like a sack of potatoes onto the cold dirt.

"This is my last job with you, Snori. I have had it. Once the Festival is over, I have other plans, better plans. Plans away from the old and decrepit." Ivan opened the passenger door to the van, kicking Snori's feet on his way past. Lighting a cigarette, he rolled the window down slightly and slammed the door shut behind him.

Snori took a few moments to catch his breath again. He coughed and choked as his airways began to expand once more. He knew there would be bruising on his neck in the morning. His wife would blame it on the Festival and tell him it was his last one, for sure. He could picture the fight now, the same one they had every year.

Snori made his way to his feet. The hum of the engine was now drowned out by the loud music Ivan was playing inside. A barrage of fast crunching noise, Snori could only imagine it was maybe guitars before it was altered and passed through a multitude of guitar pedals. The pounding beat was the only thing to be heard over the clinking of bells and ropes on the masts of the fishing boats in Keflavik Harbour, once rich in the whaling trade.

Snori gave the back doors another last check as he walked around the long way to the driver's seat. Getting in, he strapped his seatbelt, leaned forward, and took a cigarette of his own. He didn't lift Ivan's lighter. Instead, he waited for the interior lighter of the Ford Transit to heat up. This usually took a while in the old van. Snori gave his signal ahead on the CB radio that they would be joining the rear of the cattle convoy now. They would meet on the motorway just passed the exit to the blue lagoon. After five minutes or so, they were onto the main motorway towards

Reykjavik, passing the "Bonús" and the "10-11" both of which were closed now. The Festival would be in full swing, everyone would be gearing up for the finale, the Festival Blood Run. Ivan wore a Blood Run t-shirt under his overalls, last year's one, with the names of the winners and high scorers on it. Snori was sure he would go looking for the newest shirt once they arrived.

It was only a 40-minute drive from Keflavik to Reykjavik. After 35 minutes, the lighter clicked out, indicating it was now hot enough to light a cigarette off of the three glowing rings. Snori lifted it out with his forefinger and thumb and brought it to his lips, but dropped it just before it met the cigarette. Ivan was unaware as he had not so much as looked at Snori once they had started driving. He had his head against the window, watching the green and purple lights snake and dance overhead on the clear October evening. This was almost prime time to see the lights, just as the snows were beginning to appear.

Snori frantically patted at his crotch in search of the lighter. Not knowing where it was, he was scared he would grab the warm end of the lighter unknowingly. After a short while of frantic tapping, he saw the lighter fall onto his boot. He gave a cry and leaned down forward to grab it as it began to burn into his black work boots. At this point, Ivan had noticed the large rear of a cattle truck getting closer. Snori was pushing his foot down on the accelerator as he scrambled for the lighter, taking both hands off the wheel.

Fredrick
Reykjavik
31st October

She had left him a note that day.

My Love,

The flowers will continue to blossom; the water will continue to nourish them.

Like my love for you, it shall not leave, ever, but I must.

Your petal,

Marta.

The note is on the refrigerator, stuck on with a Las Vegas magnet, a trinket from their last holiday. She wanted the sign, and he the dice. Her decision was to flip for it, and she won.

Fredrick closed the cabinet above the refrigerator after reading the note again. He tore the plastic from the back of the adhesive strip and wrapped the Band-Aid plaster around his finger, stopping the last trickles of blood from dripping.

Perhaps a rest was all he needed. He needed to reboot his mind. It was in a form of standby and needed to be working overtime if he was to not only smash his personal best, but survive the festival tonight. Clicking the 'on' button and flicking to the news channel on the touchscreen remote, he slumped back into his Lazy Boy retro chair. It was just like the one his grandfather used to have. His armour was sitting up now on the table in the dining area of the apartment, like a sleeping monster on the table. Like that monster, Fredrick let his eyelids slide over his now watering eyes. He prayed before the nap took him that he would not dream of Marta. Seeing and thinking of her all day was enough, he longed for a release in his slumber.

Snori
Keflavik to Reykjavik motorway

October 31st

"SNORI, YOU OLD FUCK!" Ivan yelled as he grabbed the wheel, forcing the truck to the hard shoulder. Snori managed to grab the lighter, sit up, and, with a calm ease, he lit his cigarette in his teeth and smiled a toothy grin at Ivan.

"I think you should get out here, don't you?" Snori said behind eerily calm gritted teeth, pressing down harder than need be on the butt.

"Yeah, I've had it with you, old timer," Ivan said while unbuckling and climbing down from the cab. "I will be seeing you real soon, you suicidal old fuck," Ivan said. He waved with his middle finger as the truck indicated and moved slowly off onto the road again.

Ivan knew it was only a 30 minute walk to the main event, but he powerwalked it none the less. His Skogarcorp pass should make it a lot easier navigating the streets and security checkpoints to get where he needed to go. It wasn't the festival he was determined to get to now, it was something else.

Snori followed the convoy into the city centre. The trucks were almost bumper to bumper as they made their way through the windy tight streets. As they reached the festival heights near the top of the hill, just outside Hallgrímskirkja church, the front lorry slammed the brakes and sounded the horn. A man in an exoskeleton combat suit stumbled from the front of the convoy, continuing to run towards the assembly point of the Blood Run. Snori laughed to himself as he thought that one had no hope or chance, but he had been wrong about winners before.

Fredrick

Reykjavik
31st October

The sound of a siren broke the pleasant sleep that had eluded Fredrick for so long. Rolling from side to side on the chair, his cheek sticking to the faux leather seat, he slowly opened his eyes. A frown was worn heavy on his face as he looks both ways trying to make sense of the siren breaking his slumber.

Could it be?

Fredrick's heart beat in his chest like a sledgehammer through a supporting, load-bearing wall. As the ceiling fell, so did the gravity of the situation. He was late, fucking late, for the biggest night of his life so far! He clicked the leg support down on his chair with such force that he fell forward onto the carpeted living room floor. Half crawling, half scrambling, he made his way to the table still on his knees. He grabbed the armour and weapons off the table, pulling them to the ground. He twisted his way into his suit and darted to the door, holding the two weapons by his side. He had heard the year before, that many competitors had forgotten their entrance cards and id, therefore not allowing them to enter the Festival at all! He took no chances and had them already in the slots he fashioned on his chest. Hallgrímskirkja church was within walking distance of their... of his apartment. Running down the road, it was almost empty of traffic. Only four large, articulate lorries passed him, almost knocking him down. The cattle trucks were putrid smelling as they passed. Only once he had moved onwards did he realize what they contained.

He could hear the cheers and music from the Ritual floating on the icy October evening air as he drew closer to the building. The large, sloped sides blocked the lights but he could see the reflections of the projections on the night's clouds as he approached. Showing his id to security, he was granted access to the main area. The Ritual was drawing to a close but the Prime minister had not yet made her speech. He had made it, just. He wished Marta was here. Maybe he would bump into her? Maybe she was competing? Maybe she was with someone else? He could not even think about it.

Fredrick spent the remainder of the speech tightening his straps and checking for holes or gaps in his armour. A small part of him was using his peripherals to look for signs of Marta. A smaller part was listening to the speech. Finally, the horn was sounded. The people had turned, facing down the hill now towards the bottom of Reykjavík. The first gunshot was sounded. The lorries and trucks that had passed would be in position now, the rear doors would be open and the dead would be flowing out. Wasting no time, Fredrick set into a healthy jog, as fast as he could move comfortably in his suit. With hands raised, he gave one last check of his weapons. The smile was wide on his face now, behind the Icelandic flag mesh helmet. The moment had arrived. His moment. The sprinters would be approaching the safe zone now. The fan zone zeppelins were lowering into visible positions. These were the best signposts he knew. They hovered above large areas of the dead, looking for the best brutal experiences.

Snori
Reykjavik
31st October

Once the trucks pulled into place, Snori reversed his transit to the side of the starting crates. The rest of the staff made their way to him to collect the remaining dead they needed for the festival.

"Cutting it close there, Snori, eh?" Jon joked, nudging Snori with his elbow to the laughter and banter of the other drivers and crew.

"Yes, had a little slip up with Ivan, the boy will no longer be working with us, he just didn't have what it takes," Snori lied. The rest of the crew looked concerned and confused. Until today, Ivan had been one of the better recruits, a real natural at this line of work. Snori had never liked him. The crew knew this but were never sure why.

The crew nodded and agreed as Snori gave the orders to where they were to be positioned and the signals to unleash the horde when the siren is sounded. Snori decided he would take it easy this year and open the sliding grate at the side of the van from the rear, after the first wave had been unleashed. The undead very clearly have a herd mentality so if they see the horde of dead walking in one direction, they will follow before they check their immediate surroundings.

Celebrations had begun for the build-up to the Blood Run. All the crew and staff were in position. The competitors were ready and the president was giving her speech before the gates open, honoring the dead and the rest. Snori smoked his way through the boredom. He had done enough festivals to not care now. He just waited for the siren. When it sounded, he would pull the lever on the roof of the van, opening the side of the cage into a sort of walkway and release the tension behind the chokers. Then he would lock up, wait, and smoke some more before coordinating the clear up. Afterwards, he'd go home to have an argument with his wife about him working too much at his age. He would just rest his eyes for a short while now, as it was the only opportunity he would have for a while.

Fredrick
The Festival,
31st October

Veering left, Fredrick turned down one of the only side streets available tonight. Usually, a week before the festival, around mid-October, large steel walls are erected that border the centre of the city for this evening. All residential areas were closed and locked the day before, but the larger streets were still open season.

The first group was in front of him. He gave a war cry and charged into the fray. The saw worked better than he had ever imagined. Like a warm knife slicing through a freshly fried egg, the body parts came apart from their base. Red mist covered Fredrick's mask. He kept his mouth shut to avoid anything getting into it, just on the off chance. Using the pike to launch the dead back, he disposed of them with the saw. Five, six, then quickly up to thirteen, then fourteen! All in a matter of minutes.

Once the group was dispersed, he had well and truly smashed his record already. The kill count stood at 25 already. The festival climax is only an hour long. He had 45 minutes to find another 25. Continuing down the streets he managed to come across a few stragglers, bringing him to 30. The road swept round to the left, joining the main street. There, he found a group dining on an unfortunate partici-pant. He was face down, meaning he was caught unaware or running away. Either way, he deserved it, Fredrick thought.

Up the hill again slightly, there was a group of three

surrounded by overwhelming odds, they were firing frantically but two were reloading. Given time, they would fall
surely. Using all his energy, Fredrick charged up the hill. He
exploded the head of the closest rotter with his piston-
powered chisel gun, then with a roundhouse swipe of the
blade, he decapitated the five at the back.

The rotters were five deep now, easily. Hacking and
slashing, he screamed as he dove deeper in. That was when
the dead turned to face him. The three previous targets were
of no concern and they ran at the first available moment,
leaving Fredrick alone and overrun. He kept his balance but
felt the pressure of the rotter closing in on him, teeth and
nails scratching his armour and trying to find holes in the
joints to sink their teeth into. They would find none,
however. Just then, the blade stopped spinning. Fredrick
squeezed the trigger over and over, but there was no power.

One of the rotters behind him had torn the linking cable
from its base in the backpack. It was useless now. He
unlinked the blade from the exoskeleton and pushed his
gloved hand out the wrist slot. Punching hard, he pushed
some back to give himself a little more room. Swarmed now
like a blonde teenager in a piranha movie, he swung and
thrashed until he had forced enough of the infected to the
ground to give himself a chance to step over and clearly pick
the slower ones as his next prizes. 34, 35, 36! He was using
both hands now, his right-hand grabbing and his left firing
the pike through the skull of the dead ones.

37, 38, all the dead on their feet were now dead, the
fallen were struggling on their backs like turtles in the sun
on a dry sandy beach. Fredrick's heart was pounding with
exhaustion and excitement. Pushing through the fatigue, he
was becoming angry. This drove him on, giving him strength
and power. Stomping on head after head, his total kept

rising. He could feel camera drones hovering overhead now as he stepped on the skulls, like cracking eggshells on the street.

Looking up at the rooftop screens, Fredrick could see his festival pass photo id flashing with a giant 49 beside his name. He couldn't believe it! He was so close! This could be the year he was hoping for, everything else could come around again. Maybe Marta was watching him now! He knew that being at the top of the board will assure his place on the vision screen in every house in Iceland, if not the world! All eyes were on him, he needed that final point now.

The rooftops all housed advertisement boards and moving posters. From the sky, a giant blimp with a four-sided clock face flew low over the street arena. The numbers were just visible to Fredrick now. A fog horn started and rhythmically boomed every second. The giant 58 was now a 57, then a 56. Under one minute. Panic set in as Fredrick's eyes darted up and down the streets. Where were they all? Cheers and chants could be heard now from the fan zone zeppelins over the hum of the engines, feet stomping on the glass floors and claps to a rhythmic chant.

Snori
The Festival
31st October

The siren sounded and Snori almost jumped out of his skin. How could it have happened so soon? He had loads of time left, after the silence, the second part of the speech, the Ritual, the reciting then the cheers before the siren. Had he slept through this? He checked his watch. Yes, he had, a solid 35 minutes of sleep. The slam of the cattle trucks on either side of the church was usually booming and echoing down the cold Icelandic streets. Not this time, though. He had slept through it. Snori did not want to be too far behind as he could see the dead shuffling aimlessly now, joining together to head down the main street after the competitors ran to the safe zone. He pulled the release switch, nothing happened.

Again, he pulled the switch. Again, nothing. He reset the fuses from his control panel, still nothing. He would have to do it manually. The blimps were overhead and heading down towards the safe zone and main street. He could hear fans cheering from the airships as they passed.

He climbed down the ladder, missing the last four rungs, swung around to the side of the van, and pulled at the door. The old van had seen better days. The lever was both stuck with cold and wedged behind the side panel after a bump from the motorway earlier. Snori put both hands on the handle and pulled as hard as he could, slowly the door scraped to the side, revealing the inner cage and the dead staring out at him with red and yellow eyes. Snori was shocked, he felt vulnerable now, away from the safety of height, weaponless and armour-less, only a cigarette in his mouth and a fist in his right hand.

Just as he reached to manually open the lock-release mechanism, he heard a whistle, He looked up just in time to see Ivan throwing a small hand-axe toward him. The burning sharp pain forced Snori to the ground. The axe was deep into Snori's leg. Ivan said nothing but stared with a grin of vengeful satisfaction. More worryingly, however, he stared with a grin of enjoyment, pride, happiness, and a bloodthirsty face of excitement.

"End of the road, Snori. End of the road," Ivan said as he pushed the release button. The iron cage front fell forward, landing on Snori's legs, the weight of it snapping his shins instantly and pinning him under the grate walkway. The last thing Snori saw was Ivan fixing his competitor number to the chest on his vest, the night's sky overhead, the green northern lights dancing above him, and then a circle of red and yellow eyes, drawing closer until the biting began and everything disappeared.

Ivan did not win this festival but he was placed on the score-board under the record-breaking high score of this year's winner. The fire was ignited in Ivan's belly that evening, however, not just for the festival and dealing with the dead, but for murder. Knowing that there was one night a year he could get away with it, like he did with Snori. Ivan's blood-lust grew. He wore the charismatic, lovable rogue persona like a mask, disguising who he really was underneath, living in his secrets and his shame, his trophies and rewards, running from the truth and evading the consequences. Ivan was sure his name would be spoken of in lore and legend in years to come. It was.

Fredrick
The festival
31st October

That's when he saw it. Just turning the corner onto the side street he had just come from. He turned on his heels and sprinted. The suit slowed him down so he unclipped the armour from the clip at the front and it fell from his shoulders like a shell crashing on the ground behind him as he ran onwards. From his thigh sheath, he pulled the curved climbing pick he carried as a last defense. It hooked round and he had modified the entire length of it from the light carbon fiber pole it once had into a razor-sharp doubled edged blade. His foot slipped on fresh blood as he turned the corner. Sliding slightly, he used his left hand to steady himself on the ground. Kicking forward, he tried to get traction again. The countdown chant had begun now, 28, 27, 26. He ran with all his energy, using muscles in his legs he did not know he had, propelling himself forward until he was almost in reaching distance. With his left foot, he leaped forward, landing on his right, while turning his body to get the full power he could muster behind his swing. With his arm extended the blade sliced through the air, making impact with smooth precision. Not a fraction of resistance was felt as the razor slid through the skin and muscle in the neck, slowing with a crunch for only a millisecond as the spine was severed with such severe pressure that the head seemed to pop from the body, launching it backwards over Fredrick's shoulder. It rolled down the sloping side street. The cheers were deafening now as one of the zeppelins was directly overhead. Looking up, he could see his id card on all of the billboards. The words "New Record" were flashing with a confetti animation falling down from every screen down the hill in Reykjavik city from Hallgrímskirkja church to the old harbour. A feeling of relief was bubbling from his toes and moving upwards, from his legs and stomach to his chest then to his throat and, like Eyjafjallajökull, it erupted in a bellowing roar of elation. Falling to his knees, Fredrick heard the countdown continue.

10

9

He looked down at the unfortunate soul who had made

such a welcomed sacrifice for him. He wished he could find the family of the deceased to thank them for what had come from their loved one's decision.

8

Looking closer, Fredrick recognized the shirt the deceased was wearing. A thick, fur-lined, red and black button down cheque blouse, a "woodcutters special" as he used to call them when women began to wear them in the city. The jeans seemed familiar too.

7

Shuffling over on his knees Fredrick got closer to the body. His heart beating faster and faster, his stomach was turning and tying itself in knots now. His worst fear was beginning to rise.

6

Could this be? How?

5

He rolled the body over and lifted up the left arm.

4

Turning the hand over, it was clenched in a fist, taped closed by white electrical tape.

Fredrick snapped the tape and opened the hand.

2

A ring was on the engagement finger. A ring Exactly like the one he had given to Marta.

I

Inside the closed fist was a crumpled and folded note, stained with blood and sweat from being clasped by the deceased for so long. How could he say 'the deceased'? He knew exactly who this was.

This was Marta....

o

A foghorn sounded to the reply of cheers and music! The zeppelin overhead was circling and an explosion of confetti and sparks descended over the entire city now! Claps, laughter, cheer, and songs filled the cold night air.

Fredrick simply lay on top of Marta's body, crying now. His emotions were so mixed. He was to be celebrated as the highest scorer in the festival's history soon. The prime minister would award him with the medal and, after the performance he put on tonight, he felt a shoe-in for the Holy Trinity. The time for celebration and happiness would come soon enough, he knew. Now was a time for heartache and loss all over again.

He held Marta's hand with his left hand, intertwining his gloved fingers with her ice-cold ones. He squeezed her hand tightly, hoping, hopelessly, that she would return the gesture, wishing that she would squeeze his freshly cut finger from the sharpening stone earlier, praying for the pain that would give him courage. Unfolding the letter with his other hand, he began to read. His tears fell on the page as the fireworks lit up the sky behind him, illuminating the street enough for him to read for a few seconds after each explosion.

Dear Fredrick, my love,

   I hope this letter finds you, but more so, I hope you find it.

   I must start with an apology. My departure was never about you, or because of you.

   It was for you.

   I could never have told you all the things I wanted to in

person, so this note will have to suffice. I love you more every day. Since the moment we met, you have been everything to me. I need not tell you this as I am sure that you know.

I am sorry I grew distant in the days leading up to now. I had news I could not possibly share. The morning I left for the doctor, I was hoping to get answers as to why we could not conceive. The answers were worse than I feared. The problem did not lie with you at all, it was the cancer in my blood. I am sick. Very sick. I was given a month at best but I feel in myself I will not have that long. I know you, my dear, you would drop everything for me, nothing else would matter to you, but your success and happiness matter more to me than anything. I did not want you to lose focus. This Festival will be your greatest yet. I know from the training we did together that you have greatness. You are better than your brother, better than this city. You will be on the world stage soon! You can go as far as representing the trolls in the "Tournament of the Dead." I know you can. I hope that your anger at my departure brought you drive and passion. I know it will have, you are a strong Icelandic giant! You will make me proud, I know!

I signed over my body to the festival today. The payment was transferred to me this morning and I placed it all on a bet.

I bet you would get your goal, 50 points. If you have, the prize money will go to you, my dear. I hope this is a truly great gift I can give. Even more so, I hope I can help in another way. I hope I provide a point to you, my dear. That way I will always be part of you.

Some people get a lifetime of love in their life. We may have only had three years but I would not trade them for anything in the world. These years have made me happier than I could ever have dreamt. I will be with you always, my dear.

As I said, each flower that blooms is a reminder to you of how you made me feel each day. Each bloom brings hope to the world.

The flowers will continue to bloom.
As will you, my love.
With everything I am, my heart and soul are yours.
Your petal,
Marta

ABOUT CHRISTOPHER MAHOOD

Chris is a professional musician, husband, songwriter, author, reluctant poet, video gamer, comic book collector, Metal, rock, and music worshiper of all things alternative and an enthusiast for all things zombie related. He is also ¼ of Belfast based rock/grunge band @Plagueartists. So, when he is not making lots of noise, he loves spending time with his Wife, dog and two cats.

Story edited by Sarah from Lobster Press.

The festival started as a one off short story, but has evolved into a series and will continue only through various Zombie anthologies. Find them on Amazon.

To connect with me to talk about...well anything really, you can follow me on the social media sites below.

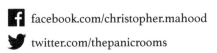

facebook.com/christopher.mahood

twitter.com/thepanicrooms

21

THE UNDEAD POOL: THE ZOMBIE NIGHT

PROLOGUE

Prologue

Mace Murdock, A.K.A. The Undead Pool, held his katana tightly as he watched several zombiefied clown soldiers shamble through the tall cornfield off of US Highway 6 in Hobart, Indiana. His gray and black mercenary outfit with a matching mask was covered in the blood from several of the zombies he decapitated.

A large semi-truck jackknifed as it tried to avoid crashing into a large zombiefied deer as it jumped out of the cornfield and onto the highway. Its trailer took out two smart cars as it slid sideways down the highway. Its cab burst into flames as it came to a screeching halt.

Mace, engrossed in the fiery spectacle, failed to notice the horde of zombiefied clowns salivating behind him. As he heard their groans, he spun around and decapitated all of them with one swoop of his katana.

"Now that's how you defeat a group of zombies. Yes, it's The Undead Pool bringing you another exciting adventure.

This one promises to be epic," Mace said, looking up toward the reader.

"Mace, are you talking to yourself again?" Tigernaut asked as he walked over to him. He was a muscular human-tiger hybrid. He lit a cigar and shoved it into his mouth.

"No...maybe."

"Let's kill the remaining zombies and head back to the base."

"I hope this is the last of the clown zombies. I want to put this Zarathustra nightmare behind us. Now that he's been defeated, I don't feel we should have to deal with his minions."

"Mace, I know how you feel, but we have no idea how many zombies he created before we destroyed his facility."

"After all the zombies are eradicated, I want to go to the Japanese buffet. I'm hungry."

"Not while wearing your blood soaked outfit," Tigernaut said, watching the blood fall from his sleeves like rain.

"It wouldn't be the most disturbing site at the buffet. Have you seen how disgusting their kitchen is? The cockroaches wear hazmat suits."

"And you want to eat there?"

"I'm a zombie. I've eaten worse."

Chapter One

Amaya Himura, the owner of Feast of the Orient Japanese Buffet, stared at the empty wall across from the men's bathroom and back at the painting which laid against the wall collecting dust.

"Iwao, why haven't you hung the painting yet?" Amaya shouted.

Iwao, her nephew, ran down the hallway and stopped in front of her avoiding eye contact. "Sorry, I got busy."

"Stop whatever you were doing and hang the damn painting. I paid a lot of money for it. I want our customers to admire its magnificence," Amaya explained.

As Amaya walked away, Iwao lifted the heavy painting and placed it on the nail. He stared at the image of the balding Japanese man with long black hair wearing a blue samurai outfit. Even though it was just a painting, the man's eyes appeared to be real, following Iwao's every move.

As Iwao touched the painting's right edge to straighten it on the nail, lightning shot out from the man in the painting's eyes.

"I, Mage al Ghoul, command you."

"Oh command me," Iwao said, kneeling down and bowing.

The man cleared his throat and continued. "As I was saying...I, Mage al Ghoul, command you to bring me a vessel so that I may be freed from this prison."

"A starship?"

"No, not a starship, you nitwit! A baby!"

Iwao's eyes glowed bright red as he was turned into a mindless zombie under the control of the painting. "I shall find you a baby."

Iwao ran down the hallway toward the foyer of the restaurant crashing into Mace Murdock. He pushed past him and ran out the entrance almost being hit by a black pickup truck.

"What a strange little man," Mace said.

"Did you see his eyes?" Tigernaut asked. "They were glowing red."

"Must be some good Japanese wacky weed here," Mace laughed.

"He did look extremely high. Let's go to the restroom and clean up. We are both covered in blood."

Tigernaut led Mace down the hallway toward the bathroom. Mace stopped in front of the painting and stared.

"I didn't peg you as the art loving type," Tigernaut said.

"It's hideous," Mace said.

A lightning bolt shot out from the painting and engulfed Mace, electrocuting him. After contorting for several seconds, Mace punched the crotch of the man in the painting and his eyes rolled back in his head. The sky behind the man disappeared replaced by dark storm clouds.

Tigernaut pulled Mace away from the painting as a miniature tornado dropped to the ground. Mace jumped over the tornado and slammed his fist into the painting causing the man's head to spin.

"Come on, Okamura, I can do this all day," Mace taunted.

"My name is not Okamura! I am Mage al Ghoul! You shall pay for your insolence!" Mage al Ghoul then chanted an evil spell.

"Frank, I forgot the sweet and sour sauce," Helen shouted to her husband.

As Frank grabbed the metal ladle in the sweet and sour sauce, a zombiefied hand reached out of the serving tray and grabbed his hand. He screamed as he fell backward. A zombiefied samurai soldier pulled itself out of the serving tray and slammed its head on the glass casing above him. It rubbed its head and then jumped down and bit into Frank's neck.

Zombiefied samurai soldiers crawled out of all the

serving trays and shambled toward the unsuspecting diners. The dining area was filled with screams as the zombies enjoyed a buffet of their own.

"Somebody must have seen a rat," Mace said.

"I summoned some of my best soldiers," Mage al Ghoul boasted.

Mace slammed his fist again into Mage al Ghoul's crotch. Two marbles rolled out of the man's mouth and his eyes rolled back into his skull.

"Samurais, kill these two nitwits!" Mage al Ghoul screamed.

Several samurais shambled into the hallway holding katanas.

"First clown zombies. Now samurai zombies. This is not my day," Mace said. He slid across the hallway slicing two of the samurais in half with his katana.

Wooden-spikes ripped through Tigernaut's fingers as he ran toward the samurais. He impaled two of them in the head and then ripped the heads off another one.

Mace spun in the air like Samus Aran from *Metroid* and decapitated five more samurais. He spun back into the air, collecting several golden coins in the process decapitating the remaining samurais.

"Mage al Ghoul, give up. Killing zombies is what we do best," Mace boasted.

Mage al Ghoul remained silent. Mace walked over to the painting waiting for him to attack, but he remained motionless.

"Careful, Mace. He may be playing possum," Tigernaut cautioned. "We should take the painting to the base and have the professor run some tests."

Mace stabbed the side of the painting with a small dagger and cut along the painting's edges. He rolled the painting up and shoved it under his right armpit. He could hear Mage al Ghoul gagging.

"Take it all in," Mace laughed. "I haven't showered in days. To think of it, I don't think I've used deodorant either. Smells real ripe, doesn't it?"

"Iwao, come to me," Mage al Ghoul chanted and then puked.

Mace and Tigernaut placed the painting on the professor's desk at Zagar's School For Special Power Needs. Professor Charlene Zagar examined the painting. The bald leader of the Why-Men lost her lower half when her protégé, Dark Moler, sliced it off with an energy sword several years back. Using her strong mental abilities, she could move her remaining half about with her mind.

"What is he?" Tigernaut asked.

"He's an evil spirit trapped inside this painting," the professor explained. "I'm using my mental abilities to subdue his powers."

"For how long?" Tigernaut asked.

"I don't know. He's a powerful spirit."

"If we destroy the painting, will he be destroyed?" Mace asked.

"There's a powerful magic protecting it from being destroyed. Mage al Ghoul wants to escape his imprisonment. We can't let that happen," the professor explained.

"Can we send it to parallel Earth? He can be their problem, not ours," Mace asked.

"That's unethical," the professor pointed out.

"Place it in the vault," Tigernaut suggested. "His powers should be rendered useless in there."

"That should work...for now," the professor agreed.

Iwao ran toward the front door of his sister's house and smashed through it.

Haruna ran into the room shouting. "You broke the front door! It was unlocked!" She dropped her coffee mug which shattered on the floor as Iwao's zombie-like appearance frightened her. His skin was dark gray and maggots crawled all over his body. A finger dangled from his mouth. "What the f...."

"Where's Aika?" Iwao growled.

"You're not going anywhere near her," Haruna said as she grabbed the broom from behind the couch and snapped it in half over her knee. She held the pointed end toward his head.

"I'm a zombie, not a vampire," he growled.

She tried to jam it into his head, but it wasn't sharp enough to penetrate his skull. He grabbed her by the throat. As he lifted her in the air, she kicked him in the groan. He flung her to the side and shambled toward the bedroom where Aika was sleeping. Before he could reach the room, he heard Mage al Ghoul call out to him. He forgot about Aika and ran out of the house. His master needed him urgently.

Chapter Two

Mace and Tigernaut sat in front of the television in the living quarters watching a *Batman* marathon on MeTv.

"This is the real *Batman*," Tigernaut proclaimed.

"I agree. There hasn't been a good one since Michael Keaton," Mace added.

"I don't know who is worse: Ben Affleck or George Clooney."

"Affleck," they both said in unison.

The lights flickered as a severe thunderstorm tried to ruin their marathon.

Staring at them through the window while chewing on someone's leg was Iwao. Golf ball-sized hail bounced off his head. As he continued his gaze, a bolt of lightning struck him in the head electrocuting him. As smoke emanated from his ears, nose, and mouth, he staggered to his feet. The storm had knocked out the power. If he was going to rescue his master, now would be the perfect opportunity to sneak in unnoticed. He shambled toward the entrance of the school. He cautiously opened the front door and entered the school. To his surprise, there wasn't anybody in the front of the school. It was almost like the author didn't have the rights to use any of his other characters in this anthology.

ⵏⵉⵉⵉⵉ

"Now what do we do? Do we sit here and talk about our feelings?" Mace asked staring at the blank television screen.

"It looks like the whole power grid is down. The forked lightning looks cool," Tigernaut said as he stared out the window. He could see a tornado in the distance. A cow flew past the window. "That cow sure gets around."

The room lit up bright red as an alarm went off.

"The vault!" Mace shouted as he jumped off the couch.

"The painting," Tigernaut said as he followed Mace out of the room.

They ran down the long corridor leading to the vault.

The door to the vault was wide open and Iwao was holding the painting.

"Where's the baby?" Mage al Ghoul questioned.

"I was going to steal my sister's. I was only a few feet away from her room when you beckoned me," Iwao explained.

"Idiot!" Mage al Ghoul screamed. "You could have grabbed the baby and then came to my rescue! No matter. Your body will have to do."

The painting burst into flames as Mage al Ghoul crawled out of it. He ripped open Iwao's mouth and then crawled down his throat. A few seconds later, Iwao's body morphed into the form of Mage al Ghoul. He spun around and flung several daggers at Mace's head - all direct hits. His hands glowed purple as he fired an energy blast at Tigernaut knocking him into the back wall.

Mace grabbed Tigernaut and jumped out of the vault as he threw two grenades at Mage al Ghoul and then slammed the door shut.

The door burst outward and Mage al Ghoul walked out of the vault unaffected by the explosions. He waved his hands bending reality around them. He jumped from one side of the school to the other.

Mace and Tigernaut found themselves standing on the ceiling while Mage al Ghoul ran across the floor below them.

"Tigernaut, for some reason I'm in the mood for Lionel Richie."

"Mace, be serious. How do we get down?"

Mace jumped downward landing on the floor below. Tigernaut landed next to him. They could see Mage al Ghoul in the distance running out the entrance of the school. As they followed him outside, Mage al Ghoul bent reality again and was running above them on the bottom of the storm clouds. Mace spun upward and landed on the bottom of one of the clouds. He looked downward and waved at Tigernaut.

"This is strange," Tigernaut said to the doctor standing next to him. "How is this even possible?"

"How would I know? I'm a doctor, not a scientist," the doctor said angrily as he walked away.

Mace grabbed the edge of the cloud that Mage al Ghoul was on and yanked it from underneath him sending him headfirst into the ground below. Mace jumped downward landing on Mage al Ghoul's chest.

"Give up," Mace suggested. "Defying the laws of physics is what I do best."

Mage al Ghoul shoved his katana through Mace's chest, the blade holding on to his heart as a trophy as it ripped through. Mace collapsed.

"Mace Murdock, my love. Wake up," a beautiful voice echoed in Mace's head.

He opened his eyes in amazement. Standing before him was a tall, beautiful woman with a black painted face with white symbols tattooed all over it as well as her body. She was adorned in a black cloak and held a large black scepter.

"Lady Deadra, I missed you. I guess I died again."

"In every novel, it seems," she laughed.

"You know I die on purpose. There isn't anyone as beautiful as you in the land of the living."

She giggled.

He heard screams in the distance.

"That sounded painful."

"Another supervillain brought down to the underworld for eternal damnation," she laughed. "They're using rather large pineapples these days."

"Yikes!" Mace exclaimed, clutching his butt cheeks. "As much as I admire medieval torture methods, I need to get back to the land of the living."

"Try not to get killed this time," she said as she jammed her scepter into Mace's skull crushing it.

𓀀𓀁𓀂𓀃𓀄𓀅

Mace opened his eyes and looked at Tigernaut.

"He's gone," Tigernaut informed him. "How's Lady Deadra?"

"Beautiful as ever. Remind me to pick up some Vaseline when we are at Target."

"Why?"

"No reason in particular," he said as he stood up.

"Mace, we need to find him quickly," the professor said as he hovered over to them. "I did some research on him. He's responsible for wiping out a majority of the samurais. Several samurais gave their life imprisoning him in the painting. I found references to his existence all the way back to the Egyptian days. After wiping out a civilization's warriors, he enslaves everyone else. The Why-Men are the warriors of this timeframe."

"How do we kill him?" Tigernaut asked.

"Stab him with the Dagger of Neferka. It possesses ancient Egyptian powers. It's at the Field Museum of Natural History in Chicago," the professor answered.

"You know what that means," Mace said, smiling at Tigernaut. "Off to the museum, but first we need to stop at the store."

Chapter Three

Mace and Tigernaut walked into the secret entrance in the back of the museum. It was nighttime and the museum had closed hours ago. They walked into the foyer of the museum where several cavemen and soldiers from the Revolutionary War and the Civil War were partying.

"Hey, look! It's The Undead Pool," a ten inch cowboy with long blonde hair said.

"Hey, Owen. How's it hanging? Tiny...right?"

"Funny," Owen said as he flicked Mace off.

"Where's Coogan?" Tigernaut asked.

Owen stared at the ground sadly. "Rat got him. Blood - so much blood."

Mace walked over to a large stone-faced statue and held up a large bag of gum.

"You brought gum gum!"

"Yes, Brad, I brought a lot of gum gum."

"What brings you guys by? Not a friendly visit I take it?" Safari Irwin, a bald muscular man wearing a safari outfit, asked as he greeted them.

"We're looking for the Dagger of Neferka," Tigernaut answered.

"It's in the Egyptian hall. Unfortunately, you have to go through the new Jurassic exhibit to get there. Deadly dinosaurs. A velociraptor or two," Irwin explained. "We keep that section locked up tightly."

"I'm not afraid," Mace said, grabbing his katana.

"You will be. You will be," Owen warned him.

"Safari Irwin, will you help us?" Tigernaut asked.

Safari Irwin grabbed a large multi-barreled rifle off the

wall and motioned to them to follow. He led them toward a large cage door separating the main part of the museum from the Jurassic exhibit. They could hear the roar from a large dinosaur.

"That would be Bessie," Safari Irwin explained.

"Exactly what type of dinosaur is Bessie?" Tigernaut asked.

"That kind," Mace answered, pointing toward the Tyrannosaurus rex that was staring at them licking its lips.

"She's a feisty one," Safari Irwin explained.

The massive dinosaur smashed through the cage door sending Mace and Tigernaut airborne.

"I am Turok!" Mace shouted as he jumped onto Bessie's leg and climbed up her back. He ran up her neck and then stabbed her right eye with his katana. He held on tightly as she slammed her head into the wall trying to crush him.

"Keep her busy!" Safari Irwin instructed as he aimed his rifle and then fired several rounds.

Bessie turned her attention on Safari Irwin and tried to crush him with her head. Mace pulled his katana out of her right eye and then climbed across her face and jammed it into her left eye. Bessie slammed her head repeatedly into the wall until Mace lost his grip on his katana and fell to the ground.

Safari Irwin grabbed an ancient spear off the wall and tied several grenades around its base. He waited until Bessie's head was only a few feet above him and he then threw the spear into her mouth. Several seconds later, her head exploded and she collapsed.

"Safari Irwin has done it AGAIN!" Safari Irwin celebrated.

"We have a dagger to steal," Mace said.

"We still have to deal with the Velociraptors," Safari Irwin reminded him.

They cautiously walked through the fake forest of plastic trees and plants toward the Egyptian exhibit. Ahead of them, the plants moved as something ran through them.

"I'll keep them occupied while you retrieve the dagger," Safari Irwin instructed them.

As a velociraptor jumped out of the bushes and stopped in front of Safari Irwin and stared at him, he motioned to Mace and Tigernaut to run. The Velociraptor paid no attention to the other two and kept her gaze on him.

"Clever girl," Safari Irwin said as the bushes to the left and right of him shook. Two Velociraptors pounced on him and ripped open his abdomen. They feasted on him as he screamed in agony.

Mace and Tigernaut ran out of the plastic forest and into the Egyptian exhibit. Two large Egyptian statues bowed their heads as they opened the entrance to the small pyramid for them. They entered the pyramid where an Egyptian man wearing a golden crown sat on a stone chair shaking his head in disgust.

"Amenhotep, what's wrong?" Tigernaut asked.

"I just got back from the theater. The new *Mummy* was terrible. I prefer the Brendan Fraser ones."

"You go to the movies dressed like that?" Mace asked.

"Are you crazy? I'd get mugged wearing a golden head-piece in public."

"Amenhotep, we are looking for the Dagger of Neferka," Tigernaut said.

"It's in the display case in the back corner."

Mace walked over to the display case and smashed it open with his fist.

"Idiot!" Amenhotep shouted as he threw a set of keys at

Mace's head. "Thank goodness we deactivate the security alarms at night."

Mace grabbed the dagger and placed it in his right pocket.

Amenhotep grabbed a broom and angrily handed it to Mace. "Remember to bring the dagger back when you're done with it."

"We will," Tigernaut promised him.

Mage al Ghoul stood outside the entrance of the school with several zombie samurais standing behind him waiting to attack.

"Find the Why-Men and rip them to shreds!"

The zombies shouted out a war cry and shambled through the gate toward the school.

Stable, a tall, muscular man with a shiny, silver metallic horse head stood in front of an army of Why-Men waiting to engage the zombies. His brown, metallic body resembled a human, and he had several metallic weapons attached to it magnetically.

"Why-Men, attack!" Stable commanded in a thick Russian accent.

The Why-Men ran toward the zombies decapitating several of them as they collided with them. The zombies shambled into the schoolyard in en mass and the Why-Men took heavy casualties.

Stable detached two swords from his chest and decapitated several zombies. He plowed through the horde as he headed toward Mage al Ghoul.

Mage al Ghoul slammed his fist into the ground causing the ground underneath Stable to collapse sending him into a sewer tunnel below. He landed on a pile of empty pizza boxes. He grabbed a grappling hook off of his utility belt and flung it upward. He quickly climbed out of the hole and decapitated another zombie as he emerged.

Mage al Ghoul slammed a baseball bat wrapped in barbwire into Stable's head putting a small dent in his metallic cranium. Stable looked at him angrily.

"It worked on Glenn," Mage al Ghoul said as he threw the bat to the side.

Stable grabbed him and slammed him to the ground. As he swung his sword downward, Mage al Ghoul disappeared and reappeared behind a horde of zombies. Stable plowed through the zombies and flung his sword toward Mage al Ghoul's head. He deflected it with magic.

"Give up! You will all die by my zombies' hands."

A large ship landed on top of several zombies crushing them. Mace and Tigernaut ran out of it and killed several more zombies.

Mace turned his attention toward Mage al Ghoul. "Your arrogance will be your downfall!"

"You two and your Why-Men are no match for my magic!"

Bolts of electricity shot out of Mage al Ghoul's hands electrocuting Mace. Mace's body glowed causing his skeleton to be seen through his outfit. Smoke emanated out of his ears and mouth. His body burst into flames.

Tigernaut and Stable jumped toward Mage al Ghoul knocking him to the ground.

Mace staggered to his feet. He reached for the dagger and held it in his right hand.

"I see you have the Dagger of Neferka! It won't be able to kill me! This I promise you!" Mage al Ghoul slammed his fist into the ground and his body glowed bright red. Thousands of Mage al Ghoul clones appeared. They spun around one another.

"Which one is the real one?" Tigernaut asked.

Mace jumped forward ready to stab one of the clones, but passed through its body.

The clones continued to spin around one another. Every few seconds, they all shot out electrical charges.

Mace spun in the air trying to avoid the charges.

As the clones continued to spin, Mace observed that one of them was standing still as the rest of them spun. He lunged forward pretending he was trying to stab the spinning clones as he slowly etched his way for the one that was remaining still. Tigernaut and Stable, realizing what Mace was planning, pretended to attack the spinning clones from the other direction.

As Mace reached the real Mage al Ghoul and was about to stab him, Mage al Ghoul jumped to the right into Tigernaut's wooden spiked fingers. Mace spun around and jammed the dagger into Mage al Ghoul's chest.

"Impossible!" Mage al Ghoul screamed as his body burst into flames. He fell to the ground as he burned alive.

Mace held a stick with a marshmallow on top above his burning body and made s'mores for Tigernaut, Stable and him. They enjoyed the chocolate snacks as the rest of the Why-Men defeated the zombie samurais.

ABOUT DEREK AILES

Derek Ailes is a demented post-apocalyptic science fiction and horror author serving his readers one plateful of horrific terror after another. He is the mastermind behind several horror anthologies including *Musings from a Demented Mind* and *Catfurnado, Zombies and One Killer Doll*. He recently ventured into the vast superhero universe with his first comedy/horror novel *The Undead Pool*. Derek openly admits that he is a nerd. He reads comic books and graphic novels along with watching every DC and Marvel television series, cartoon, and movie.

The Undead Pool series can be found on **Amazon**.

To find more information about Derek Ailes please follow him on the social media sites below.

facebook.com/authorderekailes

twitter.com/derekailes

AFTERWORD

Dear Reader,

We hope you have enjoyed the collection of zombie filled tales we have presented here. Don't forget to connect with the authors online through their social media links, or you can find all of us and almost two hundred more zombie authors at **The Reanimated Writers Zombie Fiction Authors and Fans** group on Facebook. Where we promise not to spam you with a bunch of ads, but provide a space for zombie filled fun! We would appreciate it if you could take a moment to leave a review on Amazon, Goodreads, or both! Reviews are like gold to indie authors.

On a side note, I wanted to mention how wonderful this experience has been. This project started as a whim one day when I blurted out, "We should do an anthology!" I am prone to moments like that, but what was new and amazing about that moment was the reaction of my fellow authors of all skill and experience levels jumping in to make something we could all be proud to share with you. The Reanimated Writers is a group that many of us feel is more like our creative internet home. So please, come join us. We love authors and fans, and can't wait to share our home with you!

Thank you for reading Undead Worlds,

Valerie Lioudis

Reanimated Writers Vice Chairwoman and Undead Worlds Anthologist

22

MORE FROM THE REANIMATED WRITERS

UNDEAD WORLDS 2

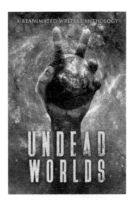

THE REANIMATED RUMBLE

2 authors write a story based on the same theme,
you decide who wins!
Check out the first ever Reanimated Rumble!
www.reanimatedwriters.com/rumble/

REANIMATED WRITERS PODCAST

Join host RJ Spears as he interviews the authors you love
to read!
www.reanimatedwriters.com/podcast

THE REANIMATED READER

I f you'd like to keep up with our latest announcements and projects, please sign-up for The Reanimated Reader, this is our monthly newsletter where you'll get all the latest scoop on Reanimated Writers Projects, Promos and More!

Plus when you sign-up you get special bonuses from some of our authors! There are free books, cool tidbits and more!

Sign up at www.reanimatedwriters.com/newsletter

FACEBOOK FAN GROUP

If you've enjoyed these stories and want to meet and hangout with authors and fans, come find us on Facebook and join the
Reanimated Writers Facebook Fan Group!

There is something happening just about everyday, games, prizes, author takeovers, live events and more! Come interact with your favorite authors and your fellow fans!

You can also find us on Instagram & Twitter!

REANIMATED MERCH

Get our latest designs and more at
www.reanimatedwriters.com/tees